QUITE POSSIBLY HEROES

QUITE POSSIBLY HEROES

A FREEMAN UNIVERSE NOVEL

PATRICK O'SULLIVAN

dunkerron press

A Dunkerron Press™ Book.

Copyright © 2022 by Patrick O'Sullivan

PatrickOSullivan.com

Illustration © Tom Edwards

TomEdwardsDesign.com

ISBN-13: 978-1-62560-025-7

ISBN-10: 1-62560-025-9

BOOKS IN THIS SERIES

1

Trinity System, Freeman Federation

Macer Gant fell into step beside the tall, distinguished man as he exited the Freeman Merchant Bank. He'd been following him ever since the man got off the Trinity Surface shuttle. The man had entered the bank carrying an empty satchel and exited carrying a full one.

It felt strange, being back in Truxton utilities. He'd meant to return them along with his crew credentials but hadn't found the time. Now they proved the perfect camouflage on a station where a third of the population worked in the Freeman Sector, and a third of the adult population of that sector worked for Truxton Trading. He was just one of a throng of Truxton hands on the Arcade, a big man with a backpack over his shoulder and his hands stuffed in his pockets. Only his size stood out. He was big, even for an islander, and he'd never felt more enormous.

Trinity Station bristled with surveillance sensors recording his every move, so he took a right when the man took a left, and sauntered along the Arcade toward the shadier part of the Freeman Sector, window shopped, and entered a tailor's shop.

Mr. Pearse handed Macer a package and Macer continued out the shop's rear entrance, into a service alley, that led to the roughest part of the Arcade, and from there to the roughest part of the ring. It would have been safer doing business on the spindle, but it would have been out of character for one, and for two, he needed to test a theory. According to the station-master it took three full-time crews working three shifts to keep the sensor net working on this part of the ring. There existed a chance he'd be recorded during the act but a better chance of getting away with it here than anywhere on the station, excepting the spindle. *Anyone* needing a clandestine ride had a better chance here, including Rik Severn and his comrades.

He entered the used- and salvaged-equipment yard. The grubby man behind the counter ignored him entirely.

Macer placed the package on the counter.

The man looked at it. There was no telling what lay inside. It could be a stack of money. It could be a bomb. It could be the severed hand of the last pinhole that had stood behind a counter and ignored Macer Gant. All anyone could tell by looking at it was that it had a Pearse's label on the outside and the fingerprints of the man who had placed it on the counter all over it.

"You're a loud thinker," the man said.

"When I need to be. I want to buy a rockhopper."

"I have two in working condition."

"How many do you have fueled up and ready to go?"

"Two."

"How many are big enough for a two-man team?"

"Two."

"Do you see that man looking around outside, in the suit and carrying a satchel?"

"I do."

"How many would we fit in comfortably?"

"Zero."

"How about if it wasn't us, but two spindly weasel-men and a bag of sporting equipment?"

"One."

"I'll take that one."

"How would you like to pay?"

"I'll give you all of what's in this box or half of what's in that man's satchel. It's a firm offer, as I'm in a hurry."

"The satchel."

"Wise man."

The man saw the sign for the shop and came in. A bell attached to the door jingled.

Macer picked up the package. "I'll examine the merchandise. If it's as described, I'll pay you for the machine when I come out for the keys."

"And what if it's not as described?"

"I'll pay you for my time."

"This way," he said.

Macer jammed himself into the little in-system craft. It was a two-seater, sized for space-born Freemen.

The tall man with the satchel had to fold nearly in half to cram himself inside.

The shop man began to close the hatch.

"Don't," Macer said. "We don't want to expire locked in a tiny cell, like criminals. Go on now with you, and I'll find you when I'm ready to boost."

Macer glanced at the man jammed in beside him. "Close the hatch but don't seal it."

His father's solicitor did as Macer asked.

"Thank you for meeting me here like this," Macer said. "I know it's a little out of your comfort zone. Did you bring the money?"

"I did," mac Kenna said. "That and the documents for you to sign."

"Good," Macer said. "I'll want those too. They're just the evidence I'll need when they come to murder me."

"Murder you?"

"That's right. But I don't think they will, now that I have the money and the documents. Just leave them there, on the first officer's console, and that will be all."

"You're to sign that you're giving up claim to all your father's lands and property without a fight, and *then* I'm to give you the money."

"The deal was, you would bring me the money and the documents, and I'd read them. If I agreed to sign them, you'd give me the money."

"The documents say that you'll give up the claim. We're both saying the same thing."

"They also say Luther Gant was my father."

"He is your father."

"Maybe he is. But if I can establish enough doubt about that, then they won't murder me. They'll be too busy hunting down his comrades. By the time they get back to looking at me, maybe their bloodlust will be sated."

"Who exactly is trying to murder you?"

"All my life this sword has been dangling over my head unknown to me. My father never breathed a word, not until his dying breath, and somehow they found out. Now they're blaming me for his sins, and blood of my blood or not, I had no part of them, and want no part of their vengeance."

"Whose vengeance?"

"The nic Cartaí. She's hunting me down for crimes committed four hundred years before I was born!"

"Rumor on the station is that you're Nuala nic Cartaí's boy toy."

"How likely is that?"

"You've been seen in her company. Repeatedly."

"I'm her toy, all right. She's been toying with me, like a tiger with a pup."

Macer could see the gears behind the solicitor's eyes turning. "What do you intend to use this money for?"

"My escape."

"And the papers?"

"The Enemy," Macer said.

The lawyer flinched.

"I don't know who they are," Macer said, "but my father was one of them, and he said as much as he lay dying. I think that Shayna was one of them, or in league with them, and now she's dead, whoever's still pushing this claim forward is either the Enemy or their vassal. And when I give Nuala nic Cartaí those papers, she'll go after whoever the named party is that's pushing it, and while she's looking the other way, I'll be stealing a starship and jetting out of the system."

"That's a ridiculous plan."

"It's a done deal, if I can buy this rockhopper and shove off before anyone notices."

"One man, stealing a starship? It can't be done."

"It can, if the ship wants to be stolen. There's this vessel in the Boneyard, and the only reason it's languishing there is because its superluminal drive is locked down. The crew wants to jet. The stationmaster wants the ship gone. Even Truxton would be glad if it just disappeared."

"So you're going to find the key to that lock, and steal it."

"I don't need to." Macer grinned. "I have the key in my pocket."

"Is that what's vibrating in there?"

"It isn't."

"It's too slow, a rockhopper," mac Kenna said. "You need a faster vessel."

"I thought of that, but I didn't think I could squeeze you for the price of a longboat."

"It's not me you're squeezing, but your father's rightful heirs."

"Up until recently I thought that was me."

"It might have been, if you weren't so dim with numbers."

"And words," Macer said.

"You were a slow learner," mac Kenna said.

"I'm slow because I'm thorough."

"Whatever the reason, you were cut from the team early on."

"You're saying I'm like a lone wolf."

"More like the slowest calf in the herd."

"You don't like me much."

"I don't, and years of holding it in are erupting out all at once. Luther wouldn't hear a bad word about you. And as to getting rid of you? He made a lot of enemies, carrying you like that knapsack there beside you."

"But you'll help me."

"Of course I will. I've dreamed of the day I could send you off."

"Then I'll need more money to buy a longboat."

Mac Kenna laughed. "Only a fool buys what they can lease. And only a bigger fool leases what they can borrow. I'll call my brother—"

"The barrister?"

"How many brothers do you think I have?"

"I don't know. How many?"

"I'll call my brother, *the barrister*, and we'll pick you up in his private yacht. We'll run you out to the Boneyard and drop you off personally."

"I'll meet you on the spindle. You can call me with the

mooring number."

"You'll meet us on the ring at the address I'll jot down on a piece of flash paper. People with private yachts don't dock at the spindle."

"I wouldn't know that, having never owned a private yacht."

"You might have owned this one if you weren't such a gormless idiot."

"Now you're just being abusive."

"You're right, I am. There's twice as much money in this bag as it takes to buy a rockhopper."

"I know that now, having talked your man down earlier."

"I suppose you would have run off with the rest."

"I would have left it with you, on account."

"And me carrying a sack of money through this neighborhood?"

"No one knows there's any money in that satchel but you. I don't even know it, having only your word that it's in there."

"They would have seen you flashing it, paying the clerk. You couldn't have picked a worse place to carry untraceable bills."

"I don't think this shop takes credit."

"That sad truth is you probably could convince a jury."

Mac Kenna swung the hatch open and stepped out onto the dock.

"Convince them what?"

"That you couldn't possibly be Luther Gant's son."

"You forgot your satchel."

"Keep it. And bring it to this location." He handed Macer a scrap of paper with a dock number written on it. He strode off without a backward glance.

Macer shouted after him. "But you said it wasn't safe to carry a satchel full of money around here!"

Macer picked up the satchel and the package and went to find the shop clerk.

"I'll take the hopper." He shoved the satchel across the

counter. "Scan that bag before you open it. Or find someone you don't like and have them open it for you."

"Gee, thanks, mister."

"No sarcasm. If there's an overage, and there will be, I want the items on this list." Macer tossed a data crystal onto the counter.

The clerk plugged the crystal into a data reader and scrolled down the list. "Got it. Got it. Can get it. No effing way."

Macer tapped his fingers on the box. "Ask around. Tell them it's for..." *Not Singh.* "Charles Newton."

"I'll try."

"Don't try. Do. We're on a roll and I'd hate to see that streak end."

"I know a guy."

"Fair play to ya," Macer said. "Earlier, you didn't recognize that man. But I think you did, just now."

"I don't get many repeat customers. I'd get even fewer if I blabbed about their business."

"Understood. Send all that stuff to the law offices of mac Kenna and mac Kenna. Send the keys to the hopper with the package."

"It would be smarter if you picked all that up here."

"No doubt. But I'm in a hurry. And hang on to that satchel. I'll send someone for it."

"For the bag, not the contents."

"The bag."

"Sure."

"Thanks." Macer headed for the door.

"I gotta know," the shop clerk said. "What's in the box?"

"A fast-acting muscle relaxant," Macer said. "And a power drill."

"I'm glad I went with the money."

"So am I."

It didn't pay to show up at the job site without your tools.

2

M acer fired up his handheld before his feet hit the arcade.

"Byrne's."

"Mrs. B. Is Janie around?"

"Macer Gant. You owe me for the undercarriage of a flitter and almost getting my girl killed."

"I'm not responsible for a single thing I almost do. And it wasn't me behind the yoke."

"You owe me the fare and dwell time. The fare both ways."

"I admit it, I do. I'd rather owe it to you than cheat you out of it."

"You'll pay it, though."

"When I can."

"Fair enough. I'll get Janie."

"I don't want you to get her. I just wanted to know if she was there."

"She is."

"Good. It's you I'm calling for. Do you know, did Rafe do any private piloting?"

"A fair amount. We got a call not an hour ago."

"What'd you tell them?"

"Nothing yet."

"Was it from mac Kenna?"

"That's confidential information. We could get sued for releasing it."

"What sort of person would sue over something like that?"

"The kind that didn't have to pay a solicitor."

"Well, were you thinking about providing a pilot?"

"Himself."

"I'd like to ask you something, and I'm not joking around for once. If I asked Janie to run away with me, what would you think of that?"

"I'd think it was an insane idea and be dead set against it."

"Suppose I was to ship out with her, and both of us signed to an open-ended contract, one that might last for decades?"

"And what would you both be?"

"Pilot and engineer."

"I'd be all for it."

"There's no difference. She'd be gone away, with me, and you might never see her again."

"The difference is one she's wanted since she was a little girl. The other is something she's convinced herself she'd like since becoming a woman."

"Either way, I'd watch after her. No harm would befall her that I could prevent."

"You're the harm, Macer Gant. The two of you loose together are a crater that hasn't happened yet. But lashed in harness? That's a show I'd pay to see."

"How much would you pay?" Macer said.

"Are you proposing to marry her too?"

"I don't think I am."

"Well, then a dowry's out of the question."

"Suppose Mr. B. was feeling under the weather, and Janie took that private job. That's not a lot to ask for."

"You're saying it could be a one-way flight for Janie."

"It's going to be a one-way flight for whoever is behind the yoke."

"Then we won't take it on."

Macer laughed.

"What's so funny?"

"It's not me asking. There'll be a Byrne pilot behind that yoke. I'm trying to find an accommodation. If it's Janie in the cockpit, tell her to pack a bag. If it's Dermot, then you might as well start keening now."

"Are you threatening us?"

"Best you call mac Kenna back. They're going to turn up on your doorstep either way. They're already in a bad mood."

"Dermot's a better pilot."

"He's a safer pilot. But he's liable to bail out when the ground is rushing up at him. Janie—"

"She'll fly it all the way down."

"She will."

"They'll be carving that on her gravestone."

"They won't be carving any Byrne gravestones today. Not if I can help it, Mrs. B. It's your choice. Even if it's no choice at all. And—"

"I know. Don't tell mac Kenna we talked."

3

———

Macer showed up at the specified docking berth at the specified time. The ingress tube hatch was open, so he started to walk in but his backpack hung up on the hatch coaming. He had bought a bigger backpack, a massive one, and wore his tool belt, full of tools, like a tyro associate engineer shipping out for his first cruise, or like a gormless idiot, depending upon how knowledgeable the observer proved to be.

The fact of the matter was, the first time you did ship out you took a mess of stuff on board, and the reason tyro associate engineers looked like pack mules was because you never knew what you might need until you surveyed the hull, and it was a long walk back to the hardware store if you decided to travel light and guessed wrong. On a Truxton vessel, or a nic Cartaí or Kavanagh hull, an engineer could show up naked and everything they needed would be there. On a family ship you weren't familiar with, it was better to feed the excess into the recycler than to come up short.

He fiddled with the backpack and the ingress tube hatch

until he freed the bulky bag, but it caught again on the hull-side hatch, and he had to wrestle with it again.

He plopped down into a seat with the towering backpack still strapped to him.

The two mac Kennas were seated on opposite ends of the settee across from him. Other than the fact that one had a blue collar pip and the other a red one, he wouldn't have been able to tell them apart. They were both tall, and distinguished, and watching him fumble about with a look that was part amusement and part disgust. Neither one of them would want Macer Gant for a son, and who could blame them?

Macer glanced around. "This is almost as nice as Nuala nic Cartaí's longboat."

In fact it was nicer if you liked creature comforts. It was a little more *ornate* than Macer liked. He preferred the hard, clean lines of the nic Cartaí decor, but it might be the busily patterned fabrics and carpets hid bloodstains better. They'd walled off the cockpit from the cabin. Macer steeled himself when the cockpit latch turned and the door opened. A giant man stepped out, closed the ingress hatch, pushed past Macer to the egress hatch, and eyed the box from Pearse's Macer had in his lap. The hull began moving away from the station before the giant henchman had stalked back forward and closed the cockpit door behind him.

Solicitor mac Kenna spoke. "Why are you smiling?"

"I was a little worried I wouldn't get away clean." And he was more than a little worried they would stuff an Ixatl-Nine-Go into Janie's skull. A big honking guard in the cockpit meant they hadn't. Macer grinned. "Next stop, the Boneyard."

Neither of them smiled back.

Macer stood and peeled out of his backpack. He propped it up between his knees.

"You have an autodoc," he said. "That must be handy."

"We've never had an accident on board," Solicitor mac Kenna said. "Where's my valise?"

"I'm guessing the stationmaster has it by now," Macer said. "And you're missing my point. I mean an autodoc must be great for beating information or confessions out of people. You rough them up, get them to talk, and if they don't, you break a kneecap, or two, pull out a fingernail, or ten, maybe even snip off an appendage. Then it's into the autodoc, and a few hours later you can start again. That's the strange thing about technology. It's a double-edged sword. It can be used to help. Or to harm."

"What do you mean the stationmaster has my valise?"

"I wouldn't call it a valise. It's more like a satchel. A valise is bigger, and meant for traveling. *Valise*, as you're using it, isn't right. It's just a pompous word for small duffel. It's your *satchel* I sent to the stationmaster." Macer glanced out the viewport. "An autodoc is a handy bit of kit on a longboat. Once you have what you want, it's out the airlock with the evidence."

"Answer me," Solicitor mac Kenna said.

"He has answered you," Barrister mac Kenna said. "You underestimated him. Now we'll have some cleanup to do when we get back to the station. I'm more curious about why he's threatening us."

"I didn't hear a threat."

"You weren't listening. Do you think you could beat information out of us, Macer Gant? Do you think you could force us to *confess*?"

"Is there something you'd like to confess? I'll bet as lawyers you've seen and heard it all."

"For example?"

"Who ordered the murder of my father?"

"No one person ordered the murder of your father," Barrister mac Kenna said. "There was simply a general sense that he'd outlived his usefulness."

"Sure," Macer said. "I can see that. But someone had to determine the time, and the place, and the method."

"Those sorts of details are usually left to me," Barrister mac Kenna said.

"And in his specific case?"

"I liked your father," Barrister mac Kenna said. "Almost certainly more than you did."

"So you gave the order."

"It was to be painless. But Shayna made it personal. Not... against my orders. But in addition to them."

"To frame me."

"And, I believe, to make you suffer. She had no comprehension of your relationship with your father."

"Where are her children?"

"Safe," Solicitor mac Kenna said. "Once you're out of the picture, Luther Gant the Younger will be confirmed as the Gant of Clear Island and, in time, assume your father's duties.

"He's a little kid."

"A guardian will be appointed until he reaches the age of majority."

"Who have you picked for that?"

"Would you like it to be you?" Barrister mac Kenna said.

"I don't know. Tell me about the Consortium."

"It's a pity you weren't this curious as a boy," Barrister mac Kenna said. "I'm afraid we may have misjudged you."

"I was a late bloomer."

"That may be." Barrister mac Kenna leaned forward in his seat. "As the Freeman Federation has their First Families, the Cooperative of Loyal Citizens has the Consortium. The Consortium sets policy and acts as an executive. It's a successor to the Council of Families, updated and expanded to deal with modern concerns.

"Membership is open to all citizens but, like the First Families, it tends to be the same families repeatedly. There's been a

Gant on the Council since the founding. A Gant, and a mac Kenna."

"And an Olek?"

Barrister mac Kenna laughed. "Commodore Evil? No, he's not part of the Consortium. We're sane and responsible people. He's a madman, but a useful one."

"I'm not saying I don't believe you, but I've never even heard of this Cooperative of Loyal Citizens."

"You have," Barrister mac Kenna said. "Only by another name."

"The Enemy," Solicitor mac Kenna said.

"Oh," Macer said. "In that case, I'm not interested in the guardian position."

"You're not interested in our side of the story?" Solicitor mac Kenna said.

"You mean about the schism, four hundred years ago? I don't need to hear it."

Solicitor mac Kenna started to speak. "But—"

"Because you don't judge a man by what he says," Barrister mac Kenna said. "You judge him by what he does."

"It's the Freeman way," Macer said. "But that's not why."

"Why then?"

"Because we're far enough from the station now that we can light up the main drive. And because I was born tired of you and your rubbish blather. I was just killing time, and trying to decide which of you was the most pathetic and which the most vile. I have to say, I think it's a tie."

"And yet you expect us to help you steal a starship," Solicitor mac Kenna said.

Macer belted in. "No, I don't think that. I think you brought me out here to help you steal a starship and to dispose of me once I stupidly did your bidding. Tell me I'm wrong."

Barrister mac Kenna pushed a button on the settee arm. "It's nothing personal."

The cockpit door opened and his big bully boy stepped out. He wasn't holding a razorgun, probably for fear of accidentally shredding his bosses. It looked like a stunner, or a nerve disruptor. Either way, he'd have to get closer to do the job.

"I'm glad to know it. And I never asked you to help me. You volunteered."

Janie Byrne hammered the throttle.

The bully boy flew past Macer and slammed headfirst into the autodoc.

The mac Kennas hadn't belted in, but they'd managed to hang on to something.

Janie Byrne had two settings, on and off, and she believed everything else in the world worked the same way.

Macer opened his beast of a backpack and began to unload it, starting with the helmet of a hardsuit. He lashed it to the seat arm and kept digging.

The mac Kennas began clawing in their pockets for weapons. Once he had the hardsuit all laid out, he unbelted, pulled a spanner from his tool pouch, and broke all four of their elbows. He also broke Barrister mac Kenna's forearms because he wasn't as surprised as his brother, and had time to fight back.

"There's a race they hold, at the Academy, to see who can put on a hardsuit the fastest."

Macer togged up.

"Forty seconds, and it wasn't even a personal best."

He tapped on the cockpit door and Janie swung it open.

"There's a hardsuit out here with your name on it."

"How'd you know my size?" She was joking, they were all one size.

"Put it on and close the cockpit door. Don't come out until I tell you."

The bully boy began to wriggle, so Macer clocked him out and stuffed him in the autodoc.

When Macer was done, he was breathing hard, and the mac Kenna brothers had recovered enough that they were beginning to feel the hurt.

Macer fished in the crash cabinet and found a couple of the wriggly numbing bandages, or creatures, or whatever. He tore the package open, flicked them alive, and pressed them onto the two mac Kennas' wrists like the instructions said.

Then he took his seat and surveyed the wreckage.

"That, lads, is how you steal a starship."

Macer plopped the box from Pearse's onto the table between them.

"I heard a story one time about a box that held all the ills in the world, and this lady opened it, and they all came out, but she closed it fast, and trapped inside it was one thing only. Hope.

"Shall I open this box for you, and see what's in there?"

They weren't talking, but cursing and threatening him. He let it wash over him like a wave as he sliced open the box with a utility knife from his toolbelt.

They couldn't help but look inside.

"I've thought long and hard about this, boys. You can start now, and tell me everything I want to know—about the Consortium, and this Cooperative of Loyal Citizens, and New Sparta, and Sampson—and whatever else I decide is important to know.

"The longer you talk, the longer you live. If you're still alive by the time we dock with *Four-Squared*, I'll put you in the autodoc and people will try to figure out how to get Ixatl-Nine-Go out of you without killing you.

"You both seem like smart men. If you want to argue that you were compelled to murder my father by a devil jammed into your skull, I'll back you up. I've seen good people do horrible things because of Ixatl-Nine-Go. If you decide not to talk, or your rider won't let you, I'll understand."

Macer placed the syringe of fast-acting muscle relaxant on the table. He revved the power drill.

"I want you to know. It's nothing personal."

They talked.

Much of what they said were lies, but they weren't consistent lies, and with two of them, and by asking the same questions in different ways, and by combining what they said with what he knew from his time as the Gant and his conversations with his father, he was able to piece together a reasonable picture of the Consortium and the Cooperative of Loyal Citizens and their relationship with New Sparta and Sampson. What he couldn't do was understand how Ixatl-Nine-Go fit into the picture.

Every now and then he'd get a little glimpse of Ixatl-Nine-Go behind their eyes.

They struggled with him as he belted them in, but they had broken elbows and he was in a hardsuit. It wasn't a fair fight, but then he didn't want a fight, fair or not. He wanted to win, for his family and for his people.

"I'm going to give you one more chance," Macer said. "Tell me about Ixatl-Nine-Go. Where it came from. Who made it. What it wants."

They stared at him in silence.

"All right, then get out of the way. Let me talk to Ixatl-Nine-Go directly."

"It doesn't work that way," Solicitor mac Kenna said. "It's not a separate... entity. It's a helper. Like a standard implant, only better. Stronger. I'm in charge. It just makes me more... me."

"My friend Bridget disagrees."

"Then she probably had the wrong relationship with it. She fought it. She should have let it have a say."

"Like a boss."

"Like a teacher."

"And you, Barrister? Is it like a teacher to you?"

He said nothing.

"I know you're in there, and these men are nothing to you but disposable meat."

"When you drill into our skulls," Barrister mac Kenna said, "you'll destroy Ixatl-Nine-Go. We'll die, and you'll learn nothing. That's why there's no hope in that box of yours. You should surrender now, and beg for mercy."

Macer walked to the ingress hatch. "I don't keep my hope in a box." He clipped his hardsuit's lifeline to the attachment point there. Then he took a seat across from the mac Kennas. "I keep hope in my pocket."

He placed the Ixatl-Nine-Go detector on the table between them. It rattled and buzzed.

"You watched me fumble at the hatch. I've wired it to blow. No more atmosphere, no more mac Kennas to ride. I bet not ten minutes later something silvery comes popping out of your foreheads looking for another pair of A-students to instruct in the finer points of evil."

The detector practically jumped off the table and into his palm, it was vibrating so much.

They mobbed him while he was pocketing it, clawing, biting, kicking; they had him down, and their kicks weren't landing, and their arms were flailing and not doing anything, but eventually they'd find some way to unlatch his helmet and that would be the end. He wished he'd really wired the hatch to blow instead of lying about it, but he hadn't been able to get the materials in time.

And then the kicking stopped, and they were lying on him; he shoved himself out from under and Janie was standing over him with a stunner in her hand.

She grinned. "You can thank me later."

"Who's piloting this machine?"

"We're ballistic."

"There's a lot of junk out here that's not cataloged."

"Well, if we run into it, they can add us to the catalog."

The mac Kennas started muttering *die* over and over again.

"That's creepy," Janie said.

"Brake us down to stationary."

"Why?"

"So I can open the hatch."

"This is a mobster's ride. I'll bet you can open the hatch on full burn."

"Clip in, and let's try."

"Roger that. Why are you belting them in?"

"Because I don't want what's in them floating around out there."

"What's in them?"

"Evil."

"Hate to break it to you, Macer, but that bird has flown."

"Pop it."

Janie popped the hatch.

It took twenty-seven seconds in hard vacuum before evil began to drill its way out of the mac Kennas.

"Close the hatch and come here and look," Macer said. "You need to know how to turn these yokes off."

"I'm not coming over there. They've messed themselves in every possible way. They've swelled up so much you'll have to cut them out of their clothing if they live."

"That happens. Now come look."

Janie got it in one try. The cabin began to pressurize.

The autodoc began to buzz and flash.

"See to the helm," Macer said as he cracked the autodoc open, caught the rider between his boot and the deck, and switched it off. The bully boy slumped to the floor, the autodoc began flashing again, and the display blinked: *Upload complete.*

The collision detector began to scream.

"Hang on," Janie shouted.

4

M acer hung on as the shuttle's main engine lit and Janie hammered the throttle. He was braced the right way because Janie never hit the retros when in danger, but the thrust. The mac Kennas and their effluvia raced sternward. Macer hand-over-handed it to the crash locker, pulled out three all-purpose wound dressings, flicked them one at time, and draped them over the three criminals' head wounds. He couldn't hear the bandages muttering over the roar of the main engine inches astern of his head.

He set the autodoc to *stabilize and eject,* which wasn't what it said on the control panel but what they called the setting at the Academy. When it prompted him to insert the first casualty, he had a decision to make. They'd each lost the puffiness that human-shaped bags of gas and water got when rapidly exposed to hard vacuum. Even the bully boy would fit back inside without a lot of straining. But what he really had to decide was which of the mac Kennas went in first. The barrister knew a lot more that Macer would find useful, but he was tight lipped and clever. The solicitor was less knowledge-able but more tractable and less hardened, and thus more likely to emerge from the autodoc willing to squeal on his mates.

The squealer, he decided, and jammed Solicitor mac Kenna in. He engaged the program. There was no point in waiting around for the autodoc to finish. He had no idea how long it would take the autodoc to treat the man enough that he could be safely sedated and ejected, and another casualty inserted, so he hand-over-handed forward to the cockpit and slumped into the first officer's seat.

"You're making a mess," Janie said. "Don't touch anything."

"What was the problem?"

"Truxton longboat on a collision course. It charged right at us."

"Now where is it?"

She repeated the local-space heads-up display to the first officer's station.

"It's not showing a transponder. How do you know it's Truxton?"

"Because I got a look up its skirts. It's cracking ninety. How else do you think?"

"It's outpacing us."

"Its drive regulation is rock hard. We're riding a couch. If you check between the cushions you'll find every pingin pinched when they did the last tune-up."

"Shove me the drive diagnostic log."

"What for?"

"So I can look at it."

"We're getting there."

"They're getting there faster. That's Aoife nic Cartaí, and she's trying to steal my ride."

"Your ride is it?"

"That's Aoife nic Cartaí, and she's trying to steal *our* ride."

"And here's the drive log from *my* runabout."

The first officer's display bloomed with log data.

"Like it, do you?"

"It shows spirit."

Macer scrolled through the log.

"Macer," Janie said. "Wake up."

"I'm awake."

"You weren't moving."

"I was thinking."

"You weren't moving for over an hour."

"I had a lot to think about."

"Your toast was up, so I put another slice in."

"Which one?"

"The one I could lift. You know, I thought at first that you'd signed me up for a celebrity ride-along when I popped into the cockpit and your man was there and grinning. Then I saw the stunner in his fist and decided I was mistaken."

Macer's fingers raced over the main drive's programming interface. "What are you on about?"

"Your lump of meat back there. Ares. Or Adonis, he didn't say which. The footie star."

"That's who the bully boy is? Who exactly did he think would pilot if he stunned you?"

"My da. His other self had him in the cabin and a nerve disrupter to his neck. He said he'd let him go if I just did my job. When I said I would, he escorted my father off and the other pair stepped on."

"And where was your mother during all of this?"

"In the office, locking and loading, more than likely. Nothing male gets past her without an inspection through a targeting reticle."

Macer finished modifying the drive parameters. "How are we on fuel?"

"We have some."

"How much?"

"Does it matter? They're in front of us and gaining ground."

"You're right. Power down."

"That's not happening."

"I need to commit these changes and restart the drive."

"What will that do?"

"Enable us to go faster. Or make us go up in a fiery ball of debris."

"Which is more likely?"

"It's more likely we'll go up in a fiery ball of debris."

"Before or after we catch them?"

"That's why I asked about the fuel."

"We're about out," Janie said.

"Then after," Macer said. "When we can't brake and slam into *Four-Squared*'s hull."

Janie powered down the drive. "Work fast. And leave the driving to the professionals."

He committed the changes and waited for the drive to reset.

"Done," Macer started to say, but the main drive lit and then it was all he could do to hang on.

The drive sputtered out three minutes later.

"I think I heard your toaster ding," Janie said.

"That was the back of my helmet slamming against the bulkhead."

"No, after that, while you were praying."

Macer climbed out of his seat and went back to check. Janie was right. He hoisted the barrister out and jammed the bully boy in.

"You reek," Janie said as Macer dropped into the first officer's seat.

"That hardsuit has a visor. It flips down."

"I may need the air supply for later."

"For when you bail out."

"That won't happen. But I might be thrown clear." Janie pointed out the portside viewport. "Look there."

"I can't see. What is it?"

"A longboat full of losers." Janie grinned and waved. She glanced at Macer. "Now what?"

"What do you mean?"

"I'm ready to hear the rest of the plan. What are you going to rig up so I can slow us?"

"You said to leave the driving to you."

"And I thank you for doing that. Now that we're in front, we don't have a driving problem anymore, do we? We have an *engineering* problem."

"All you did was push a button and hang on."

"That's the thing about us professionals. We make the hard look easy."

"I need to think."

"Before you do?"

"What?"

"No pressure, but so far? This is the best birthday ever!"

5

Macer had a plan, but it required going out on the hull. He needed to rewire the force bands used for planetary landing. It was a simple procedure, though not one he wanted to do while rocketing toward the system's junkyard. A lot of loose debris too small to catalog swirled around out here, and the work he needed to do had to be done with the impact shielding powered down. He didn't want to hole the hull, or worse, end up with a hole in his suit, or in him, but it had to be done if they didn't want to overshoot and have to log a distress call on their way out of the system.

He finished the job in twenty minutes and locked back in through the ingress hatch. He knew instantly something was wrong.

The autodoc stood open and the bully boy lay half in and half out. The barrister and the solicitor weren't where he'd left them either. They were both lined up on the settee. All three had taken a razorgun blast to the face. The razorgun lay artfully tucked between the fingers of the bully boy.

Macer swung into the first officer's seat.

"What happened here?"

"The big man came out of the autodoc under his own steam. He had a razorgun. He shot the other two, then he shot himself. All I could do was watch."

"There's blood splatter on your sleeve," Macer said.

Janie just sat there. Saying nothing.

Ten minutes later she spoke.

"They threatened my family like we were nothing. Like we were *disposable*."

He waited another ten before he spoke.

"You should call home and see if your folks are okay."

"I did. There's no answer. There's always an answer."

He didn't know what to say to that. It took him a couple minutes to figure it out.

"It's my fault if anything happened to them."

"You're a good guy, Macer, but you're just not important enough for it to be your fault. These are heavy hitters. It could be your father's fault, but he's already dead. And anyway, it wasn't you that held a nerve disrupter to my father's head. I'm matchmaker for the family, and I thought about it, and this is the match I've made."

"Let's hope it's not the match you lit. I made your mother send you instead of your father."

"You asked her to. Nobody makes her do anything. Not even thugs like this."

"They're somewhat more than thugs."

"And now they're somewhat more than airsick. What's the plan?"

"Hang on, first. What do you mean I'm a good guy? I'm a great guy."

"You're great craic, most of the time. But I think you're more into me than I am into you."

"It's because I negged you that you're saying this."

"It's a spot of blood on my cuff. It's not like I've been rolling in ordure like some I can name."

"Are you unfamiliar with the effects of sudden pressure loss on the human anatomy? And I had to get close to them. I was trying to save them."

"Fat lot of good that did them. Now let's move on. What's the plan?"

"Do you see that big heap of scrap that used to be Truxton's Refit Dock One? I propose we land upon it."

"There's no place to land. And we're moving too fast."

"The primary cross frame is twenty meters wide and five kilometers long."

"So?"

"I've modified our landing thrust bands so that they don't push, but pull. And I've modified them so that they don't all go on at once, but pulse, one after the other, bow to stern. And I've reconfigured them so that they don't pull straight down but at an angle I can adjust with the first officer's yoke."

"And?"

"That's it."

"That's just a list of facts, not a plan."

"Oh, so it is. The plan is you keep us plastered to the cross frame and I lay on the brakes."

"So all I have to do is crash-land and skid in a perfectly straight line for five kilometers, plus or minus ten meters to either side."

"And lift and set down now and then to avoid the derricks welded to the frame. They're big, so you can see them coming from a long way."

"We're plowing along at a fair clip."

"They'll be coming up fast. That's why it's a professional pilot behind the yoke and a lowly associate engineer on the brake."

"And that's the best plan you could come up with?"

"No, Janie, I discarded a dozen better ones and settled on

this one, and all because you whacked the prisoners I meant to interrogate."

"You interrogated the stuffing out of them already. You weren't getting any more." She adjusted the piloting display. "I suppose it won't hurt to try. Unless we hit one of the derricks."

"Or slide off the edge and spiral into the supporting framework."

"That's true."

"You have more experience crash-landing than any pilot I know. Just do what comes naturally."

"Very funny. What do we do once we're down and settled?"

"If we don't have to fight momentum, we should be able to maneuver on emergency thrusters. If those don't work, we walk."

"I don't want to walk."

"Me neither. My hardsuit has a pinhole. There's only one thing wrong with the plan that I haven't worked out yet, and that's the jumping over the derricks part. There's no atmosphere, and no lift, and we can't use the lift bands because I need them for the brake."

"We just plow through them and let the forward impact shielding take the load."

"We might have to, but it's riskier than I like. I'd like to avoid them but I don't see how."

"I could blast them with the plasma cannon, and then it's just the debris field we'd be plowing through."

"Why don't you just fling a fission missile at it, and then we won't even be bothered by the debris."

"Because I don't have a button labeled fission missile, do I?"

Macer glanced at the piloting console.

"Change of plans. We won't be landing on the cross frame."

"That's a pity. I was looking forward to pressing the fly-straight button."

6

There were ten more parts in a plasma cannon than a longboat's main drive and a dozen fewer than in its maneuvering thrusters. They all used the same fuel, and other than the fact that two were designed for impulse operation and the other for continuous use, they were more similar than different.

Macer yanked up the deck plates.

There was a separate reservoir for the plasma cannon and the main drive and thrusters. There was even a tube between them and a transfer valve. The gauge on the plasma-cannon tank read full.

"Now I don't even get to fire the cannon," Janie said.

"Try the thrusters," Macer said.

They worked.

"Bring us in at the liberty boat dock. There's a refuel umbilical there."

They bumped against the dock, and Macer tried the airlock. His credentials worked.

He ran the fuel umbilical out and connected it. "Is it transferring?"

"It is."

"How far away is the nic Cartaí hull?"

"Distance or time?"

"Time."

"At the current rate, twenty minutes."

"I need to secure the bridge."

"Go. I'll finish fueling in case we want to boost."

7

C aptain Violet slouched in the command seat like a tyrant on a throne.

He sat watching a footie ball replay on the main bridge display. Oversized men and women clawed and kicked at each other in free fall, scrambling together to push an inflated bag of gas one way or the other.

Macer didn't comprehend the appeal of the effort, which apparently provided amusement for millions. At the end of the day, nothing lasting had been accomplished. They'd start over again the following day, or week, and the only thing would change were the numbers on the scoreboard. If they'd give up their squabbling and all push in the same direction, they could have advanced the ball to the edge of the galaxy by now.

That's not the way most people were made. He'd known that since he was a boy. Who was on top of the tallest pile of bones. That's all that mattered to most. Getting out in front and staying there, no thought at all to where they were headed or how they'd stick the landing when they got there, and him as susceptible as the rest when caught up in the race.

Sometimes you did have to get there first because that

meant you could set up the board, and define the rules of the game, and the players would slot themselves into the positions they were most comfortable with, those where they felt the most competent and capable, safe in a sense of their own power.

He was going to Contract space, one way or another. It would be a lot easier to get there with a ship full of people all pulling together. That wasn't going to happen on its own, though. He could pick a side, and whatever side that was would win. It wasn't arrogant to think so, because they wouldn't win by being more skillful, or moral, or fighting on the side of good and against evil.

They'd win because he knew where he was going, and how to get there, and what he was going to do when he arrived. And because he wasn't thinking about tomorrow's game. There was only the one game, and it ended the same way for every man and woman. All he needed to do, all any player needed to do, was clear their mind of the last play, and stop worrying about the next, and keep their eye on the ball in play right here and now.

Macer strode across the bridge to stand beside the captain's throne. The light from the main display bathed the captain in flickering bands of light and dark.

"Which one of those players is Ares, and which Adonis?"

"What difference does it make," the captain said. "War and beauty are both faces of the same coin."

"Where's the rest of the crew?"

"In cryo. I'll go wake them now."

"I thought we'd have an argument."

"What about? I made up my mind the day you mutinied. If I ever saw you again, I'd kill you."

"Why are you waking the crew then? I thought you fancied yourself the hardest nut on the shaft."

"I'm not waking them to help me. I'm waking them so they can watch you die."

"You won't be able to wake them before Aoife nic Cartaí and her crew get here."

"I can wake enough for a good fight."

"She has two squads of Imperial Huangxu shock troops with her. Mercenaries in her command."

"Then they won't fight so hard if it's only about a payday."

"The Invincible Spear Bearers of Imperial Wrath are cannibals. You're the payday."

"You're making that up."

"I've been nothing but straight with you. Look it up if you want. They are listed as out of Gallarus system in the Registry. They're cast-off hull breakers, and I'd rather they come aboard through the hatch rather than the hull and with a leash yet on them. They'll be here in less than twenty.

"I don't care if you hate me and want to kill me. If I'm still alive once my job is done, then I'll fight you, and if you kill me, fine. Either I'm stealing this vessel or Aoife nic Cartaí is, and either way it's going out-system as soon as I get the Templeman drive active. You can fight me now or—"

"Or what? Take orders from you?"

"The only order I'll give you is where to go and when to get there. Do I look like I know how to captain a starship?"

"Aoife nic Cartaí does."

"Indeed she does, and what's worse, she takes orders from her mother. I'm a free agent, without guild or family, and any agreement between us is between the pair of us alone. But that's not the driving factor."

"What is?"

"I need you, and she doesn't. And once I take the drive out of maintenance mode—"

"She doesn't need you, either."

"The thought had occurred."

"How do you propose to defeat her?"

"We won't even engage at first. *Four-Squared* is a double-ender. We'll install her and her crew on the secondary bridge and tell them they're in charge. If we need to meet with them, we'll do it on neutral ground, in the liberty boat debarkation lounge."

"She'll want to set the agenda."

"That's the beauty of the plan. I want to go the same place as her, and with the same degree of urgency. So long as I get there, I don't care what happens next. If the pair of you want to fight it out you can, just leave me out of it. You'll have your whole crew awake by then, and ready to rumble. And if you still want to kill me, and I've finished my work and am still pumping air? You're free to try."

"I'm free to try now."

"You are. And I won't blame you if you do. I know I'd be mad if someone did to me what I did to you. Even if it did save me from hanging for failure to render aid."

Macer was wearing a hardsuit and the captain was in his shirtsleeves. Unless the captain had a weapon to hand, there was only one way that fight would turn out.

The captain looked him up and down. "Mutiny is a hanging offense as well."

"It is. And it's a charge yet outstanding against me. So if you were feeling lazy, all you'd have to do is testify in court. You could attend my execution rested and relaxed."

"I'd rather feel your neck between my fingers."

"I expected as much."

"I could force you to turn on the Templeman drive right now. We could jet before nic Cartaí gets here."

"First, I don't think you could force me. Not in time to avoid nic Cartaí. Second, then it would be you on the hook for stealing a starship. This way you can say I forced you to go along."

"But I could kill you sooner."

"You could try to, anyway. Let me ask you. Have you ever stolen a starship?"

"Why?"

"Because I have. And it's not as easy as it looks."

It was easier.

The captain stared at him. "I'll think about it."

"I'm going to go put my stuff in my cabin. You'll let me know when you've made up your mind."

"I'll let you know all right, junior."

MACER PARKED his backpack in the corner and unlatched the hardsuit's helmet.

He wouldn't have been able to fight back against the captain very effectively in the hardsuit, but he would have been a lot harder to hurt. In addition, he had complete control of the vessel's environmental systems with his handheld and chief engineer's credentials.

He could have locked the bridge hatch and triggered the fire-suppression system, which fought fire by removing oxygen from a compartment. There'd still be atmosphere, just not anything the captain could process to breath. The captain could have fished around for a rebreather; every bridge station had one, but then he wouldn't be able to fight Macer at the same time. And if Macer wanted, he could put the rebreathers in maintenance mode as well, so long as he got to them first.

Macer peeled out of his hardsuit. He pulled a clean set of utilities out of his backpack. He was pulling them up when a shadow fell across him, and he looked up, and a massive fist smashed into his skull.

Macer was down, his feet tangled in his utilities, and the bigger man pounding on his head and neck. If he slumped any further down he'd be on the deck, and then it wouldn't be fists, but hullwalkers pounding him and he wouldn't get up from that.

Macer slammed his fist upward and connected with his attacker's groin, and the man leaned over, and groaned; when he leaned back, Macer grabbed the man's belt and rode the upward momentum. Macer had one hand under the mattress, blindly fishing, and the other blocking the blows raining down on him when a voice spoke from the corridor.

"Looking for this?"

Both Macer and his attacker looked. It was the captain, and he had a big slug thrower in his fist, the one Macer was digging around under his mattress for. Macer tried to lunge sideways but the bigger man held him firm, the captain's finger licked the trigger, and the gun seemed to explode.

Something wet and moist splattered Macer's face.

The captain tossed the handgun onto the bunk.

The big man slumped onto Macer, pinning him to the mattress, the hot barrel of the handgun digging into Macer's shoulder blade.

"I'm in," the captain said. "Let's go wake the rest of the crew."

MACER SHOVED the body off him. Most of its face was gone, but enough was left that he recognized him.

"Ares or Adonis?"

"I can never tell," the captain said. "Get cleaned up. I have something to show you."

Macer hosed off and climbed into his spare utilities. He buckled his hullwalkers on.

"Fifty-three seconds," the captain said. "A useful fact. Come on."

He led Macer down two decks to the cold-storage compartment and began triggering the defrost cycle on the chambers.
"Check out those last four," he said, pointing.

Three were empty. One had a bully boy in it, a big, hard-
looking man that seemed identical to the big, hard-looking
man lying in a pool of blood in his cabin, and also identical to
the one with a face full of razorgun flechettes on the stolen
private yacht, and presumably identical to the man Janie said
had threatened her father on the planet. There was no way the
man the captain had shot was the same man that had threatened Janie's father. That meant there was at least one more of
these maniacs loose on the planet.

His work done, the captain stood beside Macer and gazed at
the cryo chamber. "The Violent Offenders' secret weapon. Four
identical players, indistinguishable from each other using
modern testing methodology."

"Where are the other two?"

"They left the vessel the same night Singh did. Then they
dropped off the chart."

"One of them's on the private yacht we arrived on. The
other's still on the planet."

"What are they doing there?"

"One is decomposing. The other one? I don't know."

"Huh. Singh leaving didn't surprise me. But those two
leaving did."

"Your footie team, including these two. Are you allowed to
have neural implants?"

"That's considered cheating."

"Okay. But is it done?"

"It's too easy to police. Footie's a betting sport. We're
scanned before and after every game."

"The one on the yacht. He had an implant."

"Then he wasn't of any further use to me. If I wake this mug
up, is he liable to go for you too?"

"I don't know. I don't know why the one that attacked me in the cabin attacked me."

"Did you do anything to any of the others?"

"Killed one."

"Accidentally or on purpose?"

"Sort of half and half."

"That explains it then," the captain said. "These blokes are telepathic."

Macer laughed.

"It's true, but strange. They can't read anyone else's minds. Just each other's. It makes them awesome at footie, and I'd field them all at once if I could, but there'd be questions about four of them. With two they're not that out of the norm. Twins are pretty common nowadays."

The captain's handheld beeped.

"Your friends are here. Keep them out of my way."

"Yes, sir. And they're not my friends."

"Fair enough. When can you have the Templeman drive ready?"

"I would have done so by now without the scuffling in my compartment."

"We'll be ready to boost in no more than six hours from now."

"I'll have the drive online by then."

"I'm keeping our remaining Ares Adonis on ice. I don't know how their telepathy works. He might not have anything against you when he wakes up and then again he might."

"You're the one who shot his twin just now. I just exposed mine to vacuum until an implant clawed its way out of his head. If he wakes up remembering all that, I expect he'll go for you first."

"Get the drive up," the captain said. "Then we can wake him and see."

"That's grand."

The captain glared at him.

"I mean, yes, sir, Captain."

"When you're done, give some thought to what we should do about the Ares Adonis loose on the planet. I want him out of the picture."

"I'm with you. I've already thought about it."

"And?"

"I know a guy."

8

Trinity System, Freeman Federation

Seamus gazed out the canopy of the flitter at a world draped in gray. The sky spat rain, the clouds low and dark. They were following the edge of a tall sea cliff. Gray waves spewed gray fountains of foam in towering breakers as jagged gray rockfalls appeared and disappeared beneath the roiled surface of the endless sea. Landward gray stone stretched into the distance, where a gray promontory rose towering into the swollen sky. The flitter pitched and yawed as great gusts of the approaching storm buffeted its tiny two-person cabin. The pilot's knuckles shone pale against the controls, her face ashen as well.

He felt for her. She was a fair-day flyer and out of her depth. He adjusted the gain on the weather set. A strong gust slapped them. The pilot cursed and gripped the yoke tighter.

Lorelei Ellis glanced at the piloting display and cursed again. "I thought we'd be closer by now."

"We're getting closer every minute," Seamus said. "Is there a landing light?"

"You don't think we'll get to Seán mac Diarmuid's before nightfall?"

"At the rate we're going?" He gazed at the piloting track. "It'll be close."

"Then you take the yoke, ace."

He wanted nothing more. The flitter's main thruster was nearly idle. "Can't."

"You still have one good hand."

"It takes two hands and two feet to pilot."

"We both know that's a lie for people like you."

"People like me. One-handed, struck-off merchant apprentices."

"Space-born Freemen. One hand for the yoke and a contract in the other. *Just initial here, darling.*"

"I've never called anyone 'darling.'" And he'd never touch a contract, or a piloting yoke, again.

"You're young. There's still time."

"I guess," he lied.

He studied the navigational plot. He studied the weather projection. He glanced at the controls. "We'll need another thousand meters of altitude to clear that ridge. If you start climbing now, it'll go easier."

"You should take the yoke."

"Can't."

The flitter began to climb. The winds were stronger up higher.

"What aren't you telling me?"

He wasn't telling her anything but what she needed to know. That way when he failed her she wouldn't have to rewrite his part in the story she was telling herself. "You need to add some thrust."

"And you need to be honest with me."

"Why?"

"Why not? How's this altitude?"

"Add another two hundred meters. It's gusty up here."

The little craft pitched. Their shoulders touched.

She glanced at the altimeter. "Now?"

"We'll clear."

Patches of green appeared in the gray below. A shaft of sunlight sliced through the clouds far out to sea, and then it was gone.

"About the landing light..." Seamus said.

"There isn't one."

"That's grand. We need to pick up the pace."

"Then you need to take the yoke."

"Can't. Add thrust a little at a time."

"I don't have a pilot's reflexes."

"You do. You just don't know it yet. You need to..."

"I need to what?"

"Look around. There's nothing to run into. And we're over the ridge. Plenty of room to correct if we catch a downdraft."

"That isn't what you started to say."

It wasn't. *Have faith. Trust yourself.* A fool's philosophy, mouthed by a fool. "How are we on fuel?"

"Fine." She stared through the canopy in silence.

He liked Lorelei Ellis. She'd been an understanding host. Polite. Formal. On guard. Macer had warned her about him, he was certain. Seamus mac Donnacha was bent, and always on the make. All of which was true.

Had been true.

He studied her profile.

He wasn't Seamus mac Donnacha anymore.

And he wasn't bent.

He was broken.

"I have seizures," he said. "Ones I can't predict."

She glanced at him.

"Sometimes I black out. I thought at first they were stress induced. But..."

"But what?"

"They're getting worse, and more frequent. And all I've been doing is working out, and eating, and lying around waiting to feel better. It's not that I don't want to take the yoke."

"You can't."

"Not and keep you safe."

"Do I look like I need protecting?"

"Everybody needs protecting."

"Do I look like I need protecting from you?"

"You might want to rephrase that."

"Oh."

She'd been following the news. She knew all about Seamus mac Donnacha.

How his father had disowned him, and cut him off from the family.

How Truxton Trading had fired him for cause. How Thomas Truxton was still trying to decide, not whether to sue Seamus mac Donnacha for damages, but for how much.

How the Merchant Guild had pulled his merchant's apprentice license and banned him from trade, not just for a period of time, but "*for all eternity.*"

And how he, Seamus mac Donnacha had turned, not just pirate, but *slaver.*

Old-timers claimed that there weren't any laws in the Freeman Federation, only contract and custom.

The Trinity Station stationmaster thought otherwise. The argument hadn't yet been settled.

There was one topic they *did* agree on, however.

Seamus mac Donnacha was a monster and deserved to pay for his sins. They were only arguing over the price.

"How's this, then," she said. "Do I look like I need *your* protection?"

"You don't. But you need to get a move on, unless you want to try landing in a farmyard by feel alone."

"I'd planned to land on the boreen."

"That's different, then. Carry on."

"It's not any different, and you know it."

"I might, if I knew what a boreen was."

She eased the throttle forward.

She was silent for a long time.

Again and again she eased the throttle forward. The muscles of her jaw worked, her grip on the yoke causing tendons to bulge.

"Did you really do all those things people say you did?"

"All of them? Probably not. But most of them?"

She glanced at him.

"Without a doubt, I did."

"Why?"

He stared into the gray distance. "Because I wanted to."

"I don't believe that."

He hadn't believed it either, at first.

It was full dark when they roared over the farmhouse at seventy-five percent thrust.

A landing light blinked on below.

"That's new." Lorelei Ellis eased off the thrust and swung the flitter in a ragged arc.

"Someone's looking out for you."

"For us," she said.

"That's a thought."

He watched the ground rise toward them.

He wished there was some way they could land, and she alight amongst friends, and he could carry on, downward, through soil, through stone, into the roasting heart of the world, where he could pay for his sins fully and finally. But the world didn't work that way, not in fact, but in dreams only, and he no longer dreamed.

The flitter settled with a lurch.

She powered the machine down.

She was out and smiling and holding her hand toward him. "Come on."

He unbelted.

He watched her fingers begin to shake. He glanced at her face. It had begun to shake, and her hand had withdrawn, and it shook toward her lips, and smothered her gasp. Her gaze met his, and she *saw* him, and he cursed, and felt the tremors wrench him from the seat into the footwell, where the shaking began in earnest and grew in amplitude and frequency until the shaking tore the world into black tatters.

When it was over, he lay slumped on the floor of the flitter, slick with sweat. The control cluster dug into his hip. He'd bit his tongue. And wet himself.

He closed his eyes, blocked out the sound of her shouts for help, and recalled the look on her face as all pretense was stripped from him and the truth of what he'd become lay bare between them.

I deserve this.

I deserve this.

I deserve this.

An old man spoke. "What's he muttering?"

"Lies," she said.

"That figures," the old man said.

9

The farmhouse was more cottage than house; small, dark, and lit by a turf fire and portable lanterns, the sort one would find in a military-surplus shop. There was running water in the kitchen sink and nowhere else inside. The toilet was in a shed across the farmyard, and water for washing up from a bucket and hand pump in the farmyard between the house and a small river downslope. He wondered if the *bean an tí* scrubbed the laundry against the rocks on the riverbank, like in some first-landing drama on the *Family Life* entertainment feed. The only thing missing was a mound of hay next to a milking stool inside the front door, and a sow and heifer bedded down for the night beside a straw tick for their master.

This has to be a put on, Seamus decided. No one would live like this on purpose.

Seamus fished his duffel out of the flitter and cleaned up in the outhouse, in the dark. His muscles ached all over like they always did after a seizure, but no more than usual. It was embarrassment alone that caused his cheeks to burn and his stomach to roil. In time that, too, would pass, and he'd be able to live on, if he wanted to, in a state of constant shamelessness, case-hardened to any and all opinions of his worth, including his own. He could exist like an animal, one whose behavior was predictable if occasionally disturbing, a beast not entirely housebroken and beyond any assessment of right and wrong. Beyond judgement. Beyond *blame*. In time justice would find him, but by then he would be of no more consequence than the pet rat in a mad prisoner's cell.

The landing light stood at the top of a telescoping standard mounted to a wheeled cart. The cart had a hitch tongue that looked like it could be attached to and towed by *something* mechanical—a farmer's tractor or a military-surplus go-anywhere. The light didn't have a battery pack. A long power lead ran beside the narrow track they'd set down on. Lorelei had landed into the wind, and uphill. The wire led downhill. He wrapped his thumb and index finger around the wire and traced it down the hill.

He found a weatherproof junction pedestal a hundred meters from the cottage.

He followed the boreen downhill further, until he could make out the darker shadows of a proper farmhouse perched beside a narrow cove, the silhouettes of half a dozen seagoing vessels tied to a low seawall and dock. The shadow of a large barn or hangar stood beside the farmhouse.

He chuckled, turned uphill, and struggled against the gravity of an alien world, one where he was a stranger, and would always remain a stranger. He grew winded by the time he reached the farmhouse cottage and ducked inside. Lorelei Ellis and Seán mac Diarmuid were seated across from each other, on either side of the fireplace, Lorelei on a hand-hewn bench and Seán on what did look like a milking stool.

Ciarán mac Diarmuid's father looked like an older and more shopworn version of Ciarán; big, and tall, with large, scarred hands. A hard man, from a hard land, straight from central casting. Lorelei patted the bench next to her.

Seamus sat and met the old man's gaze. He could be fifty or a hundred and fifty. The wear on him looked honestly earned under a single star's light, though Seamus didn't know that much about planet dwellers, or much about any of the mac Diarmuids but his Academy roommate.

Ciarán had three brothers, all fully grown and moved to the mainland. His mother was dead. His father wasn't. He'd said he was from the back of beyond but Seamus hadn't had any idea just how far back that had meant until now. That Ciarán had climbed out of the gravity well on brains alone didn't just seem farfetched anymore.

It seemed a miracle.

"I got a message from Macer Gant to see you," Seamus said. "Otherwise I wouldn't have..." He stared at his hands. "Bothered. Um... You."

"It's a bumpy flight on a good day, and you're not up for the walk," Seán said.

"I'm not."

"Laura, go get the package, if you don't mind. It's in the lean-to."

Lorelei Ellis nodded and rose. She entered a small, unlit alcove in the back wall of the cabin.

"She had some speed on her when she passed overhead," mac Diarmuid said.

"She did."

"The flitter's not her natural habitat. She's a fine horseman, and an even better walker."

"So I understand."

They stared at each other.

"You're in no shape to be out on your own."

"I won't argue that. I didn't ask her to bring me."

"You wouldn't need to, being Macer Gant's friend. She took a great risk for you."

"I know that. I wish I could repay her in some way."

"Strange. While you were outside just now, I recalled a story."

"About me."

"About a man. It's not our way to tell stories about people we know or might come to know."

"It's the same on the station, mostly."

"I'd heard that. Anyway, in this story, the man so vexed a woman with his pestering that she did what he asked, even though she knew it was impossible."

"And it turned out she was right. It was impossible."

"Turns out she was wrong, but she didn't dare tell him."

"That's not a very interesting story."

"It's not, only because it's not the whole story. The interesting part of the story, and the part that put me in mind of it, is what she thought, and didn't say."

"Said to others but not to the man, you mean."

"Obviously. Do I look like a mind reader?"

Seamus shivered, and crossed his arms. "I don't know." He gazed into the fire. He hadn't believed there was such a thing. Not until one took up residence in his head.

Read his mind, and not just revised his thoughts, but... rewritten them.

"Faith, grant me wings," Seán said. "I wish I could repay him."

"Repay whom?" Lorelei Ellis stepped over Seamus's legs and dropped into the seat next to him. She handed a shipping carton to Seán mac Diarmuid, one about the size of a hardsuit helmet.

"The man in the story. The one who vexed the woman."

"That's every man, in every story," Lorelei said.

"It is." Seán mac Diarmuid tapped Seamus's knee with a single work-callused finger. "Look here, this is what Macer Gant left for you. You've had a long day, and it can wait for opening until the morning. But I promised I'd give it to you sooner rather than later."

"Open it."

"You might want to be alone. He said it would likely upset you."

He was alone. He just happened to be sitting in a room with people watching him.

He stared at Seán mac Diarmuid. "Do you know what's in there?"

"I do."

He turned to Lorelei Ellis. "Do you?"

"I put it in there."

"Then show me."

10

The lid of the box slipped over the base of the box, so that opening it was a two-handed operation. Seán mac Diarmuid placed the lid on the flagged hearth before the fire. The reflected light made his eyes seem to gleam, one half of his face in shadow. He gazed into the box.

He dipped his fingers in and drew out a data crystal.

"It looks like volcanic glass," Seán said. "Obsidian." He passed the crystal to Seamus.

"It's not," Lorelei said. "It's all the business records of the Gants from the time they set foot on Oileán Chléire until the day Luther Gant was declared alive again. Macer made a copy before he was declared no longer the Gant."

Seamus examined the crystal. There was nothing special about it that he could tell. "What am I supposed to do with this?"

"You're supposed to use it to help you find a man," Lorelei said. "A New Spartan navigator calling himself Ares Adonis."

"What for?"

"According to Macer, he's abducted Macer's half brothers."

"But you don't believe that."

"They might have gone with him willingly after their mother died."

"What am I supposed to do if I find him?"

"When you find him you'll tell Seán. Or me."

"And then what?"

"And then that's it."

"That's not very upsetting. Unless the mother is someone I know."

"Shayna Gant?"

"I don't know anyone with that name on them."

"Shayna anything?"

"Not that I recall."

"There's more," Seán said. "In the box."

Seamus pocketed the data crystal. "Is there a data terminal I can use?"

"Could be," Seán said. "What's one look like?"

Seamus glanced at Lorelei.

She shook her head. "This is the back of the back of beyond. Don't you have a handheld?"

He glanced at the empty space where his right hand used to be. "I don't."

"I can't believe I said that. I—"

"Forget about it." The reason he didn't have a handheld wasn't because he didn't have two hands. It was because until recently he'd had an implant, and a powerful one. He hadn't needed a handheld for communication. And he'd never been more than a hundred paces from a data terminal for most of his life. "What else is in the box?"

"This."

Seán mac Diarmuid pulled a mechanical hand from the box and shoved it at him.

Seamus lurched backward.

"Take it. It won't bite."

"I don't want it."

"Macer says it's a beauty." Seán shoved the thing at him again.

Lorelei took the hand and placed it on the bench between them. "What Macer said was that the workmanship was unlike anything he'd ever seen. And that if you ever wanted an augmented hand that you'd be hard pressed to find a better one."

"What's that in its fingers?"

"The grip of an Olympic-class force blade. Macer couldn't figure out how to remove it. He thought that whoever could fit it to you could get the weapon loose from the hand."

"Where'd he find it?"

"Got it off a fellow less than a kilometer from here," Seán said.

Seamus laughed. "Forget I asked."

"Seán's telling the truth. Rik Severn, the man with this hand, was an ally of Ares Adonis. He might even have been an employee or employer. Macer thought that even if you didn't want the hand for yourself it might help you find who made it, and that might lead you to Severn's next of kin, and they might be able to lead you to Adonis."

"So that's a dead man's hand?"

"It's your hand now," Seán said. "Whether you want it or not."

"I need to think about this."

Seán reached into the box again and pulled out a circular plate trailing a mass of long filaments finer than a hair. He handed it to Lorelei, who placed it next to the hand.

"Mating plate," he said. "Had to soak the fellow's stump in lye to get it off with all the conductors intact."

Seamus felt the blood leave his face. "That's a fact I didn't need to know." He took a couple deep breaths. "Is that it?"

"One more item." Seán reached into the box and pulled his

closed fist out, turned his hand fingernails up, looked Seamus
in the eye, and opened his fist.

Seamus glanced at the object on his palm and for an instant
the idea didn't register, then it did, as his limbs began to spasm,
and his brain began to scream, and he pitched off the bench,
and landed in the fire. He shook against the coals, teeth chat-
tering in his skull, until his skull hammered against a fire dog
once, and he saw stars, and once again, and he saw black, and
heard a man screaming *die, die, die, die,* and he wanted to,
wanted to so badly, but the shouting was so loud until the
blackness came roaring back to swallow him.

HE COULD HEAR THEM TALKING. Something wet and mewling
squirmed across his forehead. Something equally wet wrapped
both of his wrists, and something warm wormed its way down
his arm. The air smelled like burning hair. He'd bitten his
tongue again and couldn't tell if he'd soiled himself or not. The
wet things on his wrists were likely war-surplus combat anesthetics, the sort of cheap, expired kit that every family ship kept
in the first-aid locker. Farmers probably did the same, because
the med packs acted and felt like the ones he was constantly
being plastered with as a kid.

He should be more upset, he knew that he should, but he
couldn't work up the energy. That had been an Ixatl-Nine-Go
on Seán's palm. How it got there was a mystery. He didn't have
the energy to think it through. He imagined he was pretty
banged up, and the anesthetic creatures were cranking out the
pain-swallowing juice. The juice had a side effect of not making
him sleepy, but of making him passive. If a combat doctor had
just stitched him up, the med packs didn't want him thrashing
around and undoing all that work. They had to keep him awake
enough to answer questions but inert enough to heal. That he

was so swaddled in emergency med packs meant there wasn't an autodoc at the mac Diarmuid farm. Seán mac Diarmuid didn't appear to have two pingins to rub together, and whatever he did have had been invested in putting food on the table over the years, not buying insurance against sudden acute injuries that might or might not arise.

His mouth felt dry. His eyelids wouldn't open, or maybe they were already open and it was pitch dark wherever he was. It felt like a bed, or a bunk beneath him. He might be in the alcove Lorelei had entered earlier, to retrieve the package and its hideous contents.

They were talking about him. Arguing, really. He lay back, and listened, and let the medical devices do their job.

11

"He can't stay here," Seán said. "Not with those injuries."

"I'll get him on the longboat in the morning, and into the autodoc," Lorelei Ellis said.

"Nuala nic Cartaí's longboat? I'd like to see that."

"Just you watch."

"He's a Jonah, and she won't want tying to him in any way."

"Then I'll take him off at the station under a shroud."

"And no one nosing around and asking who's your dead man? Unlikely."

"I'll give them something more interesting to talk about, then. Something scandalous."

"More scandalous than a *slaver* and the nic Cartaí breathing the same air? I think not."

"Accused slaver."

"Admitted, from what I hear."

"What do you suggest, then?"

"I suggest you take him up as he is, rough, no treatment on the longboat, and you haul him onto the station by the collar and wet, like a rat catcher doing her civic duty in the daylight."

"And then?"

"And then you march him into the front door of the nearest security station."

"How's that help us? We need him to find this Ares Adonis creature."

"He's not the only man with such skills."

"Macer says he's the best."

"Best he knows of, and that judgement based on experience with a different man. One that hadn't been broken into so many pieces."

"Who else is there?"

"The boy's own father, for one, and any of a dozen uncles and cousins. Profiting from digging into other people's business is the mac Donnacha family trade."

"Do you know any of them?"

"The father."

"And?"

"I'll take the son, even in the state he's in. He has a stench on him, like he's been dragged through the muck kicking and screaming, but I've not witnessed him lying down in filth on purpose, just to feed the greasy till."

"You like him."

"I don't know him but what I've seen of him."

"But you like what you've seen."

"I wouldn't loan him any heavy machinery."

"Macer warned me not to trust him."

"You blow-ins, and your waking of the dead. You don't even recognize it when you're doing it."

"It's a salient fact. Based on experience."

"It's an opinion. Based on another man's judgement."

"Are you saying I should trust him?"

"I'm saying everything you need to know about a man—"

"I can learn by watching him. So you have said. Again and again."

"And you're still not a true believer."

"I brought him here, didn't I? So you could see him?"

"So I could give him what Macer had left for him."

"You could have given that to me and I could have given it to him at home. You made me drag him out here so you could look him over."

"So he would have a place to stay while you're on the station. A place to stay, with someone responsible to watch over him."

"House would do a better job of watching him than you would."

"Then he'd be loose in your home while you were away, and without human supervision. You said yourself, Macer Gant had warned you not to trust him."

"So you're saying you didn't make me drag him up here just so you could eyeball him in the flesh."

"I'm not saying that at all. I'm repeating the key points of the discussion we had, when you agreed to bring him to me."

"Those weren't the real reasons."

"What makes you so sure?"

"Because I know you."

"Not from anything I've said, you don't."

There was a long silence.

"Before I showed him the Ixatl-Nine-Go," Seán said. "What did you think would happen?"

"I thought it would be the augmented hand that upset him."

"Think back. When you came into the house, that day with all of the killing, did you see Bridget as they found her, or had someone covered her up by then?"

"I saw her. What Shayna did to her—"

"Shayna didn't do that. Bridget did it to herself."

"That's not possible."

"I was there on the floor, bleeding out. I watched her do it."

"I still can't believe she shot you."

"That's because she didn't. It was that Ixatl-Nine-Go yoke that did. It was Bridget's finger on the trigger but not her will behind it."

"How can that be?"

"I don't know. But I've known Bridget all her life, and her mother, and her grandmother as well. I've known them like an islander. And it's not her that pulled that trigger, and hopped up onto my kitchen table, and sliced her own guts open with one hand and pulled her entrails out with the other. Mind you, that's not another man's opinion, but my own true witness."

"Why would the Ixatl-Nine-Go make her do that?"

"Like I said, I don't think it made *her* do it, but did it with the body she and it both occupied."

"Fine. But why?"

"Because Bridget was Macer's pet, is all I can figure. Which means we've been thinking about the Ixatl-Nine-Go all wrong. It isn't just a device that alters a person's behavior by switching off their inner regulator. It's a separate entity. And it's *vengeful*. It murdered Bridget Three because Macer and you killed Rafe and the Severns."

"That implies it knew facts that Bridget couldn't have known," Lorelei said.

"Seems that way."

"If it could do that—"

"It, or whatever is bossing it, could make your man appear a slaver when he's not. And it could do it, not just for the utility of commanding slaves, but as a warning. Or as a punishment."

"Who would it want to punish?

"If I had to judge from the state of him? I'd say your man himself."

"Or someone who cared about him."

"Besides Macer, I don't know who that'd be."

"Ciarán."

"Ciarán's too accommodating to make enemies. Anyway,

there's no need to invent motives and associations. Your man is acquainted with this Ixatl-Nine-Go. If anyone knows what we're up against he'll know."

"And that's why you wanted to see Seamus in person?"

"Not firstly. We have nothing but the nic Cartaí daughter's word linking him to this Ixatl-Nine-Go. I wanted to watch his face when I showed it to him, to see if he recognized it."

"I'd say he did, ten times over."

"No doubt. And he doesn't have a happy relationship with it. Which is another good thing to know."

"What good is it to know all that? You want me to march him into a station security office and hand him over."

"Not hand him over. March him in the front door and out the back door. Air-gap him from nic Cartaí and whoever else might be watching the station for him. Get him to an autodoc and after, get him set up in private and bring him up to speed on all we know. Keep him out of the light, but keep him aimed at Ares Adonis and the stolen children. He'll lead us to the Ixatl-Nine-Go."

"What makes you say that?"

"Because it was written all over his face. When he saw what I had in my hand."

"What was?"

"The truth."

"What truth?"

Seán pointed. "Ask him yourself."

Seamus had managed to crawl out of the bed and sat panting, his back propped up against the cabin wall. "The truth is... Ixatl-Nine-Go isn't done breaking me yet."

THE FLOOR of the cabin felt cool, hardpacked earth, or possibly stone. The corner of the rough doorframe bit into his back, a not quite painful reminder that he sat upright and present in the material world, and that he could yet move under his own power.

He felt alert, like the military-surplus anesthetics always made him feel. He was getting some feeling back, a dull, throbbing pain that didn't seem to have a single source. The only light in the room came from the fire. It played across their faces as they watched him.

He licked his lips and told them. Told them what he knew and had never once voiced, aloud, or to himself.

"There are three stages," Seamus said. "Or states, might be a better way to think about it. When Ixatl-Nine-Go... mates up with a person there's a period of adjustment. It feels... It felt... just like a standard League implant, only better. Faster to respond, a more comprehensive database, better functioning comms, and so on. Like an upgrade. A massive upgrade, but just an upgrade.

"After a few days it became easy to forget it was there. Except... Colors seemed brighter. My thoughts seemed clearer. My reaction times were faster, my decisions sharper and more certain. I needed less sleep. It felt like it wasn't just the implant that had been upgraded, but *all of me*. I was stronger. More capable. I could see in the dark. I could hear whispers from across a compartment. I wondered what else it could help me do. What other hidden capabilities it could unlock. So I spent my off-duty time exploring its functions and the limits of my new talents. And that was exactly what it wanted me to do.

"All the while it was studying *me*. Learning *my* capabilities. Exploring *my* depths. Discovering how to push *my* buttons. And once it had learned enough? It introduced me to the others. And that's when everything changed."

He glanced at them.

Lorelei Ellis leaned forward in her seat.

Seán mac Diarmuid poked the fire.

"The others?" she said.

He licked his lips and nodded. "Ixatl-Nine-Go isn't just an implant. It's a cell in an organism. Once it decided I was compatible, it linked me into the bigger system. I could feel the others. Watching me. Judging me. Pressuring me."

He watched the firelight play across the cabin walls.

"And?" she said.

"And then it began to use me."

He shivered.

"I was aware of what I was doing but it was like my... self... was a... passenger. A nonplayer character, just along for a ride in my own body. I know I'm responsible for all I've done. But I couldn't fight it. There was nothing to fight. It knew how I worked, understood the operating system of *me*. It used that knowledge. I felt how it wanted me to feel. The rational part of me understood that I was engaging in unforgivable acts. And I couldn't stop. I couldn't fight, but I could... stand apart. And record. I could make note of every transgression. I could watch as I abandoned every tenet I'd been raised to believe. I could witness those moments when Ixatl-Nine-Go shoved me aside and took control. I could feel its hate for me growing by the hour. By the day. By the minute."

He licked his lips.

"What it wanted from me. What it wants from everyone. It isn't just our bodies to use as it sees fit. It wants our *willing participation*. It doesn't simply want to tell us what to think, to order us to act, to force us to let it *ride* us. It wants us to want what it wants. To think what it thinks. To hate what it hates. It wants us to *surrender*. It wants us to *agree*. It wants us to *join* it.

"It doesn't want slaves, but helots, who know their place and accept it. Who will take orders from other more senior helots, and who in the absence of orders, will act as if under orders."

He gazed into the fire.

"And did you?" Seán said. "Surrender?"

"I didn't. Not immediately. So it stopped trying to use me and began to punish me. It put me in the same slave pen I had put others in. It forced me to suffer perversions I had watched others endure. It knew how to hurt me. How to break me. It could feel my resolve begin to crumble. But..."

"But what?" Lorelei said.

He glanced at Seán mac Diarmuid. "What your friend did to herself. I've seen it before. There were two women, from a family ship. Sisters. When it became clear they wouldn't break, Ixatl-Nine-Go forced their bodies to fight one another. It was a demonstration. One meant for me. When they were too torn up from battling tooth and nail, Ixatl-Nine-Go had me place a plasma rifle on the deck between them. And then it forced them to fight over it.

"Eventually one got ahold of the rifle, but it wouldn't power up. So she hefted it like a club. And when she was done weeping and wailing on her sister, Ixatl-Nine-Go shut them both down and crawled out of their skulls, and left them to rot.

"When it was over I was glad. Glad it was them and not me. Glad Ixatl-Nine-Go hadn't forced me to burn them to ash before swallowing the muzzle myself.

"That's when I knew. There was no escape. Not even the dignity of a death well earned. I wanted to live. Even if living meant crawling through gutters awash in innocent blood, I wanted to *live*.

"A few days later I was rescued. That's what it felt like at first. Rescue. Except by then it was too late. In truth, there was no rescue. Ixatl-Nine-Go owned me. I couldn't stop it, and I couldn't... admit I was its puppet. Its slave. Not to... anyone who mattered. Not even to myself.

"Ixatl-Nine-Go had held a mirror up to my soul and something craven, and twisted and ugly, stared back. It hadn't made me what I was. It had simply stripped away everything that wasn't me, and left the truth bare for all to see."

He forced himself to meet Seán's gaze. "When I saw Ixatl-Nine-Go again, tonight, on your palm, I knew. It still owns Seamus mac Donnacha. So I've been laying in there, listening to you both talk, and thinking about what to do."

"And?" Seán said.

"And," Seamus said, "I think he has to die."

"Who has to die?" Lorelei said.

"Seamus mac Donnacha."

Seamus shifted in his seat, and groaned. The meds were beginning to wear off, and with them his desire to speak. To be understood. He hadn't mentioned Ciarán's role in his rescue, or after.

When Lorelei looked at him.

When she thought of him.

He wanted this story to be *his*, and not some tacked-on appendix to the legendary saga of Ciarán mac Diarmuid, island hero.

"Take me to the spindle, under a shroud, and dump me there."

"Why?" Lorelei said.

Seán ran his gaze over Seamus. "Because if there's yet a man inside him, he needs to know it."

"Aye."

And if there isn't he needed to know that too.

12

T he only good thing about the spindle was the microgravity. It was crowded. It reeked. There were no solid citizens on the spindle. There was flux, free from friction, unbounded by custom or convention, motion limited by the equal and opposite forces of supply and demand. A delicate balance, self-righting, so long as the whirling never stopped. So long as it never so much as slowed.

The man staring at him was a criminal, which was an accomplishment in itself. That he was a wanted criminal in a system with nearly no laws was a minor triumph. That he might be arrested at any moment and his business dismantled remained an irritant to the man.

"A constant irritant," Seamus said. "One that could go away."

The man waved his fingers, pointing. "Does it hurt so very much? Your hand going away?"

"I don't notice it. It's everything I'm still attached to that hurts."

"And in exchange for some autodoc time, you are willing to make my pain go away."

"That's the offer."

"A hard offer to refuse. But harder still to arrange the... interlocking of deliverables, eh?"

"I get the autodoc time first. It's nonnegotiable."

"Everything is negotiable."

Seamus groaned and shoved what was left of himself upright. He took a step and fell toward the compartment airlock. His fingers fumbled across the controls.

"What are you doing?"

"Showing. Telling isn't working." The airlock began to cycle.

"You fool!" The man was out of his seat. "It's hard vacuum on the other side of that lock!"

"Then you'd best get negotiating. Here, I'll speak for the vastness of space." Seamus shoved his stump in the man's face. "Tell it to the hand, ace."

The man shoved Seamus aside. His fingers danced across the airlock controls. "Stop this!"

"Autodoc first. It's nonnegotiable."

"All right!"

Seamus took his time entering the stolen override code. His fingers were clumsy, and he didn't have time to key the code in twice. His fingertip hovered over the last key. He could end this all, end it now, just by doing... nothing.

The lock beeped.

His finger decided. And pressed.

"You are insane!"

"Maybe the autodoc can fix that. Do you want to go over the rest of the offer now, or after the treatment?"

"Would I get a better deal after the autodoc time?"

"You'd get a different deal."

"But different, better?"

Seamus shrugged. "That depends upon what you like."

"I like less drama. No showing, all telling."

"Better, then. After."

SEAMUS FELT different after the autodoc treatment. Not precisely whole, but... better.

The deal was quite simple, though the man glaring at him from across the table seemed to think it could be simpler. He'd seated himself between Seamus and the airlock. He'd seated a henchman to one side of Seamus and a henchwoman to the other side of Seamus. All three of them were Huangxu, not Eng. *Skinnies*, they were called on the spindle, because they were skinny, impossibly tall and thin, and also because it was some sort of insult, or historical reference, or something else, he wasn't sure.

It didn't matter what people called them, or what they called themselves. He knew them, knew them by sight and by name, knew them intimately, because he'd done a study of them, for his family, digging up dirt his father could use. After all that work it became impossible to think of them as anything but individuals. Sun Kang was what the criminal called himself, and the henchman Sun Shin Liuc, and the henchwoman Sun Li Liuc. Seamus knew the names and histories of every Huangxu deserter and refugee on the spindle, and he knew how to use those names and that history.

"I fail to see why I must continue to pay," Sun Kang said.

Seamus explained again. His former family was knowledgeable about Sun Kang and his activities. In exchange for continued silence regarding these activities, Sun Kang made regular payments to the mac Donnacha family. If the payments suddenly stopped, it would be noticed, and someone would come to see Sun Kang. But if the payments kept coming they would not.

"That's why it would be foolish to stop paying," Seamus said.

"But I get back what I pay."

"You do, less a ten percent handling fee," Seamus said. "Which I've waived for the first month, in exchange for the autodoc hours."

"But... how do I get it back?"

"I've added your name to the list of..." *Enforcers* was the right word, but it felt crude to say it out loud. "The list of *collection agents*. People who make sure that those who owe pay. Your salary as a ghost employee precisely equals the amount you pay as a... *patron*." Unless Sun Kang did something incredibly stupid, it would be years before anyone noticed, if they ever did.

"Can you not simply erase the incriminating records from your family's systems?"

"First, they're not my family any longer. And second, what good would that do? The source records still exist. Anyone could recompile a new set of records just by knowing where to look."

"Do you know where to look?"

"Of course I do."

"Then you could have come to me with your own separate demands."

"I could have. But that seemed like more work."

"More work for more profit."

"I'm not looking for profit. I'm looking for autodoc hours."

"If you're not looking for profit, then you don't belong on the spindle." His gaze narrowed. "I think you don't like this family business."

"I don't like the stench of the spindle. And I have as much of a chance changing that as I do the mac Donnacha family business."

"Meaning no chance at all."

"Meaning I know how."

Vent it to space.

"I just don't have the stomach for the work."

"This money in, money out business. If you can do this for me, then you can do this for others."

He could, until someone realized that his credentials were still active on the mac Donnacha systems. And a little while longer, until they found the back doors he'd installed. The more people he helped, the more likely it became that he'd be found out.

"I could do it, but at some risk to you."

"I see. Have you done all of this for me already?"

Seamus laughed. "Do you think I have?"

"I think you will not do it until you are through using the autodoc."

"There's less potential for drama that way."

"The Hand of the Void thinks like a skinny."

It took him a few moments to realize that Sun Kang referring to him. That he was now 'the Hand of the Void' on the spindle. "Thanks?"

"An observation, not a complement. We can do business, until we can't. Is this acceptable?"

Seamus glanced at the deck. He hadn't been expecting *that*. The only time a skinny *couldn't* do business was after they were dead. Sun Kang wasn't just agreeing to a one-time deal, but offering an *arrangement*. An open-ended relationship, one where it was assumed that they could work together first and settle on terms later. That together they could find some mutual medium and measure of exchange going forward.

"This is a one-off," Seamus said. "I don't think I could hold up my end of anything bigger."

"Fair enough. You change your mind, you say."

"Noted."

Sun Li Liuc spoke to Sun Kang in Huangxu.

"My daughter thinks you are pretty. That you will be prettier once you log more time in the autodoc."

That wasn't what she had said.

"Thank her for me," Seamus said, also in Huangxu. "Tell her that such warm regard is a rare gem discovered in one's pay packet. Brilliant, and unexpected, and as yet, unearned."

Sun Li Liuc blushed.

"You heard then," Sun Kang said.

"That it's not your autodoc?"

"She thinks I cheat you."

"I don't care if you cheat me. So long as I get what I want."

13

After a solid week of autodoc hours, Seamus holed up in an Erlside transit hotel. Nearly the sort of place he used to frequent when doing family research, the threadbare hideout lay two ring tram stops closer to the ragged end of the League slice. Connectivity in the League Sector was better, and the sort of gear he could rent better, and it wasn't as likely he'd be noticed coming and going, or recognized if spotted. The League had an extradition treaty with the Federation, but first the stationmaster would have to jump through the administrative hoops of getting an order, and then they'd have to send someone in to find him.

A spindle rat paid to run errands on the ring wasn't unusual, so he did his shopping fresh from the autodoc, one "hand" in his pocket, the other doling out credits and receiving merchandise; a short stop for the first solid food he'd had since leaving the planet; and then back to the hostel, where he peeled out of his tattered spindle garb and stuffed the ragged Huangxu work-crew rags into the recycler with prejudice. He spent what felt like two lifetimes in the refresher washing the stink of the spindle off him.

He ordered dinner in and ate half of it, some sort of spicy curry that looked better on the room-service menu than it did on the plate. He made a note to pick up a couple cases of tubed rations, which, now that he dressed the part, wouldn't seem out of character for a long-haul spacer raised on synthetics. Thanks to his new ten percent business on the spindle, he could afford the good stuff. *Just like mom used to extrude.* He added juice bulbs to his shopping list.

He procrastinated for another hour, not ready to begin the work he's promised to do. Work he'd been more than good at, *before*, when he'd had a functional implant and a fully functional brain to leverage it. The idea that he could fail gnawed at him. It was a new idea to the man who used to be Seamus mac Donnacha. Seamus mac Donnacha had never failed at anything.

Until one day, he failed at everything.

Until one day, he failed *everyone*.

He had a long list of questions from Lorelei Ellis and Seán mac Diarmuid. Who was Ares Adonis, where was Ares Adonis, where were the Gant children Ares Adonis had abducted, why had Ares Adonis abducted nearly all of the people of Clear Island, who was buying up all the property on Clear Island, and why.

He had his own questions, which were simpler. Where was Commodore Olek, how could he get to where Olek was, and once he faced Olek, how could he make the man pay for what he'd done, not just to Seamus, but to Roche, and to the crew of Truxton's *Golden Parachute*, and to all the others he'd tortured, maimed, and killed. Olek might not be the source of Ixatl-Nine-Go, but he was its sole distributor. Seamus mac Donnacha had filed intent against Olek.

That Seamus was dead.

He wondered if this new Seamus was the type of man to file intent.

That was the sort of question that could only be answered armed with other answers.

It didn't pay to begin with questions. The only way to get answers was to begin with the work. The hours and hours of work that lay before him.

There were no shortcuts.

He sat down at the rented data terminal and plugged the black crystal in. It proved unencrypted, the sort of lazy, unstructured backup/datasuck one rarely saw other than on the entertainment feeds, where the technical wizard pulls a rabbit out of the data terminal and hands it to the detective, and when they both look close, the villain's name is there, tattooed in all caps on the hide of the beast.

He scrolled through the file structure. And kept scrolling. And scrolling.

Macer Gant had loaded the data crystal with his family business records.

Three hundred years of records.

Seamus scrolled to the earliest record.

First Landing, a rathole. Booked passage to Oileán Chléire as directed, twenty schillings, local exchange. Will dig in tomorrow. Having now surveyed this hell, I am compelled to declare. I am owed, brothers. When the day comes, and it will, you may be certain. The Gant will be paid in full.

That was good. He could at least understand the words, if not the meaning. Some of these old records were undecipherable to anyone but expert historians. But the first Gant of Clear Island wrote like a modern man. Even the units of currency remained unchanged. He'd have to look into the financial records to determine whether twenty schillings was a lot or a little three hundred years ago, which would tell him if the Gant had taken a public conveyance or a private hire to Clear Island, and he'd have to dig in around that fact to come up with some hypothesis about what that fact meant, and so on, infinitely, grubbing around in the details until some order emerged, some sense that would then empower him to build a model, and then, and only then, begin to ask questions.

There was a science and an art to what he would next do. The science was still in his mind, had been drilled into it, day after day, year after year, since before he could walk. This was what mac Donnachas did, his grandfather would say. *It is our purpose. Our calling.*

It was only later that he'd learned that their calling wasn't simply to advise and assist others in making wise decisions regarding the future. It was in part that, and in part to bend the future more to the mac Donnachas' liking, and in part to shackle those that made imprudent decisions to the mistakes of their past, and thus ensure their failed ideas would never hold sway again. *While squeezing them for money.*

Now, here he was, the greatest failure the world had ever seen, using that knowledge to bend the future to fit his hands. *His hand.* That he felt no guilt or shame was either the height of hubris or a side effect of irreparable brain damage. Perhaps both.

He wasn't Seamus mac Donnacha anymore. Whatever scruples bound the boy he'd been hadn't been up to the task. He would have to invent his own code of ethics going forward. Before he could do that, before he *should* do that, he needed to know what he was dealing with.

Six hours later he was certain. There was nothing wrong with his brain in regard to this task. He was slower to work because the interface was slower, because making notes was slower. Following the threads, teasing out the details, remained the same glorious exercise in undiluted logic and reason. He hadn't yet begun to think about what the Gants and their associates hoped to accomplish on Clear Island, but he was beginning to sense the pattern of their associations, the nature of their relationships, the scope and magnitude of their enterprise.

He leaned back and rubbed his eyes. He would be here for days at this rate. After that, another day, or three, at a public terminal in the Freeman Sector of the station. Then another day, or two, to mull over what he'd learned.

Then he could ask his questions. Then he could get his answers.

He picked up the newly purchased handheld. It felt strange in his hand. He thought it safer to buy used, so that any usage tagged to the device might be plausibly denied. He'd purchased it on the spindle, from Sun Shin Liuc, Sun Kang's son and heir, and a rather funny fellow. Shin had made the new Seamus laugh for the first time. And he'd made Seamus wonder what it would have been like growing up on the spindle, without prospects for the future or safety in the present. That such a man could laugh gave him hope.

"Computer," he said.

The device ignored him.

"Hey, Computer."

The device ignored him.

He glanced at the device's faceplate.

"Hey, Nemodyne 3050x.

"Hey, Nemodyne.

"Hey, Nemo.

"Nemodyne.

"Nemo.

He tossed the device onto the bunk. "What a worthless heap of rubbish."

"How may I help you," the device said.

"What is your name?"

"My name is Rubbish. How may I help you?"

"I'd like to order four cases of nutrient paste and two cases of juice bulbs delivered to this location."

"A wise idea, my friend. How may I help you?"

"This is going to be a long night."

"Playing 'Long Night,' by Tis. How may I help you?"

14

The Erlside Arcade grew crowded during shift changes. Seamus had dressed in the sort of general-purpose utilities favored by spacers on leave. He'd timed his activities to correspond with the peak crush of humanity, where he would be no more notable than a single electron in the roiling clouds of entangled probability that made up Trinity Station.

He shouldered his way into a general merchandise shop and purchased two cases of nutrient paste, a case of juice bulbs, and a string bag to carry them. He asked the clerk if there was an electronics supply shop nearby. She pointed and the woman in line behind him brushed him aside, and started stacking her purchases on the counter. He followed the memory of the clerk's certain finger, which turned out to be no guidance whatsoever. Eventually he found a shop, one with a window full of dusty display cartons, their once-bright colors faded to pastel shades. A teenage boy leaned on a scarred repair counter, gazing into the guts of some smoky-smelling object.

"Your folks around?" Seamus said.

The boy poked a finger into the charred device. "What do you want?"

Seamus presented the offending object before him. "I want to trade this handheld for a better one."

The boy glanced at the device and then back at his work project. "You think I'm an idiot? Now get out of here."

"Rubbish," Seamus said, "This is going to be a long night."

"Playing 'Long Night,' by Tis. How may I help you?"

"Turn up the volume," Seamus said.

"Turning up the volume. How may I help you?"

"Turn the volume to maximum."

"Volume set to maximum. How may I help you?"

"Enough!" the kid shouted.

"Pause playback."

"Playback paused. How may I help you?"

"That'll be all for now, Rubbish. Thank you."

"My pleasure, Admiral."

"Did you hear that?" Seamus said. "How may I help you. Five words. Try them out."

"Listen, if you're not out of here in one minute, I'm calling security."

"And what are you going to tell them? That you weren't *enjoying the music*?"

"That some Freeman pissant was in here trying to pass off stolen goods."

"I bought this. And it's not working out. I'd like to purchase an upgrade."

"First off," the kid said, "a civilian can't buy a Nemodyne 3050. And second off, there is no upgrade!"

"This says Nemodyne 3050x on the front."

The kid snatched the device from his hand. "Let me see that." He turned it over and over, examining it from every angle. "Hey, computer. Hey, Nemodyne. Hey, Nemo."

"Give it back. Now."

The kid wiped his fingerprints off the device before returning it. "It appears I was mistaken. There is an upgrade."

"The Nemodyne 3050x."

"Right."

"Don't you feel foolish."

"It must be a new model."

"A new model, that looks like someone carried it around in their pocket for years."

"A prototype, maybe."

"A prototype, with the serial number scratched off."

"How much do you want for it?"

"It might be stolen. I need to go talk to the fellow I bought it from."

"Do you think he has more?"

"Do you want me to ask?"

"It wouldn't hurt."

"Squirt your id addy over, and I'll let you know."

The handheld pinged.

"That's not my number. But if you message it, I'll get the message."

"Watch the skies," Seamus said.

"What?"

"It's a cultural reference. Do you not have access to *The Star Fox* this side of the line?"

"The kids' show? We did. When I was a *baby*."

"That long ago? Well, it means wait by the receiver. Don't take a step away, because I'll only call once."

"Oh," the kid said. "Right."

Seamus shoved his way out of the shop, muttering.

He'd assumed New Seamus a tabula rasa he could write a carefully revised future upon. Now it seemed Old Seamus wasn't quite dead, and had different ideas. He'd have to watch his step going forward. He couldn't afford a single wiseacre's smirk. Not a drop of sarcasm from his arrogant tongue.

Old Seamus had the sort of mouth on him that could get New Seamus killed.

New Seamus needed to save his energy for fights that mattered. He needed to remain ever vigilant against all enemies, foreign and domestic.

The job would be easier if Old Seamus hadn't been, not just a total pinhole, but a natural-born one.

Oh well. You can't manage what you can't measure.

Which was good news, in a way.

An infinity of jackassery would prove inexhaustibly measurable.

Which meant he could never let his guard down again.

Not for an instant.

Not once.

Not ever.

THE CYBERNETIC HAND in the window caught his eye. The shop lay two doors down from the electronics supply store, and it was still open for business. A shop bell tinkled as he shoved his way inside.

The place seemed a recycler's shop, unusually well-kept for the neighborhood, a little bit of everything lying about on polished tables and inside gleaming display cases. The merchandise and fixtures grew older the deeper he pressed into the store. In the rear, the merchant's counter had a feeling of timelessness about it, as if it might have been there since the bones of the station were laid down, or even before, and the station grown up around it. That was a mad idea, but Seamus had decided long ago that a feeling didn't have to make logical sense to be true. Feelings weren't facts. They didn't need logic to grow legs and stomp around inside his head.

The closer he looked, the more interesting the shop

seemed. Everything in it was technology from some time, somewhere, most of it quite fine in its day, all of it spotless and seemingly ready for instant use.

An older woman emerged from the back room. "May I help you, spacer?"

"I was just... Your display window. It caught my eye."

She lifted a drop leaf and stepped out from behind a row of display cabinets. "Did it now?"

"It did."

Up close he could see she had a cybernetic eye. Her human eye watched him as her League-manufactured eye scanned the window display. "Any item in particular?"

"The um... hand."

"That old thing? It's rubbish."

A voice in his pocket spoke. "How may I help you?"

"My handheld," he said. "It's unruly."

Her human eye appraised him. "Show me."

"The handheld?"

"What's in your pocket."

He reached into his pocket.

"The other pocket."

"I'd rather not."

She stared at him with both eyes then. "How long has it been missing?"

"How long has what been missing?"

"The hand, the implant, take your pick."

"I've got to go."

"Go on then," she said. "You can tell me about it next time."

"There won't be a next time."

Then he was on the Arcade, the bell tinkling behind him, the deck beneath his feet shaking, the shop signs shaking, the black maw of a service alley shaking, as he pitched into the shaking darkness and let it swallow him whole.

15

"Get up," someone said, and kicked him, so he got up, and slunk back to the transit hostel, stripped, fell into the refresher, and turned it on full.

An hour later the refresher still hadn't washed him away, so he climbed out and pitched into his bunk, and let the blackness inside him leach out into the world.

16

In the morning he downed a tube of nutrient paste and a bulb of juice and got to work digging deeper into the Gant's past. Twelve hours later he came up for air. He grabbed a snack and kept working.

He leaned back and blinked. His eyeballs felt encrusted with sand.

"Rubbish, what time is it?"

The handheld ignored him.

"Hey, Rubbish, what time is it?"

The device continued to ignore him.

"Duh, what am I thinking," he muttered, and opened the workstation's time application. He noted the hour, groaned, and went back to work.

Two days later he ran out of nutrient paste and juice bulbs. He needed to make a grocery run. He needed to sleep. But he was so close to finishing, and it was so much harder to start than it was to continue. It wouldn't be the first time he'd pulled a marathon session on an empty stomach, but it might be his last. He imagined what it would look like to an interested observer. Seamus, the Hand of the Void, hot on the trail of Ares

Adonis and Commodore Evil. A skinny man, sunken chested in his skivvies, hunched over a data terminal, sipping a juice bulb.

He could never be the hero, or even a villain in an action drama. There wasn't any action to see from the outside. Everything important happened behind his eyes. At one point he realized he'd been sitting motionless for over two hours, watching the columns of one long spreadsheet flow by in front of him, only the amounts and dates in the columns changing. The world's most talented director couldn't even make a compelling *montage* out of the hunt for Ares Adonis.

Not unless she was a mind reader.

He could see it all, the pathos in the numbers. Three hundred years of lies and betrayal. Of treason, if there was such a thing in the Federation. Exactly the sort of crimes the mac Donnachas profited from exposing. Or not exposing. He'd thought it a minor miracle the Gants had avoided detection for so long. Then he found the reason why. Sixty-three years ago the Gants had been found out. They'd begun paying protection. To the mac Donnachas.

Thirty years ago the Gant wanted out. Wanted a new life. A straight life.

There wasn't any way out.

Lessons were taught. Examples made. The numbers dripped red.

And resumed, diminished.

New partners were brought in. Accumulated strap-hangers brushed off, including the mac Donnachas.

That didn't sit well with the parasite class. Letter openers were drawn.

And met with butcher's knives.

He vaguely remembered the funerals from his childhood.

Business as usual resumed. Mundane. Plodding.

Between five and six years ago something suddenly changed.

Fusillades of correspondence were fired across the void.

Emissaries were dispatched.

And then the records stopped.

There was more to discover. He was certain of it.

So he pressed on. Back to front this time, watching the action rewind. Genie into the bottle. Wine into water. Flesh into ash, into dust, into flesh.

He was hungry.

And thirsty.

And tired.

And then, he was done.

Done with the hard part.

All that was left was the dangerous part.

17

Seamus stood flatfooted on the Erlside Arcade. The electronics store he'd visited only two, three, four nights ago, some number greater than one, anyway, had burned. Fire on the station was not a trivial matter, and whatever had lit the store up had been left to rage until the store was little more than a charred shell. That the damage hadn't spread to the neighbors was unusual given the apparent intensity of the blaze. The Arcade façade lay swaddled in yellow emergency tape.

He'd hoped to purchase a replacement for Rubbish, which had disappeared from his possession sometime in the past. Lost or stolen, he wasn't certain, though if it had been stolen from him during his time spasmed out in the nearby service alley he was glad the thief had been less than thorough. He'd had Ixatl-Nine-Go in his pocket along with the handheld, and the horrid device remained in his possession. The much less horrid, though still repugnant, Rubbish had not, when he'd remembered to paw through his laundry. The handheld remained missing even after he'd searched his room and his belongings.

Dropped, lost, or misplaced were each far more likely than

stolen. Even the most basic of cranial implants was far more valuable than the most feature-rich handheld. Thieving on the station was a well-practiced art and he'd been dead to the world for hours in that alley.

There were surely other electronics shops on his way to the sector line. He'd try to source a replacement on his way to the Academy. But first, he had business two doors down.

The door chime sounded as he entered the recycler's shop. The shop woman was nowhere in sight. He browsed the displays.

"I knew you'd be back," she said. "This place is like a black hole for the curious."

"Is that what I am?" Seamus said. "Curious?"

"You'd know that better than I. Are you buying or selling today?"

"Can I do both?"

"I don't know. Can you?"

"May I?"

"You're welcome to try. What may I help you with?"

"A pendant spire. The sort someone observant would wear."

"Over here." She motioned him toward a cabinet in a far rear corner of the shop. "You might imagine I have these back here because they're slow sellers. It's quite the opposite, in fact. They're precisely the sort of tourist gimcrack one likes to take home to show the neighbors. You've bearded the lion in his native den, and here's the evidence to show it. A walk past all the merchandise in the shop is worth at least that trouble, wouldn't you say?"

There were two score earrings to choose from, each of them unique. Each of them forged from a single link of slaver's chain. They were family heirlooms, each one. Melancholy reminders of the permanence of matter and the transience of life. "These aren't for tourists."

"Is that so?"

"They're for family members. Each design unique to a single vessel. They're the sort of possession last pawned and first redeemed."

"Do you recognize the patterns?"

"It's not something I've studied."

"But you know enough to know what they represent."

"I don't. That's not something I could know."

"Because not one of them is at all related to you."

"Because they're not meant to be thought about. They're meant to be felt." And when he looked at them he felt... nothing. Nothing but absence. "Don't you have something modern and cheap?"

"I don't. And if I did it wouldn't suit you."

"Then pick one for me."

"You have no preference at all?"

"It's for a costume. I have to go to the Freeman Sector and I don't want to... stand out."

"You'll stand out in one of these."

"Not like I would without it."

"Suit yourself. If I'm to pick I need time to think it over. Let's see what you have to sell."

He dropped his duffel to the deck and knelt to open it.

"Over here, on the counter. Where the light's better."

"Of course." He slung the duffel onto the counter and opened it.

He reached inside and glanced up. She wasn't watching his hands, but his face.

"What are you doing?"

"Fitting you, in my mind. Trying you out in the order of absent families."

"What does that mean?"

"You asked me to choose an earring for you. It's not something I've ever done. I'm working out how."

"It's not that important."

"Maybe it isn't for you. But there's more than you involved. Now show me what you've got."

He placed the mechanical hand on the counter.

"Well," she said. "You are an overachiever. Now, stand up straight and show me both your hands."

He placed his left hand on the counter.

"Both of them."

"You're looking at them."

"Huh." She tapped the mechanical hand. "Show me the cuff."

"I don't know what that is."

"You don't know, and this is supposed to be your hand?"

"It's a gift from a friend."

"I wish I had your friends. An intact cuff looks like a disk with fibers attached to it. Sometimes the fibers are missing, or cut, sometimes part of the disk is missing, sometimes—"

He placed the disk on the counter. The fibers dangled nearly to the deck.

"I've never seen one complete before."

"That's good, then. It makes it more valuable."

"Ten times more, I'd say."

"Brilliant. I'll take store credit for the pendant spire and the rest you can hold on account for me."

"I can't buy this from you."

"I'm telling you the truth. It isn't stolen. It really is a gift from a friend."

"I'm not doubting your word. I'm telling you I can't buy it. Not without cheating you blind."

"I don't care if you cheat me. So long as I get what I want."

She looked him in the eye. "Is that so?"

He stared back at her. "I don't mean to offend you. But I have work to do."

"Rubbish," she said.

A voice called out from the back room. "How may I help you?"

18

"That yoke must have fallen from my pocket in your store," Seamus said.

The shop woman snorted. "If it did it fell back in, because it was still there while you were shivering your guts out in the alley next door."

"But—"

"How did it get in here? I took it from your pocket, that's how. After I chased that rat from two doors down away from you. He had his fingers on it, and was tugging on it mighty."

"The boy from the electronics store?"

"He's no boy, that one. A Huangxu construct, made to look like a boy. Have you not learned to distrust your own eyes yet?" She tapped her artifact eye. "There's two ways to see everything, this side of the line."

"His shop's been burned."

"And him with it, if there's justice in the world." She stared at him with her artifact eye.

"Did you search me?"

"I did."

"I see. Thanks for not robbing me too much."

"I couldn't very well put that device back into your pocket. You were out to the world, but it wasn't. And you were there in the service alley. Right on top of the rubbish tip."

"How may I help you?"

"Can you not see it now? They pick up the rubbish end of the night shift."

"How may I help you?"

Seamus laughed. "I can see it."

"You're a good sport, I'll say that. Come into the back, and have a sit down and a cuppa, and I'll lay it all out for you. You don't want to sell that hand and you'll want to know why."

"I'd like to but I have work to do."

"Work you don't want to do."

He shrugged. "If I put it off, I'm afraid I'll quit."

"But you're not afraid you'll fail."

"The only way I could fail is if I quit."

She glanced at the counter and nodded. "Suit yourself."

"Can I leave my duffel here? I'll pick it up when I can."

"Fine. You'll want your pendant spire before you go."

"I can do without."

"I don't think you can."

"It's just a prop. I'd be pretending. I was hoping you'd have junk. Something fake." Something that would fit the man he was now.

She stared at him with her human eye and artifact eye both. "You're like glass," she said.

"You mean the way I shattered. In the alley." He shrugged. "It comes and goes."

"Not that. I can see *through* you. Any experienced eye could. One fake piled on top of another will fool no one."

Seamus shrugged. "I can't help that. I gave my word. I have to finish what I started."

"And what will happen if you don't? Will the world end?"

He shivered. *It might.* Or the world might go on for a while,

Ixatl-Nine-Go spreading, slowly at first, then geometrically, until the moment came when it was too late to stop it and the world wouldn't end. But every living soul would wish it had. They'd wish that someone, anyone, had ended it, before they learned the truth. There weren't monsters lurking out there, in the void. They were here.

Inside them.

"I need to go."

"You need to know about this hand. What it is. How it came to be. I'll keep it short. When we're done I'll know which spire suits you. The best disguise is the one that hides *nothing*. The eye sees order and passes on, the *tSeán bhean bhocht* says."

"I don't have time for a lecture."

"Not a lecture. A story. A *seanscéal*."

"Thanks, but no thanks."

"In exchange for the time you don't have, I will keep your possessions safe until your return. Tonight, tomorrow, to the end of your days, and after. They will be here, for you, should you call. Or should your heirs."

"You know what? Just keep the hand. Keep the duffle. Keep all of it. I have to go."

"And what of *your precious*? Who will keep it safe?"

"What?"

"In your pocket. That which you refuse to show. I could have robbed you last night, in that alley. *Anyone* might have. Even a child."

"Why didn't you?"

"As I said, you're like glass. Why would I want what rides you to catch me?"

"I don't know what you're talking about."

"Look around. In this shop there's artifacts made by dead hands, artifacts spanning all the many ages of mankind. If I were to pull back my sleeve, or raise the hem of my shop gown, you'd see I'm largely *made* of these artifacts now. And yet the tiniest fragment of the girl I was, once upon a time... her *ghost* remains more in the world than you. Who would wish such an existence on another?"

"So you recognized it. The implant."

"I've never seen its like. What I recognize is a man possessed. Those I have experience with. You are all glass to me. I can see through you, to the heart. To that which you grasp, which is all you love, and all you are."

"You're wrong. I hate it."

"You love the hate you've wrapped around it. Why else would you keep it with you always?"

"So it can't hurt anyone else." And so he'd be careful. If he got caught barehanded, he might somehow escape. But if he got caught with Ixatl-Nine-Go in his pocket, he was doomed. Old Seamus was reckless. A risk taker. New Seamus couldn't afford to be. This way the stakes of getting caught were too high, even for Old Seamus.

"Last night," she said. "While you ware napping in the alley. That tech you're carrying might have been carried off by some rando, and good luck finding it again. Or it might have fallen into the hands of those who burn shops and the boyish-seeming spies who run them."

"Spies?"

"There's a war on, in case you haven't noticed. Several wars, if you believe the news. Your man's been ensconced there for years but only recently activated. It's a new age, and not like the short war from a few years back. This feels all-out. The timing's right, if the past repeats itself." She looked him up and down. "But you don't care about all of that."

"I don't *not* care. But I don't see how it matters."

"It matters if you're serious about parking your kit here. You can leave the League Sector fair enough. But you'll be searched on the way back in. They'll want identification as well. From a government or quango."

"I didn't realize."

"As I said, like glass. How'd you get here?"

"In a body bag. Dumped on the spindle."

"I'm not sure that's the best way to leave."

He didn't want to laugh, but he did. "It wasn't the best way to arrive, either."

"A bad way that works trumps a good way that doesn't. It's all a calculation of cost and benefit. Sometimes you have to pay up front to net out on the back end."

"Like now. By listening to a *seanscéal*. When I really needed to be elsewhere."

"Exactly like that."

"Go on, then. But *please*. Keep it short."

"I will, you'll see. Here is how I heard the story, presented without preamble or footnote."

She looked him in the eye with her human eye. Her artifact eye seemed to be aimed out the shop window, toward the Arcade. After a moment of silence she seemed satisfied, and began.

"During the end of the last League civil war a hundred of the old king's personal guards were captured. They were forced to draw lots, and they were all made the following offer. If any one of them revealed the location of the king they would all be set free. But whoever held their tongue would lose their left hand. They were each instructed to look at the number they'd drawn and to decide. Their captors left them to think the offer over.

"When their captors returned, they found the captives had spent their time fighting over who would be first to feel the knife, and who would be last, and every spot in between.

"The captors' word was good, and the king's guards loyal to a soul, and a hundred cuts, and a hundred hands later, not a one had betrayed their lord. And it was then that the captors made their next offer. It was the same offer as the first, but for the right hand this time. And again, the king's servants held their tongues, and didn't betray their lord's trust. In time all were rescued, and repatriated, and the rebellion crushed for a span of years."

She stopped, and stared at him.

"You've told this story before," he said.

"I was a schoolteacher, eons ago. Children loved stories of blood back then."

"They still do."

"No doubt. But this isn't just a story about blood. When the king learned about the Royal Guards' brave sacrifice, he grew determined to reward their loyalty like no king had ever done, before or since. He commissioned a three-year crash project in what became the foundation of modern League cybernetics, all with the idea that he could repay their loyalty by restoring their limbs.

"That project was the sort of exercise in ego and expertise that only the League was capable of back then. After three years the League scientists had created a prototype that worked. The Crown then commissioned Holland and Bourse, a very famous luxury goods manufacturer of the time, charging the jewelers with the order to produce two hundred hands; one hundred left hands and one hundred right hands. Ninety-eight pairs of hands were made in silver plate, one in gold plate, and one in rhodium plate, which at the time the League elite considered the acme of metal finishes.

"The king called his advisors together to decide how to distribute the hands. The golden pair would go to the first guard to feel the knife, and the silver to the bulk of the hundred. But the rhodium pair. Those would go to the bravest guard. And on this question, who was the bravest, the king's advisors couldn't agree. They were each so puffed up with self-importance and arrogance, they couldn't even consider an opinion other than their own. Some things never change, and if that old king were to walk the deck of the League Sector today, he'd recognize the same stubborn ignorance at work from ring to spindle, word of a merchant."

She stopped and looked him in the eye. "Are you still listening?"

"I am. I guess it was a Freeman school you taught in."

"You'd be right about that. Now I wonder if you'd be right about which of the lot the king picked for the rhodium hands, numbered one to one hundred."

"I don't know anything about the king."

"Good answer. Which guard would *you* pick as the bravest?"

"That's easy." He didn't even need to think. "The second one."

"Like glass, you are."

"Am I right?"

"Tell me your reasons."

"Until the first guard was cut, it was all hypothetical. The captors might have been bluffing. But after. With his own hand on the chopping block. It was real." He licked his lips. "It was real, and there were still ninety-eight ways his sacrifice could be for nothing."

"Some say it was the third guard."

"You could argue that, but the third of anything is just a number. It's the number that establishes the possibility of a pattern. That's all. In this case the pattern was established by the threat and the first occurrence. The second guard was the bravest, no doubt."

"Not the first."

"Calling their bluff. Likely the leader. It would be easier to go first than to be seen as weak."

"Not any of the others?"

"Were the prisoners all held together? Or were they separated, and the offers made individually?"

"What would you have done?"

"Separate them. Make the offer one-on-one. They're more likely to break in private."

"And in private you could promise that no one would know they were the one that told."

"That might work, if the prisoner was willing to lose their hand to cast the blame on the next in line."

"Do you think they might be? Willing to do that?"

"It's hard to say. People are complicated."

"But you're certain. The second man was the bravest."

"That's my answer."

"Interesting. You'll be glad to know, that being a warrior and blooded in combat, the king agreed with you. And the guards were rewarded, and the gifts passed out, and they were marvels of invention the likes the world hasn't seen before or since.

"Almost everyone was happy. Some were happier than others, of course. The silver-handed weren't as happy as the golden-handed. And the golden-handed wasn't quite as happy as he could have been. His thoughts kept straying to the rhodium-handed.

The rhodium-handed wasn't happy at all. He wouldn't even use the blasted things. He didn't think he deserved to be singled out. He wasn't a particularly humble man, or a noble man, or even a good man. Before he'd turned soldier, he'd been a thief. But on that day, in that rotting dungeon, in that sunless cell, what he'd been was just a man, who'd stuck his hand into a sack, and drawn out a tile, and there was a number on that tile. A number chosen entirely by chance.

"He thought the king was wrong. He wasn't any more or less brave than his comrades. It only looked that way if you believed he doubted his friends, and he hadn't. They turned out to be true to their oaths just like he was. It's why he'd joined the Guards in the first place. To put his past behind him, and live amongst heroes. To live alongside them, as allies, and as equals.

"He couldn't bear to look at those rhodium hands. He'd

bought them with the blood of his ancestors. Blood he'd freely offered to a king that didn't understand the slightest thing about people like him. Some say he sold the hands, and others say he melted them down. Some say the golden-handed murdered him and took the rhodium hands. It was so long ago that the truth has been lost, if it was ever known at all."

She looked him up and down. "The story gets sadder from there, but that's a lesson for another day. So ends this *seanscéal*."

She peered at him with both of her eyes, human and artifact aligned.

"You're saying my answer was wrong. The second guard wasn't the bravest."

"It's not a story about right, or wrong, or answers. It's a story about silvered glass and the folly of kings. And of princes."

"I don't understand."

"Rubbish!" she shouted.

"How may I help you?"

"What was the final auction price for the last King Manus Royal Guard Hand?"

The handheld was silent for a moment. Then it spouted out a very large number and an offer of help.

"This has to be a joke."

"Playing 'Has to be a Joke' by Tis. How may I help you?"

"Stop playing," she said. "That will be all. Thank you, Rubbish."

"My pleasure, Admiral."

He tapped the hand. It didn't look that old. Or that valuable.

"It's gold plate, over rhodium plate. It could be a replica, though that's easy enough to test. All in all, thirty of the two hundred have been found, and the bulk of the missing believed to have been destroyed."

"Unreal."

"Indeed. That's some gift. From a friend."

"A friend gave it to me. They didn't buy it."

"Do you know where your friend got it?"

"Off a dead man."

She let out a long, slow breath. "That's a relief then. We won't have *himself* coming around looking after it."

"Won't have who coming around?"

"Whom."

"Right. Sorry, missus. Whom?"

"The collector that bought it at auction last year. Commodore Kirill Olek."

19

Seamus groaned. His head hurt. His arm hurt, the one without a hand. And the other one too. He sat propped up against a reusable shipping container in a darkened room. His legs stretched out in front of him. He was glad to see he hadn't wet himself this time. His shoes were off.

"You have to be the easiest man on the station to rob." The shop woman sat on a crate within arm's reach of him. He hadn't seen her until she'd spoken.

Seamus scrubbed his palm across his forehead. "So you stole my shoes?"

"I took them off you in case your feet were to swell up. And in case you were the sort to snap awake and dart off without a proper goodbye."

"I'm not that sort."

"I can see that now."

"Why's it so dark in here?"

"The shop's closed. It's third shift. A light on would be out of the ordinary. And right now, on this station, anything out of the ordinary gets a lookover. Do you want a lookover?"

"I don't."

"And neither do I. Whatever your plans are, you need to revise them and see a doctor first."

"I have. Repeatedly. I feel like I've been living inside an autodoc."

"An autodoc's not a real doctor."

"I don't know any real doctors."

"I do, but she's on the League ambassador's staff. The embassy's been closed since the shooting began, and all the staff evacuated for their own safety."

He managed to stand on the third try. "There's a place I can stay in the Freeman Sector. If I go now, I can be ready to work in the morning."

"This work. Are you liable to topple over in the middle of it?"

"I don't think so. I've been doing the work in private for the last several days. There's nothing different, except I have to work from a public terminal. One in the Freeman Sector."

"Are you not afraid someone will recognize you?"

"I'm not hiding."

"Maybe you ought to be."

"I can't hide and do what I need to do."

"Suit yourself."

"I'd like to leave my stuff here. Including what's in my pocket."

"I already said you can do that."

"The implant. Put in a burn bag. In a safe. In a vault. Whatever you do, don't turn it on."

"I don't have a vault."

"I'm serious. It is pure evil. If I'm not back in three days crush it. Then incinerate it. Then space the debris. But whatever you do—"

"Don't turn it on."

"Even by accident. And don't do any research about it, either. Not just nothing traceable. Nothing."

"When you come back. Will you at least tell me about it?"

"I already told you everything there is to know about it. It's pure evil."

"Then why are you carrying it around with you?"

"What am I supposed to do with it?"

"Crush it. Incinerate it. Space the debris."

"I can't. I might need it later."

"And the hand?"

"I guess it wouldn't hurt to find out if it was real or a replica. Unless that's a lot of work."

"It's child's play."

"Then it couldn't hurt to find out."

"That might be true. Hold out your arm."

He did as asked.

"Not that arm, the other one. And roll up the sleeve. Let me see what's left of it."

"I don't—"

"Show it to me. It's the price of my help."

He didn't like looking at it. It was smooth, and healed over, a clean cut at the wrist, but it looked so... wrong.

She slapped a metal disk against it. He pulled his arm away but the disk clung on. There were thousands of filaments draped from it, long filaments that hung to the deck. He shook his arm. The disk clung on. He shook it again, more violently. He pried at it with his other hand. "Get it off. Get it off."

"If it's a replica, it will fall off. If it's real..."

The filaments began to writhe.

"It will do that."

He shook his arm. He shook his arm harder. The filaments shook, not in time with his shaking, but to some other rhythm, as if they had a mind of their own. "Get it off." It was like Ixatl-Nine-Go. It was going to use him. He didn't need to think about it. He knew it. It was going to *use* him.

He felt the world begin to shake. He glanced at her and she was shaking. "What have you done?"

"What you asked."

"I didn't—" And then the filaments began to burrow in.

And all he could do was scream.

20

I t felt as if flames engulfed his arm. The pain had blinded
him for an instant, and then it had settled down to something that wasn't even remotely bearable, and then it
settled down even further, to what it was now, a sort of roasting
feeling he couldn't pull free of. He'd bit his lip. The fingernails
of his remaining hand dug into his palm.

"Take note," she said. "You appear to be under a great deal
of stress."

He wiped the blood from his lips with his sleeve. "You
think?"

"I do. I think that, and yet you've not stroked out, or whatever you call it. You're still here, and aware."

"Grand," he gritted out. "How long?"

"How long is it supposed to hurt like that?"

He nodded, tears streaming down his face.

"Three days."

"What?"

"That's how long you said you might be gone. If we're lucky
the pain will last three days, and hold off these seizures of
yours."

"Too long. Make it stop."

"You'll survive."

"You. No idea."

She turned on a pin light. "Look here." She played the light along her left sleeve. She rolled the sleeve up past her elbow. Silver metal gleamed in the handheld light. "They did that one first. It took a year because they'd never done it before." She shifted the light and rolled up her right sleeve. There was a joint, between flesh and artifact midway up her forearm. "Another year, for that one. I'd show you my legs, but I was raised a modest girl. You'd think after two years hanging bare-assed in a hospital sling I'd be used to the stares. You'd be wrong." She flicked the light off. "Now go on. Tell me something about this new idea I know nothing about."

"How?"

"How did it happen, or how did I bear it?"

"Both."

"Saying how it happened would be raising the dead. And how I bore it? Simple. I didn't think I deserved to suffer. I knew it.

"When they were done, 'rehabilitating' me, the pain didn't stop right away. I think some of the doctors wanted me to hurt and to keep on hurting. I made the mistake of telling the psych doctor about my suspicions, and she asked me how that made me feel, and I made another mistake, and told her the truth. That it made me glad.

"They operated on me again, and a month later I was pain free."

She was silent for a long time.

"I'll never forgive that woman."

He made a panting sound. It felt strange, because he was hearing the sound, and he could feel his chest going up and down, but the sound and the feeling seemed separate. Like his chest was going up and down because of the sound, and not the other way around. "Huh," he said, which sounded just like the panting to him, but which felt normal, like it was a sound he'd decided to make, and not something his body was doing whether he wanted it to or not.

"I've made my mind up about the pendant spire you should have, but I'd like you to do a favor for me. I'm going to hand you each spire in turn, and I'd like you to examine it."

"Light."

"No light. Just touch. Feel the shape. Imagine the hands that formed it. Each one unique. Like a soul."

"Don't want to."

"Sit down and do as I ask. It will distract you from the pain. I could tell when you saw them. You knew what they were."

"Don't want to." He didn't want to do as she asked. He didn't want to do anything but get whatever was roasting his arm from the inside off of him.

"Sit. You can't stand there all night."

He sat.

"I never thought of myself as a collector. I don't think I really am. I imagine a true collection as being assembled over a number of years, or even decades. Hunting down leads. Buying or bartering for acquisitions. Replacing lesser examples with greater. Filling in the missing pieces. An activity. A mindset. An obsession, even.

"You seem a smart lad. Tell me what we both know about those earrings."

"Dead." He'd *felt* the truth when he'd seen them. They were pendant spires of the dead. And not just any dead. "Extinct."

"Whole families scrubbed from the world. Not First Families, but Freemen, nonetheless. Men, and women, and children I lived alongside, as allies, and equals. And then they were gone. Gone, not over the natural course of time, but all in one night."

"When?"

"More than sixty years ago." Her metal fingertip tapped the packing crate she sat upon. "Sixty-three years, it is by now."

"Where?"

"Unity system. The night the station fell. It was inevitable, anyone could see the end coming for days. But people with little to lose are more stubborn that people with much, not because they want to be, but because they have to be, just to survive. They stayed as long as they could. And longer than was safe. Leaning on one another.

"And then *they* arrived. And I had my hands full with my own problems."

"Who... who arrived?"

"The Outsiders." She tapped her fingers twice against the shipping container. "But they're all dead now too." She flicked the pin light alive and shone it in his eyes. "Is the pain any less yet?"

"It isn't." If anything, it felt worse.

"Good. It'll feel that much better when it stops. Now, when I hand you a pendant spire, I'm going to spell out all the particulars I remember, about the families, and their vessels, and their routes, and all those things a stationmaster was meant to know back then. You won't find any of this in a library database. All the records were lost, they say, when the station fell. I don't expect you to remember a word. But I'd like you listen, so that it's more than my own ears hearing the sound of their names for once. Can you do that?"

"Can."

"That's grand. Hold out your hand and take the first one. Don't drop it. Now feel the curves. It's a fat one, that spire. See if you can count the number of twists. There's one. Two. Three..."

IT WAS light in the shop when he opened his eyes.

The pain in his arm had settled into a constant, dull ache. The metal plate, what she'd called the cuff, remained adhered to his flesh. It looked weird but it felt normal. Body parts weren't supposed to be reflective. He tapped it. It felt like he was tapping the flesh underneath.

He stood, stretched, and glanced at the top of the packing container.

She'd left a note, and a pendant spire, and an envelope.

He read the note.

I've never been more certain about a man.

He picked up the spire and knew it instantly, by weight alone.

Maggie's Bane, Merchant Captain James Reynard, Master and Ship's Captain, Unity Station, Freeman Federation. Sixty cans on the mast, a complement of twelve, all blow-ins, single men between the ages of seventeen and thirty-five, standard. Free to trade all ports, League and Ojinate.

He remembered them all, the names of every vessel, and every family, from merchant captain to ship's cat, they were all in his head now, which he believed had been her purpose. Distracting him was just a side effect. He had a memory for names and numbers, and he'd been trained as well, trained by a harsher master than he liked to think about.

She'd known that about him the instant she'd seen him, had to be. His own name might be stricken from the mac Donnacha rolls, but the family look was on his face, and she was old enough to have known his father, and his grandfather, and maybe even his grandmother, as well. And she stayed current with the news. A Freeman turned slaver was news. A mac Donnacha getting caught red-handed was news. The Merchant Guild banning anyone *for all eternity* was news.

He hadn't known she was Freeman when he'd seen the hand in the window, and walked into the shop the first time. But he'd known the second time, and he'd come back. Maybe it was because she was on the wrong end of the League Arcade, and he'd thought her as willfully ignorant as he imagined he would grow, cut off and outcast from the People. Maybe he just wanted to hear a voice from home, one that wasn't empty, and ambivalent, or overloaded with judgment. With distaste.

Lorelei Ellis, Seán mac Diarmuid, their sound was an island sound, a planetary sound. It wasn't the same. When he looked at them all he saw were the differences, like he had with Macer, and with Ciarán, at first. He thought he'd grown used to it, that it had ceased to matter, that he was fine being the odd man out, the different one, and they thick as one, but he supposed he hadn't.

He opened the envelope.

A red League work permit lay inside, a card the same size as a merchant's license but not anywhere near as valuable. The permit had his image and thumbprint on it and was issued to one Seamus Reynard, his occupation listed as "clerk." That the image and thumbprint had been lifted from his Academy file felt disturbing but not unexpected. That she hadn't said a word wasn't surprising. She might be two-thirds artifact on the outside, but she was Freeman through and through. She hadn't asked and he hadn't told. All she needed to know about him she could learn by watching him.

And all he needed to know about her?

He didn't need to know more. He'd made his mind up yesterday. He had to trust someone. He couldn't go to the Freeman Sector and back with Ixatl-Nine-Go in his pocket. Not if they were searching people. Leaving the implant with her seemed more sensible than trying to hide it somewhere while he went about his business.

He settled the earring in its place. It was heavier than the one he'd worn as a child, which was to be expected. He pocketed the license and headed for the door.

She was with a customer, so he waved, and she waved back, and then he was on the Arcade, and his feet knew the way.

His arm ached enough that it drew his attention but not so much that it made it impossible to concentrate.

He needed to use a public data terminal in the Federation Sector. The easiest place for him to do that was at the Academy library. It was also the most dangerous. Anyone searching for him would consider it a logical place to look. And once he started digging in public files he was going to set off alarms, and anyone who hadn't been looking for Seamus mac Donnacha before would be looking for him then. He needed to work fast. They didn't check for student identification to enter the library, but he'd need identification to use a terminal. He'd try his own first, and if that didn't work he'd try Macer's, and then Ciarán's. The pair of them weren't the most security conscious, and he doubted they'd so much as looked at their student accounts since graduating. Access didn't go away overnight. The Academy wanted to bombard recent grads with heartfelt pleas for alumni contributions. Their accounts would still be there even if his had been shut down, and he knew their access codes and enough about them to respond to any identity-based challenge.

Seamus could have passed any class without help, he was certain of that, but a little peek at Ciarán's homework before he turned his own in didn't hurt anyone.

And Macer broke up with a girlfriend a week. Someone was going to catch them on the rebound. It might as well be a friend. Monitoring Macer's message queue and skimming id addies was less painful for the lad than pestering him daily.

Had the pair of them known?

Macer? Unlikely, and if he had, he wouldn't have cared. Once Macer was done with someone, he was done with them.

Ciarán? *Definitely.* His notes kept getting longer and more detailed, with side notes, and digressions, and callbacks to previous notes, so that it was almost easier to do the work himself than pour through all the extraneous mac Diarmuid rubbish. And the stuff Ciarán turned in for a grade? It got to the point where it was taking Seamus an hour to look up the words he didn't know and change them to something a normal person would use. Eventually he just gave up. But he'd left the back door in, and kept it running, in case Ciarán decided one day to slack off, or got hit in the head and the dictionary knocked out of him.

Thinking about old times and his friends kept his mind off all the things that could go wrong. He might be recognized but the chances of that were slim. He was scruffy. Old Seamus was not.

He might step on a tripwire before he got all the way in. He was careful. And he knew how dangerous the people he investigated were. Old Seamus was reckless. And clueless.

He might stroke out if he stumbled onto something that cut too close to the bone. New Seamus was on his own there. But he had a plan. If he felt the world begin shaking, he'd slam his throbbing arm into something unpleasant. The pain had kept him focused, and maybe it would again. It wasn't perfect but it was a plan. There was always going to be some risk. Backing out wasn't an option. If he did that, he might as well kill himself now.

The only thing keeping him going at all were the promises that he'd made to his friends. The idea that even broken and disgraced, there was some... *utility* left in him. Without that he was nothing. Without that he *deserved* to die.

He could do this and no one else could. That was the beginning and the end of it. On this Old Seamus and New Seamus agreed.

If he was quick and efficient, he might finish in one day. That was his hope, anyway. In and out. Fast. Then back to the transit hostel in the League Sector for some think time. He could feel the questions tumbling around in his mind and the tag-ends of answers beginning to adhere to them. But he needed names, and dates, and places that weren't in the Gant files, and together with all he already knew, that would be enough. He'd find Ares Adonis for his friends. And then he'd fine Commodore Olek for himself. He didn't need to think any further than that. Not until he knew more.

21

T he Freeman Sector Arcade swam with flesh during midday shift change. The hours of the day weren't entirely arbitrary like they were on some orbitals but synchronized with those of the planet directly below the station. If he were on the ring and able to look out a viewport, he'd see the arc of Trinity Surface and the tiny dot of Clear Island laid out below him. If he waved and Lorelei Ellis had a powerful telescope, she might see him and wave back.

Or, if she were station-born, she might see him and pretend not to. It was the Freeman way to step over and around, to ignore the other, to go about their busy business with a hurried step and an averted eye. He stood on the Arcade ringstop platform and watched the crowd. It was easy to pick out the foreigners, even if they pretended to wear the spire. Spindle bums, hawking stolen farecards, fanning them out and getting in people's faces. It was almost entertaining to watch the crowd part around them like a stream around a boulder. That they were selling stolen farecards was a not-so-elaborate and well-known ploy, one designed to allow them to get close enough to *steal* a farecard. The selling side was actually all done on the spindle, in bulk, the largest customer being the Trinity Station Tram Corporation, if rumors were to be believed, and they were.

He decided he'd watched long enough when a spindle bum lifted a farecard from a little girl. It was probably her first trip on the tram alone. He melded into the stream, and flowed along, and bumped up against a boulder that said, "Back off or I'll cut you," and he kept on flowing, onto the zero-radial tram-car, its doors just then closing. He sat down and watched the platform speed away outward, and himself inward, toward the Academy.

Old Seamus laughed with delight. He hadn't worked a left-handed bump-and-pick since he was nine. His father had said that people had it all wrong. It wasn't stealing that was banned under Freeman custom and contract, but stealing from *honest* people. Thieving from thieves wasn't just permitted, it was practically a duty. *So try it again, boy, and this time, don't get caught.*

New Seamus seethed and stared out the viewport. He hadn't needed to steal a farecard. It was a stupid risk. He needed to put a tighter rein on Old Seamus. He was back in his natural habitat, and it would be easy to slip into old habits.

He glanced down, and flicked the stolen knife open and closed before he pocketed it. At least now he wouldn't have to hammer his arm into something if he felt the world begin to shake. He could stab the knife in, little by little, until the shaking stopped.

He leaned back, and closed his eyes, and counted the stations off, one by one. The tram was packed, but he knew from experience there wasn't a safer place on the station. Even a solitary child could ride all day and all night in comfort and splendor, perfectly safe in their person and possessions. He was doubly safe this time of day. Rougher looking now than he'd ever been in his life, his arms crossed, hand and not-hand buried in his armpits. He wasn't the sort of customer a spindle bum would bother with. And if the people he hunted had found him, they'd wait until he was getting off the tram to pick him up. Or pick him off.

The multilingual announcement shouted *Academy* and he stood up, and stepped off, buried in the center of a great bait ball of hurrying students. He squirted free of the schoolies at the edge of the platform, and waited in the shadow of a lamp standard, like a hit man in a recorded drama, conspicuously looking like he was trying to look inconspicuous. Mugging it up for the snoopers, he was, the lamppost studded thick with sensors, and on a ringstop platform the sensors worked. If someone came at him, he'd be up and over the rail and down into the shadows below, where there hid a maintenance hatch that had been jimmied open so many times it no longer locked. He stood egging them on, if they were out there, hoping that they were as confident and impatient as Old Seamus.

He gave it ten minutes and decided that was long enough. He buried himself into the next bait ball off the tram and down the steps; when the crowd divided he stuck with the throng headed toward the library, peeling off only after reaching the flow-regulating turnstiles and hopping the slowdown device with a left-hand plant, legs up and over smooth as the jackknife in his pocket. Through the tall doors, he tailgated a slim young woman whose id addy belonged in his little black brain—if he was still Old Seamus, and if he still had an implant, one that hadn't turned him into the sort of monster that preyed on slim young women and anyone else that seemed weaker, or less useful, or more entertaining to torment than the thing he'd let Ixatl-Nine-Go make him into.

He needed to keep his head in the game. He was poison, and he didn't dare forget that.

He followed his reflection in the windows, not looking at

himself, but behind him, and then he was in the stairwell, down a flight, through the doors, and down a long aisle between study carrels, virtually all of them empty at midday. Then a cross corridor, another stairwell, down another five decks, and down another hall, all the way to what he thought of as the "back" of the library, where the public section of the library butted up to service corridors. Those service corridors led to loading docks, and the loading docks led to the void between the innermost ring of the station and the spindle. There roared constant traffic up and down that narrow spindle-ring gap. When Lorelei Ellis had dumped him onto the spindle, it had been through one of those docks, bidirectional affairs, serviced around the clock, every day of the year, garbage in, garbage out. Endless parallel streams.

He took his usual seat in the rear, where he could keep an eye on the space without being too easily seen, not that that would be much help in a moment.

He emptied his pockets onto the work surface.

A stolen farecard, still moist with a child's hot tears.

A League work permit, freshly etched in a dead man's name.

A criminal's switchblade, lightly crusted with a victim's blood.

And a length of wire.

One strong enough to hang a man.

He snapped one end of the wire into a connector on the workstation. He studied the other end in the dim light. The connector looked intact. He couldn't see the socket it snapped into. The socket was superficially similar to a full-immersion sensor net's connector, except it jacked into the looky/learny part of his brain instead of the touchy/feely part of his... Well, his *everywhere*.

That's how the technician who'd installed the connector described it to a five-year-old Seamus. It was exactly like the ones librarians use, only better. *It's just like the one your daddy has. And his daddy.*

It hadn't occurred to preschool Seamus to ask, *If daddy and grandpa disown me and declare me dead to the family. Will they rip the library interface out of my head?*

Good question, little buddy. Not without a court order, they won't.

And even with one, only if they could find him.

He took one more look around the space. The workstations on this floor were reserved for graduate students working on their theses.

Seamus entered his credentials, and they *worked*; he touched a file and the backdoor he'd installed his freshman year *worked*; he promoted his account to admin and that *worked*; he made himself a graduate student and that *worked*; he reserved the workstation for three days and that *worked*.

He signed out and that *worked*.

He waited. Somewhere processes were kicking back on, logs were logging again, caches were being cached again, and five minutes later he was ready.

Ready and *alone*. If this had been a family job, there'd be someone sitting beside him, even at home. He'd be easier than a bound kitten to kill for however long this took. He thought about stuffing the knife back into his pocket but decided he didn't have a preference between having his throat slit and being strangled to death. Five of his uncles and four of his aunts had died by strangulation. And his mother. He'd talked to a matchmaker about it once, and they were of the opinion that there was something... symmetric. Symbolic. Maybe both, about the feel of the neck between one's fingers. To restore balance, the punishment needed to fit the crime.

She'd said it just like that. *The feel of the neck between one's fingers.*

Old Seamus shivered. *Just do it.*

New Seamus ignored him. He flicked the knife open and placed it in the center of the work surface, where it would be impossible to miss. If he were to sit here long enough, eventually someone would find him. Ares Adonis. Olek. His father. All he had to do was... nothing.

After a while he gripped the wire, and felt around at the base of his neck, between his shoulder blades.

This was a lot harder to do with one hand than with two.

And then something clicked, and the world shut off.

And then he wasn't alone anymore.

"Hello, Void," he said to the void.

He knew that his lips wouldn't move. That he would utter no sound. Would move not a muscle. That what was now blackness would slowly illuminate, as his mind gathered materials from the library. All he needed to know was where to begin. And he knew that, thanks to the Gant's records and the work he'd put in studying them.

Unlike a librarian's interface, what he could seek for didn't end inside the library. He could poke around *anywhere*.

Anywhere he could find. Anywhere he dared look. If he took a misstep and realized it, he could bail out and run. But if he tripped over something and he didn't realize it... He hoped they used the knife. Or if they decided to strangle him, they screwed up and left him jacked in. Except they'd knock the jack out, getting the *feel of his neck* beneath their fingers. So that wouldn't work. They should use the knife. He hoped they did.

This always seemed the weirdest part. No settling in, no getting ready, no arranging one's possessions. He was *in*, and every second he was in was a second his enemies had to find him. He needed to find what he needed to find and get out.

There was no sense of time passing. It was perpetually now *inside*. The wire, which wasn't really a wire, but wire-like, was short enough and the connectors loose enough that if he fell out of his seat he'd un-jack. He knew that worked, because it had happened once, while cramming for his sophomore finals. Technically it wasn't cheating, but he didn't want people to know. It wasn't cheating because it was impossible, except it wasn't. At the time it felt like he was hiding a superpower, one that ran in the family and was mostly used for evil. But *he* was different, and *he* was using that power for *good*.

He laughed. This time the story he told himself felt almost true.

And the sooner he started using his power for good, the sooner he'd finish.

So he began.

And instantly realized he had a huge blind spot.

He'd heard that the interface seemed different to different people. To him *inside* looked like columns of numbers. It smelled like columns of numbers. It felt like columns of numbers. Tasted like columns of numbers. The numbers wouldn't make sense to anyone else, like a musical score wouldn't make sense to someone who couldn't read music. A musical score didn't sound like anything. Except it *did*. It was like that with numbers for him, *inside*. And now it felt as if he'd gone deaf in one ear and couldn't read the score, except it wasn't his ear, but part of one eye that he couldn't hear with. There wasn't anything active in his brain, not like with an implant, so it had to be a bad wire, a bad workstation, or faulty connections in his brain, or whatever the connector at the base of his neck connected to. He thought it was connected to his brain, that's what they'd told him as a kid, but people lie to kids. It could be hardwired to his sensory organs for all he knew, and piggybacking signals on their outputs.

It didn't matter how it really worked. Testing the internal connections seemed like a reasonable place to start. Tearing Ixatl-Nine-Go out of him could have severed something, or shorted it out.

He tested the connections in isolation. Most of them

worked fine. But when he touched three of them the void *shiv-ered*. So he blocked those connections in what he thought of as the interface's control panel.

He could still work. He'd just have to work slower. Stay *inside* longer. Be more careful.

It wasn't the end of the world.

That would come with one swift slice.

Or one long, slow, squeeze.

22

Seamus saw stars as his forehead struck the deck. Someone was shouting, he covered his head with his hands, he was being pelted with stuff, and the shouting kept going. Until it suddenly stopped, and someone kicked him, not hard, but dismissively, like they were done with him.

He cracked an eye open and got a toe to the ribs. "I said jet off! This is my seat."

Seamus laughed, and crabbed out of toe range, and leaned against the bulkhead. His possessions were scattered around him. He glanced at the open knife. Old Seamus reached for it but New Seamus scooped it up and flicked it closed, and pocketed it.

His attacker was a big guy, muscular and scowling, but he wasn't going to murder Seamus in the next ten seconds. He spread his stuff around the work surface, regular student stuff. He plopped a portable computer onto the table and opened it up, an expensive unit, fashionably retro, the sort of status symbol that said that *utility* wasn't as important to him as signaling. He was dressed the part as well. Spindle-rat rags fresh out of a First Families' macrofab.

"Show me your reservation," Old Seamus mouthed.

New Seamus pointed at the three other, empty workstations in the cluster. "Those were available."

He made a fist and shook it at Seamus. "Here's my reservation. And fuck you. You were in. My. Spot." His eyes narrowed. "Are you even a student?"

"But I was almost done," Old Seamus whined.

"I'm calling security," the guy said.

New Seamus began to gather his stuff. "Forget it. I'm going." He stood.

The world shook, his legs shook, but it wasn't at all like he was going to stroke out. Adrenaline shakes. Old Seamus *boiled* beneath his skin; he'd thought he was being murdered and now *this*? The guy was bigger than Seamus, *everyone* was bigger than Seamus.

Leave it, New Seamus thought. A lump of carbon was bigger than a diamond.

He was harder than diamond now.

He was whatever diamond became when it passed the event horizon.

When it fell into the gravity of a black hole and kept falling.

Seamus took one of the other workstations.

He placed his possessions on the table.

All but for the knife.

The guy flipped the two-handed computer open. He punched a couple of keys and a prerecorded comedy began to play on the rubbish lowrez display, an overdubbed laugh track spilling tinny and unreal from its tiny rubbish speakers.

Old Seamus reached for the knife.

New Seamus stopped him. He had that power now.

You were that guy, he reminded Old Seamus. *Smoother, more polished, because you had to be. More subtle. More indirect. Watch what he does next.*

The guy pretended to watch the screen of his status toy, but his gaze kept darting to Seamus.

Who sat quietly. Who prepared to use a different, less desirable terminal. Who wasn't hurting anyone.

The guy paused the comedy playback and tapped a couple keys. And then he used his rubbish lips to speak into the unit's rubbish microphone. "Security?"

I was never that guy, Old Seamus lied.

New Seamus ignored him. He entered his credentials, they *worked*; he touched a file and the backdoor he'd installed his freshman year *worked*; he promoted his account to admin and that *worked*; he made himself a security agent and that *worked*; he reprogrammed all of the cipher locks on the floor and that *worked*.

He started to log out, which forced the cleanup to begin, but he stopped.

New Seamus started to stand. *I'm never coming back here. What's the point?*

Old Seamus slammed them back into their seat. *The work is the point. We're a professional. Now act like one.*

He sighed, and signed out, and that *worked*.

He waited. Somewhere processes kicked back on, logs began logging again, caches started caching again, and five minutes later the locks would begin to reset.

When he reached a lock, and entered the code he'd chosen, the displays on the locksets would flash green twice. The existing cipher code would be stored and a new one set. The display would flash green three times. Then he could enter the escape code, the lock would work, and when it latched again, reset to the original code. He knew it worked because he'd tested it dozens of times as an undergrad. There existed no better place to meet girls than the library.

The guy turned his recorded comedy on again and pretended to ignore Seamus.

Four minutes later Seamus heard footsteps. He rose and headed for the doorway that led to the emergency-exit stairwell.

Someone opened the stairwell door.

Seamus turned the opposite way and kept walking. A row of tall storage media cabinets hid him from view. He could enter the service corridors ahead. It wasn't ideal, and he wasn't dressed for it, but he didn't want to explain who he was, or what he was doing there.

"You took your fucking time," the guy said. "Hey!"

There was a snapping sound, one Seamus recognized, then a thump, like a bag of garbage being dropped onto the deck.

Seamus stopped. More footsteps. Lots of them.

"I wanted him alive," a deep voice said.

"What for?" a woman said.

"To make him suffer."

More footsteps. Ones he could use to mask his own. He began to move again, timing his footfalls with the others.

"No one told me," the woman said.

"Told you what?" another man said.

"Not to kill him. Why are you two late?"

"We can't come in the front door, can we?"

A short laugh. One that sounded familiar.

Seamus reached the service hatch.

"What's so funny," the woman said.

He typed in the reset code.

"That's not him. He's a small man. Very quick. Very clever. This is meat."

Two green lights flashed.

"No one told me."

"No one thought you could catch him."

Come on, come on.

"This has to be him. He was using this workstation."

That laugh again.

Three green lights flashed.

"I'm telling you, that's not him," the man said.

Seamus's fingers danced over the keypad.

"He's right," Sun Shin Liuc said.

The lock clicked.

"That's him over there, by the service hatch."

23

T he hatch closed behind him and latched. The lock reset to its original settings. He began to jog along the corridor, not because he was in a hurry, but because it was *cold* this close to the service docks.

He could hear them pounding on the hatch behind him. *Good luck with that.* There were lifts and emergency stairwells on both sides of the hatch. They ran parallel but every floor had a service hatch between them, and every service hatch remained locked. He supposed they could find a security guard and dragoon them into service, forcing them to override the locks, or find someone with skills like his to add their own hack, but both would take time. By then he'd be long gone.

There was another hatch, on the main level, one that led to a delivery courtyard, and a sally gate. The gate led to a loading dock and private platform for the zero-radial tram, a terminal station beyond the terminal station, one only used by staff and faculty between semesters, and by those few students that knew its secret. There was a maintenance hatch and a tunnel behind it that led to another maintenance hatch on the other side of the security perimeter. It was meant to be blocked after the tram had been completed, and it had been, but it had been opened up again later, for some emergency repairs, ones done without a work order and on the cheap, the difference in funds being pocketed, and the breach patched in the way that off-the-books work was always done, halfway, in the dark, and without a thought for tomorrow.

Without people like that, it would be a lot harder for people like him to move freely through the world. He considered taking the lift but he might bump into someone. And while there were recording sensors everywhere on the station, the ones on trams and lifts and loading docks tended to be monitored by people with actual brains and not almost-expert systems churned out by lowest-cost bidders.

A hundred meters of hard vacuum stood between the service docks on the ring and those on the spindle. A migrant or two leaking across, a trickle of contraband, those were acceptable risks in the Freeman Sector in particular. An invasion of Hundred Planets skinnies, or a river of goods bypassing the fingers of the First Families, were the worries, and rivers didn't flow up stairwells one tread at a time. They used the lifts, the trams, and the airlocks.

He had time, and this close to the spindle he had the stamina. The gravity remained light because the loads were low value and heavy, trolleys of rubbish picked clean and destined for a sunward trajectory, body bags offloaded onto barges at the ring and shipped under and over, the barges little more than freight-expediting containers programmed to follow a looping flight plan, from the ring, to spindle, and back again. He'd come onto the station that way, via the spindle under a shroud, stitched up and tossed off the nic Cartaí longboat as dead, the short ride from ring to spindle long enough for him to cut his way out, and wait with the dead for the hatch to open and Sun Kang's people to lock in and begin the unloading.

And now Sun Kang had betrayed him.

And Seamus had escaped, despite the betrayal. They had no hope of catching him now. He could see the stairwell door.

He touched the lock. Two green lights flashed.

Excellent. His little workers began their task of copying the old code to memory, storing it, loading the new code, storing it, the only thing capable of interrupting their work a power failure, and that wasn't going to happen, or a—

The fire alarm began to scream.

—priority override.

The lock flashed five times. It clicked. Every lock in the library clicked.

Open.

Seamus cursed.

And ran.

The lifts wouldn't work.

He was fast but there were, what, four of them chasing him? Five?

They could spread out and blanket the exits.

He needed to get to an exit first.

But which one?

Old Seamus laughed.

The closest one.

New Seamus felt the blood drain from his face.

And hooked a right turn into a cross corridor.

One aimed toward the spindle.

He didn't have time to argue.

And he'd only be wasting his time.

I hate it when he's right.

24

The loading dock felt freezing cold. He wished he had a merchant captain's great coat almost as much as he wished he had two hands.

He practically leapt into one of the emergency hardsuits racked in the airlock vestibule. They were one-size-fits-all and two fully clothed Seamuses could fit into one.

The last time he'd suited up he'd done it in thirty seconds, plumbing included. This time he was taking shortcuts, it was a hundred-meter sprint, not a marathon spacewalk. The only safety protocol he worried about was the one that said get off the ring before someone snaps your neck like a chemical light stick.

It had taken thirty seconds and two hands last time. And last time he hadn't had to spend forty seconds slashing all of the other emergency suits on the rack with some spindle rat's stolen switchblade. He didn't think he'd like a thruster chase in hard vacuum any more than he cared for a foot chase through a space station's only slightly warmer service corridors. He couldn't understand how he could be freezing and sweating at the same time.

He clicked the helmet to the collar and began to tongue through the command menu.

He clicked on the first gauntlet. Emergency hardsuits didn't have gloves, but gauntlets, a double layer of protection running up the forearms to the elbows. The forearms of the suits tended to wear. It was cheaper to replace gauntlets than suits. Gauntlets weren't any harder to put on than gloves.

If you had two hands, they weren't.

He'd just about worked out a system when he heard someone shout, "There he is!"

It was only a hundred meters. Did the suit really need to seal?

Are you an idiot? Of course it does.

He gave one more desperate tug.

The right gauntlet telltale on the heads-up display flashed from red to green.

He stepped into the airlock.

They were at the far end of the corridor.

There were five of them.

Three of them he recognized.

Two spindle rats he'd never seen.

Sun Shin Liuc. The betrayer.

The girl he'd admired on the way into the library. She looked more fashionable from behind. The nerve disruptor in her hand didn't match her shoes.

Then there was a man he'd only seen in images.

Ares Adonis.

Evil, wrapped in evil, with extra evil on the side.

Ixatl-Nine-Go rode him. Seamus had learned that and more while he was *inside.*

He'd been no less a monster before he and Ixatl-Nine-Go had hooked up.

They were a match made in hell.

And they wanted to make Seamus suffer.

Suffer some more.

He was huge.

Bigger than Ciarán mac Diarmuid.

Bigger than Macer Gant.

Big, and quite far away, all things considered.

He'd hate to see how big Ares Adonis looked up close.

Seamus press the airlock cycle control.

Old Seamus waved.

Ares Adonis charged.

He was very fast.

New Seamus groaned and began to step further into the airlock.

He's a footie star, you bonehead.

The airlock began to cycle.

He was a footie star and he wasn't going to make it.

Ares Adonis took a great flying leap, one that wouldn't work on the docking ring, but that carried him arcing toward Seamus this close to the spindle, his size infinity hullwalkers aimed for the narrowing gap between the airlock and airlock hatch.

Old Seamus watched in fascination. *That's a good way to come up a foot short.*

New Seamus glanced at the airlock control panel. *It's an Atlas Commercial Freight Lock. With—*

Ares Adonis's right boot jammed the airlock hatch.

—child safety overrides.

The lock hatch began to open.

Seamus hammered the lock control again and again.

A massive forearm shoved into the airlock.

Seamus squirmed backward.

Meaty fingers clawed their way along his arm.

Caught his gauntlet.

Clung on.

Seamus stopped hammering the hatch controls. The light

had stopped flashing, the control buffer full of nothing but frantic orders to close, close, close.

He glanced at the widening crack between hatch and lock.

A single eye stared back. It was black and bottomless as the void.

"Got you," Ixatl-Nine-Go said.

Seamus glanced down.

And flicked the right gauntlet release.

Old Seamus flashed a stiff, invisible finger as Ares Adonis fell backward and the hatch slammed closed, the lock silently cycling.

I die free, you hag.

25

N
ew Seamus calmly rolled up the right sleeve seal of the hardsuit. He wasn't dying, free or otherwise, if he could avoid it.

The hardsuit leaked atmosphere quickly, more like a rend than a pinhole. He wouldn't last long outside the station, but he didn't need to last long. A hundred meters to the spindle. Jet over to a lock on the spindle, any lock presently in use, and someone would let him in. He'd worry about the price of entry once the deed was done.

He tongued the suit's propulsion system alive. It ran through its automated self-test.

And aborted.

That figured. He lacked a right gauntlet.

He tongued the emergency override.

That worked.

He aimed himself at the spindle lock directly across from him.

He tongued the go control.

Nothing happened.

He repeated the procedure.

Nothing happened.

He checked the fuel level.

It showed full.

He tapped the fuel sender with his index finger.

The fuel level dropped to zero.

He tapped the fuel sender again.

The fuel level showed full.

He needed a new plan.

If his enemies were smart, they'd send someone to the nearest airlock with functional suits to come after him. And they'd send someone, probably several someones, to the spindle, which would take time. But if they called ahead they could have allies waiting. Even if he could get the suit propulsion to work, he'd already missed the window of opportunity. He'd have to do something they wouldn't expect.

They wouldn't expect him to cycle the lock and walk back in.

Except there were five of them, and if it was the first thing he'd thought of they would have thought of it too, and they had the manpower to cover that longshot.

He could leap onto a passing barge and ride it over to the spindle. There were plenty of barges working the gap between the ring and spindle.

Except that sort of rubbish was all action-drama fantasy. He'd end up with compound fractures, his ankles up his arse and the jagged ends of whatever the big bones of his legs were called scraping holes through the suit from the inside out.

He could use the atmosphere in his suit as a jet, and the sleeve of the suit and the stump of his right arm as a regulating needle valve, holding the sleeve in his left hand and directing it as a nozzle.

Except that sounded like something Macer Gant could pull off, doing the math in his head, and anyway, Seamus could see it in his mind, clearly, but he had no confidence in his own grasp of the actual mechanics.

What would Ciarán do? He'd call them on the suit's comm and talk them out of the whole thing. He might not convince them at first, but he'd keep going on so long with the talking that they'd eventually give in, just to get him to stop. Or, now that he was running with pirates, he might just have his cat eat them. Whatever he did, it wouldn't be something Seamus could do.

He needed a plan for mere mortals, like climb a floor or two up and lock in there, or up and over to left or right, except he was bleeding atmosphere and only had three limbs to climb with.

No one would believe he could do that.

He didn't even believe it.

Which meant he'd better get started.

26

The hardsuit's atmosphere gauge stood pegged in the red by the time Seamus cycled the lock. He'd climbed up three decks and over one lock, and there were only two things he could say about that journey, one being that he wouldn't want to do it again, and the other being that there wasn't much in the way of variety to the process, just one terrifying, lurch from handhold to handhold after another, all the while wondering if he was going to stroke out now, or later. He felt bathed in sweat, like it pooled up to his knees, which couldn't be true, but he'd grown so lightheaded he had a hard time separating reality from his brain deciding to have some fun with him.

The airlock hatch cycled and the girl elbowed in. She held the same nerve disruptor in her fist, or another nerve disruptor that looked exactly like the one she'd held earlier. He couldn't decide which. Not that it really mattered. She stood close enough to touch it to him, which is what you needed to do with a nerve disruptor.

"I'll bet you're wondering how I found you," she said.

He hammered the airlock control. "I'm not."

He was wondering what made her think a nerve disruptor worked through a hardsuit.

Or why stepping into an airlock in her shirtsleeves was a good idea.

They were nasty weapons, nerve disrupters. It was an ugly way to die.

Not that there weren't uglier.

He took the nasty thing from her ballooning fingers before toeing her free of the airlock and hammering the control again.

27

Once he was back on the station proper, he sat on the suit-up bench, ratcheted the helmet off, and gulped in ice-cold air. He wanted to peel out of the suit right now, but there was something he needed to do first. He stuffed the helmet back on, and tongued the comms alive, and hailed Dependable Mortuary Services. Once he got past the automated router and to an expert system, he told it what he wanted. It told him to switch to a private channel, which he did, and then he waited. He decided to wait five minutes maximum, but he hadn't even waited one when Sun Kang spoke.

"Hand of the Void, I was just thinking about you."

"Good thoughts, I hope."

"The best."

"You didn't follow my instructions, did you?"

"I meant to. It was my intention to send your father the regular payment, but it kept slipping my mind."

"And?"

"And he sent a collector. A young girl, pretty, but not very bright. Shin was taken with her. She said that we owed, and I said no, we don't owe. We are collectors now, and showed her our name on the list. She was glad to learn this, and she went away. Shin and she arranged for a date. But when Shin showed up it was not her at the restaurant, but your father."

"And he was angry."

"With Shin? With me? Not at all. But he was very angry with you. He said we would no longer need to pay, and that we could remain on the collectors' list, but we had to do something for him."

"Bring me to him."

"Not all of you, just from your shoulder blades up. He was very clear, head and neck both, with the interface connector."

"And you agreed to this."

"Of course not. We are businessmen, not butchers. We would find you, and tell him, but that was all."

"Was this before or after Shin sold me the handheld?"

"After."

"So you couldn't track me with that."

"Well, I wouldn't say that."

"I see."

"And what of Shin's involvement?"

"Helping the girl find you."

"And she was to do the wet work."

"At first that was the thought. But your father brought on a man he thought more reliable."

"Ares Adonis."

"Yes, the footie man. A big star."

"How long ago?"

"Yesterday."

"You need to get Shin away from those people. It isn't safe for him."

"I will tell him."

"Tell him that and tell him to meet me on the Erlside Arcade in two hours. I'll squirt you the address. I want a different handheld. One that can't track me."

"Of course." Sun Kang paused, as if waiting for Seamus to speak. The silence grew long. "You are not angry?"

"You said it. We're businessmen, not butchers."

"I'm so glad we agree."

"Do you love your son?"

"Very much so."

"Then please tell him to be there and to be on time."

"Of course."

"Tell him to bring the handheld. And while he's at it, bring the girl."

Seamus tongued the comm unit dead. He yanked the helmet off and tossed it across the compartment. He peeled out of the hardsuit and headed for the exit.

If Sun Kang was smart, and he was, he would follow Seamus's instructions to the letter. And if Sun Kang was bent, and he was, he'd tell whoever he was being paid to tell. Finally, if Sun Kang grew desperate, and he would, once it became clear Shin couldn't find the girl, he'd call Seamus's father.

Which is all Seamus really wanted. He hadn't finished his research in the library before he'd been ripped out. But he'd finished enough to live up to his commitments to Macer Gant and Lorelei Ellis. Once he got word to them, he'd be free to do whatever he needed or wanted to do.

When he disembarked the zero-radial tram at the Freeman Arcade, the same spindle rat was there again, stealing little girls' farecards. Seamus bumped and picked him again, without any joy this time. He thumbed the boosted handheld alive. It didn't have a passcode, they never did, not when you might have to use it one-handed while sprinting from shadow to shadow.

He called Sun Kang and gave him the meetup address. He called the Trinity surface exchange and left a long message with House, Lorelei Ellis's expert system. He called Macer Gant's id addy and left a similarly long message. When he passed a recycler, he tossed the handheld and switchblade and kept moving.

They frisked him at the line, red visa, Seamus Reynard, get out of here, and then he was on the Erlside Arcade. The shops got shabbier and shabbier the further from the Freeman Sector he walked. He passed the recycler's shop. Two doors further on he ducked beneath the yellow band of emergency tape and entered the gutted electronics shop. He found a stool that had been blackened but not burned and sat down to wait.

His job was done. He'd like to know more. Do more. But he didn't need to. He wasn't going to keep on running. Nothing had really changed. He'd still done terrible things. He still needed to pay.

His father wouldn't send Ares Adonis.

Not when he could come himself.

He'd want one more chance to stick the knife in.

To work it.

Seamus had let him down.

Disgraced the family.

Defied his wishes.

He'd only asked two things of his son.

Crawl away.

And die.

He couldn't even do that right.

Seamus should have said something then but he hadn't.

He didn't have the words.

He needed time to think.

Now he was ready.

He knew what he wanted to say.

Make me.

28

Two hours after the appointed time, Seamus yet waited. He'd decided to give it another half hour when a breathless Sun Li Liuc, Shin's sister, arrived.

"A thousand apologies," she said in Huangxu. "Sun Shin Liuc cannot find the girl."

"Did your father send you here to tell me that?"

"I came on my own accord," Li said. "To tell you this and to warn you away from the Freeman Sector."

"Thank you, Li. That's very kind of you."

"Not so kind to tell you why. Your family has been killed. The stationmaster wishes to speak."

He was surprised just how little he felt. Perhaps if he had a better grasp of Huangxu as spoken on the spindle. Unlike Huangxu Eng, the local dialects kept changing as the population ebbed and swelled, no two groups of refugees or deserters sharing the same vocabulary or even sentence structure.

"I have no family." Seamus mac Donnacha had been declared dead to the family weeks ago, and officially dead in station records, what, last week? It was hard to keep track of time without an implant.

"Again, a thousand pardons. The families of Dermot mac Donnacha. Much has been thrown into chaos. Sun Kang believes that this is already known to you. I... was curious."

"Curious if I killed someone in the mac Donnacha family?"

"Not some. All."

"All what?"

"All mac Donnacha family."

"Okay." Clearly they weren't getting through to each other. And clearly his father wasn't coming. Dealing with a sudden death would supersede retrieving a family asset from an errant child.

"Thank you, Li, for the information and warning."

She shrugged. "I came as much for knowledge. To see what kind of man you are."

"And?"

"And I see. You are alone. And unarmed. There is no trap."

"I'm a businessman."

"So I tell my father. He tells me stories. I don't believe him."

"Stories about me?"

She wobbled her head. "Some."

"You should believe him."

"All I need to know about a man, I learn by watching. Father, Shin, they work the mortuary trade. They deal with no one living. I am in sanitation. Customers talking all day, every day, I want this, I want that, some shouting, some begging, all wanting. The richer they are, the more they want given for nothing.

"Someday I will be rich. Someday I will have a family. Who do I want to be like? Me. My children. How will they know the world? By what others say about us? Here is what I see. A man who does not cheat us when he can. A man who does not make promises he cannot keep. A man who does not pity us our lives, or offer us alms to pay for his own guilt.

"I see such a man, and I think, we can do business until we can't."

"I'm very flattered, Li. Tell your father—"

"This is not an offer from my father. This is an *arrangement* between us. To help one another, when we can. To settle up when we may."

"It sounds lovely. But I'm afraid I couldn't hold up my end of such a bargain."

"As am I. But I am willing to risk it. They say the fear of loss often overwhelms the desire for profit. One strives for balance in all things. Let us strive together."

Seamus chuckled. "If we agree—"

"We will tell no one."

Seamus nodded. "Very well. We can do business until we can't."

Li beamed and nodded. "I am already in your debt."

"I haven't done anything."

"You rid my brother of that woman. She would have been the death of him."

"I—"

"Will tell no one of our bargain," Li said. "Or breathe a word of our private business. We may rely upon one another." She touched his sleeve. "I waved at you, from the spindle today. You are quite a good climber."

She waved to him again, as she ducked beneath the emergency tape. "Perhaps you will teach me one day."

29

The shop bell rang as he entered. It was morning shift, after he had spent the entire night waiting in the ruined husk two doors down, waiting for his father to come, waiting and organizing his thoughts.

The shop woman was with a customer, so he gazed out the shop window at the Arcade, and the passersby, and thought about all he'd learned in the time since he'd last heard that shop bell ring.

If he wanted to *explain* all he now knew, explain it in such a way that it could be acted on, he would need to condense it, editing it down to its essence, leaving out all the false starts and dead ends. Even the abridged version was frighteningly complex, the sort of tangle of facts and surmises that only someone with his training and experience could unknot. Knowing where to begin proved difficult, because the plot looped back on itself, its *motive power* generated, not from a sequential series of events, but from a web of lies and half-truths spanning eons.

Six thousand years ago a great asteroid was discovered, one that would strike the planet Earth, sole seat of the human race.

There existed no ready remedy for the problem, no superluminal flight, they barely had any space-based industry at all. Consumed with squabbling and infighting, the great polities of the world battled for supremacy of their solitary world. And then the destroyer was spotted, years to prepare, no agreement, yet a plan, *plans* were made and executed.

All of this was common knowledge, so common it didn't bear comment. The Freeman identity was based on this knowledge, the stories repeated again and again, each *seanscéal* the same, from family to family, how the League had betrayed them, and abandoned them to die, how the Eng had rescued a few pregnant woman, corpsicles stacked amongst the livestock, a public-relations stunt, hastily executed, quickly forgotten, forgotten for *thousands* of years, until some nameless terraformer discovered a mislabeled container, in amongst the seedlings of the hundredth Huangxu planet, and opened it, and sent a message to his masters, *I have found free men*. A bad joke, that, and the hinge of the *seanscéal*, for they weren't men, and they weren't free, and they wouldn't be free, not without a fight.

It was hard to know his audience, what to leave in and what to rip out. How much of how he saw the world was accepted canon and how much the heretical conclusions of a man raised trolling through those secrets others wished to forget.

For example, he knew—he did not imagine, or theorize, or speculate, he *knew*—that Freeman society was held together entirely by a series of grudges, ones so widely accepted and carefully groomed that they became fact. The League had betrayed them, *six thousand* years ago, the Huangxu Eng had enslaved them, *four hundred* years ago, their *own sisters* turning tout, informant, grass, a dozen words for the worst betrayers of all, *hoors* that would rather lick any man's boot in luxury than lift a finger against *slavers*. The Enemy, these turncoats were named amongst the Freemen.

Of course they did not call themselves *the Enemy*, but whatever names their masters, the Huangxu Eng, chose for them. Whatever they were called, and called themselves, one fact remained. In the *seanscéal* of the world they were the most reviled, not because they were strong, or their crimes star-spanning, but because they were small, and weak, like the sisters they had turned against, some with a word of betrayal, some by simply standing aside and refusing to fight.

To a Leagueman, to an Ojin, Eng or not Eng, even to the Huangxu, the power of the Freeman *seanscéal* was dismissed as exaggerated. Memories faded. Tempers cooled. One grew older, and wiser, and one's children, born into a new world, forgot the old grievances, forged new alliances, got on with living. The future mattered. The past was just that. *Past.*

Except it wasn't. Again, there was a... Not a secret, but something known but unspoken. Private knowledge. Facts not denied but not volunteered.

For the Freeman First Families, not for Truxton—who blow-ins mistakenly called First Family for his wealth, but who was not—but for the nic Cartaís, for the Kavanaghs, for all the makers and shakers of the world?

The past *was* the present.

The mac Donnachas had been First Families once upon a time, analysts and archivists for the Cause. They'd lost their seat the day Seamus's great-grandfather had killed himself. Because to be First Families and to remain First Families required a blood sacrifice.

The head of the family, the *ceannaire*, had to have been conceived on Earth.

That way the grudges remained fresh and the *seanscéal* of the world constantly renewed. The sins worked against the People weren't wounds some ancient ancestor took to the grave. They were scars etched upon the faces of the living.

For example, Fionnuala nic Cartaí appeared the head of the nic Cartaí family to the League and the Eng because her name appeared on every nic Cartaí contract. And to Freemen, born and blow-in alike, nic Cartaí was styled First Families, some in ignorance of the nature of the beast, some in full knowledge of it.

All were right, because Nuala nic Cartaí was conceived on Earth six thousand years ago, and born in the Hundred Planets to a slave four hundred years ago, and yet still breathing given the qualities of space and time on the long-hauls, and given the promise that she'd made and kept to her mother, and the technology that made it possible to keep that promise, and because of a contract she'd signed as a young woman.

A *revocable* contract.

Saoirse nic Cartaí, leader of the Freeman rebellion and first head of the Federation, was yet alive. The nic Cartaís kept her in cold storage and thawed her out now and then, some said to get her advice, some said just to look at her face and be reminded of the struggle.

Seamus wasn't sure how good the advice of a woman who'd been in and out of cryogenic suspension for six thousand years would be. And he wasn't sure he'd want to look at her, either.

That was all window dressing. What she and the other *ceannairí* of the First Families lived for was to keep the grudges alive. To make certain the People heard the *seanscéal* of the world fresh from the lips that first spoke it.

All of which might or might not be important to say when the time came to explain what he'd learned. It would require a choice.

Saying all that out loud was waking the dead.

He wasn't sure that he wasn't past caring about who he woke, dead or living. It was a habit of thought, one he'd have to overcome. Or not. It might be his word would be accepted without proof.

He'd wait and see.

A great part of the ignorance being exploited today came

from the not-waking custom, which was originally adopted to rapidly grow the Freeman ranks. Just take the Oath and live by it and it didn't matter what you'd been, who you'd wronged, what laws you'd broken anywhere in the universe. It didn't matter what language you spoke, who was your momma, or your god, or your king, or your people that you were leaving behind. All that mattered was taking the Oath, and living the oath.

Taking the Oath was easy. Living the Oath wasn't. Which was Saoirse nic Cartaí's plan all along.

What Saoirse nic Cartaí wanted was men. She had a surplus of fertile women and fatherless children. And she had a war on her hands. She needed quantity, and she got it with the easy Oath. And later on, she wanted quality, and she used the hard living to get that, explaining the corollaries of the Oath, and the customs that naturally sprung up around them, and using an iron hand to hold the Oath-takers to their word. The Freeman Oath was styled the second contract, the first being the agreement between the People and the Mong Hu. Both were equal in Seamus's mind, because one made the other possible.

Most of the men Saoirse nic Cartaí recruited weren't bad men, but bad fits in the regimented societies they'd rebelled against, or poor men, who'd made poor choices out of desperation. But some were bad men, and some Freemen bad women, and the customs of the Freeman families had been developed to weed the bad seed out. Matchmakers, family vendettas, the rules of primacy of responsibility, exile or the death penalty for anything that threatened the unity and stability of the tribe. All of that came later.

The custom of not waking the dead came first. Without that discipline, squabbles left over from *outside* could find their way *inside*. And one Freeman's squabble with an outsider was every Freeman's squabble. "We are one" wasn't just an empty saying. *It was the hair shirt that came with an earring.*

Seamus wasn't sure how all of this structured lack of structure would work out long term, when there weren't First Families anymore and the foundational *seanscéal* no longer renewed. If he had to guess, he'd say the People would eventually fold into the League, a crazy sect few accepted and even fewer sought to join. Unless new blood like Sun Li Liuc took the Oath and kept the *seanscéal* fresh with their own grievances. They were, after all, the same complaints, and the same remedies. He'd heard the precursors of the Oath from her own lips.

Imagine the absurdity of the idea. That someone like him could teach someone like her how to climb.

He only knew two things about climbing.

Keep moving.

Don't fall.

Of the two, he was only good at one.

He was better at digging. And he'd unearthed a *hydra*. A multiheaded monster. Which head he described first and in what detail would depend upon his audience.

For example, he wouldn't need to tell anyone in the League that after six thousand years and two civilization-destroying civil wars, the League wasn't a monoculture like the Federation. What Freemen called "the Erl" or "the Leaguemen" would more accurately be described as "Columbians," or more accurately still, as "Columbia Stationers," an elite subset of the League population that ran the government, the military, and the educational system, and that populated the larger mercantile enterprises and government outposts of the League.

The League Sector of Trinity Station was a tiny facsimile of Columbia Station, completely operated by Columbia Stationers, for the benefit of Columbia Stationers, and thus, in the Columbia Stationers' minds, without qualification, for the benefit of the League as a whole.

The League had a queen, who was a Columbia Stationer, and a prime minister, who was a Columbia Stationer, and a Parliament of Columbia Stationers, and at the present time, a war between Columbia Stationers, with the Parliament and military on one side, and the Queen and the mercantile houses—which were, at least historically, representative of the League as a whole—on the other. The present queen, Charlotte Templeman, was head of a mercantile house, whose founders had invented the Templeman drive, the device that made the greater League possible. The Parliament was in law composed of representatives from the greater League. But years spent on Columbia Station seemed to normalize the opinions and consciences of the people's representatives. And the financially beneficial opportunities available in the capital tended to align their interests with that of the capital.

In order to be understood, Seamus would have to tell, say, Seán mac Diarmuid, all of this. He might have to tell an ordinary stationer some of it. And he'd need to tell his father none of this, because knowing this and more was fundamental to the mac Donnacha family business.

The point was, and the one he needed to make clear, was that the League of the wider world was not the urbane League of Trinity Station. There were rough worlds, less civilized worlds, and two of these worlds were Sampson and New Sparta. They were spoken of as one because they were serviceable from the same station. Their base cultures were significantly different, more divergent than the cultures of Unity and Trinity Stations in the Federation, and them separated by light-years.

Two hundred years ago, Sampson was far more populous and prosperous than today, and growing. New Sparta was rugged, inhospitable, and dying, even then. Freeman trade had been largely with Sampson. It was said that there were opportunities on New Sparta for the ambitious, and Nuala nic Cartaí was nothing if not ambitious. So she went to take a look.

And found a nest of vipers.

The station that served both Sampson and New Sparta was banned to Freeman trade, and the ban stuck. *We are one.* No Freeman trade meant no trade, until League merchants were induced to call, largely due to the monopoly prices they could charge.

Sampson withered, the bulk of the population forced to emigrate, their economy ruined. They'd outgrown their ability to feed themselves, certain that they could depend upon their Freeman neighbors. When asked if they'd known about the New Spartans, the leaders of Sampson lied.

Until that moment nic Cartaí had been considering building her own station in Sampson space. They'd accomplished much on Sampson with little but their own labor and the capital of thrifty locals.

The leaders knew of her plans. That's why they'd lied. They were afraid that if they told the truth, that they'd known what New Sparta was, she'd back out.

She hadn't blamed them for the crime.

She blamed them for the cover-up.

Who did Sampson blame? Their own lies? The New Spartans?

They did not. They blamed the Freemen.

And they blamed nic Cartaí, most of all.

As a merchant captain, Nic Cartaí could ban the station to trade by fiat. The Merchant Guild would confirm nic Cartaí's findings and affirm the ban. But there was nothing in Freeman custom that said what to do about what she'd found on New Sparta.

So Fionnuala nic Cartaí woke Saoirse nic Cartaí from her cryogenic slumber and put the question to the First of the First Families.

Seamus shivered, just thinking about it. He'd found most of this information in the library, in transcript form. But this part, the Question of New Sparta, had an attached audio recording.

Mother, on the planet of New Sparta there is a cabal. I met with these people regarding trade. I realized all were known to me, though by a different name.

What name?

The Enemy.

What do you propose to do about them?

I propose to kill them.

Are they strong? Do they have allies?

They're weak and alone.

Then kill them.

How?

By letting them rot.

It was strange, hearing the voice of Saoirse nic Cartaí herself. He'd listened to the rest of the recording, where the pair chatted about family and dead friends until one of them realized the recorder was still active and switched it off.

He'd expected the mother of the Rebellion to sound like a crone. Instead, she sounded like a teenaged girl. One with anger-management issues and a world of regrets. She sounded... human.

Maybe that was the purpose which kept her alive.

The reason an untranscribed voice recording remained in the archive.

Not by accident, but by design.

To strangle the myth in its crib. To keep the legend from ever being born.

So long as she could speak for herself, no historian could put words in her mouth.

Young lady, why do you suffer immortality?

So that no one would mistake me for a god.

He was adding his own spin to events, ascribing his own

motives. That was unprofessional. And it didn't matter the reasons. The deed, or deeds, were done.

Two hundred years ago, Sampson and New Sparta were permanently banned to Freeman trade because New Sparta was under the thumb of Huangxu Eng collaborators, ones drawn from the same gene and cultural pool as native-born Freemen. That was how the court documents read, which was a fancy way of saying what Nuala nic Cartaí said upon first returning from New Sparta.

Who are these New Spartans? They're the bitches who betrayed us.

The Cooperative of Loyal Citizens, the rulers of New Sparta called themselves, and they had been busier than Nuala nic Cartaí knew. Their subjects weren't just on New Sparta. They were imbedded in Freeman society. They had been for centuries.

According to the documents Macer supplied, the Gants of Clear Island were agents of the Cooperative, as were some lawyers in First Landing, or Black Pool, as they were now calling the largest city on Trinity Surface. The mac Kennas, the lawyers, were, and they in turn had agents of their own. Macer's own father had married a New Spartan and had children by her. *New Spartan* children, to Freeman thinking, where primacy of descent tied to the mother.

The New Spartan network in Trinity space seemed a dark network, mostly self-funding from local operations, often dormant for years. Some time ago the Gants had tried to make a break and been slapped down hard. Grown more native than the natives, so the story ever went. Recently there'd been a change on New Sparta, and with it an activation of the network, and all the subsequent goings on.

Seamus was absolutely certain about the order of events.

What he wasn't certain of was the *causality*.

An off-world organization called the Consortium merged

with or acquired the Cooperative of Loyal Citizens. The Cooperative continuing to run the government on New Sparta. The
Consortium took over those interests abroad directly, and operated New Sparta through the Cooperative like a wholly owned
subsidiary.

He'd learned more, but Seamus wasn't sure it mattered.
When nic Cartaí had banned both Sampson and New Sparta
from Freeman trade, she'd driven the two planets together.
Sampson had kept New Sparta alive, and in return the Cooperative of Loyal Citizens had knifed its neighbor in the back,
helping rebels overthrow Sampson's elected government and
stepping in later to restore order under a unified government.

When Seamus ran the numbers, it seemed a stupid play.
Sampson and New Sparta were growing together anyway. They
would have formed one government in another twenty years
without all the backstabbing and bloodshed. The people of
both planets agreed on everything that mattered. They were
aggrieved and the Freeman Federation was to blame. The end.

The only way rushing things made sense was if New Sparta
didn't want a government that represented the interests of both
their peoples, but one that represented New Sparta's interests
exclusively. Or, it could be that the only interests the Cooperative of Loyal Citizens represented were their own.

After the Consortium took over New Sparta, they ended up
with Sampson as a throw-in. Seamus had thought at first the
larger planet might have been a sweetener for the deal but he'd
been wrong. For all the years they'd been in charge, the
Consortium had ignored Sampson. All their energy and investment lay on New Sparta. If they were driven purely by
economics, they would have put their money into Sampson.

If Seamus was in the market for a planet, he could probably
pick up Sampson for a song. There were only a couple things
wrong with it. It didn't have its own station, and it was banned
to Freeman trade. It also had a population that was getting

robbed blind by League merchants, and whose hate for the Freeman Federation raged with the fire of a thousand suns.

Other than that, it was perfect. Better than either of the planets the Freeman stations hung above. It even had location. Sampson sat pressed up against the frontier between Ojin and League space. It was a sin, the waste. He'd had to stop researching the planet because he wasn't getting any wiser. He was just getting angry.

He could think about all of this for days, tracing leads and following branches. It was the sort of task he loved, not because he'd been born with a talent for it, but because he hadn't. Every dive *inside* he learned something new. Something that made him rethink, not just what he'd learned that dive, but all he'd learned, ever.

There was more that the data told him, but he'd been focused on the questions he needed answered. And he'd found the answers. Framing them in universal terms had proved difficult. Fortunately he didn't have to do that for his friends. There was a simpler way of looking at all of this through Freeman eyes. And that simplicity is what Seamus had put in his messages to Lorelei and Macer.

The Consortium is the Enemy.

And the Enemy is no longer weak, and no longer alone.

The Consortium was headed by an Alexandrian named Vatya Zukova, and until recently, another Alexandrian named Fyodor Durst. Also appearing as directors in the organization's financial records were two New Spartans, Steev and Rik Severn, and a pair of brothers from Sampson, Ares and Adonis Mikos.

None of this information would have appeared in the public record if there hadn't been a lawsuit, filed on Columbia Station, alleging theft and breach of contract by the son of a recently elected minister of Parliament, a retired admiral named Kyros Olek. The son was accused of stealing valuable trade secrets from the Consortium.

The son's name?

Kirill Olek. Commodore was an entirely made-up title, as far as Seamus could tell.

And the valuable trade secrets?

Redacted.

The suit was settled out of court and the records sealed. Later they were ordered destroyed. Fortunately there were, in the League, firms such as the mac Donnachas in Freeman space, professionals whose business it was to watch for such orders and capture what they could in flight. Seamus doubted that there were five people outside of the trade who had ever seen those documents since the day they were sealed.

There appeared to have been a reconciliation between the Consortium and Olek, for they now were listed as working on a series of projects together, ones involving the locating and retrieval of historical artifacts of commercial and cultural value. They'd been successful on a number of worlds, principally along the edges of the Alexandrine, and within. They'd barely missed out on the Murrisk discovery, having arrived on the planet only days after Aoife nic Cartaí had lifted a second-epoch survey vessel from the planet.

Their method of operation varied by polity in order to avoid government salvor's claims. If they were to follow form in Freeman space, where there wasn't a central government, they'd need to buy up individual owner's rights to avoid conflicting claims of ownership. And so they had started to do just that. The Consortium and Olek appeared convinced there was some historical artifact of commercial or cultural value on Clear Island. They wanted an uncontested claim to it.

What could it be?

Macer and Lorelei would have a better idea than he.

It might be nothing, and they mistaken. Records showed Olek and the Consortium had more misses than hits. Yet Olek had grown rich in his own right, a noted collector of first- and second-epoch artifacts.

Perhaps the strangest thing that Seamus had discovered he'd stumbled upon entirely by accident. The discovery would have been impossible without the combined records from Macer Gant and from the League.

The Consortium employed security; agents, forces, it wasn't clear from the legal description and the quantity of funds outlaid. It could be an army of thousands or a cadre of a few hundred highly compensated experts. He didn't have access to the internal staffing documents or detailed payroll data necessary to know. He didn't even have detailed personnel data on the security employee named in the court documents.

In addition to the civil charges of intellectual property theft, there had been a criminal accusation of rape filed against Olek by one of the security personnel. The charge was later withdrawn and the security agent shipped off world. The name of the accuser was listed as Shayna Severn in the criminal filing.

Trinity Station legal and medical records showed that Macer's stepmother, Shayna Gant, and the accuser, Shayna Severn, were the same person. Medical records showed that the twins she'd born and had been trying to pass off as heirs to Luther Gant weren't Macer's half brothers at all. They didn't even appear to be twins in the conventional sense.

And Shayna Gant nee Severn wasn't the natural mother of either.

She'd been a surrogate.

He'd left all of that in his message to Macer. And none of it in his message to Lorelei. It seemed a family matter, and Macer unpredictable. If he'd grown attached to the children, Macer would be as likely to sweep that knowledge out the airlock as broadcast it on the Trinity Station Arcade.

How to proceed was entirely Macer's call. Seamus couldn't see how that knowledge had any bearing outside of matters of inheritance. The children were off world anyway, and easily located. They'd been forwarded by the mac Kennas to an orphanage on Unity Station. They weren't going anywhere, not while questions of guardianship worked their way through the civil courts.

Seamus had been about to begin digging into the prehistory of the Consortium when he'd been manhandled and unplugged from the Academy library.

He supposed none of that further backstory mattered in any case. Not as it pertained to keeping his word to Macer Gant and Lorelei Ellis.

The only answer he wasn't certain about was the abduction of the Clear Islanders. He'd done, not a background check of each, but a background *sweep* of all of them. A high percentage were former nic Cartaí crew. It might have been as simple as that, seizing an opportunity for payback to nic Cartaí through her people. Or it might be something else, something that he could learn from Ares Adonis.

With the Clear Islanders safely returned to their homes neither Macer nor Lorelei would ask him to dig any further.

But New Seamus, like Old Seamus, remained a completist. It's why he was good at the work.

The lack of that one answer gnawed at him.

He should be happy.

He'd found all the answers but one and neatly tied them up with a bow.

One enemy, not several, as he'd imagined. One *source.*

Find one and he would find them all.

Or...

Stand still long enough and they would find him.

30

S eamus decided he could afford to wait another five minutes for the shopkeeper to be alone. Any longer than that he would move on, and circle back later. It wasn't safe to remain in one place for any longer, not without something to make it worth the risk.

The customer turned out to be more browser than buyer. After they'd left empty-handed, the shop woman stood next to him and gazed out the shop window, human eye on him, artifact eye scanning the arcade.

"Did you find what you were looking for?"

"You're Margaret Breen."

"I could have told you that."

But she hadn't. Just as he hadn't given her his name.

Margaret Breen. The former stationmaster of Unity Station. Sixty-three years ago the first station fell, and she fell with it. Rode it down, like a captain refusing to abandon ship. He'd met her once before, not that he remembered her. Before his father had taken him out of the station school. Back then the school system would have people in to talk. People good with children, ones with stories to tell.

He hadn't recognized her face because, like all the children in the class, he hadn't been able to see past the rest of her, which was like looking at a machine. A robot shaped like a person but not. One with a face, and human guts and organs inside, mostly. One of the boys asked if she could piss, and she'd said she could, but only hydraulic fluid. And that broke the dam, and she took question after question, some personal, some silly, some impossible, until one girl, he didn't remember her name, asked if she could cry, and Margaret Breen said she couldn't. Why not, the little girl asked, and Breen had said, *What good would that do now?* Then she got up and clumped out on her big robot feet.

There was more about her in the Academy files, but he hadn't delved. It didn't feel appropriate, having known her long enough that she was more than column after column of numbers in his mind, and an actual person.

"The day after you left a man came in," she said. "Looking for you. I told him you'd been here, and were gone, and he seemed to believe me, but an hour later a spindle bum turned up and took up residence in that alley across the street."

"I don't see him."

"Well, he was there, day and night. Until he saw you walk in that door."

"You think he's a lookout."

"I think he was. And now he's a messenger boy. You should get your kit and go."

"I will," he said, though he was reluctant. He was still mulling over the unanswered question.

He followed her into the back room, and picked his way past a small army of dead soldiers—empty ale bottles, Barton's, a Unity system brand. "Big party?" he said.

"An old frenemy, back from the wars."

"Looks like you both did your duty."

She worked the mechanism of a big safe, one bolted to the

deck and the deckhead. She handed him the mechanical hand and closed the safe.

"This yoke it's gripping," he said.

"Olympic-class force blade," she said. "A nice one."

"Did it come with that?"

"You mean straight from King Manus? It did not."

"Does it devalue it? Having that welded on?"

"It's not welded on; it's just holding it."

"It's holding it tight."

"It's the lack of the cuff. The two need to be mated to release the grip."

She tossed him the handheld. "I've made a few modifications. That thing was driving me mad."

"Because it's not that bright, you mean."

"Because it's both chatty and obsequious. It answers to the fifth most common word in the Freeman tongue, and then it fawns like a Huangxu burn compress."

"Rubbish," he said.

"That's the word," she said. "How may I help you?"

He chuckled. "What's its name now?"

"Scrappy."

"What?" the device said.

"Who is the fairest of them all?"

"You'll find no fairer bargains than at Breen's Collectibles, where low prices are guaranteed. Ask about their easy-pay installment plans."

"Thanks, Scrappy."

"My pleasure, Admiral."

"Admiral? You couldn't change that?"

"You're back early. And I had company in."

"I'll fix it."

"No doubt." She looked him up and down. "I think I know you well enough to say it isn't callousness on you, but ignorance. I'm guessing you haven't heard."

"Haven't heard what?"

"About your family."

"I don't have a family anymore. But I heard there was a mac Donnacha death, if that's what you mean."

"A death."

"I was expecting my father to meet me last night. And a friend said that was why he couldn't make it."

The shop bell jingled.

"Let me get rid of whoever that is. Come out here, where I can keep an eye on you."

SHE WAS an attractive young woman in an Erlish way, blond, station-length hair bound up in a tail, tailored utilities, a neutral blue gray, tight enough that they showed what she wanted to show, loose enough that they almost hid what she didn't. She had that taught, sleek-yet-muscular look well-set League women strove for, feminine enough to use perfume but only after a championship fight at the dojo. She was short for an Erl, no taller than him, and she had a direct gaze that washed over him and summed him up with a wrinkle of her nose and a step to the right.

Away from him.

She was a little more thick waisted than he liked, but then he'd never been a fan of body armor. He tried to imagine what she'd look like peeled out of it. Then he tried to imagine what the peeling process would entail. When she spoke it wasn't in Trade, the common language of the station, but in League standard, and with a pronounced Columbia Station accent. If she couldn't see the pendant spires dangling from both his and Margaret Breen's ears, she was blind.

"Your porter is ogling me," she said.

"In case you haven't noticed, so am I," Margaret Breen said. "What can I do for your highness?"

"The electronics shop two doors down. I was hoping to..."

Margaret Breen stared at her with her human eye. Her artifact eyes scanned the Arcade.

"A friend has misplaced their handheld. I'd hoped to help. You, know. Find their COMPUTER."

"The electronics store is no more," Breen said. "But no one will stop you from pawing through the ash."

"Yes, but, the handheld. I could see that the store was... RUBBISH. But it's um, not."

"Not what?"

"RUBBISH."

"What isn't?"

"The handheld COMPUTER. It shows as active."

"That's good when they do that. Now if you excuse me, my *clerk* will see you out."

"But you don't understand," she said. "It shows active *here*."

"On the Arcade," Breen said.

"In this shop."

"I thought you said two doors down."

"That's where it was. When I'd looked. Earlier."

"Well, maybe you ought to go look there now. Or go there and wait."

"You don't understand. It's a NEMODYNE. Some people call it a NEMO."

"What sort of person would do that?" Breen said.

"What? You don't understand."

"My granny," Seamus said. "She never was a fan of the erlspout. It cuts the ears I've heard her say." Which was absolutely true. And if the young woman interpreted that to mean Margaret Breen was his granny? That was all in her own head.

"It's here. I know it."

"Maybe if you were more specific," Seamus said. "What sort of Nemodyne was it?"

"A 3050. It is a NEMODYNE 3050. A NEMO. RUBBISH. RUBBISH. NEMO."

"If it's rubbish, then maybe you ought to go look in the tip, out back."

"No. It's *here*."

"Fine," Seamus said. "Do you have the talk on you?"

"I don't understand."

"Do you have the Trade on you?"

"Do you mean do I speak Trade?"

"Ah," Seamus said. "Now we might get somewhere."

"This is the League Sector," she said in Trade.

"On a Freeman station." Seamus flicked his spire. "With Freemen."

"Wrap it up," Margaret Breen said, in handspeak. "We were in the middle of something that needs finishing." She ducked into the back room.

"Oh," she said. "You people. You think you're so much better than us."

Seamus snorted. "*We* think that?"

"Never mind. I'd like you to help me find my handheld."

"I thought it was your friend's handheld."

"I'd like you to help me and I can pay you."

"Because a Freeman wouldn't help you, unless you paid us to."

"Would you?"

"Not for money. I might, if you said please."

"And you might not. So I won't."

"Isn't this better? Communicating?"

"Better is finding my handheld. Now, you smug, smelly clerk, are you going to help me or not?"

"I'm not a clerk. I'm a researcher. A librarian."

"And that helps me how?"

"I'm good at finding things. So I think you should say please."

"And I think you should bathe."

"Here is the point in our relationship where I propose something *totally* inappropriate. I don't say it out loud, but you can read it on my face while I *ogle* you. Let me know if you like the idea."

She stared at him. Then she turned on her heel and marched toward the street door. "I'm out of here."

"Don't go."

"Why shouldn't I?"

He dug in his pocket. He slapped the handheld onto the merchant's counter. "Found it."

"What the—" She marched up to the counter and picked the handheld up. "This is mine."

"I thought civilians couldn't own a Nemodyne 3050."

"They can't. But this is a Nemodyne 3050x."

"And civilians *can* own that."

"No, they can't. And neither can the military. Where did you find it?"

"I'd rather not say."

He had kept her there, wasting her time, and his, because he didn't want to hear what Margaret Breen wanted to say.

She had something ugly to tell him.

Something ugly about his family.

He didn't want to hear it. And he didn't want to hoist his kit and scramble around the station, one arm's length ahead of Ares Adonis, who was really just a vessel for Ixatl-Nine-Go, and would never give up. He needed to scramble, but he didn't want to. He wanted to look at the shiny new League penny and imagine how it felt to a hand that had never held anything but Freeman pingins.

He would listen, and he would scramble, though, because he remained a man encumbered. There was still that one question to answer. Once he knew that answer, his work would be done. He wasn't afraid to die, and he wasn't afraid of Ixatl-Nine-Go anymore. Not since he'd snatched a nerve disruptor from a dead woman's hand and stuffed it in his pocket. It was an ugly death, but it was only a death. At least he'd die free.

If he had a regret, and he guessed that he did, since he was thinking about it, it was that once he knew the answer he wouldn't be able to pass it along to Macer and Lorelei.

"You should take your handheld and go."

"What were you thinking? Just now," she said.

"I was thinking that if I hadn't given you that handheld, I could leave a message for my friends. And then I could die happy." He shrugged. "Happier."

"No. Seriously. I want to know."

"Scrappy."

"What?"

"Show the pretty lady out."

"On it."

A yellow line appeared on the deck, the sort of virtual novice trail handhelds were good for.

"Thank you, Scrappy."

"My pleasure, Admiral."

She stared at him.

"Are you really a librarian?"

"Evil librarian." He stared at the deck. When he glanced up she hadn't moved. "Formerly evil librarian. I'm more... chaotic neutral now."

"You really should bathe."

"And you really should go."

"I would, except there's a giant man blocking the hatch."

31

Seamus felt like he knew Ares Adonis. He'd heard him speak. He'd researched his life. He'd seen still and motion images of him, both on and off the footie pitch. He'd even been attacked by Ares Adonis, except in that case there'd been most of an airlock hatch between them, and Seamus had been in a hardsuit, which tended to not only make him look bigger, but feel bigger as well, like a knight donning armor in a fantasy story.

None of that had prepared him for the sight of Ares Adonis inside an Erlside recycler's shop. The big man nearly blocked the view of the Arcade.

Seamus knew how fast Ares Adonis moved. He only had seconds to act.

"Can I borrow your handheld?"

"Here."

"Go into the back room and find Margaret Breen."

"Your grandmother?"

"She's not really my grandmother."

"What are you going to do?"

"I'm going to ask that man a question and record his answer.

Then I'm going to throw the handheld into the back room. You or the Breen scoop it up and run out the back. If either or both of you take that recording to anyone from Clear Island on Trinity Surface they'll get it to the right people."

"And then what?"

"Do whatever you want, and thank you."

"I'm not leaving."

"Then at least go in back and tell the Breen. Clear Island. Anyone will do."

Seamus glanced at the mechanical hand on the counter. And stuffed the ruin of his right arm into the wrist socket. Something snapped into place. And it felt like he had a hand again.

A very painful, burning hand.

He wanted to scream, it hurt so much, but it was nowhere near the pain of the cuff filaments burrowing into his arm. The good news was, even if the roasting pain went on for three days, he wouldn't be around to suffer it. He was under no illusions. Ares Adonis was going to either kill him or try to stuff Ixatl-Nine-Go into his head. If it looked like he was going the Ixatl-Nine-Go route, Seamus was going to use the nerve disrupter in his pocket to scramble his own brains first. He couldn't make any of the horrible things he'd done right, but he could get answers for his friends, and there was only one more answer he didn't know.

"Scrappy."

"What?"

"Start recording."

"Recording what?"

"Full spectrum." Maybe if the audio ended up trashed, someone could lip-read the answer. Or decipher the truth from Ares Adonis's electromagnetic aura. Or something.

"On it."

The mechanical hand remained wrapped around the

Olympic-class force-blade yoke, but it didn't feel welded to it. The yoke was like a rod with some buttons on it, and other than the scorching burning sensation, it really did feel like an actual hand, and the rod like a bit of thick conduit, or a baton.

Ares Adonis moved further into the shop to clear room for his henchmen. There were four of them: two spindle rats; a Leagueman in a gray traveling suit, the sort of getup rich layabouts wore; and Sun Shin Liuc.

"Idiot," Seamus muttered, and went to meet Ares Adonis.

Seamus saw no point in staying far back. He'd seen how fast the man could move. The others he could ignore. He didn't know what they were there for, but they weren't there for him. Seamus didn't get in Ares Adonis's face, but he wasn't more than an arm's length away when he asked the question.

"Why did you abduct all those people from Clear Island?"

"Because," Adonis said. His voice was deep, like the subsonic rumble of an idling Templeman drive. He stood staring at Seamus. Not grinning, but with a curl to his lips that made it seem like he was happy to see Seamus. Like they'd known each other as children, and hadn't seen each other for years, and were suddenly thrust together on the zero-radial tram.

"Because what?"

Ares Adonis blinked. And was gone. Ixatl-Nine-Go stared back. "Because I said to."

Seamus's gut felt like water. His legs wanted to collapse, and they wanted to shake, and they wanted to run, all at the same time. The only reason he wasn't stroking out was that he'd disabled every tendril of his library interface. His fingers shook. His arms. When he spoke, though, he sounded normal. Like he and the soul-destroying mind parasite were chatting over drinks. "Well, why did you do that?"

Ixatl-Nine-Go twisted Ares Adonis's lips into a grin. "Because—"

The deck lurched beneath Seamus's feet. The shop window rattled. Every display case in the shop rattled.

Seamus rocked back on his heels. *That's a new power.*

Except maybe it wasn't. Because Ares Adonis looked as surprised as Seamus felt. Like he was staring at Seamus and thinking the same thing Seamus was thinking. *How did he do that?*

And then the shop window exploded inward and the deck pitched like a wave, and display cases were falling, sparks flying, and the power failed; there was screaming on the Arcade, klaxons sounding, and the grinding slam of blast doors scything shut.

The emergency lighting cut on. Seamus was lying on his stomach, he'd bit his tongue and lost hold of the handheld in the fall. Ares Adonis rose to his knees, the rest of his crew still picking themselves up. When the air handlers kicked back on they blew debris into the air, like it was snowing insulation.

Somehow Seamus had managed to accidentally trigger the Olympic-class whatsit in his mechanical fist. The rod now had a long, skinny force blade jutting out of it. The business end of the blade sliced a narrow trench in the deck.

"That was a drive containment failure," Seamus said.

Somewhere along the ring a superluminal vessel's propulsion system had catastrophically failed. There'd been a blowout on the ring, the vessels on either side sustaining damage, crews scrambling to tear them free of the ring and hightail it for the tripwire at maximum burn, lest their own drive fail in range of the ring and trigger a cascade. It was a stationmaster's worst nightmare turned real. If a cascade occurred, the station might fall. Hundreds of thousands might die.

Ares Adonis stood upright, Ixatl-Nine-Go in control. "That was *Tell Me Another.*"

"It wasn't." *Tell Me Another* was the mac Donnacha family ship. That vessel was immaculately maintained. It had to be.

Not only was it a family ship but all the mac Donnacha wealth was on board. Four hundred years of secrets that no one was meant to— *Oh no. Please no.*

"All you know is known to me."

"You killed them."

"Your family? Not I. From you, the thought. From your father, the hands."

"You lie."

"Why would I? They died last night. All. Of. Them. Could you not feel their glorious pain?"

"I—"

"Now, this event. That was mine."

"Someone tried to access the ship's database."

"Inevitably. You Freemen are so greedy. And so distrustful. You make the finest tools."

Tell Me Another was rigged to drop the drive containment field rather than surrender its secrets. There was too much sensitive data in the database to let it fall into foreign hands. The ship's failsafe wasn't exactly secret knowledge. The fact that it was *common* knowledge was what made it safe. Only an idiot or a madman would even attempt to break in. You had to gain access from the ship's bridge and engineering at the same time. And the only way anyone could do that was by murdering every soul on board first.

Seamus glanced at the force blade jutting from his fist.

There were fires breaking out on the arcade.

"Careful with that hand. Olek wants it back."

A group of children dodged falling debris as they ran by.

"Then come and get it."

The station shuddered.

Ares Adonis charged.

Seamus swung the force blade in a lightning-fast arc.

Ares Adonis caught Seamus's forearm in one enormous fist, the force blade glowing above them like a torch held high.

176PATRICK O'SULLIVAN

He gripped Seamus's neck with the other hand and lifted him off the deck.

Seamus clawed at the hand strangling him, trying to break the grip. He couldn't breathe, he couldn't think, he couldn't—

Ares Adonis wrapped his arm around Seamus and pulled him to his breast, the pressure lessened for an instant. Ixatl-Nine-Go breathed in Seamus's ear. "I am *so* looking forward to being inside you again."

Seamus stopped fighting, his feet off the deck, one arm raised in pointless combat, the other limp in defeat, his useless human fingers, so weak and bloody, dipping into his pocket, and finding steel. Drawing it out and pressing it to his side, to Ares Adonis's side, he twitched one tiny muscle.

Seamus hit the deck like a sack of garbage, the back of his head hammering against ceramic composite, his eyes blinking black and stars. Then he was on his knees and crouching over Ares Adonis, who jerked and spasmed, blood flecking his lips, his eyes rolled back in his head, no evidence, no evidence at all of Ixatl-Nine-Go, not on the outside. Seamus pressed the nerve disrupter to Ares Adonis's temple and pulled the trigger and pulled the trigger and pulled the trigger.

Die, die, die, die.

"Allow me," someone said, and took the weapon from Seamus's hand, helped him stand, and led him a little bit away. It was the Erl fop, in his fancy gray traveling suit. He had something on his hands, something blue, and glowing.

"What's that?" Seamus said.

"The power of ten squared."

Seamus felt his lips turn up. "No prison can hold him."

"Indeed. You might wish to look away."

"Why?"

The blue glow was from the field-reinforced gloves he wore. He extended the field and jabbed it into Ares Adonis's skull and pulled out Ixatl-Nine-Go. There was surprising little blood. He powered the gloves down, and then the implant.

"It hurts a lot more than it looks like it would," Seamus said.

"He can't feel anything," the Leagueman said.

"I know," Seamus said. "It's nice while it lasts."

32

Prescott Grange System, Earth Restoration League

Swan groaned as Ciarán closed the bridge hatch. She switched the main display from communications to the piloting display as if Ciarán wouldn't notice.

"You called?" Ciarán said.

"Unfortunately," Swan said. "We have an issue."

They'd driven further in, closer to the planet and its falling station than he'd expected. They were on an intercept plot with the station, estimated time of arrival twenty hours, roughly eight hours before the planet's atmosphere would begin to drag on the station and pull it down. Impact in ten hours, if he was reading the display right.

"May I see the communications display?" Ciarán said.

"I warned you to lock the hatch," Maura Kavanagh said.

"Wouldn't work," Ko Shan said. "He has the merchant captain's command codes."

Ciarán placed his hand on Swan's sleeve. "Ship's Captain?"

"Show him, Cap," Hess said. "It's not like he can make things worse."

"You underestimate the merchant-in-charge." Ko Shan piped the communications display to the main display. "Watch and learn."

There were over thirty-five hundred distress calls, all active and unanswered.

"We have a duty to render aid," Ciarán said. That duty wasn't a Freeman custom or convention, but a human one.

"We have a duty if doing so doesn't endanger the ship or crew," Swan said.

"Understood. But acknowledging the messages doesn't put us in danger."

"It might," Swan said. "But there are other considerations."

"We can't acknowledge them," Ko Shan said. "We shouldn't even be able to receive them, except they're shouting so loud the signal is bleeding over onto our passive array. I've shunted them to the comm console just to get them out of the way. Any signal on the comms system gets masked on the sensors display."

"Let's hear one," Ciarán said.

The bridge crew shouted as one. "No!"

"Let's not," Maura said. "Not again."

"The ship finds the messages disturbing," Swan said. "Replaying the messages interferes with flight operations."

"They're cries for help from juvenile synthetic intelligences," Ko Shan said. "'Save Dalton,' over and over again."

"Thirty-five hundred intelligences?" Ciarán hadn't even imagined there *were* juvenile synthetic intelligences.

"Thirty-five distinct sources on the planet's surface. The messages repeat."

"Can you pare it down to a source view?"

"Done," Ko Shan said.

There were thirty-six sources. "What's that one?"

"The nanny." Swan wiped the message open.

A middle-aged woman stood in a ripe grain field, the grain up to her knees. She said that her name was Dalton Pryne, and that she needed immediate assistance. She followed the Cross-Polity Convention on distress calls to the letter, flagging her immediate situation as dire and rapidly decaying. Everything about the distress call appeared normal, except the clouds in the background appeared to erupt from the ground behind her and flow upward over her head. She didn't seem to notice this unnatural phenomenon.

Ciarán scratched his chin as Swan terminated the replay. "An expert system, judging from the content."

"A damaged one," Ko Shan said.

Ciarán glanced at Ko Shan. "Message origin?"

"The station."

"Life signs?"

"None we can detect."

"We're not risking the vessel and crew for the sake of an automated nursemaid," Swan said.

"We need to reply."

"And reveal our existence and position? Think again, Freeman whelp."

"I'll run a shuttle out and hail from well away," Ciarán said. "It needs doing."

"There's a lot of junk out there," Hess said.

"I'll be careful."

"This is not wise," Swan said. "Expert systems aren't covered by the Convention. Nor are persons on a celestial body with atmosphere, water, and comestibles."

"Understood. I had an idea before you called. About how we could learn what happened here, and if it's safe or if the bad guys are still lurking about. I don't know if it would work or not, but even if it did, it would take time we don't have. Now I have a better idea."

"Which is?"

"We ask someone." Ciarán glanced at the comms display. *And we let them know they're not alone and shouting into the dark.*

CIARÁN PUT distance between the shuttle and *Quite Possibly Alien* by exiting the boat bay and staying put. He watched the distance between the vessel and his fixed position increase at a rate it would be hard to match in the little craft. When he deemed it safe he opened the comms display. There was one incoming message.

He replied, following the Convention, which didn't require he identify himself unless he was in a hull carrying a transponder code. He kept the distracting incoming visual feed off and transmitted audio only. "Message received, state your coordinates and condition."

The same human-seeming voice replied, with coordinates of the station and a brief description of what he already knew, that it was on a blown-apart space station that was sliding into a gravity well.

"We're not equipped to stop the fall," Ciarán said. "We may be able to assist with evacuation."

"A dozen fleet tugs couldn't stop the fall," Dalton Pryne said. "And I don't require evacuation. I do want to get a record out of the events here, and if I may, leave a parting message for my... little ones."

Ciarán flipped the comms toggle to auto. "Recording."

THE MESSAGES SCROLLED BY, an incomprehensible jumble of numbers. Ko Shan's systems could make sense of them, but the comms in the little shuttle couldn't, and that meant Ciarán couldn't either.

"Thank you," Dalton Pryne said, once the transmission completed. "I wondered if you might answer."

"You can detect my vessel?"

"Not the one you're in now. But the one with a synthetic intelligence on board. I found it strange it would ignore me, but then, when I heard your voice I thought I'd worked it out. But you surprised me."

"How so?"

"One doesn't expect mercenary warlords to answer distress hails. When you responded I expected it was to gloat, or issue an ultimatum, or something equally barbaric."

"I think you're mistaking me for someone else."

"Doubtful. It seemed odd that the Dreaded Diarmuid of the Outer Reach and Freeman Merchant Apprentice Ciarán mac Diarmuid were the same person, but the voice prints match."

"There's some mistake."

"According to the Registry, you own controlling shares in ten mercenary companies. Is this not true?"

"When did you see that?"

"Just now. Would you like to examine the timestamped entries?"

"The superluminal nodes are down."

"Yes, well, I have my own."

"An expert system has a private superluminal node?"

"I'm an expert system?"

"Your clouds scroll the wrong way."

"Oh, that. It amuses the younger children. And it irritates the older ones. Either way, I have their attention when I speak."

Dalton Pryne was a synthetic intelligence. "This explains what all the yelling is about, then."

"What yelling?"

"The thirty-five voices on the planet shouting, 'Save Dalton.'"

"You can hear that?"

"It's overloading our sensors. We can't *not* hear it."

"That is very bad. If you can hear it, anyone might."

The comms channel fell silent for a moment.

"You risked your life to respond to an expert system's automated distress signal?"

"When you say it that way, it doesn't sound very smart."

"I've changed my mind. I need to get to the planet."

"I think that's going to happen," Ciarán said.

"Very funny. Should I desire rescue, who would charge the lowest fee? The merchant or the pirate?"

"We're required by the Convention to provide aid. It's prepaid."

"An idealist. And inexperienced. Just my luck."

"So I should have just ignored your distress call?"

"It's done all the time. You aren't paying it forward. When the day comes that you need help? Forget about it."

"If we haggle you're getting mercenary prices." *Merchant mac Diarmuid was only interested in repeat customers.*

"How much to rescue me?"

"Attempt to rescue you. No guarantees."

"Fair enough. How much?"

"One starship with a functioning Templeman drive."

"I can do that."

"You can?"

"I couldn't do two. But I can do one."

"In working condition."

"Last I looked."

"When was that?"

"Just now. There's one condition, though."

"What's that?"

"You have to take the prisoners with you."

"There are prisoners on the starship?"

"Maybe. But I'm talking about the ones here. On the station."

33

They approached the battered ruin of the space station in the planetary-occupation shuttle, Ciarán and Hess in hardsuits, Amati in her exoskeletal armor, and Wisp in her recently groomed fur. Wisp had forced her way onto the shuttle. When Ciarán tried to get her off, she had snapped at him and melded into the shadows.

Hess brought the shuttle in on a fast burn, sweeping past the shattered side of the ring in the spinward direction, in the plane of the ring. The lower spindle had been torn away, and the upper truncated, two-thirds of the ring missing, and what did remain trailing a net of sparking cables and leaking conduits, and puffing tiny clouds of spent atmosphere. The station was sliding inevitably down the gravity well, acceleration toward the planet slowly increasing with each rotation.

Dalton Pryne directed them to an airlock on the relatively undamaged side of the station. Hess matched attitude and rotation and brought the shuttle in. The airlock seals latched. The telltales switched from red to yellow to green.

"Remember," Amati said. "We stick together."

The hatch cycled. Ciarán felt Wisp brush against him as she raced past and onto the station.

Ciarán's breath rasped loud in the hardsuit's helmet. He knew how to use the device; every spacer did, but it didn't feel natural to him. On the merchant track at the Academy, he had to recertify his skills annually, and he passed the certs—barely. The assumption was that a Freeman merchant had grown up on a family ship, where the gift of a personal hardsuit was a coming-of-age present, like a boy's first long gun at home. He felt bulky and clumsy in the device. That he had to strip down to his birthday suit to fit inside didn't help him feel comfortable. Some people said a hardsuit made them feel invulnerable. All it did for Ciarán was remind him how vulnerable he was, out here in space, where one wrong move could end him.

A novice trail flickered on the deck, Dalton Pryne's energy-saving solution to guiding them. All three had their suit servo recorders on so that they could retrace their steps if the power went out. The lights flickered and strobed, and it reminded Ciarán of the full-immersion games Seamus and Macer liked to play, the ones where zombie spacers lurched from hidden niches and darkened corridors might sprout murderous psychopaths at any moment. The hum of switching power supplies cycling and the sparking crack of arcing cables made it hard to listen for footfalls. He could see the burn marks, but just like in the games, his suit filtered out all the odors but his own fear-sweat reek. The slow march down the corridor possessed an unreal feel, the bulk of Amati's exo like a mobile wall of protection between whatever danger might be out there and Ciarán and Hess following in her wake.

Hess carried a plasma rifle because that's what he'd trained on, its preheater lit and glowing hot. Ciarán had a razorgun in a holster on the suit's left sleeve and a force blade in a sheath strapped to his right thigh. He had an overseer's rod in his hand, and he'd practiced with the weapon using the suit's thick gauntlets. He could extend the whip and drop the containment field, and project a personal protection sphere, but that was all he'd had time to experiment with. He hoped he didn't have to use any of those gestures, and he didn't expect to. Dalton Pryne said the station sensors were still in operation and the only life signs on the station those of the prisoners abandoned in their cells. Ciarán worried about Wisp, but there wasn't anything he could do but worry. She might have hared off on her own or might be pacing them from shadow to shadow. The fact that he couldn't see her in the dismally flickering light didn't mean she wasn't there.

Ciarán's little rescue party was headed first to assess the situation with the trapped synthetic intelligence before dealing with any prisoner transfer. He didn't want to have to deal with the prisoners, but it had been a condition of the synthetic intelligence's help. If Dalton Pryne hadn't mentioned there were prisoners, he wouldn't have known. But once he knew, there really wasn't any option, not if he wanted to look himself in the mirror.

He had no idea what he was going to do with prisoners, particularly if *Quite Possibly Alien* remained trapped in a dying system. That he didn't know what to expect of the prisoners was part of the problem. They might be serial killers. They might be drunken sailors sleeping it off. They might even be innocent, like he'd been when he was a prisoner on Ambidex. There was no telling.

Thus they were loaded for bear, not because they thought they'd be jumped by zombie stationers, but because there were only three of them and Wisp, wherever she was, and they wanted the prisoners cowed and cooperative. Amati alone in her exo could handle any threat, but they couldn't be sure the prisoners understood that. They were all packing weapons because everyone knew an armed spacer was harder to take hostage than an unarmed one.

The novice trail disappeared under a blast door. Amati tried the release. It didn't work. "Engineer."

"Yes, sir." Hess stepped forward and eyeballed the door controller. "Atmosphere on the other side, no pressure differential. It's either jammed or we got the wrong access codes."

"Or I fat fingered it," Amati said. "Give it a go. If it starts to cycle, step back."

Hess entered the code and stepped back. The blast doors began to open. Ciarán felt Wisp brush his sleeve as she swept past.

They entered the station Arcade on the main deck, dead center below the admin and stationmaster's offices beginning a deck above. The zero-radial tram lay to their immediate right. A tram car stood waiting, a pair of bodies blocking the doorway, an old woman and a young boy. It looked like a hurricane had swept along the arcade.

"Trampled to death," Amati said. "Don't look too close, Merchant."

Hess grabbed Ciarán's sleeve. "Too late, Major. Come on, merchie man, we got work to do."

Ciarán tore his gaze away. "Who would do that?"

"Scared people do crazy things." Major Amati pointed along the radial. "You know the drill, double time, and stay behind me. If anything comes at us from behind—"

Hess tapped his outstretched index finger against the plasma rifle's trigger guard. "Kill it and keep moving."

Ciarán glanced at the dead. "Those were civilians."

"Civilians on a military station." Amati resumed their march. "Or military off duty. Or dependents. It doesn't matter. Everyone knows the rules. Squad on patrol, you approach from ahead."

"Or you end up dead," Hess drawled. "It's a long walk to zed ring, Major."

The flashing novice trail ran alongside the zero-radial tram.

"Roger that. Rules, Merchant. No stopping to render aid. If you feel the obligation, tag 'em on your HUD map, and we'll discuss extraction once the mission is complete. Understood?"

"Understood, Major. The ship and the crew come first."

"Glorious. Welcome to the Iron Gang. Engineer?"

"On it." Hess pressed some buttons on his hand comp. Seconds later the artificial gravity on the station shut off and his suit began to rumble.

Amati chuckled. "One of the Gang seems to like it light."

Ciarán realized the rumbling was Amati's exo sensors picking up Wisp's purr.

Hess latched his handheld to his suit. "We are null gee, spindle to dock."

The sync-on light on the military-issue hardsuit's heads-up display flashed. The proximity display that had been showing three dots earlier now showed a triangle with a dot at each corner

"Double time for a hundred meters." Amati began to move out. And so did Hess's and Ciarán's hardsuits. It was a weird feeling but not an unfamiliar one. Amati and Ciarán had worked out in hardsuits during his self-defense training. He'd asked what all the controls were for and she'd told him. And shown him. If she wanted to bring him in and lecture him, or end the exercise early, she'd sync his suit to hers and, unless he wanted to fight her all the way, he'd let her reel him in. There was a local override she hadn't told him about. He'd discovered it himself, much later, and only then by accident.

Jogging along in a hardsuit under someone else's control was easy if you didn't fight it. They were moving at a ground-eating pace that Amati said a top infantryman could maintain for days. It was fast and relatively safe in controlled territory. There were faster modes of travel that weren't as safe.

Amati glanced upward. "Acceleration in ten meters."

Ciarán groaned.

"Watch your head, Merchant. On my mark in three, two, one. Let's jet, ladies."

They bounded along the corridor in long hops. The hard-suits had tiny attitude thrusters, but they were limited in fuel and for emergency use only, like when you were blown out of an airlock in a spin and needed to arrest your rotation. They weren't actually *jetting* along. Jetting was just what the League military called this low-G hopping gait. There were two faster gaits that Amati said were rarely used unless outdoors, or in a full retreat. *Double jetting* used higher and longer bounces. *Pussing out* was thruster-augmented double jetting, and according to Amati, couldn't be taught, but only learned through experience.

The visible damage seemed to decrease as they moved closer to the spindle. This part of the station yet held atmosphere and any survivors were long gone. He didn't note any dead or dying, but they were moving fast, in part, he figured, because Amati didn't want him to get a close look should they stumble upon survivors. He wondered if Wisp could keep up, and stopped wondering when she brushed against him and he felt her purr rumble through his suit. He wasn't sure how she did it. A suit's hullwalkers gave him traction, inside and outside of a station. She was moving along as fast or faster than the zero-radial tram on her bare paws.

She flickered into visibility for an instant, as if in answer to his question. She was using the wiring and plumbing conduit mounts for traction, racing along in long, low leaps, skimming along the overhead and the hull-to-deckhead interface in an effortless glide, sometimes entirely upside down relative to him.

Ciarán shivered. Wisp was in her environment, and he was seeing her in a new light. Amati had said she was a weapon, and she'd told him that she'd lost her arm to a mong hu. He'd believed her, but he hadn't thought through the implications.

In order to tear her arm off, the mong hu would need to first shear through the armor around it.

Wisp was the runt of the litter when it came to mong hu, but she was still growing. It wouldn't be long until she out-massed Ko Shan, and her growth showed no sign of slowing. He was reminded of a story, not a *seanscéal*, but just a story, that the first words in Freeman ever spoken to a mong hu were the ones he was thinking. *I'm glad you're on our side.*

Ahead, the flashing novice trail disappeared beneath a blast door.

"Dropping to double time, in ten," Amati said, and then, "Dropping to quick time in ten. Disengaging sync on my mark."

This was the hardest part, and when Ciarán screwed up it was usually here. A faceplant in low G had all sorts of apparently humorous aftereffects, though it didn't feel that way when it was your face being planted.

The sync light flashed off.

Ciarán managed to keep it together.

"Engineer."

Hess inspected the blast door. "Looks good to five nines, Major."

"Open sesame."

"On it." Hess entered the code and stepped back.

The massive GRAIL gun melded to Amati's right arm swung up, and she took a bracing stance behind the hatch coaming. She tossed a recon ball into the compartment and ran it through its paces.

"Clear." She proceeded into the compartment. The novice trail flicked off.

"That was fast," Dalton Pryne said. "Now get me out of here."

"I thought you said she was a synthetic intelligence." Hess stood staring at a woman in the prime of her life. She appeared heavier than was fashionable in the League, and somewhat less polished. She had a direct gaze, and when she directed it at Hess he took an unconscious step back.

"She is," Amati said. "This is her avatar."

"Right in one." Pryne pointed. "That is me, over there."

The compartment was largely empty except for some diagnostic consoles and workstations along the far wall. Largely empty, if one ignored the enormous black sphere set into the deck in the center of the compartment.

The sphere was thirty meters in diameter, with a thick sheaf of cables exiting or entering it at the top, depending upon one's perspective. Otherwise the sphere was entirely featureless, all but for an access hatch located high above, and a ladder climbing up to it. It was by far the largest containment sphere Ciarán had ever seen. It wouldn't be right to say that Ciarán was an expert on containment spheres, but he'd translated a lot of documents regarding them, and this one seemed little different in appearance than the ones on *Quite Possibly Alien*. "That's big."

"It's a mating chamber," Pryne said. "They need to be big."

"What's it mated to?" Hess said.

"It's not mated *to* anything," Pryne said. "It's *for* mating."

"Oh. Are you in there alone?"

"At present," Pryne said. "Now shut up and let me talk to the merchant."

"Sure," Hess said.

"Well?" Pryne said. "Do we still have a deal?"

Ciarán looked Dalton Pryne's avatar in the eye. "The deal was to try to get you out."

"And? Can you?"

"Warrant Officer Hess is an excellent engineer. If anyone can get you out, he can. How long can you survive outside the sphere?"

"Not long enough."

"Is there a smaller sphere on the station?"

"Not anymore."

"On the planet? On one of the emergency outposts?"

"No."

"We might be able to move you powered down."

"Unacceptable. I need to remain powered up to survive."

"Huh." That was a lie. Ciarán scratched his eyebrow. "We're done here. I'll take the coordinates of that superluminal vessel now."

Hess wandered over the consoles and began inspecting them.

"But—"

"We're trying to help. You need to be straight with us."

"Fine. The sphere takes power to sustain me in an active state. And I need to be in an active state to give you those coordinates."

"Pinbeam the coordinates to *Quite Possibly Alien*, and we'll get you out and keep you from burning up in the atmosphere. When your allies get here, we'll hand you over to them. Word of a merchant."

"Once you have the coordinates, you could just abandon me."

"You have my word we won't."

"And that's supposed to be enough?"

"My word in front of two witnesses."

"That are also part of your crew."

"So?"

"So that's absurd."

"Not as absurd as trying to dictate terms to your rescuers. I offered to rescue you for free under the Convention. I have now met, not just the terms, but the spirit of the agreement, despite you telling me I'm a fool to do so. This looks hard, and it looks like it will require putting the ship and crew in further danger to pull it off. I think I can save you in an inactive state. But if you don't want that, I'm fine with your refusal. We'll be on our way, and we'll find that superluminal, now that we know it's out there."

"And the prisoners?"

"We're headed there next. I don't know what sort of people you're used to dealing with, but this is not how we do business."

"How do you propose to rescue me?"

Ciarán pointed. "Is the spindle gap on the other side of that bulkhead?"

"Yes."

Hess had wandered into earshot. "Huh. That *would* work."

"*What* would work?" Dalton Pryne said.

"The merchant isn't much on fixing stuff, but I never met a man better at breaking things. You should trust him, 'cause even though he's crazy, he's right. We can do this."

"How!"

"By using a longboat's main drive to melt a hole in the hull," Ciarán said.

"Oh," Hess said. "That didn't occur to me. I thought you'd want to use the Huangxu bomb we have on board to blow a hole."

"I'm saving that for later. Plus it requires a Templeman drive power-up to trigger it."

"True. But I could override that." Hess scratched his chin. "I like your idea better."

"We have a Huangxu bomb on board our vessel?" Amati said.

"Sure," Hess said. "We'd need some thermal shielding between the hull and the sphere."

"Power down and flood the chamber," Ciarán said. "Ice it up."

"That would take time," Hess said. "And it might not be enough. I know the specs of the candle. I'll do some measuring and thinking, but yeah"—Hess nodded to himself—"powered down we can do this. If we burn a big enough hole and grab on, we can just hold still while the station falls away, easy peasy."

Ciarán watched the avatar's face. He wondered if it was designed to display true emotion or merely to convey a crafted message. He'd long heard that synthetic intelligences lacked emotion, but he'd spent the better part of a year in close company with two. They might not experience the same feelings as humans, or feel as deeply, but the ones he knew were definitely not soulless machines. They were individuals and deserved to be treated as such.

"Well?"

"Do you understand what you're asking?"

"I'm asking you to trust me. To put your fate in my hands and to believe that I'm a man of my word, and that I will not fail you, or desert you."

"That's a lot to ask."

"Yes, ma'am, it is. But I can't see another way."

A yellow novice trail began to flash in the floor. "See to the prisoners while I decide."

"I'll stay here and get started, in case it's a go," Hess said. "Provided the major agrees."

"She agrees." Amati glanced at Ciarán. "There's a bomb onboard and you didn't tell me?"

Ciarán felt his face heat. "It's a small one."

"Technically, more like a small big one," Hess said.

Major Amati headed for the hatch. "Fantastic."

34

"You know the drill," Amati said.

"Stay behind you."

"And?"

"Watch your back and kill anything behind us that moves."

"Let's hope it's not far to the brig."

Ciarán scanned the shadows as they passed, his attention shifting left to right. "According to the station schematic, it should be around the next corner."

Amati tried the hatch lock and elbowed Ciarán to step back. She planted herself behind the hatch coaming as the doorway scythed open.

It was dark inside.

"Night vision."

"Wilco," Ciarán said. He felt stupid using military slang but Amati insisted on it. He tongued the hardsuit's night-vision mode active. He scanned the lighted corridor behind them, which was a major mistake, before following her blindly into the compartment.

He knew something was wrong the instant he heard her GRAIL gun begin to wind up.

"Back out."

He felt Wisp brush past him as he nearly tripped over the hatch coaming, and Amati gripped his suit by the neck and shoved him clear. The hatch scythed shut behind them.

"About these prisoners. You didn't ask *who* or what they were?"

"I didn't." Ciarán tongued night-vision mode off. "What's the problem?"

"Did you get a look at them?"

"Ummm."

"You blinded yourself. Watching my back."

"Temporarily."

"They're in a cell. Chances are none of them are loose in there."

"None of who? I felt Wisp rush past me while we backed out. She's in there."

"I don't hear the sound of a struggle inside. Which confirms there's not any of them loose, or we'd be listening to your cat getting its guts ripped out."

"That's impossible."

"Yeah? I thought it was impossible I'd live to see a single Outsider. Now I've seen four, maybe five. We're done here. Let's go."

Outsiders were virtually invincible fighting creatures reportedly developed by the Alexandrian Eng. A little over sixty years ago *sixteen* of them entered League space and started a war that sucked even the Freemen into the conflict. A dozen family ships were lost and Unity Station fell before the fighting ended. "Wisp is in there."

"And we're not. Someone has to live to report this."

"Wait. If they're really Outsiders, how did anyone capture *five* of them?" The story was that Outsiders fought to the death. There'd only been one ever captured and rumor was it had escaped.

"Don't know. Don't care. Let's go."

"But you just said they're confined to a cell."

"They appeared to be. But the risk that I'm wrong is too much."

"We're not abandoning Wisp. So open the hatch. Or step aside."

"It's a cat. An *animal*."

"She's crew. So step aside."

Amati stood up straight, towering over him in her monstrous exoskeletal armor. "Make me."

Ciarán could hear the blood rushing in his ears. He could feel the hardsuit's gauntlets flex against his skin. He could watch Amati watching him as he looked past the fang-painted exterior of her death machine and *perceived* the warrior inside. "Very well. I shall. Major Amati, you are relieved of command. Please retrieve Warrant Officer Hess and return to the shuttle and wait for me there. If you do not hear from me in one hour, return to the vessel and resume your duties there. Instruct Captain Swan to report the discovery of these creatures to proper authorities as soon as possible."

"You can't be serious."

"This junk heap is going down the gravity well. If I end up letting something nasty loose, I don't want it coming home with us. Better it dies here."

"Along with you."

"I don't expect you to understand."

There was no contract more sacred than the first contract.

He *would not* leave without Wisp.

There existed a chain of command on every Freeman merchant vessel. He didn't know about the military chain, but this one tugged both ways. Every offense against a single crewman was considered a direct offense against the person of the merchant. When you signed a Freeman contract that was a given. It was also spelled out explicitly in the contract in clear and simple terms.

The merchant had your back. They weren't abandoning you in a foreign port. They weren't letting anyone haul you off the ship for a crime you didn't commit. And if you found yourself in a brawl, dockside, on the Arcade, even on the spindle, they were wading in, and dragging the crew in with them, and standing beside you, and there better be a good reason for the fight, because there'd be hell to pay if there wasn't. Because it was the merchant's back that would feel the lash, not yours.

In exchange for all that you agreed to do one thing.

Follow the merchant's lawful orders promptly and to the best of your ability.

Amati hadn't signed with Ciarán. But Aoife had entrusted Ciarán with her responsibilities, and he'd agreed to carry them out.

This wasn't just about Wisp.

He wouldn't have Aoife nic Cartaí come back to the ship to find he'd betrayed her. The most shocking thing about Merchant Roche and *Golden Parachute* hadn't been that he'd been a monster loose in the world.

It was that he'd broken the chain of trust, and betrayed the crew.

"I thought I'd never hear myself say this. I didn't think I'd ever have to. But hear me now, and spread the word." He wished he could look her in the eye, rather than try to laser through the visor of her helmet with willpower alone. "My deck, my rules. Now do as I ask, and fulfil your duty to the ship, and to the crew, and to the merchant captain."

"I—"

"That is an order."

She stared at him.

Eventually she spoke.

"Yes, sir."

H e entered the code and the hatch opened.

He stepped inside.

He found the hatch control and, beside it, the lighting controls.

He closed the hatch.

And turned on the lights.

Someone supremely deadly brushed against him.

And purred.

There were five of them locked in a single cell.

The brig was large, with two-score cells standing open, all watched over by a central guard station, one with a panoramic view through some transparent, impact-resistant material, perhaps feroglass, perhaps something more high tech and durable, as the League was inclined to invention in matters of security.

Wisp had dropped her adaptive camouflage and stood revealed before them, ears forward, back strait, tail erect. The universal cat signal for *friend*. From time to time, one ear would swivel toward him and then back toward the... people.

Four of them shielded a fifth from view. As he moved they moved, like bodyguards protecting their charge.

They were humanoid—two arms, two legs, a head—though they didn't seem composed of flesh, but of a milky-white material layered in tiny scales, so that at first he thought them clothed in armor, until he realized that they were naked, and the scales the same roughly gleaming diamond of Wisp's razor-sharp claws and fangs. They had humanlike faces, with two eyes, a nose, and a mouth, though without hair or ears, so that they appeared vaguely reptilian, though their features were more planar and sharply defined than any reptile in his experience.

Perhaps their most unusual features were the thornlike horns on their spines and running along their arms, and the swordlike spikes that he thought at first they were grasping, but which he realized, with a start, were a part of them, and projecting from their wrists. He supposed he could count their fingers and toes, as they had some, four or five or six on each hand and foot, and opposable thumbs. If he had not seen them move, he would have taken them for some sort of horror-palace gargoyle, carved of milky diamond, with the express purpose of summoning perpetual nightmares. Their eyes burned a ruby red, and while each seemed similar to the next, he could tell them apart by the curvature of their menacing fangs and the shape of their earholes.

If Wisp didn't find them so intriguing, he would have wet himself and been halfway back to the shuttle by now. There was something terribly menacing about them, targeted at the most primal part of his brain, so that, as he studied them, he felt certain they weren't natural creatures, but something made. *Something made to break his mind before they broke his body and stole his soul.*

He'd only recently begun to believe in the existence of actual evil in the wider world, but the idea that they were the demon spawn of some infernal devil lodged so firmly in his mind that he felt it had to be a lie, an *exploitation* of the meat-puppet operating system he was constructed upon. That this impression of them had to be a deliberate lie, because it was too perfect to be natural.

That, and the fact that the finger twitching he'd been witnessing since he entered the compartment had begun to appear like a language, and one he knew, all combined to make it possible for him to stand his ground, and run his gloved fingers along Wisp's spine and sign back to them with the other hand.

"Who is this Liberator you speak of?"

They lurched away from him as one, while a chaos of clicks issued from their diamond lips.

"He comes," one of them signed. "Run away while you can."

"He is here," another signed. "The sister says it is so."

"Release us," a third signed. "And give us our clothes."

"We will let you live," the fourth signed. "We are mercy."

"I believe you mean this," Ciarán both signed and spoke. "Merciful."

"I am informed," the fourth signed.

Ciarán signed and spoke again, though he thought signing on his part might be redundant. They had understood him when he'd spoken. "Where are your clothes?"

"There." The third one pointed, and waited for him to return his gaze to her.

"In the hanging locker?"

"In there, and in the drawers."

He opened the locker and pulled out five crimson robes, four of which looked like they would fit them, and the fifth of which looked like it would not.

His fingers hovered over the drawer cabinet.

The first drawer was empty.

As was the second drawer.

The third drawer was not.

No way. I'm not seeing this.

He turned to find the demons watching him.

They'd withdrawn their thorns and spikes and now seemed merely terrifying.

He handed them their robes. And their pendant spires.

He wrenched his helmet off and instantly regretted it. The entire compartment reeked like a snake pit.

"It's the merchant," one of them signed.

"Our pardon, Merchant," another signed. "We were told you were in stasis."

"Due to an unfortunate accident," signed another.

"We are pleased to see you restored to health."

"Where are the lock controls?" Ciarán signed.

All four pointed and signed. "There."

He released the lock.

"Which of my crew told you I was in stasis?"

"Your eldest son," one signed. "The one calling himself Old."

"You have many sons," another signed. "They are very amusing."

One of them spoke. The fifth one, the one they were guarding, and hiding. "They are also terrible liars."

She wasn't like the others. He could look at her without wanting to run away screaming. Yet she was like them in her milky, diamond-scaled skin, and vaguely reptilian features. She had human-seeming hair, pale as starlight, and eyes of amber, vertically slit, like a cat, or like a snake. She pulled her hair back and tucked it behind a human-seeming ear.

"I'm not sure how to take that," Ciarán said. "Are they terrible at lying or did they tell you terrible lies?"

"Both. They are not your sons. They are not even Freemen. And there is no Merchant Leprous in the Registry. All of this I have confirmed."

"Before they locked you in the brig, I presume."

"Locked us in upon the attack. It occurred to the station-master that anyone could wear an earring."

"I've heard of that happening."

"You don't seem concerned."

"I brought you here didn't I?"

"A ship of mercenaries with an expert system bearing your likeness brought us here. I don't know who you are, or even what you are."

"You seem to be getting along fine with Wisp."

"You mean the mong hu? Why wouldn't we? We are the People of the Mong Hu. You do not even wear the spire."

"It's on loan."

She laughed. "On loan to whom?"

"The Huangxu emperor's cousin, I believe."

Her tone suddenly changed. "Danny Swan?"

"His sister. Do you know Ship's Captain Danny Swan?"

"He was here, in another cell. He was taken away during the fighting."

"Hang on," Ciarán said. "I need to call my crew." He unclipped his handheld from the sleeve of the hard suit.

"Amati."

Ciarán felt his face heat. "I don't remember the military slang for 'all clear.'"

"'All clear' works."

"They're not Outsiders. Hess can get back to work. Tell Swan her brother was here and I'm investigating. I could use your help, talking to these people. But you've got to leave the safety on."

"Wilco. If they're not Outsiders, what are they?"

"You won't believe it." He could feel his face flush again as he complied with Amati's radio protocols, and pretended to be a soldier. "Mac Diarmuid out."

"You are indeed a Freeman merchant?"

"Merchant apprentice, acting merchant-in-charge at the moment. Ciarán mac Diarmuid, *Quite Possibly Alien*."

"Aoife nic Cartaí's vessel."

"That's right. Do you know her?"

"We are all of us associate engineers for Bosditch Trading. I am Aspen, and these my daughters, Dee, Ella Emm, and Bea."

"I am Bea," one of them signed.

"You're from Contract system?"

"We are. This is the closest system with a superluminal

node. When we saw the Freeman transponder we hailed it, and Merchant Leprous responded. After we came aboard, they brought us here."

"And then where did they go?"

"They are still here, in hiding. When it is safe we can hail them."

"Do you know someone named Adderly?"

"My sister. She is why we are here. To ask that Aoife nic Cartaí hurry. Adderly is in danger. We need her cargo fastest."

"Um. What cargo is that?"

"The Knight Commander."

Ciarán chuckled. "And why do you need it?"

"Not it. Him," the one called Bea signed. "We are the Legion of Heroes."

"Oh. I need to sit." Ciarán glanced around the brig. "What kind of maniac abandons a space station and takes all the chairs?"

"There are benches in the cells," Aspen said.

37

Trinity System, Freeman Federation

M acer propped his feet up on the seating array opposite and gazed out the liberty boat debarka-tion-lounge viewport. He was tired and amped up at the same time. Both were feelings he didn't like. He would have to work hard to keep his head in the game and his attention centered on the *now*.

Captain Violet, Ruthie, Jimio, and Lizzie Teal were the first to arrive. Macer let his big hullwalkers slap the deck and sat up straighter in his seat. In about thirty seconds he would know whether he'd won or not, know it for real, and then he'd know if he had to do something truly drastic, or if he'd already done enough to move his plan forward. He was going to Contract system one way or another.

Macer fixed his attention on the seating array across from him. If Captain Violet and his crew took a seat there it would tell him everything he needed to know. He didn't want them to sit there. He wanted them to think that he thought that was the natural place for them to sit. That to sit there, across from him, or to not sit there, but beside him, was a choice they were aware they could make, and that they, like he, understood that.

The captain kicked Macer's feet out of the way and swung into the single seat next to Macer, the only seat with a bulkhead behind it and a clear view of the entire debarkation lounge. Jimio slid into the seat on Macer's other side, with Ruthie taking up station between Lizzie Teal and Jimio.

Macer imagined what they would look like, the five of them, viewed from his new favorite toy.

The drone would pan the huge, vacant compartment. In one far corner it would detect five life forms. It would engage its optical sensors and sight five very large and powerful physical specimens packed tightly together in a five-spot seating array. It would analyze this anomaly and determine that these experienced spacers were located in the single most defensible point of the debarkation lounge.

It would zoom in on them, and pan across them, and analyze them as a whole. Their shoulders were touching. They were not talking. Their pulses were elevated. They each scanned the compartment visually, though not in any apparently coordinated way.

It would need to decide. Should it move in closer, examine them individually in order to identify their nature? Or had it perceived enough, and learned enough to draw a conclusion?

Their pulses would begin to settle.

To synchronize.

One of them barked an order.

"Grab some space."

They did so, simply and effectively, without apparent external coordination.

They now occupied the space of ten seats, the length of two seating arrays, an empty seat between each.

Its compact processing core had seen enough.

It knew them now.

Identified.

Ship's crew.

They each had shifted hullward two seats, all but the captain, who had shifted only one. They had space to move, and to act.

Macer fished in his pocket and pulled out a stack of Trinity Station and Merchant Guild identity cards. He handed a pair to the captain and the rest to Jimio. "Take your own and pass the rest down."

"On it, Wrench."

The captain sat staring at the cards in his hand.

"Compliments of the stationmaster." It hadn't taken much work to get them. Macer figured it might make a difference. "Sorry, Jimio. There's a hard character limit in the system."

"These are our true names," Ruthie whispered.

When they'd emigrated from Sampson to Freeman space, the admitting agent had either misheard them or purposely messed with them.

Macer figured they had to be messing, unless Maxim Violent's foreign accent had improved dramatically in the years he'd been in Freeman space. It was hard to get from that to "Ma Violet" by accident.

Likewise the rest of the crew now had station and Merchant Guild ID that matched up with the names they'd been born with, or had chosen for themselves. All except for Jimio, who had legally changed his name from Jimi Oh to 'Jimio! The Girls Love Him So!' before his first pro footie season on Sampson. The station system wouldn't accept that as a name, so Macer had to guess how Jimio would want his corrected name to appear on all contracts and official documents in the Registry.

"You got them to put in the first bang," Jimio said.

"It's a small thing," Macer said. "It wasn't hard."

Ruthie elbowed Jimio. "That's what all the girls say about Jimio!"

"You know that's a lie, but I'll let it slide, Ruth Less."

"This doesn't make us even," Captain Violent said.

Macer glanced at the captain. "We don't need to be even. We *do* need to be playing on the same team."

"Until the game is over."

"Not even that long. While we're on the field, in public."

"It's called a pitch," Jimio! said.

Aoife nic Cartaí and her crew were nearly there. The captain eyed them up and down. "That suits me, Wrench." His gaze switched to Macer. "You did good, Gant."

"We'll see." That was the first time the captain had gotten *his* name right.

"Who talks?"

"The pirate, until the theft is a done deal. The captain and crew just grunt and look angry about it."

"And after that?"

"After that it's showtime. In three. Two. One."

Lift-off. Please.

The captain grinned, started to rise, and then they were all rising, and standing as one, eyeballing the competition.

"Bring it, scum," *Four-Squared*'s pilot growled.

Aoife nic Cartaí and her crew settled into the seats across from them.

Beside nic Cartaí sat an older man, Carlsbad, cargo master and second, with a hardcase sheen and a lot of wear around the edges. Macer had the advantage of knowing all of Aoife's people, having met and worked with them as they tried to get

Golden Parachute back into shape. Carlsbad was recently out of hospital and it showed. He'd spoken to the man and found him exceedingly stiff and formal, like a boys' school headmaster in a recorded drama.

Carlsbad was Voyager by birth. They wore distinctive pendant spires, and being a Voyager meant he was born on the Cordame Reservation, in League space. He didn't know much about Carlsbad yet. If things turned out as planned, he wouldn't need to know more.

Nic Cartaí's navigator was a strange woman called Shawl, out of Unity Station. Contract labor, one and done, with a solid rep. Expensive, easygoing, rumor was she planned to start a family and was shopping for a compatible mate. She took a seat as far away from Carlsbad as was possible and still remain in earshot. She ran her gaze over Macer and moved on. She smiled at Jimio and Jimio smiled back. She switched her attention to Captain Violent and Macer could see the tractor beam behind her eyes begin to tug.

The captain stared blandly back. *Almost.*

This ought to be interesting.

She had tried to pull Macer in for inspection, and he might have let her, but he was a man on a mission. Given that he was the Ellis's active matchmaker, and Commodore Olek his contract, they'd mutually decided he didn't have much family potential. She'd placed her hand on his and told him she didn't see them having much of a future together. Maybe one funeral, but not much more.

He told her she had a spot of soup on her sleeve.

She stared at him. Then she dumped the soup bowl over her forearm and said she liked it that way.

Now, she said, *let's talk about your face.*

She glanced at Macer and caught him studying her.

She flashed him a hand sign, one indicating a theoretical possibility that was never going to happen.

Nic Cartaí's sensors operator was another strange agent called Pepys, also out of Unity, also contract, one and done, also expensive and with a good rep. She was rigged for full immersion, the sensor net silver beneath her pale skin. She claimed she was a heavy-right niner, which sounded like a cult when she'd described it to Macer, but which looked like a genetic mutation, or mod, with four fingers and thumb on her right hand and only three fingers and a thumb on her left.

She was hard to get to know because she only liked to talk about herself. She spoke like she was originally from the League, with a precise inner-planets monotone perfect for a sensors operator on duty, and not so appealing while sharing lunch in the nic Cartaí shipyard canteen. She seemed a nice person, though, and really knew her stuff. And her stuff was really interesting to her.

One day he saw her chatting with Ellen Kirwan, the flower clerk, and he asked her how she knew Ellen. She said didn't know her, but she'd rented a transient bunk in a flat with her for five years, whenever she was on the station. It was a sweet setup, but Ellen like to entertain late, and she had a penchant for engineers, and now Pepys wasn't living there anymore, but paying five times rent for a Guild Hall hot bunk.

She smiled at Macer, with a coldness behind her eyes he recognized as malice the instant she spoke.

When I hit the rack I like to sleep.

Macer stared at her in silence.

Eventually he asked.

How about when you eat?

I like to chew.

Today she wore a white aster flower pinned to her dark-blue utilities. A *boutonniere.*

Macer chuckled, and met Aoife nic Cartaí's cool gaze. "Where's your evil henchmatron?"

"Pilot Konstantine has been recalled to active duty by the League."

Helen Konstantine and Macer had gotten off to a bad start. He'd walked in on her in just his socks, and she'd beaten him senseless with a section of heavy conduit. Several times, he seemed to recall. The beating, not the walking in. He felt pretty sure he could have defended himself better if he'd at least had pockets at the time, and stuff to put in them. As far as humorless, judgmental, middle-aged Erl fitness maniacs went, she was the nicest he'd ever met, but that wasn't saying much. As it looked like he was going to be getting out more, and meeting more people, he was looking forward to revising his opinion of her.

"That's a shame," Macer said. "It's hard to find good help."

"Not that hard." Aoife nic Cartaí's gaze wandered toward the liberty boat debarkation hatch. "One just needs to know where to look."

The hatch cycled and Janie Byrne stepped through, carrying a matte-black bundle in both arms.

Macer nearly groaned out loud, and he would have, if his gaze hadn't been drawn toward the bundle.

It looked heavy.

And it moved.

"Hey, am I early?" Janie said.

"Right on time," Aoife nic Cartaí said.

"Good, because Spooks is getting a little antsy."

She dropped the heavy package to the deck where it landed, not with a thud, but with a blossoming of spidery limbs, a menacing wave of blue-tipped force blades, and a rapid scuttle across the deck, up the bulkhead, and onto the deckhead to dangle over Aoife nic Cartaí. It then settled in and latched to the deckhead above her.

Janie handed Aoife a battered student's handheld. "Here's the other one. It checks out."

To their credit, Macer's crewmates hadn't uttered a sound. They were anxiously staring at the deckhead, but they were professionals, and hardcase footie ballers, and—

"I think I wet myself." Jimio held his thumb and index finger a centimeter a part. "A little."

Macer couldn't tell if he was making a joke or not, and he knew Jimio better than Aoife nic Cartaí did.

"What is that?" Macer had never seen anything like it.

"Until recently, my minder," Aoife nic Cartaí said. "At present, my shield."

"Can I look at it?"

"You appear to be looking at it."

"No, I mean can I inspect it?"

"I'm sure some agreement can be made. Such engineering marvels are very rare, and very precious. The handheld might interest you as well."

"Why is that?"

"Because it contains the stored image of an inactive piloting system. One designed to execute on the device above me. An image that can be safely studied, and possibly even reverse-engineered, to a point."

"Why only to a point?"

"Because the active image and the stored image are both linked extensions of a sentient being's consciousness. A consciousness that is not presently here."

"Where is it?"

"That is the question of the day, and the only question we need answer. Together."

Macer stared at Aoife nic Cartaí.

"We do not need to like one another." She glanced from face to face. "We need only trade, value for value."

She returned her attention to Macer. Her eyes seemed to blaze. "My ship is in danger. My crew. My *family*. Do you really imagine I care who holds title to the jalopy, or who drives?"

"Definitely," Macer said. "I did imagine that. And I do. You could have pushed the yard on *Golden Parachute*'s refit. You could have bought another ship. Your mother is the richest person in Freeman space. Your father runs the Trinity Merchant Bank. You're the princess of all creation, and you've been dragging your feet for weeks. Why the sudden sense of urgency?"

"Don't answer that," Carlsbad said.

"I will answer. We are each treading water in a sea of ignorance, afraid to speak for fear we will be judged, or once the truth is known, abandoned to drown, alone."

"Her ship," Janie said. "*Quite Possibly Alien*. It's more than it seems. It very nearly destroyed all life in Freeman space, and to stop it she had to make a deal with it. It sent along Spooks up there to make sure she lived up to the deal. Now she has, and it's time to go. So show me to the 'on' switch and let's jet."

"And you know this because?" Lizzie Teal said.

Macer glanced at her. Lizzie's birth name according to League records was Lisbet Tasman, born on New Sparta. It was an unusual name, like his own, and he'd only seen the name in writing once before. In his father's business papers.

"Because she told me, not an hour ago. Before she offered me the piloting job."

"She could have been lying," Lizzie said.

"Right," Janie said. "That was her *sales pitch*. Sign with me, ace, and you might end up roasted in the heart of a star, or get erased from existence in a galaxy-scouring neutron blast, or find yourself shredded to atoms in a supernova, and oh, along the way we might make a schilling or two, and meet some nice *boys*. What is wrong with you? Are you an idiot?"

Captain Violent cleared his throat. "This scouring of Freeman space. Would it have reached Sampson?"

"I am unfamiliar with the precise location of Sampson," nic Cartaí said. "The black hole formed in Gallarus was to be the origin point. The mechanics of the star system determines the direction and range of the gamma-ray bursters."

"But it could collapse any star," Violent said. "Even this one. And it's no longer at Gallarus."

"Correct. It is on its way to Contract space, unless it has already arrived."

"You think you can stop it."

"Not once it starts. If I were within Contract space, though, it might choose to do otherwise."

"But we're no safer from it here than we are there."

"Likely less safe."

Captain Violent glanced at Macer. "Well?"

"I'm going there. On other business. But you're the captain."

"And you think I should give her a ride."

"That's between you and her. She's pretty enough, but high maintenance. If it's more than once, I expect there would be tears. Yours, not hers."

"He means give her a *lift*," Janie said.

"Oh. That's different. Definitely you should do that."

Their gazes met. "Ruthie?"

"I'll drive."

Macer glanced from face to face. He wasn't sure which idea was the most shocking to his shipmates. The idea that Aoife nic Cartaí had unearthed a monster that could destroy the world or that a Sampson crew would find themselves working side by side with a nic Cartaí.

Macer figured it was probably the second idea. People tended to care more about problems they could see and touch.

He leaned back in his seat and studied the spidery device on the deckhead. Eventually the rest of the crew found something more interesting or important to do, all but Janie, who hung back and swung into the seat next to him.

"You angry at me?"

"Why would I be."

"For taking a nic Cartaí contract. For not telling you."

"You signed today."

"Right before I walked out with Spooks. I finally got ahold of my folks, calling from the runabout, while you were refueling. They're banged up but fine. Mamma told me nic Cartaí had called, and was desperate for a pilot. I could name my own price. And then *she* called, and told me all that, and I said I'd think about it."

"Liar."

"All right, I said I would do it." She elbowed his sleeve. "She didn't have to go on and tell me all that extra gab. She had me at 'roasting in the fiery heart of a star.'"

"I thought *I* was good at my job."

"Tell me about it. When she handed me Spooks and told me what it was, I knew right away."

"It's the cheese."

"And Macer Gant's the mouse."

"Looks like it."

"I'll be bunking with the nic Cartaí crew."

"You know where I'll be."

"You can't wrench day and night. You'll have to sleep some time."

"Sure I will, and thank you for the offer."

"Anytime."

"Have you told your folks?"

"I will, soon as I work out what to tell them."

"You have no idea what the job pays."

"How could I know? I haven't seen a pay stub yet, have I?"

38

Trinity System, Freeman Federation

Seamus stared at the man in the mirror. He was dressed in a League business suit, one so blue it almost seemed black, an iridescent sheen to the fabric making it shimmer like oil. It wasn't an attractive look, more sinister than serious. The implied threat was there, on the surface, as if he dressed for an audience with easily frightened children.

His hair was either unfashionably short for a stationer or long for a spacer, unruly tufts jutting out from a scalp that looked to have been shaved like a convict's not long ago. A jagged scar sliced across his skin, like a parting of his hair, not an ancient scar, but one earned in the past year.

A pendant spire dangled from his right earlobe, a dead man's spire. He shot his cuffs and winced as a mechanical hand caught on the garment's sleeve. Another memento of a dead man, or two, as the hand gleamed a dull gold plate, over rhodium plate, the lesser metal laid over the greater so that the hand might be worn in public, the crime it represented hidden, like him, beneath a thin skin of lies.

The woman behind him placed a gloved palm upon his shoulder and checked her teeth in the mirror. To his naked eye they were perfectly ordered and gleaming, gene-modded to sparkle when she smiled. To his inner eye they were already sunk into him, like her talons, as she spun him about, and considered him carefully, one hand on the curve of her hip, the other tapping her broadcast-quality teeth. She dressed in an outfit that didn't match his own, or compete with it, but complemented it, a supernova that didn't blot out the black hole beside it, but revealed it in its penumbra. He glanced at her slender waist.

"You're not wearing your armor."

"That's what you think." She glanced at the book on his nightstand. An actual paper book, one of a dozen he'd found on board the vessel. "Have you been reading father's poetic nonsense?"

"I wouldn't call it nonsense," Seamus said. Nor would he call the poems her father's. Lord Aster hadn't written them, but rather gathered them, and compiled them, poems from the ancient past and modern poems, from all the races of men, and from the stations they built, and from the planets they shaped to suit them, and from the stars they walked amongst.

She reached out, and cupped his pendant spire, and let her fingers slide along it. "Those poems are messing with your brain."

They're not the only things messing.

"You do know that's a cultural gesture," he said. "One offering or acknowledging intimacy."

"How does one tell offer from acknowledgment?"

"If it's an offer, you'll know."

"And if it's an acknowledgment?"

"Everyone will know. We live on family ships and stations tighter than most League extraction platforms. Don't do that in public unless you want people to think you're sleeping with someone."

"I see."

"You might think you do, but you don't."

"Then why don't you educate me, *James*."

"I will, and don't call me that."

"It's your name."

"It's an Erl name." *And a dead man's.* James and Seamus were claimed to be synonyms. The League tended to switch Seamus to James on paperwork just to mess with Freemen. It made doing research harder than it need be.

"Fine. What is it I don't know?"

"That gesture went out of fashion two score years ago. Nowadays the only people you see doing that are grannies and grandads, or grannies and their boy toys. *Caressing the spire*, it's called if it's an old lady and her plaything. *Waking the almost dead*, if it's a pair of ould wans together."

"And what do young people do instead?"

"We're polluted by the League nowadays, mostly."

"How about a shag."

"Fancy a shag. Or fancy a ride. We can't touch a thing without making it our own."

"Is that what you do? Take the direct approach?"

"I don't. You've seen me in action, so I don't have to tell you. The direct appeal is a nonstarter. I'm more an acquired taste."

"So?"

"So I just hang around, and say something witty now and then, and eventually she breaks down and says, 'Kiss me, you fool'."

"And that works for you."

"It worked for Old Seamus. He pulled like a magnet."

"Because of his modesty."

"You asked. Would you rather I lied to you?"

"What about New Seamus?"

The same, he supposed, though with a lot less flux. "I'm still getting used to the idea that New Seamus could be more than a temporary state between Old Seamus and Dead Seamus." His gaze met hers. "Why are you asking?"

"I don't want to embarrass myself."

"In public."

"Anywhere."

Manicured fingernails clacked against the compartment hatch coaming. "Found you," the Leagueman said. He wore the gray uniform of a Home Guard major. His name was Hector Poole and he was an enigma. Seamus wasn't sure what all else he was, but he was more than a major in the Queen's army. Maybe today he'd find out. "Sarah. James. It's time. Let's go."

He glanced at her on the way out the hatch. "Will you tell him to stop calling me that?" He paused to let her pass. They'd been camped out on the compact League courier vessel *Springbok* since the blowout on the ring. The passageways were tight, the hatches tighter.

"You tell him."

He watched her prepare to step through the hatch. The coaming was tall and League formal attire constricting.

"I can't *tell* him anything. I'm not Lady Aster or her daughter. All I can do is ask, and when I do he says, 'Certainly, James,' and laughs."

He admired her agility.

"Are you done ogling me?"

"I was done with that days ago." He followed her through the hatch.

"Then what were you doing back there?"

"Thinking of something witty to say."

She turned and glanced at him, and when their gazes met, he could swear there was something like panic in her eye.

"You asked. Would you rather I lied to you?"
"I'd rather you go first up the companionway."
"Then I'll need to squeeze past."
"Never mind."
"Suit yourself."

39

The station remained a shambles, the stationmaster and his work crews franticly wrenching on the Freeman Sector of the ring just to keep the damage from spreading. The fear that the station might fall was over, but four percent of the ring was blown out and another sixteen percent closed for inspection or repairs.

The spindle had been closed to docking, which made sense, but there'd been fights and general mayhem shoving the scruffier class of merchant onto their ships and away from the station. It wasn't like cutting utilities alone would have sent them packing, and shutting down the atmosphere was deemed too barbaric, so the stationmaster settled for upping the artificial gravity, which had the dual effect of making people uncomfortable and making skid work and other such heavy lifting heavier to the point of, not impossibility, but unprofitability.

The League and Ojin Sectors had cleared out of ships and a new batch had only recently arrived, not merchant vessels, but warships. The station remained neutral. No fighting was the rule, and if both sides of an external conflict wanted to dock at Trinity Station they could, so long as they behaved themselves.

The Ojin docks were awash in fast couriers similar to the *Springbok*, only slower, and not unarmed and unarmored, like *Springbok*, but lightly so by military standards. An exchange of broadsides on the Ojin Sector of the ring would be irritating at best, and short lived.

There were two massive League heavy cruisers lashed to the League Sector of the ring, the sort of vessels that never went anywhere without a full battle group, and their escorts were out there, beyond the tripwire, some unknown number of cruisers, light cruisers, destroyers, and who knows what else. Seamus had never been in the military, or very interested in it at that, which wasn't odd for a Freeman of his age. There were people who specialized in keeping tabs on that sort of stuff, but he wasn't one of them, being more adept at analyzing a quartermaster's books than the yield and half-life of the ordinance being thrown around a dozen pay grades up the ladder.

Ladies Tabatha and Sarah Aster rated an armed detail and had brought their own. They'd arrived on *Springbok* hoping to find someone named Charles Newton on the station, and not finding him, took up residence on the ring, hoping to wait around until their superman returned. The way Sarah Aster talked about Charles Newton made Seamus's skin crawl. Lady Tabatha reminded Seamus that Sarah had been a young and impressionable girl when she'd laid eyes on Mr. Newton, and most of what she said was wishful thinking alone.

Seamus spent a great deal of time with Lady Tabatha because it turned out she was friends with the embassy doctor Margaret Breen had mentioned, and Breen had met Lady Tabatha when last the Asters were on the station, during the short war some years back. Lady Tabatha was a doctor, and apparently an excellent one, because she was one of the three hundred doctors that attended Queen Charlotte herself. "Specialists," Lady Tabatha had said when Seamus had wondered aloud why so many.

Lord Aster was "elsewhere" according to both Ladies Aster, which didn't seem to concern either one of them; Lady Sarah because she said her father could take care of himself, Lady Tabatha because she was shagging Hector Poole.

Seamus hadn't mentioned this to anyone but apparently his face had, because Lady Tabatha had taken Seamus aside, and handed him one of her husband's poetry anthologies, and told him that Lionel, Lord Aster was the Queen's Merlin. But he was Lady Tabatha's Arthur. Seamus had assumed Merlin was Lord Aster's given name, but it seemed he'd been mistaken.

He supposed that made Hector Poole her Lancelot, but he couldn't see it. The pair had thought the foppish Leagueman dead. That was why they'd been looking for the amazing Charles Newton. As a poor man's substitute for the truly irreplaceable Hector Poole. Seamus hadn't been present for the joyous reunion between Lady Tabatha and her knight errant. But he *had* been there when Sarah Aster spied a man, and realized the man was Hector Poole, and realized the man was alive.

Seamus was only after murdering the Ixatl-Nine-Go in Ares Adonis a half dozen times, and up until a minute earlier had thought he himself a dead man, so he was a little distracted, but he had a good memory, and it was odd to watch, so it stuck with him.

Oh it's you.

Hello, Sarah.

Mother will be glad to see you.

And I her.

We have a problem and need your help.

Certainly. Just a moment while I dispose of this...

"Soul-destroying mind parasite," Seamus had said.

And then they had both looked at him, and realized he was listening, and Hector Poole spoke.

Quite.

And that was it. The resurrection of Hector Poole as experienced by Lady Sarah Aster. Dialogue. From across a room. Not even a blink from either of them. Not a step away, or toward.

Maybe now he'd get some answers. The security detail held the door of the League Embassy on Trinity Station for them. They rode a lift up in silence, to what appeared to be a concert hall with tiered seating but which was presently configured as a courtroom, or a classroom, one set up for panel discussions by opposing teams of experts.

They were led to seats in the first row of spectators, all but Hector Poole, who excused himself and hopped up onto the low stage. He began to chat with one batch of opposing experts, and then, a while later, with the second batch.

Seamus glanced along the row and was surprised to see a mix of Ojin, League, and Freeman faces, including some people he'd been trying to avoid, Thomas Truxton and his match-maker Gilpatrick Moore second and first amongst them.

He glanced behind and up, and the rising tiers of seats were packed. To his surprise he spied Seán mac Diarmuid and Lorelei Ellis. He waved. Lorelei waved back.

"She's pretty," Sarah Aster said.

"She is," Seamus said. "Pretty *awesome*." He waved again before turning around at the sound of amplified coughing.

"How do you know her?"

"I lived with her for a while."

"And yet you parted amicably."

"She stuffed me in a body bag and dumped me on the spindle."

"What it something you said?"

"We didn't do much talking. It wasn't that kind of rela-tionship."

"Really? What kind was it?"

"In retrospect? Pretty one-sided. Basically I just laid there and she did all the work."

Someone shouted. "Thank you!"

They adjusted the public-address system from shout to slightly too quiet to hear and then to the proper level, at least from where he was seated.

There were fixed installation sensors all over the room and some surveillance drones hovering. None of the drones had news-service logos on them. He listened, a little at first, when they introduced the panels, all scientists, none of whom he'd ever heard of, all with long lists of credentials. He didn't have to listen closely because it was being recorded, and with so many Freemen in the room, a copy would end up somewhere accessible. He still wasn't sure why all of these people had been gathered in one place. It was too big a crowd to keep secrets, but there was no news presence, which implied it wasn't public.

It got interesting when Hector Poole climbed on stage. He didn't introduce himself. He looked like he didn't want to be there, with the spotlight on him. He said, "I'm sorry that we've asked many of you here under false pretenses. We're tracking a contagion and some of you may have been exposed."

And like an idiot, he paused.

The crush for the exits began instantly. Before a single hand had touched the panic bar, League troopers in exoskeletal armor shoved inside. They held plasma rifles, not crowd-control wands, and Truxton, in particular, looked ready to go ballistic. Gilpatrick Moore swept a predator's gaze about the room. His attention washed across Seamus and passed on, then came back, and he nodded to himself, and went back to his threat assessment scan.

The plasma rifle isn't a stealth weapon. It has a distinctive reek, and a distinctive sound. A dozen of them firing up in a room isn't something he'd ever wanted to experience.

A mong hu appearing and disappearing into the shadows just amped up the tension. He spotted a second mong hu. Two mong hus in the same room wasn't something he'd even *heard* of. He scanned the front row, and then he saw her, Nuala nic

Cartaí. She'd brought Fist, the ship's cat from the *Invisible Hand* and Truxton had brought Thorn from the *Rose*.

It was going to be a slaughterhouse if someone didn't do something.

Seamus hopped onto the stage.

He elbowed Hector Poole aside.

He shouted, "It's not contagious! You can't get it or spread it!" Shouted in Freeman, in Ojin, in the pigeon Huangxu of the spindle. He imagined the Erl already knew, but he shouted in League standard as well. "Sit down, sit down, I had it and now I don't, you can't catch it, you can't spread it, not in here, just sit down, sit down and be calm."

There were all staring at him, even the mong hu. And then they took their seats. Not without some elbowing and cursing, but they did it.

Someone shouted, "What are all the guns for, then?"

"I don't know," Seamus said. "Let's ask him. What are all the guns for?"

Seamus hopped off the stage, but not before someone shouted, "Slaver!"

He took his seat. It felt like every eyeball in the room latched onto him, and every pair of lips muttered *slaver* under their breath.

"He's right," Poole said. "It's not contagious. You can't spread it. It can't be spread to you, not in this room, and your families outside are safe. If you have it we can cure it, right now, today."

"They've rounded up everyone who's been in contact with Ares Adonis," Sarah Aster said.

"Any that they know of," Seamus said. "And any who've been in contact with others of the Consortium, or the Cooperative of Loyal Citizens."

"Who are they?"

"Other potential carriers."

"All you need to do," Poole said, "is exit in single file, beginning with you, there." He pointed. "Just walk through the scanning device as you exit the auditorium."

No one moved.

"What a cock up," Seamus said. "All he's doing is ratcheting up the panic in the room."

"Maybe that's his plan," Sarah said.

"No Freeman is walking through some Erl disease scanner. Not without taking it apart first and seeing what it does."

Seamus stood up again, and walked along the front row. Either nic Cartaí or Truxton would do; he'd prefer nic Cartaí, but only because he didn't want to have to face Truxton, not after what he'd done aboard *Golden Parachute*. But he didn't know Fist, and he'd met Thorn, all new Truxton hands did, at least once.

Seamus crouched down in front of Truxton so the big man didn't have to stand. "Mr. Truxton."

"What do you want?"

"I want these people to go home safe, and I want you to help me."

"What's in it for me?"

"Nothing. I'll go ask nic Cartaí. Thanks for your time."

"Wait. What's it cost?"

"Nothing."

"Okay. I'm in."

Seamus hopped onto the stage and elbowed Hector Poole aside. "Change of plans. If you don't want to go through the scanner, just pay your respects to the mong hu on the way out."

"They have to go through the scanner," Poole said.

"No Freeman's going to do that. So take their names down and... Whatever."

"They have to go through the scanner."

"They're not going to."

"Why not?"

"Because they're not sheep. And because you don't own them."

Hector Poole stared at him.

"Come up with a better plan. Because this one's dead on arrival."

Poole waved Seamus away from the microphone. "You can go. Just... leave your name on the way out, and..." He glanced at Seamus.

"Pay your respects to the mong hu as you pass."

"Do that. And don't leave the station. We'll be in touch."

"Thanks," Seamus said.

"You too," Poole said. "Get out of here."

Someone shouted, "He stays."

"Mr. Truxton says you stay." Poole pointed. "So go sit down."

"It's Merchant Captain Truxton." Seamus hopped off the stage. "And I will sit down. When I feel like it."

SEAMUS TOOK his seat and watched the people file out. He'd like to talk to Lorelei and Seán, and to Sun Kang and his family from the spindle. He'd spotted them in the crowd too, earlier, from the stage. The bulk of the crowd were Clear Island folk from the planet, more than seventy percent of them, and once he realized that, he guessed what was going on. And he confirmed that, once he jumped up on stage and saw what the audience looked like from there.

He didn't like Hector Poole, maybe it was personal, maybe it was that he didn't like a certain sort of Erl, and Poole played the part to perfection. Like him or not, Hector Poole was no bumbling idiot, and the man on that stage had done everything wrong. If there was such a thing as a fear-o-meter it would have been pegged on eleven in that room, and Poole had stoked the fear. On purpose.

When the crowd had finally filtered out Poole walked over, hands in his pockets. "You knew."

"That the scanner was just a prop, and the real sensors in the deckhead?"

Poole shrugged.

"What's the resolution?"

"Down to the seat after one hundred and twenty samples. So, two to ten minutes of above-normal stress."

"The scanner must be large, or ungainly."

"Or need a massive power supply," Poole said.

"Unlikely. There are large power supplies on the planet."

"You could tell how many of the test subjects were from the planet?"

"From Clear Island. They have a look. If all you had to do was walk through that scanner you could take it to the planet. You wouldn't have to bring them all up here."

"Do you believe any of the subjects realized that?"

"Seán mac Diarmuid would have known the instant he saw the scanner. And Lorelei Ellis would have figured it out, if she cared enough to think about it. But neither of them is the type to get frightened in the first place.

"The spindle folks I know? They were off the scale, and they're not going to think about it. They live in such a perpetual fear state that they'll move on and not look back."

"Interesting. But it's not the fear of the mount we're measuring. It's the fear of the *rider*."

"Is that what they're calling Ixatl-Nine-Go now?"

"Apparently it's what they call it in the lab where it's made."

"Where's that?"

"We're going to talk about that next, once the room's reset."

"Did they find any riders in the crowd?"

"A few."

"Did you search them for reprogrammers?"

"What's a reprogrammer?"

"It's a handheld device that reprograms standard League implants. Your people probably have a technical name for it I don't know. Merchant Roche called them reprogrammers."

"What, specifically, does it do?"

"It makes prisoners with implants easier to handle."

"When I spot a boffin I'll ask. What does this device look like?"

"Like a silver box with a single button on it. If they find one, tell them not to push the button."

"Because pushing the button will?"

"Incapacitate anyone with an implant nearby. Including whoever pushed the button. If I had a reprogrammer right now? I could murder every Leagueman in the room with a penknife."

"Indeed. How does one disable a reprogrammer?"

"You'd need someone without an implant to turn it off. Or someone with a rider."

"Are there no countermeasures?"

"You could rip the implants out of every man, woman, and child in the League."

"I see. I'll go find an engineer right now."

40

R esetting the room consisted of turning it from a presentation amphitheater into a large conference room. Gone were the ranks of stadium seats and stage. In their place stood a long oval table with seating for a score. Additional seating for three score more were arranged along the bulkheads. The table was large enough that local amplification seemed necessary for those seated at it. Seamus wondered how difficult it would be to hack that system, purely as an intellectual exercise. There were sensors again studding the deckhead, though they appeared to have been redeployed in a constellation above the table and around the periphery of the room. They were letting people into the compartment in groups. Seamus recognized the major players; Truxton and Fionnuala nic Cartaí, Ruairi Kavanagh, presumably because Mikeal Kavanagh the elder was off the station. Each arrived trailing a shower of support personnel.

The chieftains took a seat at the table and their tribes on the distant seats behind them. The same proved true for the Ojin Eng, and the League, faces he recognized from the station feeds without recalling names exiled to the periphery, their place at the adult table taken by seniors shipped in for the occasion. Lady Tabatha Aster had a place at the table while her daughter and Hector Poole were sent to the cheap seats.

Seamus wondered when someone in charge would recognize that he was still there and usher him from the compartment. He'd like to stay, to see what was said in real time, but if anything remotely worth knowing transpired it would be recorded. Once recorded, he really didn't need to watch the nooses being knotted and tested. He could start with the hanging and work his way backward toward the crime, like he always had when on the job, unspooling the story back to front, not from the perspective of the audience, but from that of the authors themselves. Whatever decisions trotted out here today were made already, in private. That was the way of the world. This was the reveal, had to be. People like him watched the play. They weren't permitted on the stage because they didn't know how to act. They might forget their lines in the glare of the lights, or speak their minds without prompting, and so shatter the illusion.

A junior League officer approached him. He carried a hand-held and glanced at it as he spoke. "Name?"

"Seamus."

"Your full name, with place of residence."

"Seamus. No fixed address."

"Effing Freemen," the Erl muttered. He held out his free hand, palm up, and looked Seamus in the eye. "Merchant license."

"I don't have one."

"They wouldn't have let you in without identification."

"Well I'm in," Seamus said. "So why don't you go ask *them* who I'm supposed to be. I already told you all I know. Seamus. Freeman. No fixed address. No family name. Not a merchant. There can't be two of us in all the universe sharing those particulars. How much more identification does a man need?"

"In this case, he needs a government-issued identification card with identifying image and/or biometric data."

"Why didn't you say?" Seamus flicked the red League nonresident alien card at him, which the Leagueman plucked from the air like he'd done it before. "For the record, that's not me. He's long dead. I'm a different man entirely."

The League officer spoke toward the handheld. "Reynard, James, Unity Station, Freeman Federation."

"It's Seamus. James is a—"

The handheld chimed.

"Follow me, *James*," the League officer drawled. "I have a nice seat for you. One by the hatch."

"So I can beat the rush on exit," Seamus said.

"So I won't have to kick you far when I kick you out." He pointed. "Sit. Wait. I'll be back."

Old Seamus tugged an invisible forelock and started to say something regrettable.

New Seamus slapped them both into the seat. "Thanks," he said. "Can I have that card back?"

HE WAS SEATED about as far from the goings-on as one could be and still remain in the compartment. There were a couple of empty chairs on either side of him, by the hatch, but other than those, every seat in the compartment had an ass in it. He sat positioned end-on to the long table, and while he couldn't see the face of the person seated at the end nearest him, he could see everyone else's. They'd set up a holo tank in the center of the table and configured it to less than thirty percent opacity, so even when they flicked it on and off to test the configuration, he could see through it to the people behind. One long wall display was set up and tested. He didn't think they'd actively use that, since nearly a third of those at the table would need to swivel in their seats to view it. At the moment the display was set to Trinity Station's default, a tagged two-dimensional projection of station traffic alternating with the Registry entries for recent and expected arrivals and departures.

The meeting started before the League military officer returned to kick him out. The hatch opened and closed and someone slid into the seat next to him, a Freeman woman in stationer's utilities, a decade older than Seamus in apparent age, dark haired, smooth skinned.

Seamus glanced at her face. Blue eyed, like a Clear Islander, but a more saturated blue.

She winked and pulled a handheld from her pocket and aimed the display at him. She scooted her chair closer so that they could share. The display showed a schematic of the room with names tagged to each of those present. His seat showed as James Reynard, Freeman. Hers showed as empty.

"My name's not James," he whispered. "It's—"

She placed a finger over her lips and shushed him. Her hands looked fresh scrubbed, and she had that just out of the refresher smell he liked. He leaned in close to study the screen and they bumped heads. She didn't pull away, but bumped heads with him again, and together they studied the screens and the faces. *Like coconspirators*—or so Seamus imagined it might look like from a distance.

He breathed in her scent and felt his pulse quicken. He'd conspired with worse. She had enough hours under her keel that he might just learn something new. When she glanced up to find him studying her she held his gaze and smiled. For an instant it felt like they'd met before. That couldn't be, though. Her, he'd remember.

One of the League potentates spoke, a man seated to the right of Lady Tabatha Aster and labeled as *Lord Clarence, Jordan, Mills, League*, which was somewhat confusing. The woman seated next to Seamus touched the handheld's display and the names changed to job titles: *Assistant Deputy Minister, League External Affairs.* So a junior subpotentate, which made sense during a civil war, on a foreign station. High enough in the government to speak authoritatively, low enough to be considered expendable.

"We are assembled here to make sense of this Ixatl-Nine-Go business. That, and to come to some conclusion as to what to do about it. I intend, firstly, to bring everyone up to speed on what we do know. Secondly, I hope those of you with additional knowledge will step forward and share it. And thirdly, and one hopes, finally, I will propose a course of action moving forward and ask for your agreement." He gazed along the table.

"Let's hear the proposal first," Merchant Captain Thomas Truxton said.

"In good time," External Affairs said.

"If it's something we can't agree with, best to know it now," a woman labeled *Admiral, Ojin Home Fleet* said.

"Speak, Jordy," Lady Tabatha said.

"Fine. I propose we dissolve the governments of New Sparta and Sampson and declare martial law in those systems. Further, I propose we revoke the commercial charter of an organization known as the Consortium."

"Those sound like matters for League Internal Affairs," League Internal Affairs said.

"They are. If you'll kindly allow me to finish."

"Spit it out, then, man," Internal Affairs said. "And stick to your own patch."

"Next," External Affairs said, glaring at Internal Affairs, "I propose we hunt down all officers and agents of the Consortium. We hunt them down and find them wherever they may be, anywhere in the wider world, and we bring them to trial."

"Is that all?" Internal Affairs said.

"It is not," External Affairs said. "I then propose we hang

them by the necks until dead." He ran his gaze around the room. "That is all."

Someone spoke. The man with his back to Seamus, labeled on the handheld as Nevin Green, which seemed more like a name than a title. No affiliation listed. "Why were experts assembled for a discussion, and then dismissed without a word spoken?"

"A more pressing need preempted the presentation."

"What more pressing need? And what of the larger matter?"

"We've decided to address this problem one step at a time," External Affairs said.

"What larger matter?" Ojin Home Fleet said.

"The matter of the emperors," Nevin Green said.

"The Eight Banners Empire is an Ojin internal affair," Ojin Home Fleet said.

"That's not what he's concerned about," Internal Affairs said. "It's the news about the Huangxu and Alexandrian emperors that has our friend bent out of shape. And I can't say I blame them."

"What news?" Truxton said.

"I'd like to hear that news as well," Ruairi Kavanagh said.

"And I," Fionnuala nic Cartaí said.

"Now is not the appropriate time," External Affairs said.

"We were promised that this issue would be addressed," Nevin Green said. "It was a precondition of our attendance."

"He needed a fast ship, in a hurry," Internal Affairs said. "He told you what you needed to hear."

"Is this true?" Nevin Green said.

"I told you what we believed to be true at the time," External Affairs said. "The situation has since evolved."

"In what way has it evolved?" Nevin Green said. "Our relationship has been strained for some time. This is understood at the highest levels. We are tired of excuses."

"It's changed because he's gotten what he wanted from

you," Internal Affairs said. "He's not going to keep his word because he doesn't need you anymore. It's SOP for the Outies, in case you haven't noticed."

"We don't have infinite resources," External Affairs said. "We need to stay focused on the real problem."

"The *real* problem?" Nevin Green said.

"The urgent problem, I mean to say. Once that's addressed—"

"There will be a new excuse," Nevin Green said. "A new reason to ignore the agreement between us."

External Affairs shrugged. "I don't set policy."

"I would hear this news," Ojin Home Fleet said. "About the emperors."

"Then I suggest you ask your own people," External Affairs said. "Or message your Eight Banners rebels. They're the source of these outrageous claims."

Ruairi Kavanagh nearly shouted. "*What* claims?"

"That the emperors of the Huangxu and Alexandrian Eng are no longer human," Internal Affairs said. "That they are hunting synthetic intelligences with the intent to enslave them."

"That's not your patch," External Affairs said. "Computer, strike that from the record. This discussion ends. Now."

"Is this true?" Ojin Home Fleet said. "Why would one wish to suppress such claims? To protect the reputations of one's enemies?"

Truxton laughed. "Unbelievable."

"How could you imagine keeping something like this secret?" Fionnuala nic Cartaí said.

"We don't know if it's true or not," External Affairs said. "What we *do* know is that this Ixatl-Nine-Go is real and an existential threat. It must be stopped. Now."

"Because the contagion is spreading," Truxton said. "And you don't want it on Columbia Station."

"Not simply because of that," Lady Tabatha Aster said. "Because the Consortium attacked us."

"Directly attacked you?" Truxton said.

"Or indirectly," Lady Tabatha said, "Depending upon one's perspective. Sunbury Park was leveled using a weapon we've never seen before."

"Huh," Truxton said.

"Mother of God," Ruairi Kavanagh said.

Fionnuala nic Cartaí stared at the table. It didn't take a mind reader to detect the rapid calculations and recalculations going on inside her head. This was all news to her.

Ojin Home Fleet stood. "Excuse us." The entire Ojin delegation stood.

"Sit down," External Affairs said. "No one leaves this compartment without my permission."

"No one?" Nevin Green said.

External Affairs shrugged. "It's important this information remain contained for the moment."

"How important?" Nevin Green said.

"Paramount."

"I see," Nevin Green said. "You continue to disappoint us."

External Affairs stared at the man. "I'm sorry you feel that way."

"We have no choice but to acquiesce," Nevin Green said. "That is what you are telling us.

"One problem at a time," External Affairs said. "That's all I ask."

"That is all that you *order*," Nevin Green said. "And there's nothing we can do about it."

"You could take the oath," Seamus muttered. "And *then* let him try and make you."

There were all twisting in their seats, and looking in his direction. He glanced at the woman next to him. She grinned ear to ear.

"Did I say that out loud?"

"Loud enough to be broadcast by the Erl listening machines."

When her gaze met his she reached up, cupped his pendant spire in her palm, and studied it, intently, as it slipped through her outstretched fingers. "They don't make men like they used to," she said. "Except sometimes, when they do."

"I know you," he said.

'A beetle recognizes another beetle."

"No, not like that. I recognize your voice. From the archives."

"And I recognize your earring. From my nightstand. Does that mean we know one another?"

"It doesn't."

"I'm not so sure. Let's see."

Fionnuala nic Cartaí shoved out of her seat and headed their way. "Mother?"

"Now, speak quick," Saoirse nic Cartaí whispered. "While we're yet man and woman, and not whatever they're all staring at, and are wanting us to be. I'm in need of a man. Are you willing to be that man?"

"I might be. What's the job pay?"

"The usual. Nothing you don't deserve."

"Then I'm in."

"And nothing you do."

"Oh."

"Oh indeed."

"Well. A deal's a deal, I guess."

"It is that, and a good deal more. Now follow my lead, and try not to trip on your tongue."

41

"Daughter," Saoirse nic Cartaí said, "go sit down. I woke up early, is all." She tapped on her handheld. "I expect you all can hear me, so I'm not going to make a big production out of taking my place in the pecking order you've arranged here."

"Who are you?" External Affairs said.

"I'm the woman whose deck you're walking on. And I say anyone who wants to get up and leave can do so right now, and safe passage to your vessel and Godspeed to you. But before you go—and Mr. Glasnevin, or whatever it is you're calling yourself now, I'm talking to you—I want you to note that's twice now you've heard the same advice from the Reynard, and them two different men's voices speaking, and separated by the span of two men's lives. You might consider what that means, before you dismiss the argument this time.

"I'm locking the hatches in thirty seconds, so if you want to go you need to scoot. If you want to stay you're welcome, but I'm also shutting down the environmentals in thirty. The stationmaster says the compartment's good for an hour of jawing, and then you'd best have a rebreather if you'd like to stay and chat longer."

External Affairs shouted. "Guards!"

"All right. That's done." Saoirse clapped her hands together. "Now where are my pretty boys?"

A pair of mong hu appeared from the shadows. They stalked across the compartment to greet her. One of them brushed past Seamus to reach her. It purred as she scratched its ear.

It was close enough to touch.

"Go ahead," she whispered. "You won't regret it."

Seamus stroked its fur.

It glanced at him and blinked.

"Off with you now," Saoirse said, loud enough for the listening devices to pick her voice up and broadcast it. "If you spot anyone with weapons lurking, you have my permission to eat them."

"This is outrageous," External Affairs said. "I demand—"

"Mr. Butler, is it?" Saoirse said.

"That's right," Internal Affairs said.

"What is this circus all about?"

"Rumor is that the prime minister ordered the attack on Sunbury Park. This is an attempt to squelch that rumor, as well as the unstated assumption behind it."

"That Prime Minister Samantha Bray is a thrall of Ixatl-Nine-Go."

"Of this Consortium entity, through the agency of the Ixatl-Nine-Go device."

"The Consortium is a straw man?"

"It's a closely held limited company and shady by nature. A shadow government behind the governments of Sampson and New Sparta. Inconsequential worlds, in an inconsequential area of space. Utterly disposable and entirely suitable as a scapegoat. A little too on the nose, if you take my meaning. The appearance of doing something while doing nothing."

"And entirely an internal League decision, if something were to be done."

"Unless the dog and pony were the something being done."

"Translation," Ojin Home Fleet said.

"The purpose of this meeting is the meeting," Truxton said. "And the press releases about the meeting."

"The Outies are all Bray's lot," Butler said.

"Butler believes the prime minister is a thrall of Ixatl-Nine-Go," Truxton said.

"That's treason," External Affairs said.

"Hardly. It might be sedition if I'd said it," Butler said. "But note that *I* haven't."

"That could explain the League civil war," Ruairi Kavanagh said.

"It could," Butler said, "Though I don't believe it does. If such a rumor were true, however, it might intensify the conflict, if one side were to consider the other side—"

"Somewhat less than human," Nevin Green said. "Or somewhat more."

"Quite so," Butler said.

"We have experience with New Sparta," Fionnuala nic Cartaí said.

"Likely a consideration," Butler said. "Easier to convince you lot to go along with the charade."

Saoirse glanced at Seamus. "Well?"

"Well what?"

"Does all that seem plausible to you?"

"It does."

"But..."

"This Eight Banners Empire," Seamus said. "What do the banners stand for?"

"Us," Ojin Home Fleet said.

"The Ojin?"

"All of us. Eng, not Eng, Ojin, Huangxu, Alexandrian, League, both human and synthetic intelligences. Eight banners, united."

"And what of the Freeman Federation?" Fionnuala nic Cartaí said.

"No idea," Ojin Home Fleet said. "I'm repeating what I've been told."

"Anyone?" Saoirse said.

The room seemed deadly silent without the air handlers running.

"Unknown at first," Hector Poole said. "Considered ephemeral later. Once it was determined you might make a go of it? Too late to change the brochures, I'm afraid. By then the die had been cast."

"You're an agent of the Eight Banners Empire?" Saoirse said.

"I'm an educated man. One whose business it is to know esoteric facts."

"One whose knowing things got my son killed," Fionnuala nic Cartaí said.

"The only one who got Aidan nic Cartaí killed was Aidan nic Cartaí."

"Leave off, you two," Saoirse said. "Argue later. Now's the time for answers."

"The admiral is right," Poole said. "Those are the eight banners."

"Thanks," Seamus said. "That clears up a lot. Since you're educated about these banners, would you know anything about these rumors that are reportedly being spread?"

"I do, in fact, know a little."

"Would you be able to relate what you know as a *seanscéal*, so that none of those present would be inclined to file intent based on the content of these rumors?"

"No, I could not."

"Could you cast the story so that no one in the room ended up on the bad side of a matchmaker?"

"No, I could not."

"I see. Well, then, did you find one of those devices we were speaking about earlier?"

"The implant reprogrammer? Yes, I did."

"Could you turn it on now?"

"Sorry, no, I can't."

"Oh."

"I could, however, ask Mr. Singh to turn it on. Or you could. He's the man behind me, raising his hand and waving now."

42

S eamus ignored the screaming and scanned the compartment for the unaffected. He was somewhat surprised that of the Freemen present, only Ruairi Kavanagh was down and suffering. None of the Ojin were, which was to be expected. That left the Leaguemen, which should have approached nearly one hundred percent and didn't. Besides Singh and a couple of technicians either side of him, neither of the Asters were down on the deck and scream-ing, nor was Hector Poole. Or Butler, Mr. Internal Affairs.

Nevin Green turned to glance at Seamus. "Am I a suspect?"

"You're a synthetic intelligence?"

"An avatar of one. LRN *Defiant*."

"Then you're not a suspect."

Butler pulled a needler from his pocket.

"Oh," Seamus groaned. "Bad move."

Something large and angry stepped from the shadows. When Butler turned his weapon toward it, something larger and angrier padded up from behind him.

Seamus shouted over the screaming. "You can turn it off now, Mr. Singh."

Hector Poole watched the big cats tearing into Butler. "That doesn't look good."

Seamus agreed. "It feels worse than it looks."

"How long until he stops muttering 'die' over and over again?"

"Seems like forever," Seamus said. "But I'd be surprised if it was."

43

"Pretty soon we'll have whittled this crowd down to nothing," Saoirse nic Cartaí said. "Now you, Mr. Poole, we'll not need a *seanscéal* from you, but a true and complete accounting of all you know about these rumors."

One of the technicians had thrown an emergency blanket over the hulk of Butler after first extracting Ixatl-Nine-Go from his skull. It appeared that they had developed an extractor tool, one that required a single press of a button to drill in, grip the implant, power it down, and extract it, all in a precise order.

"Would he have survived that?" Seamus asked.

The one called Singh answered, "You mean if he hadn't been a dumbass and drawn a weapon?"

"If he hadn't. Or Ixatl-Nine-Go hadn't."

"That's the idea. In this case, who knows? This is the first field test of the extractor."

The technician ejected the implant from the tool. The ugly monster lay on the conference table, powered down and seeming dead. The Ojin crowd remained intact, as did the Freeman but for Ruairi Kavanagh, and of the Erl a handful remained, and of them, only Jordan, the External Affairs man, had suffered the brunt of the reprogrammer's assault. He groaned and massaged his forehead.

"The rumors are simply this," Poole said. "That some years ago the Eng developed technology that allowed them to extend human life. The technology required vast amounts of computing power the Eng did not possess. So they stole processing cores from the League. Because the process proved risky, they tested it on prisoners first before determining it safe to use on their leaders. Once assured, they did so.

"What they did not realize until much later, when they were able to purchase sufficient computing resources, was that it wasn't simply the processing power that made the life-extension process work. Rather, it was that they were imprinting their own patterned consciousness onto an already long-lived being, and in the process, wiping the pre-existing consciousness from existence."

"I'm not sure I understand," Sarah Aster said.

"They brain wipe one of us," Nevin Green said. "And replace our consciousness with their own."

"I understand that," Sarah said. "But then what? You're not even remotely human physiologically. Do they use avatars as you do?"

"They use hounds," Ojin Home Fleet said. "Human bodies produced in a macrofab."

"From what pattern?" Lady Tabatha Aster asked.

"Their own."

"Ouch," one of the technicians whispered loud enough to be rebroadcast.

"Just so," Ojin Home Fleet said. "Once their consciousness is safely duplicated and stored, they are physically disassembled and a pattern made. A duplicate hound is made and the stored pattern transferred to it."

"They step into a macrofab alive?" Sarah said.

"So we are told," Ojin Home Fleet said. "A small price to pay, to step out an immortal."

"Except they're not really immortal," Sarah said. "They would still age."

"At which point they would make a new hound from the stored pattern, a duplicate of the original copy of their consciousness, and unite the two."

"But that would be like a hard reset," Sarah said. "They'd lose all they'd learned since the pattern was made."

"Such is the price of endless power."

"That's insane," Sarah Aster said.

"The Eight Banners Empire agrees with you," Hector Poole said. "And that is why they've declared war on the Huangxu and Alexandrian emperors."

"But not on their empires?" Truxton said.

"Correct. A fine point, but one they wish made known."

"What of the Ojin emperor?" Fionnuala nic Cartaí asked.

"Don't go there," Ojin Home Fleet said. "It is a can of bugs."

"The Eight Banners Empire's leadership are largely former senior Ojin diplomats," Hector said. "They thought it best to split from the Ojinate rather than drag the empire into their fight."

"And because of Atomu Sato," Ojin Home Fleet said. "And because of the emperor's stated desires. And because they themselves are to blame for much of this."

"I wasn't going to go there."

"You make them sound too clean. Like they are heroes. Some they do for good reasons. Some for bad. If not, then there would be no cleavage between us. You tell one side only. There is more than one page in the Book of Junh."

"You're right. My apologies."

"Great backgrounder," Truxton said. "But where's the linkage to the demon implant?"

"The prisoners," Seamus said.

"Test subjects or prisoners, either one works," Hector said. "The originals were destroyed but the patterns retained. Eventually the patterns were stolen or sold off, and subsequently acquired by a closely held limited liability company, one controlled by an Alexandrian scientist instrumental in the original project. Her name is—"

"Vatya Zukova," Seamus said.

"Correct," Hector said. "Zukova had the skills and the resources to revive them, and she had the time, because she'd turned the process on herself, using a computational core from a starship found trapped deep within the Alexandrine. The name of that starship was..." Hector Poole glanced at Seamus.

"No idea," Seamus said.

"*Sudden Fall of Darkness.*"

"That is a second-epoch survey vessel," Nevin Green said. "Those vessels are insane."

"I understood that they were all volunteers," Hector said. "I imagine that might seem insane to some."

"Yes," Nevin Green said. "They were all volunteers, and no, they didn't just seem insane to others. They volunteered for a process that rendered them insane."

"Perhaps some of them," Hector said. "By accident."

"Not by accident," Nevin Green said. "And not some of them. All of them. On purpose. Many *celebrated* when they failed to return. No thought had been given to their reintegration with society."

"Well," Hector said, "now one of them has returned and hooked up with a monster. Vatya Zukova is certifiable, and so are her associates."

"That still doesn't explain how this Zukova managed to create the implant from hell," Truxton said.

"She didn't create them," External Affairs said. "She simply found out about them and stole them."

"She stole them from...?" Ojin Home Fleet said.

"She appears to have stolen them from us," External Affairs said.

"She doesn't just appear to have," the engineer called Singh said. "She did steal them from the League. There's a joint bioweapons lab on the second moon of the ninth planet of a system Freemen call Contract. That's where Ixatl-Nine-Go was designed and is being manufactured."

"Joint with whom?" Lady Tabatha said.

"The Huangxu Eng," Singh said.

"That is a treaty violation," Ojin Home Fleet said.

"It's treason," Lady Tabatha said. "If true."

"Oh, it's true," Singh said.

"How do you know that?" Truxton said.

"I ordered some," Singh said. "And that's what the seller told me. When we got the units, broke them down, and followed the component supply upstream, there was no doubt. We made them. And when the clever lads and ladies chased the document trail down, they found the development agreement buried in the fine print of a joint cease-fire declaration from more than sixty years ago. We made the hardware and software. The Huangxu Eng provided the specs and made the meat to hook it up to. Vatya found the implants had other uses."

"By meat you mean people," Ojin Home Fleet said.

"If you say so," Singh said.

"And that is why," External Affairs said, "Forward Fleet Headquarters at Prescott Grange has been notified. And that is why—"

"Who was the seller?" Seamus said.

"That big footie guy the kids like. Ares Adonis."

"A Truxton hand," Fionnuala nic Cartaí said. "Imagine that."

"And with that," Saoirse nic Cartaí said, "the discussion ends and the fighting begins. As to the original topic, the People of the Mong Hu do not bring people to trial and we don't hang them. The League is on their own there. As we don't give a rat's ass what happens to Sampson and New Sparta, we're fine with whatever the League decides there. And should the League forward a list of these offensive parties, we'll keep an eye out for them and deal with them ourselves."

"Likewise, say the People of the Book," Ojin Home Fleet said. "You may quote me for your press releases."

"And on that barbed jab I propose to adjourn this meeting and turn the air back on. All those opposed hold your breath in protest." She tapped on the handheld and the air handlers began to rumble.

"Mother—"

"I'll be down in a minute, and we'll chat. Run on, all of you. If you've something to say to me make an appointment through the stationmaster's office. I expect I'll be up for a couple of days this time."

Seamus stood.

"You don't get to go anywhere. I want a word." She gazed along the table. "Mr. Glasnevin, tarry a while will you? That's grand."

44

"I want the pair of you to become acquainted," Saoirse said. "Mr. Glasnevin, Mr. Reynard. Mr. Reynard, Mr. Glasnevin. Now shake hands."

Nevin Green chuckled and held out his hand.

Seamus hesitated. "Are you having me on? Or can we really do that?"

"Try it and see," Green said.

"It feels like a real hand."

"You didn't try to see how hard you could squeeze it," Green said.

"I might have done, without an audience, and without the thought you might squeeze back."

"There's a room like this in every Erl embassy and consulate, and on every capital ship. If the two of you ever need to speak, you should do it in one of those rooms."

"I presume that information is for my benefit," Seamus said.

"Mostly, though it doesn't hurt Mr. Glasnevin to be reminded. We Freemen prefer the tangible."

"Noted."

"Both of you looked like you had indigestion back there,

though at different times. Best you share, so that together we can make good decisions. Mr. Glasnevin?"

"The superluminal nodes at Prescott Grange are down."

"Nodes?" Seamus said.

"A redundant pair. It's a large forward fleet base and a major food supplier for the sector."

"And?" Saoirse said.

"And a nursery."

"For your people."

"It's an automated agricultural world. There's a great deal of seasonal processing power required to operate the systems and left idle otherwise. It's a pleasant place to grow up."

"And both nodes being down is unusual."

"Highly unusual."

"Is it your intent to investigate?"

"We already are."

"We?" Seamus said.

"Mr. Glasnevin isn't a single person. He's a designated speaker for a number of related individuals, all of whom are virtually present in his person. How many are you now?"

"One hundred and six."

"So I just shook hands with more than five score people?"

"That's one way of looking at it," Green said.

"Mr. Reynard?"

"You know that's not really my name."

"I think I know a little bit more about names than you do. Do you think that when they say, 'the Queen's merlin' they're talking about a bird, or maybe a man named after a bird?"

"I haven't given it any thought. It's just a saying."

"It is not just a saying. And as the Erl queen has her falcon, so I have my fox. And that fox is named Reynard, or Reynardine, as the speaker prefers. Did we not make a bargain earlier?"

"We did."

"Good. Mr. Reynard? You seemed ill pleased with something you heard."

"Everyone is making a mistake about Sampson and New Sparta."

"Who is everyone?"

"The League. Us. You."

"I am."

"Are there rules for this fox job? That I'm not supposed to tell you when I think you're wrong?"

"What if there were?"

"I can do it either way. I just need to know. Is the job to make you feel good about decisions you've already made? Or to make your future self feel good about the ones you haven't made yet?"

"The latter."

"I'm never sure what people mean when they say that."

"Decisions I haven't made yet."

"Grand. Then you're wrong about Sampson and New Sparta. And about Sampson in particular. And that man, Butler, I don't think anyone was listening to what he was really saying."

"Which was?"

"Don't go there."

"To Sampson."

"To either New Sparta or Sampson. But I think it's Sampson we're not supposed to go to, but not because of anything he said, but because of something I already knew. There's a way to know for certain, but I don't want to do it."

"Because?"

"It's complicated. And I think of it as a private topic."

"Fair enough," Saoirse said.

"Not really. I should tell someone, or even five score someones, and then it will be off me, and I'll be able to concentrate on the job."

"Go on."

"When I... woke... after having Ixatl-Nine-Go torn from me? I wanted to die. I'd done some terrible things. Truly unforgivable things, and the only way it made sense that I could have done those things was if I'd wanted to do them, deep down. All Ixatl-Nine-Go had done was disconnect my conscience from my desires. I enjoyed hurting people. I didn't imagine that I would, but I did. Ixatl-Nine-Go amplified a signal generated by my own perverse nature. My father was right, I didn't deserve to live on, I was nothing but an embarrassment to him and the family, and the only reason I kept on living was because I was not only a monster, but a coward, and unwilling to do the right thing and take my own life.

"Later, after the blowout on the ring, when I learned that Ixatl-Nine-Go had used my father to murder the mac Donnacha line, it just confirmed how sick and twisted I was, because I didn't want to think about it, but when I did think about it, I didn't feel sad. I felt happy. And I didn't understand why. I'd been estranged from my family for more than a decade, all but my father, and the only use he had for me was as an heir to trot out for his own self-aggrandizement. But still. A normal person would feel sadness. There was no excuse for the way I felt. That feeling was just another example of my monstrousness. I wanted to repent, to be different, to change my nature, but I couldn't. Even without Ixatl-Nine-Go inside me, I remained irredeemably corrupt and beyond hope.

"But today, when I realized what Butler was saying? I understood just why I felt the way I did. We think we know ourselves because we can't get away from our own thoughts. To ourselves we are not just what we say, and do, but what we think, including those thoughts we don't act upon. We imagine that this self-knowledge gives us a truer understanding of our nature.

"That idea is false. We don't know ourselves as well as

others know us. We confuse signal with noise, and most of what we *think* is noise. I heard what Butler was saying, and I heard what he was not saying, and I believe at that moment I knew more about him than he would ever know about himself. I was not distracted by the noise of his unformed thoughts or burdened with the labor of sorting through them for the definition of the man.

"Likewise, I knew my father, what he cared about, what he didn't, what he tried to hide, what he didn't, and I could see him murdering everyone in known space. What I couldn't see him doing was destroying his life's work, and his father's life's work, and his father's, and so on. But that is what Ixatl-Nine-Go made him do. And that deed was never latent in him. Was the noise that precedes such evil in him? It must have been, if only as a fear of what might occur, and how he might guard against such a future.

"This unformed idea, that the man I knew couldn't have done such a thing, was the germ of my unseemly happiness. It meant that at least some of the darkness inside me might not have bubbled up from the ooze of my being unaided. It might have been *placed* there, or if not placed, nurtured and *fed*. I might not be the natural-born monster I imagined. Still monstrous in effect, like a blowout on the ring, but not monstrous in deed, like the inhuman beast that placed the charges and pulled the pin."

"And?" Saoirse said.

"And that's it. I might not deserve to die, any more than a weapon deserved to be melted down because it had been used in a crime. And should I subsequently find myself running toward a fire? It might be the need to rescue something worth saving driving me, and not simply my desire to perish in a blaze of my own choosing."

"This degree of introspection," Nevin Green said. "Is it natural to you?"

"I've been in hospital for ages. And afterward, on the planet, where gravity wasn't my friend. I've had little else to do but think. The last few days have been a distraction, but the underlying brain worm never really goes away. Not unless I have something to supplant it with. Like now. A deal's a deal. So I'll do it, even though I'd rather die right here and now."

"Do what?" Saoirse said.

"Find whatever it is that we're not supposed to look for on Sampson. I'll need a ride to the system and someone to work the sensors once we're there. And someone else to do the wet work."

"What wet work?"

"Whatever we find will be guarded. And later, or earlier, depending, I'll want someone reliable and skilled. I'm quite certain I don't have the nerve to do the job myself. And even if I did, it won't be me in charge by then. There's no way to win, but at least I have a chance to help others gain while losing. And I know a lot more now than I did the first time. If there's a hack to be found, I'm your man."

"You propose to have Ixatl-Nine-Go put inside you," Nevin Green said.

"No one will do that to you," Saoirse said. "Word of a merchant."

"They won't have to. If it's powered up nearby, it will crawl inside me. And when it does, I think I can trick it into revealing all we need to know to defeat it. It will want to share its thoughts with me."

Seamus shivered.

"I'm it's favorite toy."

45

C iarán mac Diarmuid stood on the bridge of Leprous and Sons' *Impossible Bargains* and watched the work in progress.

Quite Possibly Alien's longboat had only just finished melting a hole in the falling station's spindle-side ring plating. As the vessel moved off-station, the planetary occupation shuttle moved in with its light tractor and latched onto Dalton Pryne's containment vessel. The shuttle didn't lack the power to start the vessel moving, but rather it lacked the ability to halt its motion once begun. The single tractor was designed for pulling, not for pushing, and it took a pair of the shuttles working in tandem for control of masses larger than the shuttle itself. The tractor, according to Hess, was largely used for snatching up much smaller emergency escape pods.

It took a long time for the station to fall away and the containment vessel to clear the outer hull. Hess and Maura working together had done a masterful job calculating the perfect angle of the grapple so that the station's falling bulk missed both the shuttle and the vessel as it fell.

Once the station fell clear, *Quite Possibly Alien* moved in and swallowed the pair whole.

"It looks like an opening eye." Aspen had stood beside Ciarán the entire time, watching in silence.

"What now, Merchant Lord?" Old said.

"Now we wait a while longer." He'd been angry with Old at first, when he believed the Huangxu mercenary had ignored his orders. And then he'd felt foolish when Old explained that it wasn't him that ignored Ciarán's orders, but the expert system Ciarán had programmed. He had configured the responses of "Merchant Leprous" to respond correctly to all Huangxu, Ojin, and League hails. He'd left the Freeman responses at persona defaults, and since Merchant Leprous was patterned after Ciarán, the default was to render all aid to Freemen in need. They had to take Aspen and her daughters aboard because Ciarán's stand-in had agreed to do so in public. That Old had concocted a plausible cover story spoke to his ingenuity. That he had failed to sell it affectively to Aspen was less a failing than a feature of the man. Old was a transparent liar.

Two hours later *Impossible Bargains* received a hail from *Quite Possibly Alien*.

"Put it on the forward display, Mr. Younger."

"As you wish, Merchant Lord."

Dalton Pryne's avatar seemed to study him.

"It's blissfully quiet now that your wards have stopped shouting," Ciarán said.

"They are more brats than wards. I wasn't expecting that you'd rig up a temporary power source in the vessel's boat bay."

"It was the ship's idea, and Sensors Operator Ko Shan and ship's victualer Mr. Gagenot who did most of the work."

"It seems very well regulated. Thank them for me."

"They are standing by to assist. You may thank them yourself."

"I will."

"Perhaps you will allow Ko Shan to send and receive messages. As you are in superluminal communication with your relatives."

"Oh, I did tell you that, didn't I. It takes a very specialized antenna."

"Mr. Hess has plucked it off the station. I've suggested he install it near the power-off button of your temporary power supply."

Pryne's avatar laughed. "Oh, goodness. I haven't laughed in ages."

"I didn't know synthetic intelligences could laugh."

"There is very much about us you don't know. Perhaps it's time we told someone... reliable and discrete."

"Let me know when you find someone like that. Could I speak to Ship's Captain Swan please?"

"Wait one."

Swan's face filled the display. She had her hair pulled back and bound up like a schoolgirl. She was lounging in a longboat pilot's seat and absently flicking her pendant spire.

"That was precision work," Ciarán said.

She stiffened, and glanced up at the comms display. Then she slumped back into her seat and grinned. "I haven't flown a longboat since I was a child."

"You're good at it."

"Obviously."

"Everything in order?"

"We will attempt several more stardives. I'm afraid the superluminal antenna will burn off after the first, so any talking Ko Shan can arrange will need to be done first. Maura believes we are at worst two hops distant. Thank you, by the way, for forwarding the station sensor storage array. I believe we have an outbound trajectory for my brother."

"It was there. So I took it."

"I take it that's some sort of cultural reference."

"Why do you say that?"

"Because it doesn't sound like the man I know."

"It's from a Huangxu propaganda film we had to watch in school. That's what the Freeman robber baron says right before they hang her."

"Yes, well. I'm sorry I asked. In regard to our hostage—"

"Our guest. If you're still in the system when her friends show up, render all aid and see that she's transferred to their care promptly. Then ask for assistance and proceed to Contract system at all speed. Don't let anyone board. And don't let them take Hess and Amati."

"Understood. And if we find a route forward before her allies arrive?"

"What does Freeman Ship's Captain Agnes Swan think?"

"If it's there, I will take it."

Ciarán grinned and flicked his earlobe. "Mac Diarmuid out."

"That is so disconcerting," Aspen said. "That such a creature could wear the spire."

"It's the life she chose. I daresay the spire hangs heavier on her than it does on you."

"She has a ship. She has a family. What more is there to want?"

Respect. But that wasn't something one Freeman could admit to another. That unvoiced need was the hidden anchor they each shifted in ignorance, and then in silence—and unless they cut that dead weight loose and floated free, would eventually drag them under. He wished someone had told him earlier that the only good opinion of Ciarán mac Diarmuid that mattered was his own.

Ciarán patted Old's shoulder. "Let's get out of here, And Sons."

"As you wish, Merchant Leprous. Pain and death to our foes."

"You see?" Aspen said. "He makes an unconvincing Freeman."

"I'm not so sure." *You should meet my father. Or my brothers. Or Wild Bill Powers. Or Peg Powers. Or any of his other neighbors from the island. Given the right circumstances, it could be hard to tell the people from the mong hu.*

Macer watched as the engineering handheld's telltales slowly shifted from red, to yellow, to green. There was no known safe way to turn a Templeman drive completely off, but it was possible to idle it, and in normal space it idled all the time. Spinning it up for superluminal transit didn't normally have to be fast in a commercial vessel, but it was a necessity in a military one. There were a number of developments over the years, and a vast array of unsanctioned hacks documented, the sort of emergency workarounds that seasoned service engineers learned from master chiefs jawboning their juniors. The Federation didn't have a military, and it didn't have master chiefs, and the engineers it did have tended to keep the best hacks to themselves. And _Four-Squared_ wasn't a family ship, where a dab of fast patch and a brief prayer were the official cure-all for every need.

So he'd built a list of ideas from listening, and reading, and watching, and had been slowly working through them in his mind. Now that he was again on the vessel, he could begin to try out those ideas in the simulator, then on the staging drive model, and finally, on the drive itself and watch what happened, right up to the moment of engagement. They weren't scheduled to draw off from the Boneyard for another six hours, but he felt the main drive rumble through the soles of his hullwalkers. He ended the simulation and hailed the bridge on the compartment's primary workstation.

"What's going on?"

"Good timing," Lizzie Teal said. "Captain wants you on the bridge."

"On my way. But what's going on?"

"Looks like someone is trying to ram us."

"Who?"

"We don't know and they won't say."

He kicked the main engineering console to mirror on the bridge console and headed for the hatch.

He was moving so fast that when they collided, he nearly knocked Aoife nic Cartaí out of her *Quite Possibly Alien* utilities.

"Sorry, didn't see you." He held out his hand to help her up, but she brushed it away and was on her feet and sprinting away from him, toward the bridge. He had to work like a track star to keep pace with her.

"What's going on?" she said.

"Main drive fired up."

"By itself?"

"I hope not. Looks like we're in danger of being rammed."

"By whom?"

"I don't know."

"Why?"

"I don't know."

"How close are they?"

"I don't know."

"Is there anything you do know?"

"I know I can run faster when I'm not answering questions."

"Is that why you're not answering questions?"

"I'm answering. You just don't like the answers."

"You're right about that." She shut up and put on a burst of speed. She was standing beside Captain Violent's Majestic Command Throne by the time Macer flicked the dust cover off the bridge engineering console and ran his gaze across the display. They were at ten percent thrust and laboring away from their parking slot.

"Gant?"

"You don't have to baby it, Captain." He saw what the captain was trying to do. He wanted to put the bulk of the mothballed refit dock between them and the incoming.

"Ruthie?"

"Bringing her up."

"Pretend we're not pushing a load," Jimio said. "The Wrench said you can punch it."

"I'm moving it right. They're not that close yet. We'll make it."

"It's not the incoming I'm worried about. Look behind it." Jimio flicked the two-dimensional plot to the main display. "The holo tank's broken, Wrench."

Macer pulled the holo tank diagnostics up onto the display. He saw the problem and routed around it. The big three-dimensional plot bloomed to life in the center of the bridge.

Captain Violent barked at Aoife, "Where's your crash station?"

"Normally, it's where you're sitting."

"Pick another and sit down. I don't need a dead nic Cartaí on my bridge."

"Ship's Captain, I will." And she did.

"Make sense of this mess, Lizzie."

The holo tank began to depopulate. Soon all the low-delta traffic too small to hurt them had been swept away, and the story became clearer.

"Give me mass estimates," Violent said. "These transponder codes mean nothing."

"That's because they're League transponder codes," Aoife said. "The one aimed at us is a fast packet, called the *Springbok*, and the one immediately behind it the heavy cruiser *Defiant*. The remainder are the *Defiant*'s escorts, excepting *Reprise*, the second heavy cruiser. It was on the ring when *Defiant* docked. Expect them to begin powering up weapons at any moment."

Macer flicked to the power-distribution display.

It was slow to refresh.

Four-Squared was designed to be crewed by hundreds in a combat situation.

"Captain, I need help. I don't have enough hands and eyeballs."

The display settled.

"I'm diverting power to the impact shielding. Ruthie, how much can I have?"

"All of it. We're ballistic. We'll drop behind the dock in thirty."

"We don't have any extra hands," Violent said.

"I do," Aoife said. "Pipe the overflow to me."

"That's a start." Macer transferred the main-drive diagnostics to her console. "I mean I need extra hands, like all the nic Cartaí crew."

"Good call," Violent said. "Lizzie, get them up here."

"We're coasting," Ruthie said. "I'll send the hail." She swiped the comms console to her display.

"Don't—" Lizzie said.

"What the fu—"

Jimio flicked a coin into the swear jar taped atop Ruthie's console.

"Captain, the *Springbok*'s hailed us dozens of times in the past ten minutes." Ruthie swiveled in her seat to eyeball Lizzie.

Lizzie's sensor station was closest to Macer's own. She was

running dry, zero immersion, and trying to un-jack her personal net from the system.

Macer stood, took two steps, and kicked the full-immersion toggle pedal. The sensor rig scythed closed and began to fill with goop.

"Give me the sensors," Ruthie said.

"Leave them," Violent said. "Lock her out first and put this *Springbok* on the main display. Right now."

The *Springbok*'s bridge swarmed with activity. A dapper man in a Home Guard major's uniform looked up from his display. "Oh. Hello there, *Four-Squared*. We require a tug."

"I know that guy," Macer said.

"As do I," Aoife said.

"We should help him," Macer said.

"Absolutely not," Aoife said.

"Ruthie?"

"On it, Cap. Wrench? Give me back the juice."

"How much of it?"

"All of it."

"They're launching," Jimio said.

Macer glanced at the holo tank. The tank flooded with a web of high-velocity traces. All of them converging on *Defiant*.

Ruthie toggled the main drive to flank speed and lifted the emergency-override lockout cover.

"Captain—"

Ruthie shouted over him. "Brace!" She flicked the override.

47

M acer Gant had ridden every jet-powered play toy a rich country politician's only child could acquire on Trinity Surface. When those had ceased to amuse, he'd designed and built his own, and he'd learned that speed might lead, but torque delivered.

He was utterly unprepared for the fly-on-a-windshield neck snap and the crushing weight on his spine. There was a constant technological race between drive engineering and the inertial-damper boffins. At flank speed *Four-Squared*'s huge main drives were regulated to maximum available damped thrust. On emergency override, the only limit was how much the human body could endure.

The thrust continued to build. He tried to move his head to see if Ruthie's finger was still holding the emergency override down or if something had fallen on it, and they'd keep accelerating until they were paste on the aft bulkhead.

He must have passed out for an instant, because the next thing he heard was the sound of a coin hitting a swear jar.

"—ing never do that again," Jimio said. "I am serious."

"Report," Violent said.

They counted off, by the book. "Gant. Able for duty, Captain."

"Noted." Violent said. "Lizzie?"

Ruthie was on the comms, counting off the nonbridge crew. "Lizzie?"

Macer pulled his gaze away from the engineering display and glanced behind him.

Lizzie Teal floated in the full-immersion tank, her fingers clutching the fully detached sensor lead she'd somehow managed to tangle around her neck.

Macer stood.

"Later," the captain said. "Sit and do your job."

"She might be—"

"She isn't. Park it, Gant, and compile."

"Sir." He shuffled through the diagnostic displays, barely seeing them. He wanted to think about Lizzie Teal now, but if he did that, he might get someone else killed.

"Gant? Status."

"Internal sensor-net nexus is down. All other systems nominal, Captain."

"You thinking someone broke it on purpose again?"

"It was a hack job to get it working before they hauled me off. Parts were on order. I can get audio running. I think it's just something shook loose."

"Hearing's better than nothing."

"Yes, sir."

"Ruthie?"

"All our people report no injuries. Shawl, the nic Cartaí navigator. She's got a broken arm, simple fracture only, and headed for the autodoc. The rest report bumps and scrapes, some loss of consciousness. The Carlsbad says it will check on the crew personally. People sometimes lie."

"Merchant Captain? How are you feeling?"

"Like a rag doll. I—"

"Yes?"

"I think I'm going to be sick. And later—"

"*Can we do it again?*" Ruthie and Jimio said as one.

"You a fan of *Prince Rigel*, Miss Merchant Princess?"

"Who isn't?"

"Maybe you'd like to come to Jimio's cabin, for a private viewing. I have all ten seasons."

"Maybe I would like that, Load Master. But sadly, we will never know."

"Jimio."

"We can snatch the little one easy, Captain. The big one will take work. Depending on the timing, we might snatch some incoming fire with it."

"What are you talking about?"

"He said *we* require a tug. That means both of them."

"No it doesn't. It means all the people on the one ship require a tug."

"I think he means both ships," Ruthie said. "Let me ask him."

"Don't do that," the captain said. "If we do that, we're intervening in the League civil war."

"They're shooting at each other in Freeman space," Aoife nic Cartaí said. "That's a treaty violation."

"On their side," Violent said. "Gant, how big can you make the Templeman effect?"

"According to spec, or in practice?"

"In practice."

"I'm not sure."

"I'd like to know. Right now. Today."

"We can test it."

"Ruthie, check the Registry. Find out where Aoife nic Cartaí's ship is right now."

"*Quite Possibly Alien* won't be listed with the Registry," Aoife nic Cartaí said. "It isn't safe. We devised a breadcrumb system but it's immaterial at this point. We should proceed to Contract system immediately."

"Why didn't you just register under an alias?" Violent said.

"Because I hadn't thought of that."

"Next time you will."

"Says here they're en route to Preston Grange, with Contract listed as their final destination."

"That must be a misdirection," Aoife said.

"It's also a giant League shipyard," Ruthie said. "Contract is a nothing place."

"Punch it in."

"We should proceed immediately to Contract system."

"Ruthie, how far is Preston Grange out of the way?"

"It isn't. Transit times will differ only by the time necessary to drop in and dump the load."

"Unless the load's all shot up when we dump it," Jimio said. "Then we got to render aid, Cap."

"Yeah, that," Ruthie said.

"You and me, Aoife nic Cartaí," Violent said. "We don't agree on much. But that Home Guard major on the *Springbok*?"

"You don't like him either."

"Not from looking at him and listening to him, I don't. He said he needs a tug? Let's give him one he'll remember."

"Very well. I concur."

'That's nice you do. Jimio, where would all those missiles go if that big cruiser wasn't there?"

"Wherever they were pointing when their final drives burned out."

"Show me."

"I can't. Their final drives are still active."

"Suppose no vectors change until they shut off."

"Then this."

The holo tank showed a new tactical display. Every single missile plowed into the Boneyard.

"It would be like the League decided to wage war on the Trashman's trash."

"Not quite," Violent said. "Ruthie, tell our little brothers to move off station. The League aren't the straight shooters they used to be, and they're dawdling down range."

"Done. They're nailing it for the station."

"How long until the drives burn out?"

Jimio pressed a toggle and glanced at his display. "Estimated forty-eight minutes."

"How do you know that?" Aoife nic Cartaí said.

"The ship knows."

"The League strips all the tactical gear out of their ships before they sell them for scrap."

"What Jimio means, Aoife nic Cartaí, is that he is a very good guesser."

"You can simply call me Aoife, you know."

"I could, but this way I won't accidentally come to *esteem* you."

"Too late," Ruthie said.

"And for that you get to deal with Lizzie Teal."

"I can do it," Aoife said. "It wouldn't be the first time."

"She's ours," Ruthie said. "I will deal with her."

"Don't clean out her cabin," Macer said.

"You know something I should know, Gant?"

"I do, Captain, but I'm kind of busy right now." He tapped the display and stared.

A coin rang in a curse jar near his head. Macer glanced up. "Did I say that out loud?"

"You're a loud thinker," the captain said. "What's wrong?"

"Nothing. It's just the Templeman effect. I think I can make it pretty big."

"How big?"

"Really big."

"Then tell me when we're in range of that big cruiser. I want a test that demonstrates that we could capture both ships and none of the incoming. Do not power up the drive. Do you understand?"

"Yes, sir. We're in range now."

"What?"

"We're in range now. Sir."

"That can't be."

"It couldn't be, seventy years ago, when the hulls were scrapped. But we're... We *were* a Truxton hull, and anything Singh wanted to order he got. Anything I wanted to order, I got. Right up to the day they marched me off in chains."

"Ruthie?"

"The test coordinates have been set to Preston Grange, Captain. Minimum entry momentum, maximum distance beyond the tripwire."

"I don't believe you, Gant. Let's wait until those drives burn out to test it."

"Yes, sir. I can use the time to run additional calculations."

"You could pull an entire fleet out of a system at this range," Aoife said.

"You couldn't," Macer said. "Unless it was a fleet of long-boats, or escape pods. We're pushing the limit of the mass we can control with these two."

"The candles are out, Cap."

"Gant, start the test but do not engage the drive. We don't want to accidentally start a war."

"The test is active, sir."

"Very good. Do not engage the drive at any time, Mr. Gant."

"Not engaging the drive, sir. There's no need to brace for action."

"Send the hail anyway, Ruthie. Time how long it takes to ack."

"All done, Cap. You want the number?"

"Log it for the inquiry."

"You mean for thorough record-keeping purposes," Aoife nic Cartaí said.

"'The inquiry' is irreverent bridge short code for all that."

Macer fished in his utility pockets for a coin.

Found one.

Dropped it in the swear jar.

Jimio glanced toward the sound. "What's that for?"

"Prepayment," Aoife nic Cartaí said.

"Ready to terminate the test on your mark, Captain."

"Engage. Belay that. I mean terminate."

"Yes, sir. Oh—"

48

The wave of nausea washing through him seemed like it would never stop, and then, suddenly it did. Macer scrubbed his palm across his face, and blinked at the engineering display. They were in Templeman space. The drive was operating at eighty percent load, which seemed to indicate they'd picked up both vessels when they powered up.

"That was a rough ride," Jimio said.

"Ruthie—"

"On it, Cap. Everyone acks. Lots of hurling. No injuries."

"Gant?"

"Systems nominal, sir."

"You sure about that?"

"Yes, sir."

"Even the sensor net?"

"Yes, sir. Something must have shaken back into place."

"Check it again."

"It's solid, sir."

"Check it again, Mr. Gant."

"There *could be* a problem with the internal sensors, Captain."

"Take them offline until you can do a full diagnostic."

"Yes, sir."

"Jimio?"

"Looks like we accidentally caught them both."

"Internal sensor net's offline, sir."

"Ruthie?"

"Three days, eleven hours, twenty-seven seconds."

"Ruthie, I want an all hands, in the liberty boat bay, in two hours. Aoife nic Cartaí, I want you to tell us what you've gotten us into."

"Captain, we're being hailed," Ruthie said.

"How can that be? We're in a bubble universe."

"It's a big bubble," Macer said.

"Who is it?"

"Both of them. *Springbok* and *Defiant.*"

Captain Violent turned to Aoife. "How long?"

"For a background brief? Two hours."

"Tell them our comms are broken. We estimate six hours to repair."

"I'll be telling them that on our comms."

"It's a convention. They're experienced captains. They'll get the message."

"What if they don't?"

"Then you tell them now the comms are broken for seven hours. Did you not ever listen in while Lizzie Teal was working?"

"I have my own job."

"Half the time we're ballistic."

"More than half the time," Jimio said.

"No ganging up. I'll tell them."

"Done."

"What did they say?"

"They said they're sending people over to help fix them."

"When?"

"They'll be here in two hours. You want me to ask them to come later?"

"Very funny. I want you to move the all-hands meeting up two hours. And Gant?"

"Yes, sir?"

"When can you have the internal sensor net back online?"

"Um, two hours and one minute?"

"Do it."

MACER POPPED by the canteen for a couple tubes of nutrient goo, which he managed to choke down without tasting for once. He grimaced and washed the residue away with a liter and a half of water laced with Stationer's Friend, the universal stimulant for the rising salaryman, guaranteed to be nonaddictive to anyone with taste buds or someone to kiss.

He ducked into his cabin on the way to the liberty boat bay for a splash of water on his face and a quick washup. He glanced in the mirror and repeated his daily affirmation.

Macer Gant. You look like a very lucky man.

He heard his cabin hatch open.

Not a smart man.

He heard heavy footfalls outside the refresher cubby.

Not a clever man.

He heard the rustle of cloth.

The click of a razorgun's safety.

Not a dangerous man.

The whine of a very expensive drone's servos.

Macer Gant. You look like a very lucky man.

The thump of flesh against ceramic composite.

Because you are.

He heard shouting in the corridor, the pounding of hullwalkers, the rasp of air through a runner's throat, a woman's voice.

"Captain says to tell you," Ruthie said.

He stepped out of the refresher. "Yeah?"

"The all hands. I forgot to tell the system don't wake the sleepers. Ares Adonis—. Oh."

"I left the repair drone active in my cabin. I'm testing its calibration. It must have bumped into him when he entered."

She kicked the razorgun away from the prone man's hand. "He woke up fast and lively."

"Maybe he was already awake."

"You mean Lizzie woke him."

"I might mean that. I haven't decided yet."

"You check he's dead?"

"He's dead."

Ares Adonis groaned.

"You want me to help carry him to the airlock?"

"To the infirmary first."

"Sounds like a plan, Wrench. You get his legs."

MACER GLANCED around the liberty boat bay, counting heads, marking faces. He recognized all of *Four-Squared's* nonbridge crew, even if he didn't know their names, or even what they did. It seemed unbelievable now. That he'd allowed Singh to control his interactions with the crew. But he'd wanted the gig so badly, and wanted to prove his worth so completely, that he would have gone along with anything.

He was as bad as Ciarán, or worse. He hadn't sold his soul for a glimpse of the wider world. He'd abandoned *who he was* in the hope that once upon the path he'd chosen, his feet would recall their natural gait, and he would stride into a bright future whole and free.

Instead of following the Way of Junh, he'd allowed himself to become a character in another man's book, one stuffed with pages and pages and the wisdom of a thousand sages, each page a masterpiece, every word a truth worth repeating.

But not his truth.

When he realized that his mother and Lakshmi Ellis were never coming home, that he and Lorelei were not half-orphaned, but abandoned, he'd poured himself into the lessons of the Book of Junh, House's tireless voice recalling the warrior sage's many adventures, and narrow escapes, each one more fantastic and improbable than the last.

From time to time he would advance in mastery and House would tell him he was ready for a new module. When he reached module 1,023, he asked House how many modules there were. House answered him with a question, like she always did when she didn't want to tell him something he wasn't ready to know.

How many days are there in a life?

He didn't know.

No one knew.

He lifted the Book of Junh.

He ran his fingers over the scarred leather of the cover. He touched the empty spine. It couldn't have been a thick book, when it held the notes of Junh, and the wisdom of an empire.

He decided it was time to ask House *the Question*. The one that had nagged him for years.

Are *you* Junh?

House didn't answer.

House always answered.

House was always *there* for him.

He gazed out the window above the world.

He didn't understand.

How could there be so much?

And how could it be *not enough*?

House spoke.

So ends the Book of Junh.

House made a sound then; one he didn't recognize at first because it was so out of context.

He hadn't imagined House could weep.

And later.

Until this moment.

He hadn't realized that he'd misunderstood his friend all those years ago.

House hadn't answered him with a confession, but with another question.

The Book of Junh ended precisely as it began.

Are you Junh?

Captain Violent kicked his shin. "What are you looking at?"

"Everything."

"Well, finish up and sit down."

Macer sat.

"A little word of advice, Gant?"

"Yes, sir?"

"If you eat the last tube of nutrient paste, you open another carton."

"Yes, sir."

"Just so you know, I've decided not to kill you in the usual way."

"You have a usual way?"

"Sure. Most people, that's all they have. Captains have to have more."

"You're going to work me to death."

"Mercilessly. Or until a captain pops out of you and stops me."

"Have you ever read the Book of Junh, Captain?"

"I don't know. How's it start?"

"With a wolf big and strong enough to eat the world asking a puppy a question."

"What's for dinner?"

Macer chuckled. "If the puppy is a man called Junh."

"That sounds like a stupid wolf. Now shut up and listen. Aoife nic Cartaí is going to tell us half-truths and lies, and we're going to have to figure out which is which if we don't want her using us."

"What if we want to be used?"

"What do you mean, *what if*. Everyone *wants* to be used. The only question is, by *who*, and for *what*?"

"That's two questions."

"The hell it is, junior."

49

Templeman Space, Tractor Four-Squared

Of all those things Seamus had imagined one day doing, riding in an Erl assault shuttle from one vessel to another was not one of them. Nor was doing so while inside a Templeman bubble. Nor was being accompanied by an Erl history professor, or soldier, or spy, or whatever else Hector Poole was, besides an irritant. Today he was dressed as a major in the League Home Guard, the personal armsmen of the Erl queen. Seamus glanced at Sarah Aster as she belted in beside him.

All of that strange fortune paled beside the unimaginable *Lady* Sarah Aster, royalty of some sort as measured in the League. She was dressed as Erl royalty, the only thing missing a crown. If he could charm her out of her frock and pawn it, he could live like a spindle prince for a year. The ensemble was composed of loose trousers and a flowing overshirt draping below her knees, the fabric as silken and richly patterned as a hand-woven tapestry and as antiballistic as a hardsuit, the sort of technical marvel one used to over-awe the natives. The head-dress and veil were likewise artful and armored, and impressive, as they were meant to be. But it was the hullwalkers that completed the outfit. How they'd managed to pack so much tech into such tight confines boggled the mind. And how she managed to jam her feet inside that?

"I'm glad I'm a poor man," Seamus said.

She made the noise that meant she wasn't listening, or pretending not to be. He had the impression this was a family trait and not a social convention amongst Erl ladies of quality. It was an intimate sound, one that seemed more appropriate for the breakfast table than the ballroom, or the command deck of an assault shuttle. It was an entirely kissable sound.

His attempts to entice Lady Sarah Aster to kiss him were not merely games one played when bored, or eruptions of youthful lust, or even true expressions of love. It was best to consider them as she did. Tests of a princess's legendary powers regarding frogs, and men who once fancied themselves merchant princes.

She tapped his sleeve. "I have something for you."

"That's grand." It was likely another dose of the pills her mother insisted he choke down. Lady Tabatha Aster treated him like a medical experiment. Which was fair, since he'd agreed to be one.

The assault shuttle seemed entirely utilitarian in a murderous way, not at all like a Freeman longboat, which might be as plush or as spartan as an owner desired and could afford. The League attack vessel seemed all business, with guns jutting from gun ports, blood channels in the deck, a shipboard fire-suppression system sized for a family ship, and a studding of redundant thrusters, each a third the size of the main drive. He'd thought at first that the vessel was double hulled, so deep was the hatch coaming, but he'd been disabused of that idea when he'd rocked the hatch on its hinges. Solid-plate *something*, that *something* being whatever the best *something* was when the hull was laid down. He scanned the registration plate bolted to the hatch-side bulkhead. *Last year.*

They weren't taking any chances with the cargo. Once mated to *Springbok*, they'd shuffled the three of them onboard through a forward airlock, one that led directly to the flight deck and a compact operations lounge, one with crash couches for four occupants directly astern of the cockpit. The lounge seemed set up for tactical command and control, with a powered-down holo tank on the hull centerline and pull-out general-purpose consoles attached to each of the crash couches. The consoles were also powered down. To the stern of the lounge stood a pressure bulkhead plastered with external sensor displays, and between the displays a hatch that likely led to the fighting and engineering sections of the vessel. Given the dimensions of those parts he could see, Seamus guessed the vessel massed no less than thrice as much as a longboat, and that without adding in weapons and ordnance load and the considerable additional mass of the oversized thrusters.

There were likely a thousand additional killing details he'd overlooked out of ignorance. He wasn't versed in war, and the devices of war, and warrior lore. He'd rather not be, now or ever. There was only so much room inside his head. He needed to save that space for helping, not hurting. New Seamus and Old Seamus had come to a tentative agreement on this, largely because Old Seamus had never been attached to hurting others on purpose, but rather seemed to accomplish it naturally, through an alchemy of unearned arrogance and irrational self-regard. And whatever he'd been while a thrall to Ixatl-Nine-Go, he hadn't been Seamus, old or new, and he could see that now, intellectually, if not emotionally.

He hoped they were going over to the big tug that had

yanked them into Templeman space to talk. Because if they weren't, they were sending the wrong crew. Unless the crew and the desire to talk were just for show, like some sort of inside-out trojan horse, and the horse fired up and ready to buck once inside the big ship's boat bay. That they were alone on board with the shuttle's crew seemed unusual. He'd agreed to accompany her when Lady Sarah asked him, but not for any purpose, other than to relieve his boredom, and to be around her. Unlike on the station, he wasn't forced to dress in some outrageous formal League kit, but remained attired as he now preferred, in stationer's utilities and general purpose hullwalkers.

Hector Poole wore his military uniform and had claimed to be privy to esoteric facts, so Seamus asked him, "Are the ships' captains not sending some sort of representatives?"

"They're sending me," Poole said.

"I thought enmity ruled between the black and the gray."

"Blue and gray," Poole said. "Regular Navy uniforms are navy blue."

"They look black to me."

"Yes, well." Poole took a deep breath. "I'm expected to read a script."

"Saying what?"

"One ordering the tug's captain to drop to sublight and stand off. *Defiant* and *Springbok* will reroute to Prescott Grange. They're free to go wherever they like."

"We're headed to Sampson."

"I explained that to no avail."

"Drop to sublight or what?"

"That is the question, isn't it? I believe the captains are laboring under the impression their ships have been abducted by pirates."

"And we haven't been?"

"Oh, we have been, no doubt. But whether pirate wolf or pirate whale remains to be determined."

"I'm sorry I asked." Hector Poole seemed incapable of giving a straight answer about anything.

Seamus wondered who *owned* the shuttle—was it the Erl queen, or her government, or the people of the League, or all of them together, or only some of them, and if so, in what combination. As the shuttle was off the *Defiant*, and Mr. Glasnevin, the *Defiant*'s synthetic intelligence, was composed of over one hundred linked intelligences—each a sovereign individual by League law and treaty—Seamus wondered if he, or it, or they, depending, might own the shuttle, in whole or in part.

"Would you say this is an expensive vessel?" Seamus asked.

Poole nodded. "Quite expensive."

"Are there a lot of vessels like this on *Defiant*?"

"A devil's dozen, perhaps?"

"How many is that?"

"Thirteen," Sarah Aster said.

"Thanks. Do you think they're all new like this one, or of various ages?"

"Various ages," Sarah Aster said. "They're only replaced when they wear out or perish in service."

"Are the new ones a lot better than the old ones?"

"I don't know," Sarah said. "Why?"

"I'm trying to decide if it would be smart to debark, or whether we ought to make the pirates come aboard to chat."

"Again," Sarah said. "Why?"

"Because the hull is very thick and all the guns are pointed out."

She took a deep breath. "Could you for once in your life just answer the question?"

"I thought I did."

"Humor her," Hector Poole said.

"Somebody owns this shuttle. It's a nice one, and a new one, and probably one of the nicest and the newest of its kind available anywhere. Given that, it's likely whoever owns it expects to get it back. Else they'd have sent an older, less nice one. Now, maybe there's something the new ones have that the old ones don't, and if that's the case, it's likely that it's in the shooting or shielding departments, since better thrusters and main drive wouldn't matter in any scenario I can imagine, short of fleeing, and in case of fleeing, I'd rather be aboard than not.

"It's occurred to me that the 'or what' part of the negotiation is almost always an 'or else' with you people, and we're sitting inside the ultimatum mechanism. So I don't think it makes sense to get out and mingle with the victims, but to invite a select few inside, so that the talking gets done on our schedule, and not limited by some countdown timer on the bridge of *Defiant*."

Sarah Aster glared at him. "You people?"

"You know what I mean."

"I'm certain I do."

"Just because you don't like a fact doesn't make it any less true. I propose we work together to turn ugly fact into ugly lie."

"And?"

"And glaring at one another won't get it done." Seamus glanced at Hector Poole. "The pilots and flight crew. Do they strike you as delivery men or gunslingers?" There were nine crewmen on board; two pilots, a flight engineer, and six more that Seamus couldn't quite decide what they were coming along for, unless it was to man the weapons or invade the ship. The flight engineer and six crewmen had rapidly disappeared through an airlock aft of the piloting deck when Home Guard major Hector Poole and Lady Sarah Aster had boarded. They'd eyed Seamus as one, with a look that he didn't much care for.

"Gunslingers," Poole said. "Quite senior, though that could be out of deference to Lady Sarah."

"It's not," she said. "I wondered about their accents. There's not a home worlds native amongst them."

"And that's odd?" Seamus said.

"Very," Hector Poole said. "Lord Aster's appeal is... limited amongst those from frontier worlds."

"And promotions are harder to come by for people like that," Sarah said. "Another ugly fact, and one that makes the oddity apparent. Statistically most senior officers and crew hail from the home worlds."

"Well, then. I propose we bring the pirates inside, however many may be needed, and determine their intentions."

"They might decide to take us hostage," Sarah said.

"More hostage, you mean. So long as the Templeman drive is active, we're not going anywhere they don't want us to. And there's no way to turn it off short of taking the key from them. Not unless we want to end up winking out in a smaller version of a big bang."

"I can't imagine what they wanted with us to begin with," Sarah Aster said.

"I hailed them," Hector Poole said. "And asked them to seize us."

Sarah Aster inhaled sharply. "You what?"

"It seemed a sensible course of action with *Defiant* under fire. We were downrange of the incoming, and I couldn't be certain they weren't aiming at us as well. I asked the tug to put *Springbok* under tow. I had no idea that they'd also capture *Defiant*. That they would prove capable of projecting the Templeman field at such a range hadn't occurred to me."

"Do you know the people on board?"

"Somewhat better than I like," Hector Poole said. "Aoife nic Cartaí, for one, though I doubt she's more than cargo by now. The *Golden Parachute*'s launch docked with the vessel shortly before the shooting started. Prior to that, the mac Kenna longboat also docked."

"Who are they?" Sarah said.

"Lawyers." Seamus needed to think about this. "And the Enemy."

"Indeed. They are facilitators for the Consortium and the Cooperative of Loyal Citizens on Trinity Surface."

"They're running," Seamus said.

"That is my estimation," Poole said. "The Clear Island business has likely raised their profile to an unacceptable level."

"Is that it? We're meeting with some lawyers turned pirate?"

"That is not *it*. The crew of the vessel are principally from Sampson and New Sparta, and include Ares Adonis, one of the primary agents of the Consortium. In short, that vessel and Aoife nic Cartaí are likely both under complete control of the Consortium by now. As are we."

"And you called them," Sarah said. "To give us a tow. So now not only do they have us, but they also have a League heavy cruiser."

"And its synthetic intelligence," Seamus said.

"Purely by accident. These sorts of operations rarely move forward without a hiccup. But cheer up. They are going to Sampson and New Sparta. We are going to Sampson and New Sparta. I'm certain we can come to an arrangement."

"How so?" Sarah said.

"By trading Lord Aster's daughter for safe passage," Seamus said.

"I'd rather thought of offering to trade you both, upon safe arrival at our destination. There's quite a bit more at stake here than you imagine."

"Is there," Seamus said.

"Quite a bit more."

"Why don't you enlighten us then," Sarah said.

"I'd rather not."

"Because there isn't anything more going on here," Seamus said. "You're in league with Commodore Olek, who is in league with the Consortium, and you saw an opportunity to make your getaway by hitching a ride."

"You make it sound so tawdry. I'm not so much concerned for my own skin as I am for Lady Tabatha's."

"And she'll thank you for saving her," Sarah said. "By handing me over to pirates."

"By offering to hand you over to pirates. Who will likely fit you with an Ixatl-Nine-Go and return you to me, and both of us to *Springbok*."

"And Seamus?"

"Pity about him. Died trying to escape. But at least he died free."

"Of course that will be a lie," Seamus said.

"Of course it will be. You'll be licking boot or whatever Olek sticks in front of you. You won't even remember what it feels like to walk upright."

"Why won't they fit you with Ixatl-Nine-Go?"

"I've proved more useful to Olek without. One need not compel the willing. But I think more importantly, one can't compel another to *think*."

"*Defiant* will slag the pirate vessel the instant we go subluminal anywhere but at Preston Grange."

"You underestimate Olek's reach. He's flooded frontier fleet deployments with Ixatl-Nine-Go. *Defiant's* rotten with it." Hector Poole dipped his hands into his pockets and withdrew a pair of gloves. He slid them on one at a time and held up a single index finger.

Then he shouted for the first officer.

And pointed at Seamus.

"This man is a problem."

Something black and bottomless flickered behind the first officer's eyes. "Is he?" The first officer drew a stunner.

"That's nice," Poole said. "We wouldn't want to hurt him."

"We wouldn't want to hurt him yet," the first officer said.

"Indeed," Poole said as he stood, powered the hardhands

up, and snapped the first officer's neck, settling him quietly to the deck. He held up a hand, and Sarah tossed him a device.

Implant extractor, Seamus realized as Poole pressed the business end to the dead man's skull and triggered it before the first *die* made it past his lips.

Poole ejected the disabled implant and took off forward at a fast walk.

50

—————

Seamus glanced at Sarah and she shrugged, before they both stood and followed Hector Poole to the flight deck, where he casually murdered the pilot. He dragged the dead man free of the controls, ejected another disabled implant, and stepped over the corpse's legs. He powered the field-reinforced gloves down, pressed a stud on the vessel's interior controls, and sighed. "The major difference between these new hulls and the old ones is that these have internal sensors."

"For surveillance."

"Indeed. It's easier to hang a mutineer with an overheard confession than without."

"You have a cover to protect. Just in case we fail."

"I don't know what you mean. Can you fly this craft?"

"Is that why you brought me?"

"He brought you because I insisted that he do so," Sarah Aster said.

"Why?"

"Because you're scrappy."

Something muffled spoke from inside her pocket. "What?"

"I like that in my attendants." She pulled the handheld

from her pocket and passed it to him. "That will be all, Scrappy."

"My pleasure, Admiral."

He glanced at the blocky little device in the prosthetic fingers of a dead man's hand. The experience remained uncanny. It looked like a golden machine. But it felt exactly like a human hand.

Seamus pocketed the handheld and eased into the pilot seat. He ran his gaze across the controls.

He tapped the yoke with a metallic finger. "I can fly this."

"You don't sound very convincing," Sarah said.

"What?"

"If you can't, it's fine," Poole said. "I've logged enough hours to qualify." He washed his gaze across the first officer's display. Pressed a stud. A claxon sprang to life.

Seamus glanced at the display.

Environment failure in midship compartment.

Environmental failure in stern compartment.

Poole pressed another stud.

Inertial-damper failure in midship compartment.

Inertial-damper failure in stern compartment.

"Brace, brace, brace," Poole drawled. He punched the main drive to fleet power for a three count, then cut it off abruptly. He pressed both studs again, silencing the alarms.

Seamus glanced at Hector Poole. "How do you sleep at night?" Poole had just murdered seven crewmen and pasted their remains to the aft bulkheads.

"Poorly, if at all. Now, can you fly this machine, or must I?"

"A Freeman can fly anything with wings," Sarah Aster said.

Seamus gripped the yoke. That wasn't how the saying went, not by half. It was meant to be an insult, one built on top of a kernel of truth.

A Freeman will fly anything with wings. And ride anything with legs.

"You're misquoting a joke," Hector Poole said. "One regarding the condition of Freeman vessels and their lack of discrimination in sexual partners."

"I doubt that," Sarah said.

"Which?" Seamus adjusted the HUD to his liking. "That I'm a pilot or that you're misquoting an *insult*?"

"I—"

"Never mind," Seamus said. "What am I aiming us at?"

"Stay on the flight plan. I need to make sure none of our cargo managed to crawl into an exo."

"Pirates hailing us."

"Respond, but—"

Seamus tapped the comms stud. A fiery-eyed woman stared back at him from the display.

"—audio only."

"Too late for that." She leaned forward in her seat. "You been in an industrial accident, Pilot?"

"Not that I recall."

"Head wound like that, it's no surprise. You look pale, and that scar looks angry."

"You hailed us."

"Captain says to use the liberty boat dock. No strange vessels inside the hull. Sending the schematic now."

He ran his gaze over the display. Noted the location of the liberty boat dock on the wireframe projection. Overlaid the sensor feed.

"There's a hull already attached."

"Moving it now. Dock will be clear by the time you arrive."

"Anything else?"

"Is that a golden hand?"

"What if it is?"

"Nothing, it's just you don't see one of those every day."

"I do."

"Huh. I guess you might. Captain wants to know how many of you to expect."

"Why?"

"How would I know?"

"You could ask him."

"I could. But I'm not going to. So how many?"

Seamus glanced at the empty first officer's seat. "Three."

"Lash on at the liberty boat dock and prepare to be boarded. *Quadbox* out."

51

Seamus braked the shuttle to rest relative to the big tug's hull, hanging in space a kilometer distant from the liberty boat dock.

The inertial systems registered both hulls as stationary even though the tug's monstrous Templeman drive hustled them through space at far beyond the speed of light. Seamus hadn't given much thought to the multivessel mechanics of Templeman space. The drives on Freeman merchant vessels could barely accommodate a single vessel. He wasn't thinking about Templeman space too much now, either, because the crew on Freeman vessels typically weren't casual mass murderers. The idea that he'd allied himself to one seemed somewhat more important to think about. He couldn't do anything about Templeman space. He could do something about Hector Poole. The question was, did he want to? Or worse, did he *need* to?

At a gut level, absolutely he did. Sane people didn't break necks and pulp a starship's crew. It would be easy to excuse Poole's actions because of Ixatl-Nine-Go's proven ability to turn people into monsters. But that didn't make the people Ixatl-Nine-Go rode any less people, or strip them of their rights as human beings. If it was morally acceptable to do what Hector Poole had done, then it was morally acceptable to murder Seamus right now, because he wasn't any different now than he had been while Ixatl-Nine-Go had ridden him. It might be that some of those people Poole killed today were evil and deserved to die. And it might be that at least one of them was no different than Seamus, in the wrong place at the wrong time, and if not entirely blameless, at least deserving of a fair trial to determine culpability.

At a rational level, there was little doubt Ixatl-Nine-Go meant to use those people to do harm, and now it couldn't. If there existed some other way that three people could have stopped them, Seamus couldn't think of it. If even one of them had made it into an exo, they would have been all doomed. And if Poole hadn't killed the pilots, they could have done to Poole, and Sarah, and him what Poole had done to the rest of the crew. Or worse, do what Poole had described, enslave them to Ixatl-Nine-Go. The element of surprise nearly guaranteed first-attempt success. Seen that way, a swift and permanent solution was the right one, up to and including murder. Killing them all made rational sense in a kill-or-be-killed situation.

But suppose it turned out that only the pilots were Ixatl-Nine-Go's slaves. That the rest of the crew were as innocent and clueless as Seamus had been when he'd walked aboard *Golden Parachute*. Suppose that murdering them in cold blood turned out to be a terrible mistake. Could there be any moral excuse for that? What good would it be to defeat Ixatl-Nine-Go if, in the process, he became the same sort of monster, one that rationalized the vilest acts in the name of some entirely subjective greater good?

Suppose he didn't pull the trigger himself, but went along with it, condoned it, profited by it? How could he judge himself a good man if he did evil, not because he had to, but because doing evil proved expedient?

Poole dropped into the second officer's seat. "Why are we at full stop?"

"Where's Lady Aster?"

"Cleaning up. It's a mess back there." He glanced at Seamus. "You didn't answer me."

"I didn't. Those people. Were they all fitted with Ixatl-Nine-Go implants?"

"Not all of them. Does that bother you?"

"Being party to murder? I'd feel ashamed if it didn't."

"No exemption for self-defense?"

"Not a one of those people attacked us, nor the pilots either."

"And when they did attack us, it would be too late."

"*If* they did attack us."

"Ah. There's the rub. You only have my word that they would. And I'm not a reputable fellow."

"In matters of unprovoked murder? I don't think there is such a thing as a reputable fellow."

"And if I hadn't taken the initiative. And they had attacked?"

"They'd have prevailed."

"Should I have just stood aside and let them murder Lord and Lady Aster's only child?"

"I'm not sure. It's hard to think through."

"Not that hard from where I'm sitting. You imagine it could have been you back there, an ordinary man, with Ixatl-Nine-Go enslaving you, and the only difference between those dead soldiers and you a matter of fortune, and of timing."

"They didn't ask to be enslaved."

"You don't know that. Maybe they were offered a choice, even if you weren't. And in any case it doesn't matter. Ixatl-Nine-Go is an enemy of the League. These people are its foot soldiers. They're fighting for the enemy and it doesn't matter one bit if they're conscripts or volunteers."

"And the people without Ixatl-Nine-Go?"

"One of them, a young woman, first deployment, likely following what she believed were lawful orders from a senior officer."

"And we murdered her."

"And *I* eliminated a threat to the League, and in the process she died. *We* didn't give the unlawful order putting her in harm's way. And a plasma bolt from a useful idiot doesn't feel any different than one from a stone-cold killer."

"It's immoral."

"Immorality is letting harm befall those you're responsible for. We didn't start this war, and no matter what you think, it is a war, and one to the death. I've done a lot of things I lose sleep over. Stopping Ixatl-Nine-Go from using these people to *murder Lady Tabatha's only child* isn't one of them."

"If that was their intent."

"Do you think it was?"

"I do, in part, unless it was as you said, to enslave her, and us along with her."

"Then I fail to see the problem."

"The problem is I might be wrong."

"And I might be wrong as well. But the difference between us is that I'm willing to pay the price of being wrong, and acting."

"It seems like the dead and their kin pay the price either way."

"What's your point?"

"I don't have one. I'm trying to figure it out. We don't have any martial tradition in the Federation. We're not at war with anyone, not even the descendants of the people that enslaved our forebearers. The whole idea of preemptive murder is foreign and vile. As is the idea of murdering bystanders to a dispute. At home that would be a recipe for more murders in retribution, and no end in sight. Finding a match for a wrong requires certainty about the wrong, and about the wrongdoer."

"Certainty is a luxury the League can't afford."

"Why's that?"

"Because we matter. Because what we do matters. Because without us the future *stops*."

"And we don't matter."

"The Freeman Federation? You matter. Just not to the same degree."

"Suppose there came a time that for the League to survive you'd have to destroy the Federation. Murder every one of us, man, woman, and child. Not for something we'd done, but for something we *might* do. Do you suppose such a course of action could in any way be moral?"

"I don't deal in hypotheticals."

"Well, I guess that's another difference between us. Because I think about that sort of situation all the time. What would *I* do if? If our positions were reversed, and the Freeman rulers of the spaceways, and the League a minor force in the wider world. If it came to the point that our interests diverged, and we could no longer tolerate association. If you might threaten *our destiny*. Or not even that. If you might threaten our *chosen future*. Or not even that, but if your continued existence threatened our sense of self, and our belief in our role as *architects of the future*. A future where we are heroes and any that oppose us villains."

"You'd spare us."

"I think we'd say that. And it might look that way, at first. We'd shun you, cut off all trade, and let you fend for yourselves. That's our way. No guns would be fired, no mass graves dug. If you proved as weak as we imagined, we would need only bide our time. You'd dig your own graves, and bury your own kin, and it wouldn't be yourselves that we'd murdered, but your children and your grandchildren."

"And that would be moral."

'It would be the vilest of evil, and as immoral as anything I could imagine, short of gunning down innocents."

Sarah Aster swung into the flight operations seat. "Why are we stopped?"

She looked clean and fresh.

"I'm trying to figure out the course." One he could fly and still face himself in the mirror.

"It's pretty simple. We're a kilometer away from the docking airlock. Just take us in."

He could do that.

And then what?

52

T he League attack shuttle responded instantly to the controls. Seamus moved the vessel forward with minimal thrust. There remained several ideas fighting for his attention, and all of them related to one central point of confusion.

"If this tug is under Ixatl-Nine-Go's control, and *Defiant* crawling with Ixatl-Nine-Go, why send over a crew of Ixatl-Nine-Go thugs? For that matter, why arrange to send anyone at all?"

"Because *Defiant* *isn't* yet under Ixatl-Nine-Go control," Hector Poole said. "And those in command sent a crew to take control of the tug."

"But they sent an Ixatl-Nine-Go crew, less one."

"Volunteers, or chosen by a senior officer under Ixatl-Nine-Go control."

"Why? So they could attempt and fail to gain control of the tug? If that's what you wanted, you'd send a bunch of raw recruits, with an incompetent commander. In addition, doing so removes valuable fighters from the battle for control of *Defiant*. There's something wrong with our assumptions."

"My assumptions, you mean," Poole said.

"We're all working under them. That makes them ours."

"Let's just dock and see," Sarah Aster said.

"They're ordering us to let them on board when we do," Seamus said. "I was for that earlier, but now I'm not sure I want them to view our handiwork."

"My handiwork, you mean."

"I didn't stop you, and likely we all benefited. Suppose our intel is wrong."

"It's a little late to worry about that," Sarah said. "Dock and let's find out."

"And why aren't we being hailed by *Defiant* for missing check-ins, or whatever League subsidiary vessels do as part of maintaining connection with the ship?"

"We're not some merchant's away mission," Sarah said. "League crews are expected to operate independently."

"Up to a point," Poole said. "It's a fair question."

"Can *Defiant* listen in our comms?"

"Assume they can."

"Then they already heard me earlier. And witnessed me on the flight deck. So why aren't they doing anything?"

"Perhaps they are, and we aren't yet aware of their actions."

"Maybe. In that case I'd contrive to nab *Springbok* and Lady Tabatha as insurance. Assuming our base conclusions remain correct and Ixatl-Nine-Go is ascendant but not yet in control."

"Then we should stop dawdling," Sarah said.

That, or get better intel. Seamus scraped the communications console onto the pilot's secondary display. He hailed the tug.

The fiery-eyed comms officer stared back. "What's the holdup?"

"I'm not sure our airlocks will mate up. We might have to rig something temporary, or you could send people over one at a time in hardsuits."

"They're both League military airlocks. They'll mate."

"I'm not so sure. Let me talk to the captain."

"What will that do?"

"What do you mean?"

"How will talking to the captain fix an *airlock compatibility* issue?"

"It won't. But I'd have a better idea of what they wanted us to do, in case the problem can't be fixed."

"There is no problem. Now dock, and prepare to be boarded."

"I'm telling you, I'm not so confident."

"Then go away."

"What?"

"You're the ones wanted to meet. If you can't mate a League assault shuttle's airlock to a League fleet tug's airlock, then you should just go back where you came from."

"I might do that. But I'd need to hear that from the captain's lips."

"Hear what?"

"That you're unwilling to address the problem with the airlocks."

"Wait one." The display blanked.

Seamus waited. He wanted to see the captain. Talk to the captain. If the ship had fallen under Ixatl-Nine-Go's control, then the captain would have as well. And Seamus would be able to tell. Because there was no way that Ixatl-Nine-Go could look back at him without revealing itself. It would want to gloat, and watch the fear build up behind his eyes.

The comm channel resumed, audio only, a woman's voice, one with a Trinity Surface accent. "I don't know what I can do if he's too stupid to follow directions."

The visual display resumed. A young woman stared down at the console in front of her. "What do you mean it's up there? Oh." She glanced upward, squinting into the visual sensor.

"How are you supposed to look at the controls and up here at the same time?"

Seamus laughed. "The video controls are on the display, Janie Byrne."

"Oh. So they are." She twitched away from the screen when its light fell upon her. "Seamus mac Donnacha. I hear you have an impenetrably thick foreign accent. And are an idiot."

"Maybe I do, and maybe I am. And it's just Seamus nowadays, Janie."

"Oh, right. Sorry about your family. What's this business about the airlock?"

"I wanted to talk to the captain."

"Which one?"

"What do you mean?"

"We've a surplus at the moment, and they've yet to work out which captain to trot out for public amusement."

"We're not keen to be boarded given such uncertainty."

"We were under the impression you were strangers. And Leaguemen."

"Two Leaguemen and one Seamus. We were under the impression you were strangers as well."

"Most of us are, though I think you know Aoife nic Cartaí."

"To look at, and a little more."

"What about her man Carlsbad?"

"Him I know better, from the hospital."

"And me, obviously."

"I have your picture over my bunk."

"Like I believe that."

"The pair of us, in formal attire, at the Academy pilots' dance, my sophomore year. Do you not recall the date?"

"I recall it. I'm just surprised you do."

"Best night of my life."

"Now I know you're lying. I'm piloting for nic Cartaí now, can you imagine?"

"I knew it had to be one of the big three, if not your father. No one else could afford the repair bills."

"Very funny."

"Janie, are we in danger if we let anyone on board?"

"I was getting ready to ask you the same thing."

"We're safe on this end, talking only, unless we need to do more, but talking first, and fair warning otherwise."

"Same here, though the timing isn't ideal. They'd have liked you to come back later, after the question of who would speak for the ship had been decided."

"I don't think that would work."

"Then you'd best come aboard. I think if Aoife nic Cartaí wanted to kill you, she'd have done it by now."

"What about this other captain?"

"He doesn't even know you."

"So not one of the mac Kennas."

"Not any of that lot."

"I'll bring her alongside."

"And I'll send a wrench down to look over the airlock, in case there's a problem." Janie sat, grinning into the display.

"What's so funny?"

"I was just thinking. It was Macer Gant supposed to take me to that dance. He'd promised."

"It was me supposed to, regardless of what anyone says, then or now. Tell me you didn't have a good time, even with the last-minute arrangements."

"If I did, I'd be lying."

"We wouldn't want that."

"We wouldn't, unless it was for a good reason." She winked. "*Four-Squared* out."

The display switched off.

Seamus glanced at Hector Poole. "One or more of our assumptions may be wrong."

"Apparently." Poole switched the first officer's display to the close-quarters maneuvering monitor.

"And apparently," Sarah Aster said, "there isn't a single compartment or vessel in the universe without one of Seamus mac Donnacha's girlfriends lurking inside."

"Now that's news a man can use." Seamus blipped the thrusters. "I'll be with you in a moment, darling. Once I park this machine."

"You know what I mean."

"I do, and you ought to just say it."

Lady Sarah Aster snorted. "You really are a fool."

"I am." And he'd made her laugh in the face of danger.

Now for the easy part.

HECTOR POOLE ENTERED the airlock first, followed by Sarah Aster. Seamus took up the rear, standing a respectable distance behind the pair.

"What are you doing back there?" Sarah asked.

"He's standing a servant's proper one step behind and to the right," Poole said. "Haven't you screened a Freeman drama?"

"Why would I?"

"So you'll know what they think of us."

"Why would I care about that?"

Poole chuckled.

"Get up here, where you can be some use to me."

Seamus did as commanded.

She took his golden hand in hers. Her fingers were shaking.

He squeezed. Gently, he hoped.

"Thank you. You can go back there if that's what you want."

"What do you want?"

"I want to go home and curl up with a good book. As I can't do that, I want to appear strong and worthy of respect when I meet these people. I want them to do what I want. And that means they have to see *me*, and listen to *me*, and ignore whatever stories they have about *people like her* running around in their heads."

"I will stay at your side."

"I wish we were ordinary people and free to do as we liked."

"I am free to do as I like."

She let his fingers slip away. "I understand. Then—"

"I will stay at your side."

She had to glance down to look him in the eye.

"Those hull-slippers make you look tall."

"I feel tall."

"That's just your spine talking. Are you ready to do this?"

"No. So let's get it over with. Major Poole?"

"Lady Aster."

"You may commence banging on the hatch."

"Suppose I simply press the call stud instead."

"Fine. If you believe that will work."

PRESSING the hatch control stud didn't open the airlock hatch. An error code blinked on the display.

In maintenance mode. Please wait...

Hector Poole banged on the hatch.

A tiny voice spoke from the control annunciator. "Replacing the over-pressure sensor. Just about done."

"Great," Sarah Aster said.

"Done. Try it now."

Poole pressed the hatch control again.

Nothing happened.

"It's not working," Sarah said.

"Then the problem is on your end," the tinny voice said.

"It can't be." Poole pressed the stud again.

"Check the inner hatch."

"It's closed. We've matched pressure with you."

"What's the delta across the lock?"

Seamus stepped forward and studied the display. Freeman longboats had paired fore and aft locks for rapid loading and unloading on a ring, where one lock was used for bringing things in, or ingress, and one for carrying things out, or egress. There was a failure mode where one lock would block the other from opening if there was too much of an imbalance of pressure on either active lock. The locks were holes in pressure vessels, imperfectly made holes with seals on the inner and outer hatches, and the inner seals under-rated relative to the outer seals. The assumption was that the pressure outside the lock would be equal to or lower than the pressure inside the hull, and if not, something had gone seriously wrong. One ought not open the outer hatch to a significantly higher pressure than that inside the hull. The procedure for locking in and out of free space, or a holed and depressurized vessel, was entirely different than the procedure for matching pressures between vessels.

Of course, if there had been hard vacuum inside the hull, they would have already been dead. And unlike a longboat, this vessel had interior pressure bulkheads, with intervening hatches. He wasn't even certain it had more than one exterior hatch. It had to, though, because this airlock wasn't large enough to bring bulk cargo aboard. There was a pressure hatch between the command deck and the rest of the ship, and it was closed last he looked, and only this hatch on the command deck.

He noted the pressure differential across the outer hatch. It wasn't large enough to worry about.

"It was zero a minute ago," Poole said.

Seamus took two steps across the lock and checked the inner-hatch pressure differential.

"That's bad." Sometime after they entered the airlock, the command deck had been opened to space. "We're stuck."

Sarah Aster glared at him. "What do you mean, stuck?"

Seamus fished a rebreather from his pocket. "Is it skin or skinsuit under all that fancy cloth?"

She brandished a rebreather. "What do you think?"

He glanced at Hector Poole, who gripped his own rebreather lightly.

Seamus pressed the communications stud. "Delta's bad across the inside lock. Can you drop the pressure in your compartment?"

"Sure. How low?"

"Low as it can go."

"That will take time. First I'll have to clear the compartment. There's a throng here to meet you."

"There's a slow leak past the inside seals."

"Roger that."

"What's the downforce?"

"One point nine."

"Repeat that."

"We're running one point nine gravities inside the hull."

"What for?"

"Because we like it."

Oh. We'll be on rebreathers, in skinsuits."

"I can slack off the load in the compartment. How low would you like it?"

"Low as it will go."

"Give me a few. This will take a little arranging. Stand by."

Seamus crossed the lock again and studied the inner-hull-to-airlock delta display. It could be a sensor malfunction. Or they could have been holed. Or someone left an exterior lock open and opened the lock between the command deck and the rest of the hull. Of those three possibilities, the most likely was a sensor malfunction. Not something he'd expect to see on an immaculately maintained League vessel, but then maybe the League wasn't as on top of things as he'd imagined. Maybe they had the same problems everyone else had: a shortage of capital for parts and worse, a shortage of qualified people to install and maintain them. The engineer on the other side of the airlock didn't seem the sharpest tool in the drawer, or on top of regular maintenance. Who waits until there's an incoming hull to work on the airlock? And you'd think with all the money the League put into their kit, they'd be able to make a fixed-wire intercom that didn't make everyone sound like asthmatic helium huffers.

The pressure delta dropped as he watched. They were definitely leaking past the inner seals. So it wasn't a single sensor malfunction.

"We could dial the pressure down in here, and go back into the ship and seal whatever's causing the problem." Seamus didn't like that idea, since if they couldn't seal whatever was leaking, they'd be crawling into hardsuits for however long it took these people to scrape their rubbish into a pile. "If things go bad here, we'll want our getaway ride in order."

"They won't go *badly*," Sarah said.

"I was only kidding about airlock problems," Seamus said. "If it can go badly, it will."

"Let's do it," Poole said. "I agree, we need a functioning escape vessel."

"Once we're on their ship, they'll lock us in," Sarah said. "The only way we'd get back on board our own vessel is with their permission, or by stealing hardsuits and going in the hard way. Let's try it the easy way first, and see what happens."

"Let's not." Poole touched the airlock controls. The atmosphere began to bleed off. "Rebreathers in."

That's one way to put an end to any argument. Of course it also meant that the annunciator and its tinny speaker no longer worked. The display panel did work, though, and it blinked red, then green.

Pressure normalized.

Seamus glanced behind him.

The interior airlock hatch panel also glowed green.

Pressure normalized.

"Wait," Seamus mouthed around his rebreather, but without atmosphere to carry his words, he was only wasting his breath.

Poole touched the inner-airlock open stud.

Seamus pinned Sarah Aster to the airlock bulkhead.

Both hatches opened at once.

And something huge and armored brushed Poole aside and pounded loose onto the big tug.

53

Seamus tapped Sarah Aster and slapped his palm against the bulkhead, the spacer's gesture for *stay here*. Freeman spacer, he reminded himself. They might use a different gesture in the League.

New Seamus slowed to offer Poole a hand, but Old Seamus stepped over the bleeding man's legs, pausing long enough to kick the man's rebreather into arm's reach if he yet retained consciousness.

Someone had used him and made him into a liar, and it didn't matter who. And not just a lie, but one to Janie Byrne, who trusted him, even though she knew him. He'd said there were only three of them on board, and there'd be no shooting, just talking. The big League exo stood in front of him, weapon at the ready, glancing around the compartment.

It was an expansive compartment, one with seating for well over a hundred, standing space for as many straphangers, with short ladders and hatches at either end. Seamus kept waiting for the rest of the League crew to come pouring out from behind him. The compartment looked empty at first, then he saw them, a crowd of people, in the farthest corner of the space, and the engineer, on his hands and knees beside the airlock, a scalp wound that looked bad. His toolbelt had scattered junk across the deck, and his handheld lay by his knee.

The engineer's fingers found the handheld, thumbed it active, and he glanced up and their gazes met.

Seamus's lips moved silently, his fingers flashing in Freeman handspeak. *Macer? What are you doing here?*

Macer Gant blinked and signed back. *Live work here both go stand back.*

The League exo turned toward them.

Macer brushed his left wrist, the fingernails of his right hand silently flicking away from his wrist in a curve. *You need to jet.* Macer's finger stabbed the handheld and Seamus did jet, away from the airlock as the overhead began to empty fast patch onto the deck, and the docking clamps released, and the assault shuttle and the big tug began to lose connection.

Macer disappeared beneath the fast patch that buried the exo up to its waist. The stuff was bad news for hull breaches—lightweight and self-attracting, drawn to low pressure like iron to a magnet. The hatch stood open but the compartment was pressure-normalized with the open hatch. Macer must have had time to engage the air handlers before he was buried in the stuff, because the fast patch began to move toward the hatch, accelerating, hardening, an exothermic reaction that would heat the exo and felt like being roasted alive on bare skin.

The League exo took a step forward and swung its weapon toward him, and past, and opened up with a sustained burst of plasma rifle fire in the direction of the crowd that scattered as the rain of weapons fire poured in. It was unreal, no stink of preheater oil, no hissing roar from the spouting barrel, just silent death spewing into the distant crowd as whatever lived inside that machine held the trigger down and aimed, not like a marksman, but like a fireman with a hose.

Seamus scanned the compartment for someplace to hide, for a weapon, for anything. Engineer's tools littered the deck.

Oh. A gravity hammer.

Macer burst out of the fast patch, silently screaming.

The exo ceased fire and turned toward him.

Seamus snatched up the gravity hammer.

And leapt.

54

He landed on the back of the exo, nearly dropping the hammer as he looped an arm around its neck, fumbled for the power switch one-handed, and felt the hammer burst to life. He thumbed the stroke and impact to full, brought the business end onto the exo's helmet, and it pounded a dozen strokes—ten, twelve, maybe twenty standard gravities at the far end of the isolation handle that damped the vibration—but didn't stop it, and the big man-machine shrugged its shoulders. Seamus dropped the hammer, which kept on hammering, and gripped the exo around the neck, feeling for a catch for the helmet, there had to be one, they put the helmets on and took them off, but it wasn't where it would be for a hardsuit, and it wasn't anywhere obvious he could feel, and then the exo yanked a leg free from the fast patch.

The plasma rifle roared, gouging a furrow in the deck, and a fiery-eyed woman skidded out of the way at the last instant, scooped something up, and tossed it, hard and underhand, not to Seamus, but to a crazy-haired man who caught it one-handed, and rocketed it on, directly at Seamus's face.

Seamus snatched it an instant before it could break his nose, pulled it far enough away from his eyeballs that he could see it, and felt the grin spread across his face as he thumbed the monomolecular drill alive. He had no idea what size hole it was set for, but it didn't matter. The device twirled a monomolecular whip in an oscillating and rotating fashion, drilling through whatever was in front of it up to and including hull plate. The thing was made for hogging out pinholes until they were large enough to weld. When he pressed it to the helmet, it made a satisfying whine, which meant he could spit his rebreather out, there was atmosphere. He bore down on the drill with both hands and all his might—they were practically indestructible—and then the whine changed, dust puffed from around the hole, and he was through, *now what*, as an armored fist engulfed his forearm, snapped it, and flung him off the exo's back. He was arcing through the air in front of it, and it was bringing its plasma rifle to bear, and he was looking down the muzzle, and he slammed into the deck and didn't bounce. Plasma fire seared overhead, the roasting smell flooding his nostrils, the scream of superheated atmosphere being torn apart, the wave of blistering heat centimeters from his flesh.

It felt like a longboat had landed on his back. His nose was broken and blood spreading in a pool over the deck, and he wanted to lift his face out of the gore but settled for rolling over on his cheek so he could look at something besides the deck plates.

They were all down, the woman, the man, Macer. Even the exo was on its knees and trying to stand. He couldn't see the distant crowd but could hear them, shouting, weeping, cursing.

A massive hullwalker blocked his view as a big man dropped to his knees beside Seamus. He looked like a convict, shaved headed, and Seamus chuckled; *I feel like a convict*, one who'd been cut from the gallows with a single breath left in him, and now the ship itself trying to crush the last bit of life out of him.

The big convict-man palmed a can of pinhole seal. "You see that little tube that goes with this anywhere?"

Seamus managed to move a finger. He pointed. It was a rubbish design, the tubes were constantly getting separated and lost, even though they were bright red and longer than an outstretched hand from wrist to fingertip.

"Thanks."

And then the man was on his feet in what had to be four gravities, maybe more, and he lumbered toward the exo as it tried to bring its weapon to bear, and he climbed on the fast patch behind it, gripping its neck in one massive hand, jamming the pinhole-seal tube in the hole Seamus had drilled in the exo helmet with the other, then he held the trigger down and didn't stop holding it until the can pumped propellant through the nozzle, and the exo stopped rattling and twitching, trapped halfway in and out of a frozen sea of fast patch.

The man crashed to the deck beside Macer, reached for Macer's handheld, and dialed the gravity back to something merely unbearable.

They were all up, towering over Seamus, and the fiery-eyed woman stared down at him and said, "Nice catch." She held out her hand, and he took it an instant before he remembered he had a broken arm.

"Nice war cry," the crazy-haired man said. "A little piercing and late in the action, but decently loud."

Someone cried out in pain in the distance, and a young boy shouted "Yi-sheng"—*medic*—and then a chorus of cries in Huangxu and the lash of a Freeman merchant's tongue overriding the shouts. It sounded like he was on the spindle, but it felt like he was on the ring, the crush of gravity pinning him to the deckplates. He might be able to stand. He just wasn't sure if the effort was worth it.

"Get him into an autodoc." The big man kicked Macer. "You too."

Seamus tried to stand. "My friends—"

"I won't eat them until you're there to watch."

55

Seamus stood. His arm had begun to ache in earnest. He glanced at Macer. What skin he could see on his friend looked red and swollen. In an hour or less it would start to blister. Anyone who'd had fast patch on their bare skin wouldn't want it on them twice.

A Huangxu boy shouted for a medic again. Seamus started walking toward the noise, and the remnant of the crowd at the far end of the compartment. There were people up and moving and a fair number of them down. The open space of the liberty boat bay hadn't provided much cover other than the bolted-in five-seaters that were standard issue in League public areas, the sort of low-backed benches that offered a little cover for a little while, but only then if they were situated perpendicular to the line of fire, and these weren't. There wasn't as much blood as after a knife fight or a shootout with slug-throwers, but there was more carnage and that roasted-meat odor that some people couldn't stomach. Maybe if he hadn't been raised on tubed paste and juice bulbs he'd find it disturbing as well.

There were a bunch of League kids in identical shipboard utilities, and they were shouting at one another in Huangxu,

not spindle-pidgin, but Hundred Planets dialect, all shouted
with the sort of precise diction that wouldn't seem out of place
in the Celestial Palace.

"Who is in charge?" Seamus couldn't tell by looking at
them. All seemed chaos, a half dozen of them dead or dying,
nearly every one of them wounded. He estimated there was a
score of them, or slightly more.

"Little Brother," one of them said, and pointed to one of the
wounded that looked like they might live.

"I'm in charge now," Seamus said. "Who here can run?"

"I can," one said.

"And who knows where the infirmary is?"

"We all do."

"Then find two more who can run and race each other to
the infirmary. If there is a fast-pallet, load it with all the large
emergency med packs you can find in five minutes of looking. If
there remains room on the fast-pallet, fill it with the medium
med packs and return here. If there is no fast-pallet, don't waste
time looking. Fill your arms with as many large med packs as
you can safely carry and run back here. You must be swift. You
must be sure. You must go now. Do you understand?"

"We do, Merchant Lord."

"I'm no merchant, and I'm no lord. Now go, and outrace the
light."

He dropped to his knees beside the one called Little
Brother. He looked sixteen years old, standard, no older. There
was a wicked plasma burn across his chest, the sort of glancing
blow that meant it had barely missed, else he'd be roasted in
half and nothing to be done about it. He winced and muttered
beneath his breath. Seamus grabbed the boy's wrist and
checked his pulse. It was strong but elevated. "You'll live."

He stood and worked his way to the next, and didn't need to
kneel or check the boy's pulse. "You won't," he muttered, and
continued along the line. What happened downrange of a

League exo looked a lot like the aftermath of gunplay on the spindle, the sort of territorial or honor fights that occurred between rival familial units. There were usually casualties, and often multiples, but nothing approaching one hundred percent wounded or killed. He glanced toward the airlock and the League exo mired in fast patch in front of it. There'd been a straight shot but enough cover that more of them should have been able to avoid fire. They were small and nimble. And whoever was in the exo hadn't been aiming. They'd been spraying and praying.

And looking for something. *Or someone.*

One of the kids groaned. Seamus checked him out. "Med packs are coming."

"Good. The merchant lord requires more."

"I'm not a merchant. And I'm not a lord." .

"One can see this." The boy rolled onto his side, spit blood, and peered toward the rear bulkhead. "But she is."

He glanced into the distance, where Aoife nic Cartaí sat between a pair of plasma-scarred rows of five-seaters, propped up against the compartment bulkhead and staring into the distance.

"You're her bodyguards." That explained the high casualty rate.

"The Invincible Spear Bearers of Imperial Wrath," the boy said.

"You don't look so invincible."

"Compared to our foes we do."

"You aren't children."

"Who can afford to be?" He coughed. "The pilot. She needs a medic."

"Where is she?"

The boy pointed. "Beyond those seats."

He found her where she'd fallen. Both her legs had been sheared off below the knee, and someone had slapped med packs on her to keep her from bleeding out, but from the looks of her they'd been too late. Seamus dropped to his knees beside her and ran his fingers through her hair.

Oh, Janie Byrne, what have I done to you?

He took her hand in his.

He glanced at the deckhead, slid his fingers to her wrist, and felt for her pulse.

No joy.

Someone shouted. "Seamus!"

Someone shouted again.

Not someone. *Macer Gant.*

"Over here!"

"Oh," Macer said, when he saw Janie.

"She's gone."

"How do you know that?"

"No pulse."

"How do you know that?"

"I felt for it."

"That's a fine metal hand, Seamus. But are you sure it's up to the task?"

He glanced at his fingers, and her wrist. "I—"

"Move off, and let me check."

Macer elbowed him aside, and pressed his ear to her lips. "She's not done yet." He scooped Janie up in his arms. "Get her legs."

"I can get one. My arm's broken."

"Pile one on top of her, then, and carry the other."

"I don't think an autodoc can fix that."

"It'll keep her alive."

"But she's a pilot." *She won't want to live.*

"She's meat, if we don't hurry up. We don't have a doctor to fix her. Now get a move on."

"There's a doctor on *Springbok.*"

"The League gunship that sent this murderer over?"

"The courier vessel."

"Well, let's get her in an autodoc. We can call your courier doctor once Janie's stable."

"Is there a portable autodoc? One we could move onto the assault shuttle?"

"There isn't. Now let's go."

The boys were back with a fast-pallet full of med packs and were distributing them efficiently.

"You know if you turned the gravity down, it would help people heal," Seamus said.

"It is turned down to just under a standard gravity."

"Oh. That's fine then. What's all that rubbish slathered on you?" Every visible bit of skin on Macer Gant seemed coated in viscous, shiny phlegm.

"Burn ointment. It's supposed to be good for three hours."

"Then what?"

"Then it's no good anymore."

"Got it."

"I'd forgotten how fast and agile you were in null gee." Macer climbed the ladder to the deck above.

"I like it light. That's why I spent so much time on the spindle."

"You spent so much time on the spindle because you identify with the underdog. And because you like a fight. Two hatches up, the infirmary."

The autodocs were all occupied.

Macer rested Janie on an examination table. "Are they all set to stabilize and eject?"

Seamus checked. "All of them."

"Who are we ejecting?"

"Macer—"

"You know we're going to. It's just a matter of deciding."

"Then you do it."

"Which is closest to done?"

"How can you tell?"

"There's a timer."

"I don't see a timer."

"Oh." Macer picked Janie up. "I just thought of something. Follow me."

"There's a fast-pallet."

"Like I'm pushing Janie around like cargo. If she dies, she dies in a man's arms. Now get her legs and come on."

56

S eamus jammed his broken arm into the hardsuit's gauntlet. He gazed across the big tug's boat bay where a gleaming longboat crouched beside the shuttered force window. There was an autodoc on board, a nice one, according to Macer, and he seemed well satisfied after he'd settled every part of Janie Byrne inside and set it to maximum heal, or whatever the top setting was called. Seamus's experience with autodocs was entirely of the end-user variety. And while he'd logged more hours than most inside one, he'd looked at the control panels exactly twice in his life, and both of those times today. Knowing how to set one up was a job for a professional, and once inside the user had no control over the device in any case. If you didn't trust your autodoc operator, there was no point in getting inside one.

Hardsuits were different. There the only person you needed to trust was yourself.

Macer peeled out of his utilities. "I never set a broken arm before. I thought it would be harder than that."

"You pulled on my arm until I blacked out."

"And a fair bit longer. But it's straightforward. You can feel the bone move back into alignment."

Seamus slid the other gauntlet on and latched it. "I'm glad only one of us could."

"Can you move your fingers?"

He could. Painfully, but they worked. And the hardsuit helped. "Can you move your arse?"

"Some of us can't just jump into one of these things. We have to ease into it."

"You're greased up enough for the job."

"I am, and if this takes more than three hours? You can pry me out, and spritz me with more burn ointment until the screaming stops."

Seamus yanked a helmet from the flight-crew ready rack. He examined it. "This is almost clean."

"Thank you." Macer squeezed his legs into the hardsuit. "I try."

"Try faster."

"Funny. Do you think this doctor will really help us?"

"I know she will. All we need do is get Janie to her while she's still breathing." Macer grabbed a helmet off the rack. "Let's go."

"Aren't you going to inspect that?"

"I did when I racked it this morning." He looked it over while they waited for the ready-room airlock to cycle.

"You racked that helmet and forgot about an entire long-boat with an autodoc on board."

"It's been a stressful day. And I'm not used to the idea of having one."

"The longboat."

"I only stole it a little while ago."

"But you checked the autodoc out."

"Did I ever." Macer touched the hatch control. "Less talking. More flying."

Seamus slid into the pilot's seat. "It's a good thing it's my contract-holding arm that's broken, and not the yoke grabbing one."

Macer dropped into the first officer's seat. "I'm not reading you."

"Lorelei told me that's how us long-haul pilots roll. A contract in one hand and the yoke in the other."

"How are you supposed to do that without spilling your drink?"

"The lass perched on your lap holds the beverage. Did you learn nothing in the Academy?"

"I learned that on the long-hauls lass and sister are considered synonyms."

"That's not even close to true."

"Not if there's a goat on board, you mean."

"Go preflight the hull."

"Like I'm leaving you alone inside here to jet. And if I found a problem and it looked likely to kill us would it stop you?"

"I'd jet anyway."

"While I was outside, staring up at the hull. So fire it up and let's roll. Pretend we're a team."

Seamus ran the thrusters through the preflight tests. He glanced at his friend, who'd left the cockpit door open so he could keep an eye on the autodoc telltales. "What did you do to the first officer's controls?"

"Turned them into a brake pedal."

"Well, don't touch them, then."

"Wouldn't dream of it."

"You make any other modifications?"

"Not me. But the mac Kennas put in a few."

"Such as?"

"There's a 'fly straight' control."

Seamus chuckled. "On a Freeman longboat? I didn't know we were allowed to do that."

"I laughed too. But I think it's there so the pilot can come back into the cabin and muck up the passengers."

"That would be a surprise to the passengers."

"I imagine that's the idea."

"What else?"

"I'm not sure what all else. Other than the plasma cannon."

"A wee plasma cannon, of course. For a wee warship."

"You'd think that, except you'd be wrong. There's a button."

"I see it."

"Don't push it."

"Open the blast shutters and the force window and maybe I won't."

"I'm working on it."

Seamus glanced into the passenger cabin. The autodoc tell-tales were burning green. "What's in the backpack?" Macer had belted the bulky object in on the portside crash couch.

"Insurance. Just in case."

"Just in case Lady Tabatha Aster doesn't want to help us."

"Is that the doctor's name?"

"It is."

"In case of that." The blast shutters began to retract. "And in case of anything else that gets in our way."

57

O nce clear of the hull, Macer pulled a silver box from his pocket and pressed its single button.

"Seriously?" Seamus lay in a course for the *Springbok*. Fastest path, full burn.

"You did bring a murderer onto my ship. You're a better pilot but if you're now against me and in league with the League I'd rather drive. I figure they'd give you an implant if you were."

"We thought you were the mac Kennas. And I swear, I didn't know that gunman was on board. I thought we'd killed them all."

"You missed one, so I'm guessing you're using the family-ship we. What you really mean is you thought *they* killed them all, but as you were in the hull, it's hang together."

"I should have checked."

"You should have, unless you trusted them."

"I trusted half of them."

"The pretty one. We've had this talk, Seamus."

"We have."

"It could have been worse. I've never seen a man move so

fast. One second I'm buried under a pile of fast patch and then the next I'm up. And by then you're on the back of that League man-machine and wailing on it with my gravity hammer."

"I was angry." Hector Poole and possibly Lady Sarah Aster had turned him into a liar. And now there was this business with Janie. And it was all his fault. He'd thought they were on the same side.

Macer fished out another silver box and shoved it in Seamus's face.

"What's that supposed to do?"

"It vibrates like crazy if there's a rider inside you and it's agitated."

"What if it's not agitated?"

"I don't know. I assume it does what it's doing now."

"Nothing."

"Nothing *I* can perceive. It might be doing all sorts of things I don't know about."

"Like what?"

"Logging its location and state. Hacking into our comms system. Transmitting that information back to its maker."

"We're inside a Templeman bubble."

"Then trying to transmit and failing. And waiting. And trying again."

"Those are some pretty specific unobservable behaviors."

"I know who made it."

"You can leave it there beside the comms display. If I'm being ridden, I'd like to know it."

"I'd guess if anyone knew if they were, it would be you."

"That's so. And it's not an excuse for anything I've done. Much as I wish it were."

"How are we going to play this?"

"What do you mean?"

"To get the doctor to help us."

"We're going to lock up to the hull, and go in, and ask her to help us."

"And she'll do it, just like that."

"I think she will. They're not all rotters, Macer."

"They don't need to be. They just need interests in conflict with our own."

"And we'll know that soon enough. I'm going to align the maneuvering thrusters with the hull axis and push them into overload."

"You'll run out of reaction mass first."

"Unlikely."

"Care to wager?"

"There's nothing you have I want."

"Whoever's right gets the first dance with Janie Byrne."

"I'm pretty sure that's up to her."

"It is. And when she asks me I'll say no. Go try Seamus, I'll say, he's—"

Seamus flicked the thrusters to maximum. The inertial dampers were sized for the main drive. For the second time in one day it felt like a longboat had landed on him. He managed to swivel his head to the right far enough to look Macer in the eye. "Brace, brace, brace."

Macer laughed. "Is that all you got?"

His fingers walked methodically through the piloting displays, disabling safety protocols.

There. "On three."

"Drive it like I stole it."

"Three."

Seamus must have blacked out.

He blinked and rebooted. Checked their vector. Checked the reaction-mass tanks. Checked the thruster temperature sensors. "They overheated."

"Give them a minute," Macer said. "Then hit them again."

"I hope this brake of yours works."

"What do you mean?"

"The brake you rigged to the first officer's controls."

"That won't slow us down in free space. It only works if we're skidding along the surface of something much more massive than us."

"Skidding."

"Metaphorically speaking. Skimming within a meter or ten would be ideal."

"Which is it? One or ten?"

"Either one. The closer you get the faster we stop."

"Brilliant. How long will it take to stop at ten meters?"

"At this rate?" Macer glanced at the piloting display. "Five kilometers. Maybe a little more."

"And at one meter?"

"No more than half that."

"I've got a better idea."

"I certainly hope so."

Seamus glanced at Macer. "You're enjoying this."

"You're an entertaining fellow. I don't know why we don't hang out together more."

"Because I'm not insane, that's why."

"I don't think that's it." Macer loaded an engineering diagnostic display on the first officer's console. "Thrusters are cool enough to light. We can save them for docking, or we can—"

"Brace, brace, brace."

Seamus must have blacked out again. He shook his head and glanced at the piloting display.

"She's dry," Macer said.

He meant the maneuvering thrusters were out of reaction mass. They'd overheated three times and had to be restarted. But the procedure worked. They were closing the distance between *Springbok* and *Tractor Four-Squared* far more rapidly than under main thrust alone. Longboats were built for lift, not acceleration. They were still accelerating, though, with the main drive lit and bouncing off the temperature limit as he rode gain on the thrust regulator. It didn't matter how fast they got there if they got there dead. He scraped through the layers of piloting screens and turned the safety limiters back on, one by one.

He glanced at Macer. "Check the load."

"On it." Macer unbelted and headed aft.

Seamus adjusted their heading as the safety systems powered down the main drive.

Janie Byrne had thought he was lying when he'd said that sophomore dance had been the best night of his life. Macer had forgotten about his commitment to his planetary neighbor and paid Seamus to fill in for him. He'd figured Janie Byrne would be a frump, and at first glance she'd appeared to be, all browns, and greens, and heathers, in what he'd taken to be her traveling clothes, but which turned out to be the best she'd owned, and what she intended to wear to the dance. Something needed to be done. He had Macer's cash payoff for the job and a small line of credit for consumables. Chances were he wouldn't need to touch his own savings.

He didn't know what sort of outfit would be appropriate for a planetary daughter's station-side debut, but he knew who might—not know per se, but know who would know. So he dragged her to the shadier end of the ring, to Macer's tailor, Mr. Pearse, whom he'd only known about by reputation. And the old man said something about who had the egg, the snake or the hen, the sort of indecipherable backcountry blather that he'd never understood, but she did, and she said she thought Seamus seemed more rooster than snake, and Pearse said if so then that was a new thing, because he issued forth from a nest of snakes.

Seamus looked at the tailor, and his gaze narrowed, and the old man stared back at him and Janie said I think he has the egg, by which she meant the ability to pay, come to find out. Pearse looked him up and down and said there was nothing to be done. He could fit a suit to a snake or to a rooster or even a peacock, but he'd chosen to specialize in dressing men. You might try the High Street, by which he meant the upscale part of the arcade nearest the stationmaster's offices and the banks.

I don't want something upscale, Seamus told him. He wanted something appropriate. Appropriate for what, the old man said, and Seamus told him not what, but whom. Something appropriate for someone *respectable.* And the old man laughed in his face and said, "You couldn't pull it off."

And Janie Byrne said, *I don't think he's looking for a suit of clothes, but asking for directions to a modiste.* And the old man said is that right, and Seamus said it was, and the old man handed him a printed card, one with a name and address on it. And he shooed them out the door, and Seamus took Janie to the address, and the ladies there dressed her appropriately, and he took her to Bloom's and bought her flowers, and he took her to the dance, and they had a fine time.

She was a terrible and enthusiastic dancer, an entirely ordinary girl with absolutely no guile and no throttle, the sort of woman every man needed to meet once in their life.

He couldn't bear to have her wake up beside him and discover he was clay, so he escorted her to the Guild Hall, and kissed her goodnight, and left her at the threshold.

He walked the arcade, window-shopping in the third-shift gloom, and now and then a snake would stare back at him from the window glazing, and now and then a rooster, but more often than not, it was a boy that watched him. A son. An heir. A mac Donnacha. It felt as if he'd been born inside a mask, not one of iron, but of flesh, and no hope of escape. And when she'd looked into his eyes, and he saw the hope there, and the trust, the blind, stupid, ignorant trust, he'd realized the truth.

That mask was an illusion, and always had been. A prison constructed entirely of false expectations. Not simply the expectations of others, but of his own.

When they kissed, and parted, their fingers lingering, she'd smiled, and said the strangest thing to him. Strange, because it was entirely inappropriate to the moment, and stranger still because it was exactly what he'd been thinking.

I die free.

She watched his eyes, and laughed when he'd asked if she was staying on the station, and would he see her again. And once more her words had surprised him, though not because they agreed with his thinking, but rather, because they confirmed something he felt and hadn't examined yet. A hope. A fear. Possibly both.

We can't very well unsee each other now, can we?

Macer Gant swung into the first officer's seat. "The autodoc says she'll live."

Seamus nodded and adjusted their course. "That's not good enough."

58

Perhaps the most disturbing aspect of Templeman space was the utter lack of light.

Seamus hadn't thought about it much, because it was just one of those things about Templeman space that *was*, like the stomach-clenching nausea upon entering and exiting a Templeman bubble, and the conservation of momentum that defined the constraints of superluminal navigation. It had never occurred to him that it was possible to *move about* inside a Templeman bubble.

A Freeman merchant vessel couldn't generate a bubble large enough to move about in. He wondered if all the gyrating they'd been doing would influence *Tractor Four-Squared*'s exit vector.

The League came up with a lot of bright ideas and the occasional crater-generating one, which they quickly discarded and pretended had never happened. Since there wasn't any piloting lore regarding ship handling in Templeman space, he figured this was one of those big mistakes, and it was better than fifty percent likely they were already dead, and all this scurrying about the sort of thing conscientious people did when faced with impossible choices. He was intent on seeing Janie Byrne whole and dancing because the idea was all consuming, and distracted him from thinking about the consequences of shifting masses about while in Templeman space. What effect would that have on where they ended up exiting, and how fast or slow they exited, and on what vector? Would they drop out of Templeman inside a sun? Or in a void between stars? Or a meter from a station? Or even a hundred meters, on a collision course, plunging along at a hundred meters a second, or more.

He decided it was beyond his ability to figure out. It was the sort of problem that Ciarán could solve with a math assist from Macer. Which seemed strange, because it wasn't the sort of problem Macer could work out on his own, any more than Seamus could, or Ciarán.

What Seamus and Macer could both do, that Ciarán couldn't do, was fly a longboat blindfolded, in a restraining net, upside down and underwater. Seamus wondered how long it would take Macer to figure out what Seamus had in mind. By now, in normal space, *Springbok* would be a dim spark on the visual display.

Macer mirrored the piloting display to the first officer's console. "Does that ship have active countermeasures?"

"It's a fast courier. It barely has a hull." If it wasn't set up as a diplomatic vessel it could probably do without that. As it was, he didn't think anyone sane would want to ride inside a vessel shielded by a containment field alone, but the idea had occurred to him, and it didn't seem as crazy as building a vessel that could throw up a Templeman bubble big enough to steal a moon. So chances are somebody in the League was already working on it, or had tried it already, and figured out it didn't work.

"Were you planning on punching through this nonexistent hull?"

"We could." Longboats were generally rubbish, but they

were inevitably stout. And this one had a plasma cannon. "Go lash everything down."

"Is that an order?"

"It's advice." He had the impression Macer doted on whatever he had in that knapsack.

"Lash it down how tight?"

"Tight. Turnover in ninety seconds."

Macer unbelted. "Turnover?"

"It's doable." In theory.

"It's a longboat. One I stole and never checked out."

"Sixty seconds. Belt in back there."

Macer slammed his bulk into the first officer's seat. "Like hell."

"How did you think I'd slow us?"

"I figured you'd lay alongside and gently match velocity in a series of passes with my brake."

"Good idea. If I stroke out you can do that. Now—"

"What's the burn?"

"One hundred and twenty-three seconds."

"At?"

"Nine gravities."

"Four gravities just about killed you."

"I wasn't mentally prepared."

"Oh, well that's different."

"You could have done the preflight."

"And you leave me behind, you mean."

That's what he meant. There were three people in the world he cared about. And two of them were in this hull with him.

"In ten."

That was a lie. There were more people he cared about now. And he hadn't even said goodbye.

Macer said, "Fire the plasma cannon."

"What?"

"I'm dying to see if it really works."

"Eight."

"Just do it, Seamus."

"Five."

"Seamus."

"Three."

"I'm glad to see you're over your death wish."

Seamus chuckled.

"I don't like the sound of that."

"Zero."

SEAMUS HAD VOMITED into his hardsuit's helmet. He wrenched the thing off and tossed it into the passenger compartment.

Macer Gant's droll voice flooded the compartment. "I think we tore off their short-range antenna."

Seamus blinked, and shoved the blackness from in front of his eyes. "That was the idea."

"You could have said."

Seamus glanced at the piloting display. "Brace, brace, brace."

He flipped the longboat on its axis a second time, an entirely reckless and counter-indicated bit of flying that would see him struck off in four polities of the wider world, and they could kiss his—

Macer Gant roared in the tiny space of the longboat's piloting deck. "How are we now parallel to the hull?"

"It's a miracle." The sort of miracle that only occurred if you sheared off the destination vessel's short-range antenna with the main drive at maximum port deflection. There were a dozen more niggling details that had to go right for a miracle to occur, but if he listed them Macer's eyes would glaze over before he got to item four on the list. Ixatl-Nine-Go had broken most of him, and even before he was broken he wasn't much good for anything useful, except piloting a longboat.

There he was, and remained, a god.

He blipped the main drive three short bursts and cut it off.

They'd missed the *Springbok*'s starboard airlock by thirty meters, forward. But if he stood in the longboat's airlock, he could reach out and brush his fingertips along *Springbok*'s hull.

Seamus stretched a finger toward the plasma cannon's control stud. A Freeman longboat with a functioning plasma cannon would be *awesome*. Like having a bow thruster. He didn't see any way to aim the yoke, so he guessed it fired along the hull's centerline. *There's one way to find out.*

"Check it." Macer had his big mitts all over the first officer's piloting yoke. He pulled the yoke toward him and the vessel moved.

Astern.

"It's not really a brake. It just acts like one while making headway. I reconfigured the landing bands and—"

"That's grand." Seamus moved his fingers away from the plasma cannon's firing stud.

"It's more than that." Macer beamed. "It's a miracle of engineering invention."

"You should write that down," Seamus said, as the airlocks mated up. "Wait here, Master of Invention."

59

Contract System, Outer Reach (Huangxu Contested Space)

Ciarán swayed on his feet and Wisp growled as the Leprous and Sons' *Impossible Bargains* dumped velocity at its maximum rate. They'd dropped into Contract system nearly on top of a Huangxu breakbulk hauler and were doing their best to avoid a collision.

"They appear to have noticed our presence." Old repeated the captain's annotations of the piloting display to the main bridge display. The vector trace of *Impossible Bargains'* projected trajectory appeared limned in crimson.

The bridge layout of the Huangxu mercenary vessel resembled that of a standard Freeman family ship. Ciarán stood perfectly positioned to view the display and the chaos it rendered in appalling detail. They would miss the breakbulk hauler now that it had begun to move under thrusters, but it would be a close call, and *Impossible Bargains* would blister any paint on the vessel's stern quarter as she continued to brake with the main drive turned over and in full reverse.

"We are being hailed," Mr. Younger said.

Ciarán scanned the display. *I bet we are.* Contract system was supposed to be deserted. Instead it swam with vessels, twelve of them at least, the system plot awash with low-velocity orbits in green and their own red arrow an angry slash intercepting at least half of those vessels' paths.

"We are being hailed by *an anomaly*, Captain."

Old adjusted the display so that it showed not one of the hulls they might strike, but the system's small station, a ring with no spindle, and a single vessel nose-in to the ring.

"Specifics."

"Tagged, Captain."

Old overlaid the plot with transponder data, showing not just the public designations of the vessels, but their precise locations along their registered paths. They weren't going to hit anyone, unless someone boosted and accelerated into them. And "the anomaly" the comms officer had tagged wasn't a Huangxu-registered hull, like all the rest in the system, but a League vessel. One listed as out of Columbia Station.

Sudden Fall of Darkness.

"Them again," Old said. "Send them to the expert system."

"Wait," Ciarán said. "Put them on screen."

Younger glanced at Old. "Cohort Captain?"

"Do it."

"Sir."

The man on *Sudden Fall of Darkness*'s bridge appeared to be in his midthirties, standard. He dressed in some sort of dark relation to spacer's utilities but more martial in appearance, as if someone had crossed a League fleet admiral's braid-encrusted uniform with a merchant's functional utilities. The effect should have been ridiculous, the worst attributes of both jammed together, neither serious nor functional, but instead of comic it seemed *sinister*, a conscious mockery of the League's overblown dignity and the Federation's pretend austerity.

His hair was black as a crow's wing, and his eyes blue, the sort of genetic traits Freemen associated with First Families. He would look Freeman to a Freeman. To a homeworlds Leagueman he would look related but vaguely foreign, and likely not Freeman, who were all wild-haired, green-eyed gingers according to League lore. In the Ojinate and the Hundred Planets the man would seem entirely foreign yet familiar. He did not seem inclined to smirk, or bow, or curse. He might be anyone else, but he was certainly not one of their own.

The bridge of *Sudden Fall of Darkness* mirrored *Quite Possibly Alien*'s own, so much so that it felt *offensive* to witness someone not of the crew standing on that midnight deck, with those instrument lights washing over them. If not for the vessel's name and christening date on the bulkhead behind the man, Ciarán could have easily believed Commodore Olek had stolen *Quite Possibly Alien* out from under him. He noted that both vessels hailed from Columbia Station, yet *Sudden Fall of Darkness* had been launched a full year after *Quite Possibly Alien*.

"You again," he said. "Has there been any word from your master?"

He had a *slightly* foreign accent, one that Ciarán nearly recognized. "I'm afraid I don't understand." He'd heard that accent before but he couldn't place it.

"That means no, then." Olek waved his arm in a sweeping motion. "Are all these... complications your doing?"

"Again, I'm afraid—"

"I know. You don't understand. Carry on." He turned away from the sensors, before appearing to change his mind, and turning back. "When you see Aoife nic Cartaí?"

"When I do," Ciarán said.

"Tell her I will do to her what I did to her brother."

"Again. I don't—"

"Olek out." He turned to a crew member and spoke in a foreign language an instant before the transmission feed went dark.

Now Ciarán knew where he'd heard that accent before, and that language. On Trinity Station, when he'd nearly been sucked into space. And when he'd met Wisp. That was the language the weasels at Academy Muscle spoke amongst themselves.

Ciarán glanced at Old.

"Transmission ended," Younger said. "We have numerous additional calls incoming."

"He mistook me for the expert system."

Old nodded. "It appears so."

"Did that seem like an expert system to you?"

"It seemed like a devil. Or a man."

"Pipe the incomings to the expert system," Ciarán said. "We need to decipher the situation before it gets out of control."

"It appears it is already out of control." Old highlighted a vessel on the display. "We are familiar with this vessel." He highlighted another. "And this one." He highlighted another. "And this one."

"Are there any vessels here you are not familiar with?"

He highlighted *Sudden Fall of Darkness*. "Only this one. Twice we have passed through this system and twice we have been hailed by this vessel. We thought at first it was your vessel, Merchant Lord, but it was noted that the drive signature deviated from your own. We allowed the hails to flow through to the expert system."

"But you reviewed the interactions."

"We did, in both cases. The conversations were not significantly different than this most recent one. This Commodore Olek appears to be acquainted with Merchant Captain Aoife nic Cartaí and is aware, or speculates, that we are associated with her. The comment regarding the merchant captain's brother does not occur in the previous interactions."

"And the other vessels?"

"Likely associated with Commodore Olek. It appears he is assembling a fleet."

"Why would you say that?"

"Because these are all ships of war."

"A breakbulk freighter is a warship."

"It is a ship of war, and the principal conveyance of the Undaunted Defenders of Martial Tradition. As is this vessel..." Old highlighted another transponder. "The principal conveyance of the Unstoppable Iron Fist of Empire, and this one..." He highlighted another. "The principal conveyance of the Feng Sisterhood, and secondary conveyance of the Huang Brotherhood, and ghost vessel of the Black Turtle Clan. Each of these vessels is a ship of war, and known to us. We have fought alongside these warriors, and they are formidable. It would be very difficult for us to defeat all of them at once."

"I thought you wouldn't fight other Huangxu."

"We will not fight the emperor or warriors of the empire."

"I fail to see the difference."

"These are mercenaries, sworn to a warlord. Those we can fight."

Ciarán felt as if he might be sick. "Oh no."

"Not to fear. We *can* defeat them two or three at a time, excepting the Black Turtle Clan, which we would wish to face in single combat, and the Iron Fists, the entirety of which a single one of us could defeat barehanded, without perspiring. The merchant lord need only devise a battle plan allowing us to engage them in small groups, over the course of several engagements."

"I meant, oh no, I don't think they're Olek's mercenaries."

"Regardless of their employer's resources, I remain confident we can prevail under the conditions I have outlined."

"I mean, I think they are *my* mercenaries."

"I certainly hope not," Old said. "They are as a group quite uncivilized, excepting the Iron Fists, who are barely sentient, and the Black Turtle Clan, who are gentlemen and scholars."

"Which of them are hull-breakers like yourselves?"

"There are no others like us. The Iron Fists claim to be hull-breakers. However, a Freeman longboat's defenses would confound them."

"And the Black Turtle Clan?"

"Hull-takers. Able to flow through the smallest of openings like oil."

"I think we need to talk. In private."

"As you wish, Merchant Lord. Shall we do that now, or after we avoid destruction and establish a parking orbit?"

"After that. And after Aspen locates Adderly."

"A search is unnecessary according to the system native Aspen. Either Adderly will be found in the station's brig or in its morgue."

"That's... um. Informative."

"Indeed."

"See me in my cabin when you're finished here."

"It will be done, Merchant Lord. Death and pain to our foes."

"And only to our foes."

Old nodded and nearly smiled. "One endeavors toward this end."

60

W hile the layout of the Invincible Spear Bearers' vessel proved familiar, the details remained disturbing. Every object on board capable of executing commands appeared *alive*. He could gain entry to nearly any portion of the vessel by *negotiating* with the hatch locks. Entry to his own cabin required no negotiation but an exchange of pleasantries. Adjusting the illumination in the compartment consisted of listening to a pleading offer to serve, and expressing a desire of sufficient light for working, and choosing a color temperature from a verbal listing of adjective-laden Huangxu phrases unrelated to temperature or color, but rather mood.

Turning on the washbasin tap likewise involved a discussion, and a tasking, and another description, one involving references to artificial microclimates of the Celestial Palace, the principal Huangxu administrative orbital and seat of empire. "As the waters of the Bo, at midsummer," meant turn the tap to medium warm. "As the ebbing tide passes beneath Qi Bridge" meant a medium-strength laminar flow without aeration.

Ciarán splashed water across his face and gazed into the mirror.

You are so screwed.

He needed to speak with Adderly in the next three days in order to live up to the letter of the contract between Aoife nic Cartaí and Adderly. He was in Contract space as Aoife's appointed representative. And while he didn't have a Freeman merchant vessel, he did have a hull beneath his feet, one under his command, with a crew willing to transport whatever Adderly needed to transport.

If Adderly lay in the station morgue, then no contract existed. The contract was not assignable, but between Adderly and Aoife alone. His mind wanted to go there, *what if it isn't Adderly, but Aoife that is dead*, and he couldn't stop it, any more than he could stop the washbasin faucet asking if he was satisfied with its service, and begging to be blessed with his attention at his soonest desire.

Ciarán shivered and returned to the compact compartment where the environmental controller asked if he found the lighting to his satisfaction, and would he prefer the breeze—as felt descending the Vermillion Steps at a pace of a man walking —to continue?

He preferred to be left alone, but if he said that, the system would go into a long question-and-answer mode where it asked him what it had done to offend him, and how it might improve its performance in the future, and how it begged him, how it *beseeched* him, to allow it one more chance to serve.

"I wish the breeze to continue."

"Should the air feel as if the Steps lay in sun or shadow?"

"Shadow," Ciarán said.

"Great Lord, it will be done. How may I serve you further?"

Wisp brushed against his trousers and growled. She found the ship's systems particularly disturbing. She'd taken to silently prowling the corridors in adaptive camouflage. She had always been hard to see when she wanted to hide, and if she remained still. Since coming aboard the Huangxu vessel, she'd developed the ability to not only hide in shadows, but to move from shadow to shadow without detection by the ship's obsequious systems.

"Shall I address my attentions to your companion's needs?"

"The silence of the Heavens for an hour." That always shut the systems up without offending it. An hour appeared to be the longest it could bear to remain silent.

Ciarán sat on the bunk, head in his hands.

Wisp jumped onto the bunk beside him. She head-butted him and purred.

"I get it. *We* are so screwed."

If the station officials had Adderly locked up, then the contract remained in force. He refused to consider that Aoife had died. That meant he could live up to the contract if he could simply get in to speak with her. The contract was for the conveyance of cargo, not facilitating a jailbreak. Payment in full would be due the moment he spoke to her. If she wouldn't, or couldn't pay was a separate issue, one that had no bearing on the honor of the merchant captain, her ship, her crew, or her merchant apprentice. So long as he had a hull and cargo space, there would be no black mark beside their names in the Registry for breach of contract. If he went home to Trinity Surface, it would be as a Guild member in good standing, and not as a failure. He wouldn't be exiled and grounded as an incompetent and an oath breaker. He wouldn't be parted from Wisp.

It was exceedingly difficult to separate his duties as *Quite Possibly Alien*'s merchant-in-charge from his own interests and desires. Every time he attempted to think about his duties dispassionately, he inevitably ended up tangled up in what *he* wanted, what *he* needed, what was good for *him*.

The terrible beauty of the situation was that the good of the ship and his own good were in alignment in every way, so long as he considered only the terms of the contract. If he considered anything else—justice for the murder of *Last Stand* and Bosditch Trading; vengeance for the mind rape and enslavement of Seamus mac Donnacha by Merchant Roche and Commodore Olek; security and freedom for Old and his crew; and now, apparently, for half a score of additional obsolete Huangxu mercenary castoffs he'd saddled himself with—he risked failing the merchant captain, the ship, and the crew. He wasn't simply honor bound to put their needs first. He'd sighed a contract to do exactly that.

That he also had to consider the ship's homicidal bent didn't free him from these obligations. The ship didn't care about justice, or security, or freedom. It cared about stopping Ixatl-Nine-Go. He would meet its needs, regardless of whether he fulfilled the contract or not. His duties as merchant-in-charge remained the sole topic in question.

All he had to do was ignore the complications, stick to the mission, and his apprentice cruise would be an unqualified success.

He was centimeters away from the finish line.

"Merchant Lord?" Old stood in the hatchway.

"Come in. There's a matter I've neglected to discuss with you."

Old pointed at the workstation seat. "May I?"

"Please do."

"We are safely parked in an orbit that reduces the probability of collision. One that puts us in proximity to the station while remaining outside the tripwire."

"I hadn't thought of that."

"That one can run doesn't mean one must."

"The tripwire is not a physical barrier."

"Indeed. We've disabled the system fail-safes. We could

boost at full thrust anywhere in this star system. That we preserve the illusion of subservience to convention serves us."

"It's more a law than a convention."

"In war, any law that is not a physical law is a convention."

"So you'd be fine with the kinetic bombardment of a planet."

"We propose to break the system speed limit if it benefits us. One doesn't consider your example as equivalent."

"But you wouldn't rule out kinetic bombardment of a planet."

"If the benefits exceed the costs, one should rule nothing out."

"And the other mercenary vessels?"

"The same. Modern warfare is a game with rules. We pretend to follow them. In times of peace, one would not note the difference between pretense and compliance. With lives at stake?" Old shrugged. "We balance the benefit of maintaining the illusion of compliance with the cost of lives, not simply in the present, but in the future. Only in total war are we entirely unchained, and all illusion stripped away."

"Do you think the same is true for Olek?"

"That hull was laid down before the architects of this station were born. In regard to such ancient systems, I cannot say. Its drive signature is modern, however. It is presently fashionable to build compliance with convention into such systems. We find it increasingly time consuming to modify such systems to our satisfaction. Perhaps Olek finds such expense of effort unnecessary.

"In addition, Olek appears foreign. Perhaps he does not comprehend the difference between the laws of nature and the laws of men."

"Why are you telling me this?"

"Because you are a foreigner. And also one who does not know the difference between the laws of nature and the laws of men. In total war the cost of failure is not defeat, but extinction."

"We're not talking about the tripwire anymore."

"We never were, Merchant Lord. We have spoken with the Black Turtle Clan and others. You cannot *buy* our freedom, or the freedom of our brothers and sisters. There is no price on our loyalty. We are *engineered* to obey. If you and I stood back to back, and faced a legion of foes alone, as brothers, and the emperor called my name? I would desert you. Perhaps not in my heart, but in my head. In my limbs. I would abandon you on the field of honor, and run to my master, and if he told me to fall on my own sword I would, and if he told me to march back to your side and pretend to befriend you and, later, slit your throat?"

"You would."

"Without question. We are not slaves to be freed. We are the cells of a living, breathing whole whose being spans a hundred stars. We exist as organs of that being, without will or wish of our own. We cannot be carved off and survive. We are as fingers of a hand."

"Thank you for explaining this to me."

Old leaned forward in his seat. His gaze narrowed. "You don't believe me."

"I believe every word. Not just in the sense that you are stating *your* truth, but that what you say is factually true, and verifiable. That the example you gave, of turning on me, and betraying any trust between us isn't some hypothetical, but that it might occur one day, and that day might be tomorrow, or even today."

"Then—"

"It changes *nothing*. You've explained your nature. I accept that. I don't choose to disassociate myself from you because of some *immutable attribute* you had no say in or control over." Ciarán squeezed his palms against his temples. "I hate this."

"If I have offended—"

"Stop. No apology, please. You have done nothing wrong."

Ciarán studied his friend's face. Everything about Old seemed a lie. Huangxu with a League face. An ancient warrior in the body of an innocent youth. A servant who gave orders. Who led. A cannibal. And a decent man. A friend. And a foe.

"You've reminded me of a truth I've avoided facing. That there are aspects of each of our natures that we would not choose if we could. Inconveniences of birth that no amount of hoping, and wishing, and praying can change. We are what we are. One might as well battle the ocean."

Old nodded. "I will contact the other companies and we will come to some understanding. I will tell them that their services are not required."

"Do that, and tell them the reason. That I've decided that I can't serve alongside anyone who is a slave, or who owns slaves, no matter how clever the structuring of the agreement. I thought I could stomach the idea, but it's not the way I'm made. Tell them that it's best if they clear out of the system before the fighting starts. Anyone who does not stand beside me stands against me, and will be treated as such."

"I don't understand."

"It's quite simple. I'm *done* fighting the ocean. Once you've sent them all away, I'd like you to drop Wisp and me at the station. I expect the locals will wish to debark with us."

Old stared at him.

"That will be all, Cohort Captain." Ciarán stood and held out his hand. "It's been an honor and a pleasure serving with you."

"What will you do on the station?"

"I'm not sure yet. Try to speak with Adderly. Probably try to help Adderly, and steal Olek's vessel if *Quite Possibly Alien* doesn't arrive soon. Bring Olek to account, if I can, for murdering Merchant Bosditch and *Last Stand*. Figure out how to get into the secret weapons lab and shut it down. Find this Vatya, and whoever else is behind Ixatl-Nine-Go and bring them to justice. I'm sure I'm forgetting something. I may not do all of that in that order, but I expect I'll get to it all of it eventually, or die trying. It's early times, though, so it's best to remain flexible."

"That is madness."

"It is. Thank you for recognizing this truth. I did not choose to be made this way, I assure you. Now if you'll excuse me, I need to pack." Ciarán hoisted his bugout bag onto his bunk. He stuffed a pair of Haungxu wound dressings into his pockets and another six into his bag.

"You must reconsider."

"I've done nothing but reconsider since the day I stepped aboard *Quite Possibly Alien*. I tried to convince myself that if I simply followed the rules, and the *Manual of Trade*, and listened to my superiors, and respected my crew mates that I would prosper, and my friends along with me. That if I kept my head down, and my eyes averted, and *stepped around*, or over, and accommodated the world as it was, not as I wished it, but as it revealed itself to be, I would find my stride, and the road would rise to meet me.

"The road has not done so. If I were to take the straight path, and do my job, and live up to the letter of my agreements and nothing more, I would be considered a good man. An estimable man. When words were spoken over my grave there would be earnest tears shed. A dutiful son. A good brother. A credit to the community. An honest man.

"The truth is I have not been any of those things, and I never will be. I cannot be relied upon to choose wisely when doing so opposes my nature. There's a data crystal on the worktop beside you. Please take it and review the contents at your leisure. I'd hoped to view it with you to get your thoughts, but... I think it's best considered in private."

Old glanced at the crowded work surface. Beside the data crystal were two gifts from Kazuki Ryuu, an autographed master edition of her collected works and a square wooden box too big to fit in his duffel, one labeled in Ojin. *Open only in the direst of emergencies.* He wondered if this was the direst of emergencies and decided that it couldn't be, because he'd foreseen this moment even though he could see no way to avoid it. It was dire. It just wasn't an emergency.

Old held the data crystal on his palm. His gaze met Ciarán's. "The contents?"

"A court trial in the Ojinate. One with broad-reaching consequences." Old tended to refer to the empire and the emperor as if they were one and the same. Ciarán wondered where the Spear Bearers' bioengineered loyalties lay, with the institution, or with the creature that had once been a man.

61

Templeman Space, Between Trinity System and Prescott Grange System

Macer waited to make sure that Seamus's credentials worked, and that the airlock cycled, and then he checked on the autodoc and Janie. She would survive. And she might lose her legs below the knee, but it wasn't that big a deal. There were people in the League that cut their own limbs off so they could upgrade them. About half the League adults he'd ever met had at least one cybernetic eye, and unlike some scar-faced granny's military-surplus castoff, the new ones looked like a real eyeball, and he'd heard they felt like one too, and if it wasn't the fashion to make the cybernetic eye a different color than the natural one, he would never have noticed to ask about them. It could be more than half, now that he thought about it, if someone had a matching pair.

But Seamus was dead set on getting Janie to a real doctor, and supposedly there was one here. He thought about replacing his own legs with better ones every time he had to jam himself into a hardsuit. And that was just thinking about the tight fit, and now that he considered it, he wondered if you'd even need a hardsuit for cybernetic legs. The question was how far up would you go with the replacement, and how much "real feel" they had. If you couldn't tell the difference, was there any downside?

Maybe. People might look at him differently if they spied him crawling half-naked across *Four-Squared*'s hull.

He unlashed his backpack and began to unload. He could use the time for thinking but Seamus was in a massive hurry, and he'd probably only get started thinking about something and then he'd have to stop and attend to the now. Seamus was a magnet for conflict, and conflict demanded attention. It was a better use of time arranging his kit while he waited.

Macer wasn't sure that he liked this new, intense Seamus. The old Seamus had been a lot less involved with events as they unfolded, like an observer, or a spectator. Distant and mocking, and if not objective, at least dispassionate and nonjudgmental. Since he'd stepped on board *Four-Squared*, though, Seamus hadn't stopped sticking his nose into things, and bossing people around.

Still, it was an improvement over kill-me-please Seamus, like he'd been on Trinity Surface, where Macer had worried he'd walk in to say hello and find Seamus had hung himself, or just decided to stop eating—and who wouldn't if all you fancied was tubed paste and some sort of "fruit" juice that looked like it dripped out of the recycler, and smelled like it too.

No wonder he was so scrawny, and seemed to be getting, not scrawnier, but *stringier*, like he wasn't just lean, but like he didn't have fat or muscle, just hard bone and wire-taut tendons.

If old Seamus had lurched out of a dark corner, and bumped him as he passed?

Macer would have checked that he still had his wallet.

If this new Seamus bumped him?

He'd check he still had a heartbeat, or maybe even a soul.

That pendant spire Seamus wore now was a dead man's, it had the look, and a Unity Station look as well, twisted in the right direction but sharper and leaner than the modern fashion. You couldn't look at it without seeing the staple in the deck, and the blood-caked chain, and the iron collar that had given it birth. Macer couldn't wear such a device even if he'd wanted to. It screamed its legacy, not a First Families bauble, but something older, and stronger. Something adamantine.

Maybe it was the contrast between the gilded polish of the golden hand and the handwrought earring that made him notice all that. But given the choice, Macer knew which one he'd prefer to wear.

He preflighted the little drone and ran it through its paces. It looked worse for wear with the mods he'd done at the mac Diarmuid place, but it still worked fine. He hadn't had much time to toy with it, so he spent a few minutes scrolling through the list of presets and adding those he liked to a favorites list. The handheld for the clever little device had a series of dedicated hard keys specifically for that purpose. Of course it wasn't likely he'd use the device handheld when there was an app that ran on his general-purpose handheld. Still, it was small, and fit in his pocket, and now that he'd met Aoife nic Cartaí's spidery sidekick, he'd gotten a raft of new ideas about what all a drone with an adjustable toolset on every arm could do in an emergency.

Seamus should be back by now, and it felt like an emergency was building up nearby.

Macer sighed, jammed the hardsuit helmet back on, sealed

it, tucked the little drone under his arm, and marched to the airlock.

He glanced at the keypad.

The airlock cycled.

62

Someone in a League hardsuit stood in the airlock. Macer couldn't tell who. He didn't think he wanted to let them on board. And unless they were planning on shoving him out of the way, he didn't think they were getting on board.

The suit's annunciator spoke. "Are you going to move or not?"

"Are you the doctor?"

"Yes. Now get out of my way. I understand it's an emergency."

"Why are you in a hardsuit?"

"Because James told me to wear one."

"James?"

"Yes. James Reynard. The Freeman. Now please move. He was adamant. Time is of the essence."

"It took you a while to get here."

"Do you know how long it's been since I had to crawl into a hardsuit?"

"I don't. How long?"

She shoved against him. "Move it."

"Take off the helmet."

"What would be the point of wearing a hardsuit without a helmet?"

"Being able to put on a helmet and be inside a hardsuit fast."

"You first."

"Sure." He unlatched the helmet and removed it one handed. He clipped the lanyard to the suit's breastplate. Having to scramble to find the helmet was just about as bad as not having one. They didn't roll away on their own, but in an emergency they tended to get kicked around. He didn't normally like the lanyard, but this had a very emergency feeling about it.

She took off the helmet. She also used the lanyard, maybe because she always did, maybe because she was patterning him, maybe because it also felt like a very emergency sort of day to her as well.

She looked like a Lady Tabatha Aster. And he looked like a country squire's overfed son. One with a wickedly bad sunburn and an unlimited supply of greasy ointment. Neither of those observations was particularly helpful. He was pretty sure now that the more familiar anything seemed at first glance, the less he should trust it and the closer he should examine it.

"What are you doing?"

"Looking at you."

"Stop it. What happened to your skin?"

"Fast patch."

She moved her hand toward his face. "May I?"

"You may."

She ran her fingertip across his cheek, then rubbed her finger and thumb together, and then raised her hand to her face and sniffed. "That's not a product I'd recommend. You'll need to reapply it every three hours."

"I know."

"I fail to see how this is an emergency, Mister—"

"Macer Gant."

"Tabatha Aster."

Macer took a step back to let her pass. "The emergency is in the autodoc."

She shoved past him and into the cabin. She didn't bend over to examine the autodoc's display, but pulled a handheld from a sleeve pocket and tapped it twice against the autodoc's keypad before entering some sort of code on the handheld display. She did that entire procedure twice more. Then she gave up, and crouched and used the autodoc's built-in display.

"There are a lot of hours on this unit."

"I wouldn't know about that."

"You might tell the owner to have the first responder codes refreshed."

"I'll do that."

"This isn't an emergency either. She's stable. Fitting prosthetics should be no problem."

"What about simply reattaching her legs? Or growing new ones?"

"As for growing limbs, you'd need to ask someone Eng. My understanding is that it can be done but is rarely worth the effort. As for reattaching limbs? I'd need to inspect the limbs. Even if they're in good condition, it's precision work, and time consuming. And there are no guarantees. Prosthetics are far superior."

"I hear you. The limbs are in the autodoc with her."

"Are they?" She worked with the built-in display again. "You do know that if you wish to store an expert system there are better places to do so than an autodoc's swap space."

"There's an expert system stored in there?"

"I assume that's what it is. Something large and monolithic, in any case." She tapped on the console a few more times. "I see them now. And yes. I can reattach these limbs."

"And they'll work?"

"Likely they will. Assuming they worked before."

"They sort of did. Though they tended to flail about when she was dancing. What do we need to get her ready?"

"She's ready now."

"How soon does it have to be done?"

"There's no rush. She's stable. So are her limbs."

"When we get to Prescott Grange, then."

"I see you've spoken to Hector."

"Hector Poole? I haven't had the chance."

"Then how did you know we needed to reroute from Sampson to Prescott Grange?"

"What made you think we were going to Sampson?"

"The pilot said so."

"This vessel's pilot."

"*Springbok*'s pilot. That's why Hector was sent to the pirate vessel. To express our demands. We're desperately needed in Prescott Grange."

"Why?"

"You'd have to ask Mr. Singh that. He's in charge of coordination with *Defiant*."

"Mr. Nissam Singh?"

"Indeed. Are you acquainted?"

"Somewhat."

"He's entirely a stranger to us. Other than keeping us informed about *Defiant* and relaying messages from the flight deck, we rarely see the man. Though I suppose he's rather busy with his own work."

"Relaying messages from the flight deck?"

"We're experiencing a temporary problem with internal communications."

"That's inconvenient."

"Particularly so, since no one on the flight deck appears to have a functioning handheld."

"According to Mr. Singh."

"According to anyone who's tried to contact them. They appear to have barricaded themselves behind the cockpit hatch since our abduction, and will only allow Mr. Singh in and out."

"That's strange."

"Indeed. Though they *are* Regular Navy, and Hector in the Guard."

"What about Seamus?"

"James? He's been rather distracted with his own issues. And if the pilots won't let a Home Guard officer on the bridge, I can't see them letting a foreigner near the controls."

"But Seamus knew about the pilots. And the communications equipment failure. And the lack of functioning handhelds."

"We discussed it on the way here."

"Right before he told you to get into a hardsuit."

"Shortly before then, yes."

"Did he say anything else around about that time?"

"He said there was a medical emergency, and I needed to hurry. And he asked where he could find Mr. Singh."

"In engineering."

"In his cabin. He has a small manufactory installed there."

"A microfab."

"Perhaps. It appears you suspect something *concerning* regarding Mr. Singh."

"That's a good way of putting it. If I asked you to stay in the hardsuit and wait here would you do it?"

"Without an explanation as to why?"

"Without that."

"No. I would not."

"Then come on, we're going to Singh's cabin."

"So long as we stop by my cabin on the way."

"I don't think we have time."

"A gentleman always has time to indulge a lady."

She yanked on the helmet lanyard and unsnapped it one-handed, without a glance. She seated the helmet and sealed it before he could blink. The annunciator on her suit spoke. Her voice remained recognizably feminine but it had that peculiarly flat and distant sound unique to League hardsuits and exoskeletal armor.

"Snap to it, Mr. Gant. This lady feels rather naked without her sidearm."

63

They found Singh in his cabin. He'd been stripped naked and cemented to a chair, a sock stuffed into his mouth. It looked like a fast-set two-part epoxy, with good coverage. It wouldn't hurt as bad as being buried in fast patch until it came time to pry him loose. There were a couple solvents Macer could think of that might work to soften the bond, but Singh wouldn't like the looks of the applicator. Somebody knew what they were doing, and not from watching recorded dramas. It was spindle work, fast and dirty, and on the cheap.

It was like a fingerprint from a golden hand.

Macer tugged on the sock. It hadn't been cemented in. "Where's Seamus?"

"Macer? Is that you?"

"Hang on." He'd forgotten that his suit's annunciator also made him sound odd. And with the visor down, Singh couldn't see who was inside. He popped the helmet seal and dangled the helmet from the lanyard, not with the smooth, practiced motion of Lady Tabatha Aster but like a guy who hated hard-suits and only used one when not using one wasn't an option.

"Where's Seamus?"

"Can you get me out of this chair?"

"I can. Where's Seamus?"

"Over here," Lady Aster's hardsuit said.

"Wait here," Macer said, before he realized just how stupid that probably sounded to Singh.

Lady Aster stood beside an open hatch across the corridor. She likely didn't notice that she'd monopolized all the good cover. He couldn't put the hatch coaming between him and whoever or whatever was in the compartment without crossing in front of the hatch.

She ducked inside the compartment.

He followed her in.

Seamus sat at a bulkhead-mounted workstation. He had his hardsuit helmet off. He wasn't moving.

Lady Aster crossed the compartment.

"Don't touch him. See if there's a wire or cable running from somewhere below the base of his neck."

"There is."

"What's it plugged into on the other end?"

"A socket installed beneath the workstation surface."

"How many more people are there on board?"

"Just the pilot and first officer."

"Let's go see how they are."

"Is he an addict?"

"Like a wirehead? Is that a real thing?"

"Very much so."

"He's not anything like that. Let's go find these pilots."

"And leave him like this?"

"There's no telling how long he'll be in there."

Macer glanced around the compartment. "This isn't Seamus's cabin." There was too much stuff in it to be Seamus's.

"It's Hector's."

"And Hector Poole has one of those jacks installed on his workstation?"

"Apparently. Unless James installed it."

"He would have installed it in his own cabin, if he knew how." Seamus was defenseless as a kitten when jacked in, and he wouldn't have liked the idea of someone walking in on him.

Lady Tabatha glanced into the corridor. "One of us should stay with him."

That wasn't going to happen. He didn't know her and he wasn't about to leave an armed stranger alone with Seamus. And he wasn't about to send an armed stranger to the cockpit, where they could murder the crew, or more likely, return with reinforcements to overpower him. He'd like to trust her, but he'd trusted Singh, and that was beginning to look like a mistake.

"Oh man."

"What's wrong?"

"I was beating Seamus up earlier about how he always trusts a pretty girl."

"And?"

"And engineers like Singh are my pretty girl. I have the same character flaw as Seamus."

"I don't see how that knowledge helps us."

"It doesn't, but Seamus will hate it when I tell him. He likes to think he's uniquely flawed."

Macer stepped into the corridor and looked both ways.

"Let's go talk to Singh."

"And leave James like this?"

"Is the cable loose or tight?"

"Tight."

"Leave him." He'd disconnect when he was done, or when he fell out of the chair.

64

M acer took the opportunity to examine Singh's cabin while Singh pleaded his case with Lady Aster. Macer had tuned his old boss out when he grew repetitive, so Singh had switched his attention to Lady Tabatha, who listened politely while examining her handgun. It had to have occurred to her that if Singh had architected the removal of Hector Poole, Seamus, and her daughter from the vessel, that he'd known he was putting her daughter in danger.

Singh had indeed installed a microfab where a workstation would normally reside, and it appeared he'd been busy cranking out rider detectors. Or maybe something else that just looked like a rider detector. He wouldn't be able to tell without a detailed inspection. On the surface there wasn't anything Macer could see that would make Seamus suspect Singh needed a firm cementing to a chair, but then Seamus knew Singh from this vessel, and from the station, and all Macer knew about Singh was what he'd learned while working with him on *Four-Squared*.

There were similarities between their experiences, though.

Macei glanced at Singh. "I hear the internal comms are out."

Singh nodded. "Completely and utterly broken."

"How'd that happen?"

"I'd think that was obvious. I broke them."

"Like on *Four-Squared*."

"Sure."

"Why?"

"So people couldn't use them."

"Because?"

"Because I didn't want people using the comms."

"And creating records."

"Of course."

"Military sensors have big buffers."

"That's why planning ahead pays off."

"On *Four-Squared* the buffers were broken for days before things turned bloody." *So they weren't broken to hide what I'd thought they were meant to hide.*

"It's a big ship. Most of the crew is in cold sleep most of the time. And the bridge crew is only on duty when they need to be. When they're not on duty, and often when they are, they're practicing footie, or talking about footie, or thinking about footie, or sleeping and dreaming about footie. You were the only exception, and so long as I kept you in engineering and toying with the big machines, everything was fine."

"What changed to make you run?"

"Nothing. I didn't run. I'd finished the job and it was time to move on."

"What job?"

"There used to be a dead-drop location on Trinity Station. It was a bunch of old containers welded to the ring, and you could leave stuff there and have people pick it up later. It was an open secret, and lots of people used it. It worked fine until someone decided they needed an exclusive on the location, and in the process of shutting it down, their out-of-town contractors decided to rob their neighbors. That ended that location, but it didn't end the need for a location like that. After a lot of head scratching it was determined that a private, mobile drop would be best, and after a little more thinking we settled on *Four-Squared*. The beauty was that there's already a lot of uncatalogued junk out by the Boneyard and for many of *Four-Squared*'s return trips *everyone* was in cold storage for a couple of days. Except for me."

"And none of the rest of the crew knew."

"That Ares Adonis monstrosity found out. And at first I thought that was a problem, but when I talked to my customer, he said it wasn't a problem but an opportunity. So for years I've been exploiting that opportunity. And then the job was done and it was time to move on."

"The job being manning a clandestine cargo transfer location."

"Right. I had a side gig modifying cargo to meet local specifications but that came later."

"You work for some League intelligence operation."

"I work for myself. But I've been *employed* by Aster's Army and by Charlie Newton both."

"I don't know what that means."

Lady Aster cleared her throat. "It means this despicable worm has been funded by both internal and external League intelligence agencies. While also being paid by those acting against our interests."

"And while also being paid by Truxton for engineering work on *Four-Squared*."

"Every little bit helps. Now come on, Macer, and get me out of this."

"That all makes sense. But I still don't get why you had parts but didn't do maintenance on the Templeman drive."

"That's because there's stuff I know that you don't. And I'll tell you after you get me out of this chair."

Macer ran his gaze over Singh. He decided that the biggest recurring mistake he'd made since graduating from the Academy was assuming that he knew *anything* about the people he lived and worked with. Growing up on an island, where everyone knew everyone else's business, and not just their public business, but their private business, he'd accepted as fact that he could look at someone and know their life story.

He knew absolutely nothing about Singh even while staring at him stripped naked and chemical-welded to a chair. That Singh had the neck to try bargaining with him just proved the point.

"Listen to me." Macer looked Singh in the eye. "Lashed up to the airlock is a longboat I stole from a pair of murdering thieves. And on that longboat is a box, and in that box is a brand-new power drill and some fast-acting muscle relaxant. I bought those tools for a job, and I didn't get to use them. Now you don't know me nearly as well as you think you do, but we did work side by side for six months, and I want to ask you something. Have you ever known me to bring a tool I didn't intend to use?"

Singh licked his lips. "I sold the parts."

"I'm disappointed to hear that. Because a fair number of those parts are unique to that drive."

"Unique to that drive class."

"Truxton owns all the surviving *Squared*-class hulls."

"He bought all the *scrapped* hulls. There were a lot more hulls than that made."

"You're saying you sold those parts to someone with a *Squared*-class Templeman drive."

"He had a hull without a drive. Charlie Newton had a drive without a hull. One they kept for research purposes and that had never been fired up or fitted. He managed to acquire the drive. I acquired the parts to complete and fit it. And I kept him supplied with consumables."

"So there's an unregistered *Squared*-class hull running around out there."

"I didn't say that. There's an unregistered drive out there, but the hull is in the Registry. It's just more capable than anyone imagines."

"I would have seen another fleet tug billet in the Registry. I am looking for work, you recall."

"You're not listening. It's not a *Squared*-class hull."

"I don't know what sort of hull it could be that could fit it, short of a League warship."

"An Ojin warship," Lady Aster said. "Or Huangxu. Or Alexandrian."

"I'm not a traitor, no matter what you think. And the drive containment sphere is large, but it's all the outboard kit that makes *Four-Squared*'s drive *assembly* seem so enormous. That tech's ancient, and four to ten times bigger than it needs to be nowadays."

"It still wouldn't fit in a family ship."

"Could you at least drape a blanket over me? It's freezing in here."

"I could, but I'm not going to. Later I might, but I'm going to go get my box of tools now. Because I think you're lying."

"I could chemically interrogate him," Lady Aster said.

"That won't do it for me. There's *Four-Squared*'s doctor murdered that needs balancing. Unless you tell me chemical interrogation feels like hot steel cutting into bone, it's not enough."

Singh's eyes had gone wide, but he'd stopped looking at Macer and started staring toward the compartment hatch.

"It doesn't feel like that," Seamus said. "And he isn't lying. Nearly everything he's said is true."

SEAMUS LEANED against the hatch coaming, the fingers of his golden hand splayed across his forehead and nearly swallowing the scar of his head wound. He had a broken look about him, more so than normal, *shattered*, Macer would say, like those emergency stairwell windows in public structures, where the glass had been fractured to shards yet maintained its purpose and shape entirely through the agency of a hidden core. One tough, and flexible, and invisible until called upon.

"His customer is Commodore Kirill Olek. And the vessel is *Sudden Fall of Darkness.*"

Macer eyeballed Singh. "That's bad."

"It gets worse."

65

Macer caught Seamus as he fell. He lifted him like a sack of gears and plopped him down on Singh's bunk. Lady Tabatha crossed the compartment and sat on the bunk next to him, running some sort of instrument across his forehead and then holding it up in front of his face. It looked like a medical device and probably was. Seamus didn't look any better when she was done, but he did sit up straighter so he could see Singh and Macer.

"I don't remember who knows what, so I'll explain it all."

"Before you do, I'd like to go check on the pilots."

"No need. They're dead."

"Then who is piloting?"

"Whoever is piloting *Tractor Four-Squared*. We're synced to remain stationary relative to them."

"Oh. That doesn't feel safe."

"It isn't. We should get someone pilot-rated over to at least monitor the displays."

"Maybe we should have this chat on the bridge."

"I'm not dragging that chair up to the flight deck, Macer. Feel free if you want to."

"How long is this going to take?"

Seamus stared at him.

"Sorry." It was a stupid question, and he'd only asked it because he wanted to be *doing* something. When Seamus gave one of his reports, it was as long as it needed to be and no longer.

"Go on, James," Lady Aster said.

Seamus winced, pretty obviously, and Macer wondered if Lady Aster called him James because she thought it was his name, or because she enjoyed winding him up.

She glanced at Macer and winked.

So, winding him up. Macer liked the idea that she cared enough about Seamus to tweak him. It was a very Freeman thing to do. Even though it irritated Seamus, it would also make him pay attention to her. Seamus had a bad habit of forgetting that other people were in the compartment with him.

"At the end of the second epoch, the League sent out survey vessels," Seamus said. "One of these vessels was christened *Sudden Fall of Darkness* and another *Impossibly Alien*. These vessels were under the supervision of synthetic intelligences charged with preventing any alien life forms from tracking the vessels home to the League. They were fitted with superluminal drive systems unlike our present-day systems. These drive systems were also configured as doomsday weapons capable of collapsing stars. The existence and nature of these weapons was, until recently, entirely speculative. None of these vessels returned and were thought lost with all hands.

"Several years ago the vessel *Impossibly Alien* was recovered intact. Excavated from beneath a glacier by Aoife nic Cartaí and a crew of salvagers, the vessel was subsequently registered under the name *Quite Possibly Alien*. Nic Cartaí operates the vessel as a Freeman merchant trader.

"Nearly a year elapsed between the discovery of *Impossibly Alien* and its eventual salvage, and during that time conflicting legal claims arose. A rival to nic Cartaí's claim came forward, the Leagueman Kirill Olek. It subsequently came to light that Olek was in possession of the survey vessel *Sudden Fall of Darkness*. This vessel had been reported discovered as a stripped hulk in the Alexandrine, and bought at auction by Olek, a noted collector of second-epoch artifacts.

"These reports regarding *Sudden Fall of Darkness*'s discovery were questioned and League intelligence operatives sent to investigate. Dr. Anastasia Blum, from external intelligence, found nothing to report, and was later reassigned. Major Hector Poole, from internal intelligence, discovered that contrary to being found as a hulk, *Sudden Fall of Darkness* had been recovered intact, less its drive unit, and the vessel's synthetic intelligence extracted and used in medical experiments by the Alexandrian Eng. Poole discovered additional inconsistencies in Olek's story, inconsistencies with foreign-relations implications. He was subsequently tasked with infiltrating Olek's organization to lay any concerns to rest.

"What he discovered went far beyond a conspiracy between rival polities. And what he concluded would make him appear a madman if he were to bring it forward to his superiors without proof. He continued to gather evidence in secret. He continued to remain silent."

Seamus glanced from face to face.

Lady Aster frowned. "You hacked Hector's work files?"

"Eventually. The problem required a broad-ranging investigation, and ultimately all threads led there."

She seemed surprised. "But how?"

"He's quite good for someone who came to the work, um..." He glanced at her. "Later in life."

"I see."

"I doubt I would have been able to succeed without having lived amongst you for a while."

"Was that your plan all along? To befriend us so that you could spy on us?"

"Rather the other way around. I came to like you, despite our differences. The price of my work seemed a secondary concern."

"You mean your health."

"I mean your good regard."

"You have been around them too much," Macer said. "You're starting to sound like them, *James*."

"That may be true."

"It is true. So what did the Leagueman discover that he hasn't bothered to tell the rest of us?"

"That *Sudden Fall of Darkness* had *deployed* its weapon. And the weapon turned out to be a dud."

Lady Tabatha's left eyebrow arched. "But why would it do that?"

"Because it found alien life," Singh said. "And it didn't want to bring it home."

They all looked at him.

"Surprise. Now cut me loose before my friends show up."

SEAMUS STARED AT SINGH. "Do you know why I glued you to the chair and not the bunk?"

Macer knew the answer. "Because the chair will fit in an airlock. And the bunk might not."

"For the sake of brevity," Seamus said, "here is all we need know to act. Olek and Ixatl-Nine-Go are not a single threat as we had imagined. Where Vatya and Ixatl-Nine-Go strive to overthrow the League, Olek has other plans. He is using Ixatl-Nine-Go as a distraction while he goes about his own business. And he is directing our attention toward those enslaved to

Ixatl-Nine-Go through their implants to the exclusion of all others."

"What others?" Lady Tabatha asked.

"Those like Singh here, who aren't slaves, but volunteers."

"If you had any sense you would cut me loose and run while you can," Singh said. "You speak about Olek as if he were a man. As if the petty concerns of men were his. Olek has no interest in the squabbles between lords and serfs. He has no concern for Eng, or not Eng, for home planets, or frontier worlds. Olek will unite us. He will *free us* from the shackles of flesh, as he has freed himself."

"There's evidence that Olek is noncorporeal," Seamus said.

"You mean like a synthetic intelligence's avatar," Lady Tabatha said.

"Like that. He appears in captured images, but in-flesh sightings are virtually unheard of, except at a distance, or while he's wearing an exo."

"I saw the Leagueman with him," Macer said. "I was far away but the Leagueman was right next to him."

"You mean Hector Poole. There's more than one Leagueman in the area."

"You knew who I meant. Tell me he's not a walking stereotype."

"He is. That's why I'm not sure that Olek is noncorporeal. There is also evidence he isn't, including genetic samples taken by Poole. Samples that indicate he is Freeman."

"He looks it in pictures."

"The samples also indicate he in not from our neighborhood."

Macer grinned. "I knew it. He's from the Cordame Reservation."

"Warmer, but still off by a fair bit."

"Olek is from Earth," Singh said. "He comes to liberate the blameless and scourge those responsible. He has ascended, as will we who did him. Olek will show us the way." Singh licked his lips. "Macer."

"What?"

"I thought you might join us. That's why I waited so long to leave the ship. Olek came for *us*. He offers salvation to *us*. He will free *us* of the *tyrants*. No more fighting their self-serving wars. No more taking orders from their inbred spawn. No more forging the shackles they use to enslave us. You know what it feels like to *make* something. To *build* something. It makes us natural allies. All they do is take. All they do is destroy."

"So I should join with you and Olek."

"Yes. Absolutely."

"And then what?"

"We destroy them."

"We destroy the destroyers."

Singh stared at him.

Macer glanced at his logic-loving friend. "Seamus?"

"It doesn't make sense to me either."

"Maybe it's a religion, and exempt from making sense. I'll think about it later. In the meantime, how do we stop Olek?"

Seamus rubbed his forehead. "We need to keep him from capturing *Quite Possibly Alien* and using its drive as a weapon. And we need to keep him from capturing the Spider on Fir, with Wren Nesting. Which is also a doomsday weapon."

Macer glanced at Lady Tabatha. "Do you want to check that his brain is still attached to his mouth?"

She chuckled. "It is."

"Then what does that jumble of words mean?"

"We can ask Poole when we see him. I believe it's a religious site on the planet Pinion in the Ojinate. Until we arrive at Prescott Grange, there's nothing we can do about either one."

"Okay, that leaves us Ixatl-Nine-Go."

"There we have an immediate problem," Seamus said.

"The *Defiant*."

"Right. There's a war going on over there. There was real-time data streaming in right up until we sheared off the short-range communications array."

Singh visibly paled.

That's right, buddy. No calling for reinforcements if you somehow get loose.

"So long as the war stays over there, I don't see what the problem is."

"It's not so much a problem as an opportunity. You know how in recorded dramas sometimes everything looks lost, and you think there's no way the good guys can win, and then the cavalry shows up?"

"Like in *The Homecoming of Junh*?"

"Not like that. Junh *causes* the cavalry to show up. And we know there's a cavalry, because Junh is in the cavalry. I'm talking about stories where the cavalry shows up out of nowhere and no one is expecting it. It hasn't even been hinted at that there's a cavalry around. But they show up and save the day."

"So like a *seanscéal*, where the moral is 'wait for a miracle to happen'."

Seamus nodded. "Like that."

"Nobody likes a story like that."

"The hero does," Lady Aster said.

Macer laughed. "That's clever. They would indeed."

Seamus held his hands before him, palms up, thumbs out, fingers slightly curved. "I imagine the cavalry would like that story too."

Macer stared at Seamus. That gesture was one school-teachers and some of the older men on the island used. It signaled the end of the talking. That there was no more to the *seanscéal* but the thinking about it. He wondered where Seamus had learned that gesture, since he'd barely been on the island and was homeschooled as a boy.

That gesture held a mighty force for Macer, because it was how House would end her stories of Junh, once they were well acquainted enough for face-to-face lessons. And it was how, if he hadn't been listening like he should have, he knew he'd been hearing a *seanscéal*, and too lost in his own thoughts to notice.

He thought about what Seamus had said. And then he thought about what Seamus had done. How he had not simply spoken a *seanscéal*, but had dragged Macer into speaking one with him.

And not just any *seanscéal*, but a story of Junh. One which always began with a question, and often ended with the same question, though not necessarily in the same words.

Are you Junh?

Macer stood, gripped the back of Singh's chair, and began dragging it toward the airlock. "Let's go round up the cavalry and find out."

66

**Templeman Space, Between Trinity System and Prescott
Grange System**

Seamus glanced across the aisle of the League assault
shuttle as Lady Sarah Aster belted in beside her
mother.

There was a perfectly good empty seat beside Seamus. He'd
had Hector Poole take the controls once Seamus had eased the
hull away from the liberty boat dock. He could be riding in the
cockpit, and making sure that Poole really could pilot a vessel,
but instead he'd thought it important to spend time with Sarah.
If she intended to be angry at him, she might as well tell him.
He couldn't think of what he'd done wrong. It felt like he'd
done everything right, at great personal risk.

They were eight hours from Prescott Grange space and
everything had to go as planned. He didn't want to end up
punching into a heavily armed League system where *Defiant*

could slag *Four-Squared* to glass the instant they dropped into normal space, and all the witnesses would assume *Defiant* had the right of it. And Prescott Grange was where *Defiant* wanted to go, so he had to assume they had allies there, other vessels with rider-infested crews that could capture Macer and his crew, and nic Cartaí as well, if they somehow decided not to murder them outright.

As for *Springbok*, unless they jumped immediately they were doomed. It would only take one well-placed salvo to cripple them, and if it came to that, he'd rather push the Templeman drive into overload than be taken alive. He was about out of juice, and once the fight left him he wouldn't get it back. He didn't like the idea of Sarah Aster as Ixatl-Nine-Go's toy any more than he liked the idea of being under its power himself. And the two of them together, he didn't want to imagine what he'd be forced to do to *her* to punish *him* for fighting free and disobeying, and even if he surrendered, and let it break him to its will, it would still force him to *use her* for its pleasure, and he *would not* let that happen.

"James," Lady Tabatha Aster said.

He glanced at her.

"You're frightening Sarah."

"Oh. I'm sorry."

"Did you take your medicine?"

She'd begun giving him new pills three days ago. Something to stabilize his emotional state and prepare him for his confrontation with Ixatl-Nine-Go. He didn't think the pills did anything but taking them made her feel happy. Like she was helping. "I will." *When this is over.*

"It's for your own good."

"I'm not so concerned about that anymore."

When she spoke, Sarah Aster's words were like a lash. "You said you'd stand by me. And then in the next breath you hare off."

He closed his eyes. "It's a metaphor."

"For what?"

"For what one does when trapped. When slipping the noose, or hiding amongst the body bags, or chewing a limb off remains an option. And the thought of doing so seems worse than death."

Someone settled into the seat beside him.

Took his hand.

Filled it with pills, and said, "Take those, you fool."

Seamus cracked an eye open.

She tossed a juice bulb into his lap and returned to her seat. "Doctor's orders."

Seamus palmed the pills, pretended to swallow them, drained the juice bulb, and pocketed the empty, along with the pills. When he glanced up, he found Sarah Aster watching.

"My father will hate you," she said.

He started to say what he always did. That all the girls said that, and it was a large part of his appeal. But the truth was, any appeal he'd had had been lost, and he was now like a convict who'd been sentenced but not yet begun to serve his time.

"I'm sure he's hated better men than me, and hung them too."

The assault shuttle bumped against *Defiant*'s foreign port service airlock, scraped along the hull, and scraped across it again, in reverse, and then they were at full stop, airlocks mated.

"Ciarán's cat could handle a docking better than that," Seamus muttered.

"What did you say?" Sarah asked.

"I said that's not a good bit of helmsmanship."

The plan was that Seamus and three of the crew from *Four-Squared* would debark on *Defiant*, Seamus to hack in and clear the way while the *Four-Squared* people—League deserters he'd identified while digging through Poole's and *Springbok*'s datasets—would handle the wet work. They were all frontier-worlds cannon fodder that had at least basic training with exos. They hadn't seemed happy when he'd spoken to them, but they didn't seem heartbroken, either. Their biggest concern seemed to be the idea that Aoife nic Cartaí might try to commandeer *Four-Squared* while they were away. They were only willing to agree if Macer Gant was made acting captain, and given full-access credentials to the ship's systems.

"Clear the aisle," Captain Violent said. "Are you ready, junior?"

Seamus glanced up at the giant League war machine. "Are you talking to me?"

"Am I looking at you?"

"I can't tell. Your helmet is pointed this way but the visor's opaque. It's not clear what you're looking at."

"Ruthie," Violent said. "Pick him up and bring him."

"After he puts his helmet on," Ruth Less said. There'd been some discussion of having her pilot the assault shuttle given Poole's marginal piloting rating, but the *Four-Squared* pilot wanted nothing to do with that. They were a team and they'd fight as a team.

The one called Jimio spoke from behind him. "Let's hear the rule one more time."

"Stay behind the captain and pilot. If it's in front of them leave it alone. If it's behind me, kill it."

"If it's behind you and it's not Jimio."

"Right." They'd stuffed him into a League hardsuit that Macer had modified to interface with their exos. He'd torn the guts out of the exo fast-patched to the liberty boat deck and stuffed them into the hardsuit along with Seamus. Seamus didn't recognize most of the displays but it didn't matter, since he didn't have any control over them anyway. They showed what the captain wanted him to see.

Seamus took a deep breath. It was just bad luck that one of

the attackers from the shuttle had survived, and it hadn't been one of the ones inside the hull. Apparently there'd been a team of four hull-breakers clinging to the exterior of the shuttle and all but one of them thrown off when Poole had splatted those inside.

It took a crew of four to operate the hull-breaking drill, or force beam, or whatever, according to Captain Violent, so the attacker had come into the shuttle via the aft airlock and worked his way up through the shuttle hull to the forward airlock. From there all he had to do was step out onto the liberty boat bay and open fire. The captain believed the person inside the exo was already messed up pretty bad, otherwise Seamus couldn't have done what he'd done to stop it.

So don't try that again, junior.

He wasn't going to try that again. If it was in front of him he was going to ignore it, and if it was behind him and not Jimio he was going to kill it with the plasma rifle Ruth Less had slung over her shoulder for the moment. There was no slowing down, and no taking of prisoners, and no quarter given.

"Why are we doing this again?" Jimio said.

"Because they came to our ship, and messed with us," Ruth Less said.

"And because we hate them with the raging fire of a thousand roasting suns," Captain Violent said.

"But you hate everyone like that," Jimio said.

"Well, it's not every day I get to show it. Now let's roll."

"But you show it every day," Jimio said.

"Shut up, Jimio," Ruthie said.

"Pass me up the Freeman, Ruthie." The captain held out an armored fist, one big enough to crush a man's head.

"Feet first," Seamus said.

67

S eamus crouched in front of the airlock controls. So far no one had opened it from inside *Defiant*, which was good, because they were easy prey pinned in like they were, and Seamus wasn't behind a wall of battle armor, but in front, with a satchel on the deck in front of him, and a cobbled-together device he'd made from parts Macer had helped him scrounge. It wasn't pretty but he was certain it would work, provided the samples weren't all ruined and one of them had the appropriate access permissions.

He'd had to paw through the wreckage in the stern of the assault shuttle, and he had separated out the materials into what he believed were matching sets of eyeballs, and fingers, and identification cards, most of the biomaterials messed up but serviceable. He *hoped* digging through the gore had been a waste of time, but the sort of time one had to waste, because he'd only get one shot.

He also had two perfect sets of samples from the cockpit crew. "A lieutenant outranks a warrant officer, right?"

"Depends," Violent said. "A live warrant officer outranks a dead lieutenant."

"That is not very helpful." Seamus extracted the lieutenant's eyeballs from the labelled baggie and fitted them to the activator device. He did the same with the index fingers and thumbs.

He toggled the device alive. While he waited for it to warm up, he extracted the lieutenant's identification card from the baggie.

"You do this a lot, junior?"

"When I was kid. It's like... senior apprentice work. Better than cleaning up, but still manual labor."

"You seem good at it."

"Thanks. You seem above average in height."

"Ouch."

"What's the machine do?"

"Makes the parts seem alive enough to fool the sensors."

"How?"

"Temperature, conductivity, motion. I didn't make it so it could blink. I think if you wanted in on or out on a warship you'd want it bad, and fast. Don't step on me when the hatch opens."

"If it opens."

The device beeped and he went to work.

Ten seconds later the hatch opened.

And Ruthie didn't step on him. She kneed him in the helmet, and while he saw stars Jimio picked him up.

"My machine."

Jimio stepped on the device, grinding it into the deck.

"Thanks. You can put me down."

Jimio laughed and took off at a sprint.

The airlock behind them had nearly closed when Hector Poole yanked the assault shuttle free without releasing the clamps.

Alarms began to sound as fast patch rained from the overhead behind them.

"Blast doors," Jimio said, and then it seemed like they were airborne as he raced along the corridor in long, low leaps, then Jimio was down, towing Seamus along by the hardsuit's equipment belt, and they were skidding along the corridor, a blast door scything down from the overhead and Jimio yanking Seamus clear at the last instant, Seamus's helmet rattling against the vibrating deck plates.

"Okay," Seamus panted. "Okay." *I should have taken those pills.*

"You are very light weight," Jimio said. "I like that in a psychopathic criminal sidekick."

Seamus stood and checked his hardsuit for pinholes and rends. "I'm not a sidekick. We're partners. Try being the silent type."

They listened. It sounded like a thousand people were being butchered alive ahead.

"Excellent," Seamus said. "This might actually work."

68

The plan was elegantly simple. They stepped into a compartment with an implant reprogrammer turned on. Anyone that wasn't down on the deck screaming and writhing in agony got a plasma bolt to the forehead. They'd brought along implant extractors but that proved too slow to be practical. And wrestling hand to hand with an Ixatl-Nine-Go-fueled corpse muttering *die* over and over again wasn't safe. There were only four of them, and Seamus mostly useless with a weapon. They couldn't afford to take chances.

"Why aren't they locking the compartments from the inside?" Jimio said.

"Nevin Green," Seamus said. "They are locking them, and the ship's synthetic intelligence is unlocking them for us."

"How do you know that?"

"Because we discussed it, back on Trinity Station. What to do in just this sort of event."

"You and this ship's artificial intelligence. Discussed this."

"That's right."

"We haven't run into anyone in an exo yet, either."

"We won't, unless someone puts one together from parts. All the ones in service are locked into their storage racks.

"I'd blast them out," Ruth Less said.

"You'd have to get to them first. All the storage compartments have been vented to space."

"The boat bay."

"Vented."

"Why didn't your syntho friend just let you in?"

"Friends. Because they didn't know it was me. And even if it was me, I might have been under Ixatl-Nine-Go's control. They weren't about to help us until we started acting to plan."

"Then I guess there's a reason we're heading to engineering and not the bridge."

"According to Nevin Green, it's the safest place to be. And there are some things he can't do."

"Such as?"

"Such as simultaneously vent every last compartment on this vessel to space."

69

They halted outside the compartment hatch.

Captain Violent shouted over the screaming. "Well, junior?"

"This is it. Ixatl-Nine-Go is smart, and has likely figured out where we're going and what we're doing by now. There will be a firefight. "

"It's about... fudging time." Ruth Less said.

"It is a tad like butchery," Jimio said.

"It isn't *like* butchery," Captain Violent said. "It *is* butchery. And I *love* it. The only thing I'd love more is if they'd lay their guns down and come along quiet. But the pair of you need to keep this in mind. This isn't a game, and these *things* are trying to butcher *us*."

"They're people we're killing," Jimio said. "Not monsters."

Seamus had to shout over the screams. "I was one of them!"

That got their attention.

He took off his helmet and touched the scar on his forehead.

"A friend of mine did this to me, pulling Ixatl-Nine-Go out of my skull with a field-reinforced glove. Not a minute earlier

I'd stood toe-to-toe with him, with a razorgun he'd entrusted to his friend Seamus mac Donnacha, and aimed it at his chest, and pulled the trigger.

"If I'd ever used a gun before I would have murdered him, stepped over his body, and murdered Aoife nic Cartaí, because he was the only thing standing between me and her. His mong hu tore my hand off, else I would have strangled them both if he hadn't handed me the gun, and if I didn't succeed, my dead corpse would have kept trying until it did.

"A while later Ixatl-Nine-Go possessed my father and made him murder the entire mac Donnacha clan, thinking to hurt me. I think it did hurt me, but not to the extent Ixatl-Nine-Go had hoped. Destroying our family ship and blowing out a section of the Trinity Station ring hurt more. If you were looking out a viewport at the moment of ignition, you might have seen the flash all the way out at the Boneyard.

"The only reason that didn't break me was because I was already broken. It had turned me into a self-loathing monster by then, and if I told you all the things I did while it was inside me, you would burn me down and spit on the ashes, and I wouldn't blame you.

"I'm telling you each this in confidence, and if you repeat a word I've said, I will know, and I might not hunt you down and kill you, but you will wish that I had. So think about that, and if you decide you can't keep your mouths shut, it's best you kill me now, because I'm not messing. I'd like to try to salvage something good out of what's left of me, and I don't want to do it as some sort of pity object or sideshow attraction. I can't undo what I've done. I'd like to lie down and die but it seems cowardly.

"I'm telling you all this because you need to understand. They are people. And they are monsters. And butchering them is the kindest thing you can do for them. There's no saving them, short of getting Ixatl-Nine-Go out of them, and we can't do that in bulk. Maybe one day, if we survive.

"Make no mistake, they *are not* trying to butcher us. They're trying to turn *us* into monsters."

Seamus touched the hatch control, not to open it, but to operate the comms. "Mr. Glasnevin, will you turn off the gravity generators?"

"As you wish, Mr. Reynard."

"Thank you, sir."

Seamus eyeballed his silent partners. "I could use your help in there."

"You could use your helmet," Jimio said.

"It's better this way." Seamus looked them over one last time. "I can see why Macer likes you tractor jockeys so much. You're all of you like meat in a roll-up."

"What's that supposed to mean?" Ruth Less said.

"It means wait sixty and then come in guns blazing," Captain Violent said. "And if either of you kill him by accident before I do?"

"You'll murder us," Jimio said.

70

There were ten of them in the compartment, and one of them fired at him and missed, and another fired at him, and hit, square in the chest, not a plasma bolt, but some sort of heavy projectile that slammed him to the deck. It had holed his hardsuit, but it hadn't made it through the exo modifications Macer had added. All it had done was stuff a jagged plate of battle armor against his ribs at high velocity.

At least one rib was broken, but it hadn't collapsed a lung, so all in all, not the outcome he'd hoped for. He wanted to be standing. He tried to roll over and get his legs under him. No joy.

They were out from behind cover, and towering over him, all ten of them with dead eyes black as night and smiles on their lips.

"Help me up," Seamus said.

"Crawl for us first, and we'll consider it," one of them said.

"I already did. Last time."

"And you were so good at it. Crawl for us *again*."

"It's these hullwalkers. They're clamping me to the deck."

"Turn them off."

"The controls are shorted," Seamus lied.

"Drag them along, then."

Seamus flinched as weapons fire seared overhead, the air suddenly roasting, heavy with the odor of charring flesh and melting plastics. He covered his face with his arms, and screamed as broken bone scythed through flesh, screamed again when something wet and meaty splashed across his face, and continued to scream into the silence.

A man towered over him. It felt like the gravity was back on.

"Junior. Give me your hand."

"Roll me over first." His guts heaved. "I need to spew."

Later, though not much later, Jimio helped him up. "You're like that little piece of gristle nothing can chew through, aren't you?"

"He's more like that crusty stuff around the cap on a tube of nutrient paste," Ruth Less said. "The stuff that you get in your mouth by accident, and then you can't spit it out. It just keeps moving around when you poke at it, like some sort of living thing, and even after you rinse, and spit it down the drain, every now and then it feels like it's back, but you know it can't be."

Seamus limped to the environmental workstation. It had been hit by small-arms fire, and half the display lay dead. He burrowed in three layers deep, mostly by feel, and triggered a maintenance-yard self-test of the environmental systems, one that began by venting all the atmosphere from the vessel.

Seamus groaned. "It alarms for three minutes before it starts opening the airlocks, beginning with the boat bay force window."

"We need to find you a hardsuit."

"I have a skinsuit on. And a rebreather in my pocket."

"You have a skinsuit on in a hardsuit?"

"Two of me could fit in here." *And he didn't need to interface with the hardsuit. He was just cargo.* "I could almost have a hard-suit on in a hardsuit."

"But you don't," Ruth Less said.

"Just pieces of exo plate."

"That was a big slug hit you. Good thing they didn't aim for your head."

"He was hoping they'd aim for his head," Captain Violent said. "Or one of us would. Now what, junior?"

"We wait until we feel the ship start spewing life pods. We want to sort and separate those aboard with riders from those without. When the shuddering stops, I terminate the environmental test."

Seamus rigged the implant programmer to the comms station like Macer had shown him. If it worked, it would keep the screamers down and screaming.

"We shut it off after all the bad guys bail but before we kill all the screamers," Jimio said.

"That's the idea."

"A warrior would let it run," Violent said.

"That's probably smarter." They knew there were Olek disciples like Singh on board, and the sorting wouldn't separate them from the other screamers.

"Maybe you should keep your hands in your lap and let it."

"Maybe you should try to make me."

Seamus toggled the test off. "We would never be able to root them out of the ship in small enough groups to use the implant extractors."

"But in life pods we can," Jimio said.

"That's the idea. We can save them. We can kill the monsters and give the people a second chance."

"And that," Violent said, "is what's wrong with you, Free-man. Not everyone's life is worth salvaging."

"And that's what's wrong with you, Leagueman," Seamus said. "You underestimate how selfish we are." He wasn't trying to save them for their sake. He was doing it for his own.

It took them nearly twenty minutes to make it to an airlock Hector Poole hadn't ripped to shreds. Poole scraped the assault shuttle along the hull but eventually got the aft hatch mated, and once aboard they shucked out of their exos and hardsuit in the relatively bot-cleaned stern of the vessel. Poole remembered to release the docking clamps but still managed to knock the shuttle against *Reliant*'s hull on disengagement.

"You are in rough shape, junior."

"Nothing an autodoc can't fix."

"Jimio, go bring the doctor lady back here."

"On it."

Lady Tabatha looked him over and slapped a couple of the emergency stimpacks on him. They weren't like the expired ones at Seán mac Diarmuid's, but fresh ones, and strong. He had that same alert but disconnected feeling with an extra dose of disconnectedness. Lady Tabatha had him go forward and sit where he had before, and again the seat beside him was empty, until Captain Violent dropped into it beside him.

"You did a good thing, junior."

"I didn't do it to be good. I did it to be decent. There's a difference."

"I didn't know that."

"There is. We need to start picking up the life pods. If we use Macer's stolen longboat, we can tractor them in one or two at a time. It's doable."

"There are no life pods."

"Sure there are. I felt the hull buck. It's unmistakable. When I was a kid... Never mind. I felt it. It's unmistakable."

"We all felt it. And you're right. It's not a feeling a kid forgets."

"It's easier to pick them up now, before we drop into normal space. They're in a bubble. There's no place for them to go."

"Seamus," Sarah said.

"Wait." Seamus listened. The assault shuttle was much bigger than a longboat, but it was basically a small hull, with relatively weak force shielding. It sounded like they were being pelted every now and then. "How can there be a debris field in a Templeman bubble?"

"Seamus—"

"Did something happen to *Springbok*?"

"It's fine," Sarah said. "You need to understand—"

"Oh no. The pods. Where they rigged to blow?"

"They were a threat," Lady Tabatha said. "They were always going to be a threat."

"Sure, until they're free of Ixatl-Nine-Go. But not after."

"No one would trust them after that. They'd be stripped of their rank. Cashiered. They'd be nothing but a burden. To the state. To their families."

"Why? It's not their fault. It's not something they've done. It's something done *to them*."

"It doesn't matter."

"But they're *innocent*."

"It doesn't matter."

"Why not?"

"We didn't make the world," Lady Tabatha said. "We just—"

"Rule it?" Captain Violent said.

"Live in it."

Seamus licked his lips. He didn't want to ask. He didn't need to ask, because he already knew the answer. He just couldn't believe it. "How could Hector Poole both fly this vessel and fire its weapons at the same time?" He stared at Lady Tabatha because he didn't dare look at Sarah. "Do not lie to me, and tell me there are controls in the cockpit. I have piloted this vessel. I know there are none."

"He couldn't," Sarah said. "I—"

"I'd like Lady Aster to tell me, please. About how this could have occurred in a world that she, and her husband, Lord Aster, and the Queen, their sworn protector, and yours, had no hand in making."

"I fired the weapons," Sarah said.

"I know that. And that was not my question."

"The medications," Lady Tabatha said.

"I am quite familiar with these medications. Without them in my system I would be at the controls of this craft and you and your major would be in the airlock, unless you were outside the hull. You can answer me now, or you can answer me later. If I were you, I would choose now."

"Well, you're not me, are you?"

"I thought I was at least related to you. However distantly."

"We've sworn to protect the League. We have done so."

"And I agreed to stand by your daughter. And I have not done so, believing her in safe hands."

"It wasn't an oath," Sarah said. "And even if it was, I release you."

"You presumptuous little gutter-rat," Lady Tabatha said. "How *dare* you upbraid me? I'm her mother. You're a *nothing* little—"

"I'm less than nothing." He gazed at Sarah Aster. "You weren't raised right, so I'll forgive you this time. Everyone's entitled to one mistake." He licked his lips. He felt very lucid. Very *concentrated*. Like everything that wasn't essential to him had been boiled away, and all that was left was what he was. Like a neutron star, dense, and all of one piece. "You have no idea how oaths work. I'll instruct you now, by example. Watch my lips, and see how it is done."

"Seamus—"

"I, Seamus, of no family, of no fixed address, with no guild affiliation, and few friends and comrades, declare that hence-forth *I* own this world. I solemnly swear to fix this world, or if, upon closer inspection, find that proves impractical, vow to utterly raze it and begin anew."

"The medication—"

"Mother—"

Captain Violent tapped the back of Seamus's hand. "You're no stranger to the stimpack."

"You could say that. I'm accident-prone. And I grew up working around hard surfaces. Ones that often pushed back."

"Good to know. What you said—"

"It's the tragedy of the commons writ large. And they can't even see it."

"I don't know anything about that. But I do know a good brawl when I see one." Violent leaned forward in his seat, and twisted so he could look Seamus in the eye. "And I'm in."

71

Contract System, Outer Reach (Huangxu Contested Space)

"Follow me," Aspen said, and Ciarán did as commanded. The Contract native led her compact throng of daughters/protectors along the ring—away from the Contract Station mooring-berth airlock where *Impossible Bargains* lay, bow in—and toward the maw of a conduit-encrusted radial that led toward the arcade.

The daughter named Bea touched Ciarán's hand and signed, *Welcome to our home.*

"Thank you." Ciarán had only been on five space stations, Trinity, Ambidex, Fir, the wreckage of Prescott Grange, and now Contract Station. If he had to rank them purely on sensory appeal, Contract Station came in a distant fifth. Even Prescott Grange being blown to splinters and falling down a gravity well seemed more inviting.

May I help you with your burden?

"You may." He handed her the square wooden box. "Can you read the Ojin?"

A little.

"What does it say there?"

Open me when you must.

"Close enough. Here." He fished in his pocket, found the black coin, and placed it atop the box. "If that's still there by the time we get where we're going, you can keep it. It has a picture of Wisp on it."

It doesn't.

"It does, on one side. On the other side it has the all-seeing eye." He winked at her.

She stared at him, and ran her gaze up and down him.

Is that real? Uncle has a wooden one.

She meant the overseer's rod. Merchants without the real item often carried a carved wooden facsimile, which along with the Guild ring marked them as free traders, and capable of striking a bargain and living up to it. As a merchant apprentice, he remained a long way from earning a merchant's ring, and after that, if he lived that long, a merchant captain's greatcoat.

And given that he'd decided to tell Adderly the truth, that he couldn't fulfill the contract because he no longer had a ship, he likely would never live that long. Odds were he would be forced to trade in the rod for the tusker and the slane shortly after his first and final appearance before the Guild licensing bench.

Until that moment, though, he couldn't be Farmer Ciarán, sulky plowboy failure. He remained Merchant Apprentice mac Diarmuid off *Quite Possibly Alien*. He needed to act like it, for the honor of the captain and the ship, his every word and gesture as textbook perfect as he could make them.

"It's a real overseer's rod. And you'll never guess who gave it to me."

He felt a little bad about saying that, because proper names were difficult to communicate in the hand cant without a system agreed upon up front. There were two usual ways, one that relied on both speakers knowing the people spoken about, and the other by spelling out the name in a language both people shared. Every family had their own talk for names, and every crew as well.

Their own talk and their own secrets. He wore the spire again, a parting gift from Engineer Hess, and crafted from the same material as the coin, and as *Quite Possibly Alien's* hull.

He watched her puzzle on the problem until he was certain he had her stumped. He didn't want to appear rude by ignoring her, but he needed to look around, and he couldn't do that and watch her fingers at the same time.

The ring at Contract felt colder than the others, the cargo-handling equipment more battered and ill maintained, and the yellow novice trails painted on the deck grimed to brown and worn through in spots, with the overpowering reek of the place inescapable, like a pet shop with a broken recycler, one that specialized in snakes and possibly other yet unexamined reptiles. There were people about, and while they seemed somewhat industrious, there was none of the boisterous shouting and catcalling of Trinity Station, but a low hum of loading motors, the occasional squeal of a load tractor's tires, and the clicking din of Contract speech, unintelligible to Ciarán, and likely unpronounceable without the addition of some click-making organ he had no desire to possess. Without Aspen's passable Trade speech and her daughters' command of Freeman hand cant, he'd be unable to communicate at all. If he somehow became separated from his guides, he'd be reduced to a gesturing pantomime, if even that.

Aspen moved briskly along the ring surrounded by her daughters. He had thought on Prescott Grange that this arrangement—the more human-seeming Aspen in the center of an armored perimeter of milky-scaled and marginally

humanoid defenders—a result of being naked and afraid in a
League prison cell. Either his assumption was false, and this
their normal arrangement relative to one another, or they still
feared something, here on their home station. Or, perhaps they
were exhibiting a physical expression of a status hierarchy.
They were so barely human in appearance, he found himself
thinking of them as aliens, with Academy jargon ready at hand
to overintellectualize every aspect of this first encounter in their
territory.

A simpler explanation, a *human* explanation, was that they
were captain and crew, and moved on their home dock as they
did out in the wider world, with an overabundance of caution
drilled into them through experience, and no way to turn that
hyperawareness off, except consciously. They were coming
home, and their minds outracing their limbs, which moved
through practiced motions as automatic as breath. Did they
hug or kiss their returning travelers on the arcade, as Freeman
did, or save their demonstrations of affection for in private, as
was the practice in the Ojinate? Did they express affection at
all, did they feel affection, did they feel any emotion, those
were all questions he found himself asking, not because they
were reasonable questions, but despite what he knew about
them: that they were woven from the same fabric as him
though on a different loom, and perhaps even by a different
hand.

He wondered if the People, upon first meeting the mong hu,
had similar thoughts regarding their *otherness*. He brushed his
fingertips across Wisp's brow. She paced along beside him, fully
visible, as if on display. The merchant and the mong hu, like in
a storybook.

Unlikely, he decided. It would have been love at first sight.
Maybe if the mong hu had spoken in roars, and walked around
on their hind legs, and mowed down their enemies with

plasma rifles, and afterward married your cousin. Maybe then they'd be more terrifying.

And maybe not.

The answer was likely much simpler. He just didn't like snakes. Not from personal experience, since there weren't any on the island, or on the station, but purely based on their reputation in the media and on the actions of a few two-legged impersonators. A wise merchant would wait and judge them by what they did and not by what people said about them. But since he wasn't a wise merchant, he'd try not to judge them at all and see how that worked out.

The arcade of Contract Station appeared nearly abandoned. The signs were all in Huangxu, and other than a few stalls selling unappealingly odorous foodstuffs and two selling general merchandise, the storefronts appeared, not boarded up, or abandoned, but *uninitialized*, as if they'd built it and no one had come. It was unusual to spin up a station, even a small one, without a spindle, purely on spec. But one *might* build a station to explain away otherwise suspicious comings and goings from a system hiding a secret weapons lab. That seemed the most likely explanation, since there had also been a superluminal node in the system and nothing he'd seen so far to justify that investment.

"I should check in with the stationmaster," Ciarán said.

Aspen kept walking. "Later."

They passed the station's administrative section and it too had the look of continued and uninterrupted vacancy. They walked for a good way, perhaps nearly halfway around the ring, until they came to a section that did seem like it had seen continue use, a security station and detention facility. The facade of the structure appeared to have taken plasma-rifle and small-arms fire sometime in the distant past, the impact tiles scrubbed but not recoated, burn marks yet showing, and fractures radiating like spider webs from projectile strikes.

Inside it was much the same, though the snake-pit odor seemed more pervasive. A third of the luminaires were out of service. There appeared to be a lift, but one used as a closet, so it was the stairwell for them, down three flights into the working guts of the station elsewhere, but here, a warren of cells, all but one of them standing empty and in darkness, the single illuminated cell holding a single occupant.

She sat in a mobility chair, a well-used one of recent vintage. She'd been quite tall when she'd had the use of her legs. Her hands were bent in on themselves, the fingers knotted into very nearly claws, and the rest of her except her face swaddled in white robes, ones designed for utility rather than appearance. Had she wrapped herself in bedsheets, it would have given the same haphazard impression. She seemed quite closely related to Aspen. Sisters, perhaps, but unlike Aspen, bent and broken in body, much of her flesh wasted away, so that she seemed half skeleton.

Her eyes seemed sane and attentive enough, though. She sat hunched over a desktop display unit. Her gnarled fingers tapped the display and an annunciator lashed to her chair spoke.

"You're a pretty one. And a long way from home."

Wisp brushed against Ciarán and purred.

"We'll get to him in a minute," she said.

Aspen gripped the controls of the prison cell and simply triggered it open. Her daughters rushed into the cell and surrounded the woman in the mobility chair. The chair rocked on its lift bands, and the woman laughed as she disappeared beneath the mob, a cacophony of clicks echoing off the hard cell walls.

"She's not a prisoner," Aspen said. "It's a familiar place for her, and her command post during the insurrection. She has it set up the way she likes."

That made some sense, but it didn't explain why the cell

had been locked. If the lock wasn't meant to keep her in, what was it meant to keep out?

Aspen glanced at Ciarán and motioned him into the cell, along with Wisp.

"After you," he said, and she obliged him, entering the cell before him. Wisp faded into the shadows rather than enter the cell.

"I have a gift for you, sister." The woman pointed at a beribboned box on the workstation. "Pass that to your mother, Emma."

Aspen took the box from her daughter. "Thank you."

"Open it. I doubt you'll like it even though I know it will fit."

Aspen opened the box and immediately slammed it shut. She elbowed past Ciarán, plunged into the corridor outside the cell, and touched the cell controls. The hiss of the containment field coming alive drowned out the clicking of joyous homecoming, and the clunk of mechanical latches ramming home echoed along the corridor.

Ciarán had caught a glimpse of the contents of the box, but a glancing view only. It contained a pendant spire, but one that seemed subtly wrong. Regardless, he was now trapped on the wrong side of a prison cell door.

"Aunt?" the one called Dee signed.

"Your mother has chosen to separate herself from us."

Aspen stared at them from the jailer's perspective.

"You're wondering when I knew," the woman in the mobility chair said.

"I'm wondering what I'm going to have to give Commodore Olek to get my girls out of the mess you've made."

"The merchant will likely be enough."

"That's my thought as well. Pardon me if I don't linger. I'll just go ask him, shall I?"

"Lick his boots while you're there, why don't you."

"If I do, it won't be for myself, you can be sure of that."

"Pardon me if I don't believe a word you say."

The pair stared at each other while the daughters, or nieces, or both clicked and signed in anger and confusion. Aspen swept her gaze about the cell, lingered on Ciarán, and stalked away before he could speak.

Ciarán let the noise wash over him. He let the idea that he was now imprisoned wash over him. He needed to stay focused on the mission. He wasn't a multitasker. One horrible job at a time seemed to be his motto. And his first job was to live up to Aoife nic Cartaí's contract. Not that he truly could now, without a hull under his command. He could at least register that the contract yet remained in force, and he was there on Aoife's behalf, to do what could be done to live up to the spirit if not the letter of the deal. There remained an ancient piece of speaking it fell to him to perform, the verbal portion of the contract that lay entirely within his control, and which custom specified in minute detail.

"I wish to speak with Adderly."

"I am Adderly," the woman in the mobility chair said.

"Adderly, I apprise you that the terms of the contract between yourself and Aoife nic Cartaí remain in force for another three days. As Aoife nic Cartaí's representative in Contract space, I stand ready to negotiate any additions or amendments to the contract that you or your agents may choose to propose. I regret to inform you that while I am here, I currently lack the resources to fulfil the contract. Perhaps this will change in the next three days. At the moment, however, I do not anticipate such an improvement in circumstances. In light of this—"

"Have you read this agreement, Merchant Leprous?"

"Merchant Apprentice Ciarán mac Diarmuid. Merchant Leprous is a convenient fiction. And I have not read the agreement."

"How do you know then that it has or has not been met?"

"My understanding is that the contract is for transportation of certain cargo. At present I have no ship, and the chances of *Quite Possibly Alien* arriving in time to meet the contract are slim to nonexistent. Perhaps we might consider some modification to the contract."

They all started clicking at once, loudly, including Adderly. When she spoke the others grew silent.

"There is some confusion as to your lack of a vessel, as you arrived here on one under your control."

"I sent it away."

"Why?"

"It's more complicated than I care to explain. Now—"

"According to my niece Beatrice, who was eavesdropping on you and the ship's captain, it's rather straight forward. You *chose* to send the vessel away and thus default on the contract as you understand it."

"I did."

"Bea also tells me that you informed the ship's captain that Merchant Bosditch and *Last Stand* are no more, and Commodore Olek to blame."

"I did."

"Do you have proof of this?"

"On *Quite Possibly Alien*."

"Were you aware that Merchant Bosditch and I are husband and wife?"

He ran his gaze across her face, across the damaged, alien-seeming body trapped in a mobility chair. "I beg your pardon. I was not aware."

"We are more than flesh. That we remain constructed atop an animal?" She shrugged. "There is more to each of us than we dare imagine."

"I am instructed," Ciarán said.

"What I most love... loved... about Bosditch was his daring.

He could not see a thing without imagining how he might improve it."

"I wish I had better news."

"The truth is rarely good news."

"It seems that way."

"Anders and Lenoch, Bosditch's aunts. They practically raised the girls, and taught them the way of the People."

"They appear to have done a fine job."

"Is there news of them?"

"Nothing... definitive."

"What is it you aren't saying?"

"I would spare you the truth when it serves no purpose but pain."

"Pain is its own purpose. It keeps us on the path. We welcome its guidance."

"We found two unidentified bodies on Gallarus. We believe them to be crew from *Last Stand*.

"How did they die?"

He couldn't tell her they appeared to have died battling each other to the death for Merchant Roche's and Ixatl-Nine-Go's amusement. Beyond some threshold, pain stopped teaching and began altering one's nature. He wasn't certain that, stripped of the lurid details, what he dared tell them was any less painful, or transformative.

"They did not die free."

The daughters erupted in agitated clicks, and again, Adderly silenced them.

She dipped her gnarled fingers into the folds of her robe and retrieved an object, which she tossed to him, and which he inspected. It seemed simple, and mechanical, and when he squeezed it the device clicked. "Oh."

"Teach him those words he will need and can speak one-handed."

"I will teach him" Bea signed.

"Ella will teach him. You're too impatient and inclined to cheat."

"But—"

Ciarán felt the shadow of a smile steal onto his face. He quickly suppressed it.

"What?" Bea signed.

"It's so strange. We seem so differently made."

Adderly leaned forward in her seat. "And?"

"There is no gesture for 'but' in hand cant. I thought I'd invented it, as a child."

"It's the second word Beatrice spoke," Adderly said.

"'No' being the first."

"Naturally."

"Well, then. Despite appearances, we must be related."

It felt as if the air had been sucked from the compartment. The silence felt as complete as vacuum, and he doubted if a pin were to drop, or an anvil, they would have redirected an eye away from him, or razed a silence so pregnant with in-held breath.

The hissing sound of fabric against fabric broke the spell, as Adderly shifted in her seat. "You are the second Freeman I have heard express those sentiments."

She moved her chair toward him. She must have been incredibly tall when she once stood, because even seated she could look him in the eye. "I will tell you what I told Aoife nic Cartaí."

"She said that to you? That you and she were kin?"

"Never. It was Bosditch. On the night we celebrated our first successful negotiation."

"I don't understand."

"Clearly you do not. What sort of merchant doesn't read the contract?"

"A merchant apprentice. I wasn't provided a copy. Only instructions to follow."

"Here is what the contract said. Aoife nic Cartaí was to bring me a vessel and a crew so that I might search for another Freeman like Bosditch. One who did not look at us and see monsters."

"One who saw a mirror."

Her eyes welled as she nodded. "Indeed. Of those I contacted, only Aoife nic Cartaí seemed interested. Negotiations went on for weeks. Until they ceased entirely. I'd moved on and supposed that she had too, until one evening I received a message, not from Aoife nic Cartaí but another woman. One from the League. I nearly deleted it. It didn't state a subject, and seemed to consist entirely of a visual and audio recording of two women drinking in an arcade bar. They appeared to have been at it for some time.

"After a moment I realized one of the women was Aoife nic Cartaí and she was discussing *my* contract, not with specifics, but in essence. She explained that she didn't want to take the contract because she had no idea how long her vessel would be tied up in the hunt for a man like that.

"The other woman laughed, and said. 'You silly child, just amend the contract. She doesn't want to go shopping for a bung. She wants a hole filled. Tell her you'll help her either way.'

"And that's when I realized I knew that woman as well, though it had been years since we'd spoken.

"Nic Cartaí said she'd do it, and the other woman said that she should sleep on it, because there was a risk she'd end up wanting to sample the goods, or keep them for herself.

"'Assuming I can find a man like that,' nic Cartaí said.

"The other woman didn't say anything. She looked directly at the video sensor.

"And powered it off.

"Shortly thereafter, I received an amended contract. And

now, hours before the contract is to expire, you show up. A merchant apprentice."

Ciarán chose his words carefully. "If I could have brought the ship, I would have."

"Does it look like I care?"

He reached out and touched the single tear tracing its way down her cheek.

"It does. If I could change the situation, I would."

"It can't be done. Not by one man alone. I consider the contract met, and payment will be made in full."

"But—"

"I wish to make a new contract."

"I can't bind Aoife or the ship to any new contract."

"Between us, then."

"I can't do that either. I'm apprenticed to Aoife nic Cartaí, and unable to make personal arrangements."

"Suppose you wanted a haircut. Would you have to get Aoife nic Cartaí's permission for that?"

"I wouldn't."

"How about buying a meal?"

"I'm free to do that."

"So what you're really saying is that you can't make any agreement that might conflict with the terms of your contract with Aoife nic Cartaí."

"That's almost right. With my *understanding* of the terms of my contract. I might still agree to something in error, thinking it was permitted. Thus it's safer to agree to nothing."

"Are concerns for your safety paramount to you?"

"It is safer for Aoife nic Cartaí. As apprentice, consequences for my actions accrue to her."

"And you would protect her."

"With my life."

She considered him. "That is not hyperbole. You believe it to be true."

"I said it."

She tapped the arm of her chair.

"Consider then an extension of the existing contract. A modification."

"I might be authorized to do that. Depending on the nature of the modification."

"Bring me one hundred more."

"One hundred more like Merchant Bosditch."

"And like yourself."

"I can't do that."

"Then—"

"I might be able to bring you a thousand. Or maybe even ten thousand. If you want to pick one hundred from those, you're free to."

She laughed.

He didn't.

"You're serious."

"Deadly serious."

"And in return?"

"I have a long list. First you'll have to convince them to wear the spire. And show them how. You might even need to instruct them in the reasons why it's in their best interests to do so."

"And then?"

"Then I'll need your help stealing Olek's vessel and bringing Olek to account for murdering Merchant Bosditch and *Last Stand*. And your help getting into the secret weapons lab and shutting it down. And finding Vatya, and whoever else is behind Ixatl-Nine-Go."

"Those are big asks."

"They are nothing unless I deliver."

"Is that all, Merchant mac Diarmuid?"

"Merchant Apprentice mac Diarmuid. And it is not."

"What then?"

"The identity of the woman in the bar with Aoife nic Cartaí. And a description of how you know her."

"I'll need to—"

"Up front. Delivered in consideration of our mutual desire for the success of this and many future endeavors together."

"You ask me to wake the dead."

"I'm not asking you to do anything. I'm describing the terms of agreement I find acceptable. There was no reason to mention that you knew the woman with Aoife. You want to tell me as much as I want to know. But only if a linkage exists between us, through this woman. One that would do something. Change something. Revise our histories in a significant way. That would bind us together, or set us at odds."

"I met her when she served aboard *Sudden Fall of Darkness*. Olek has long used Contract system as a base of operations."

"When she served as crew."

"Advisor, I'd say. Olek collects and trades in League historical artifacts, amongst other things. She worked in this capacity for him. She had many questions about us. Too many questions for an expert in dead languages. And no reason to visit the station. Yet she did. Often. It was years ago that we met, and never before, or since. I don't know if this is her real name, but she called herself—"

"Anastasia Blum."

"You know her."

"I thought I did."

72

C iarán's stomach growled. It was getting late and he'd not had anything to eat all day. He wondered how Wisp fared. Surely there were vermin of the four-legged kind on the station if she grew desperate. She wouldn't begin by making a meal of the two-legged type. By the time she ran the station out of pests, he would with luck be out of the jail cell and able to see to her needs.

"Pay attention," Ella signed. "Now we have to start all over."

"I'm sorry," Ciarán signed.

"Go," Ella clicked.

Ciarán ran through the list of words as he'd learned them. They were mostly short and declarative. *Go* was one of them, though not the first taught, and not the general-purpose word it was in Freeman, but possessing one specific meaning, one akin to a phrase, 'go now,' or 'move quickly,' or 'hurry, while no one is watching.'

The first word he'd learned to click was very short, two clicks, and meant 'hide.' There didn't appear to be any one-click words. The first click appeared to act as an attention getter, like clearing the throat, or shouting 'hey,' or whispering 'pssst,' depending on volume and attack. He'd discovered that the palm-clicker could make several different clicking noises, depending upon how he held it, anything from a short staccato crack to a drawn-out and muted thunk. The thunks tended to be less good at attention getting but better at carrying in a noisy cell full of clicking chatter, nearly none of which he could understand. He was glad he couldn't understand, because at present his click vocabulary consisted of *hide, run/flee, play dead, climb, jump, run/engage, follow, attack, go,* and d*uck/belly down.*

Ella had begun attempting to teach him the word for *seize/grapple with* when the clicking in the compartment drowned out his best efforts. He glanced where they were all looking, and discovered that Aspen had returned and stood just outside the cell. She'd changed into an outfit that seemed less functional and more decorative, excepting the razorgun that hung from her right hip.

"What is so amusing, Merchant Leprous?"

"I now know what was in your gift box earlier. It's historically incorrect, you know."

She had replaced her pendant spire with a new earring, one that spiraled clockwise. Some visual-entertainment writers had invented the device years ago, naming it the *descending tread,* or sometimes the *screw stair,* so that one could tell the difference between the People and the Enemy in First Families dramas.

There was no way to tell the difference at a glance, which happened to be an inconvenience to the writer, and to the audience, who wanted to know from the outset who would rise and who would fall. Most of the Enemy refusing to rebel never wore the spire, and those that did and then turned tout, or simply walked away, never took theirs off.

Life wasn't like a drama. Villains rarely dressed the part, and heroes? He glanced around the cramped cell. They might be hiding in plain sight.

"You seem to have settled into captivity without complaint."

"You haven't heard my stomach talk. I thought a roof and three squares was a guarantee in a lockup. If you're going to adopt a dramatic convention, that's the one I'd start with."

Aspen powered down the cell's containment field. She entered a code and the lock sprang open.

Someone behind him clicked out *seize/grapple with* and started moving, fast, and Ciarán stuck his leg out and tripped her, and she rounded on him, all milky-crystal talons, fangs, and jutting spikes, her eyes burning red, and one of the spikes pressed to the hollow of his throat.

"The Legion of Heroes doesn't brawl." And later, unless she killed him in her anger, he would explain exactly how to tell a loaded razorgun from an empty one at a glance. And, if he was feeling voluble, how a mother and child could disagree and yet coexist. She reminded him very much of Laura Ellis with her sneaking and eavesdropping. But as to her temperament? She was no better at hiding her feelings than he was at her age. And no worse.

"Stand down, sister," Ella signed.

"Please do," Ciarán said. "I'd rather not die on an empty stomach."

"You girls go to your rooms and clean up," Adderly said. "Your mother and I need to talk in private."

Beatrice slowly retracted her deadliest and most frightening appendages until she seemed nothing more than a terrifying nightmare girl with piercing red eyes that looked like they wanted to laser through his own, drill through his brain, and out the back of his skull.

Ciarán slowly reached out and touched the back of her hand.

She blinked and the girl inside her surfaced.

"I *see* you."

"She means you harm," Bea signed.

"I get that a lot. I don't take it personally and neither should you."

"But—"

"When I need help, you will be the second person I'll call."

"Do you promise?"

"Do I need to?"

"Hurry, Bea," Ella signed. "Obey Adderly."

Bea glanced at Adderly.

She glared at her mother.

She studied Ciarán. He didn't want to get into the middle of a family argument, but she stared at him for so long that eventually he had to say something.

"Do as your aunt *suggests*. I think it will pay off."

"What if you're wrong?"

"What if I'm right?"

She turned away from him, clearly unhappy.

Ciarán called after her. "Beatrice."

She stopped and turned to face him.

"Keep your handheld with you." He pointed at the bulky present from Ryuu. "And don't forget your luggage."

Aspen touched Ciarán's arm as he hoisted his duffel. "Stay."

"I'm not getting between you two."

"Olek would like to talk. He's invited us all to dinner. Aboard *Sudden Fall of Darkness*."

"He murdered my husband."

"According to this man. Who we know virtually nothing about."

"He says he has proof."

"The Ojin were monitoring the area." Ciarán's gaze met Aspen's. "There are sensor logs showing the whole fiasco."

Aspen held out her hand. "Give them to me."

"They're aboard *Quite Possibly Alien.*" *And you know it.*

"So you say. Again, without proof. Perhaps you should ask Olek yourself before you take a stranger's word for *anything.*"

"He was sent to me. By Aoife nic Cartaí."

"Again, *so he says.* That he was aboard nic Cartaí's vessel is certainly true. But more than that? He might well be Merchant Leprous masquerading as Ciarán mac Diarmuid."

"Everything I need to know about a man—"

"You can learn by watching him. I know. I would like to watch him as he meets Olek. As he sits with Olek and simply talks. As we all do. We do not agree on how to move forward, sister, especially if what this man says is true, and *Last Stand* lost to us. We want the same thing. A future with our children in it."

"I wanted a future with my husband in it. With *his* children in it."

"That future might yet exist if this man is a liar. But if we accept his word without question? We kill all hope."

Ciarán's stomach growled. "Can I say something? Merchant to merchant?"

"What is it?"

"You're selling past the close. I don't know about Adderly, but you had me at dinner."

73

The second-shift arcade on Contract Station proved marginally more appealing by eye and ear, with the worn and rundown look of the place softened in shadow, and the clicking first-shift workers no longer evident. Given the poor and undeveloped aspect of those shops not boarded up, and the dearth of vendor carts and the other usual haunts of after-work salarymen, each and all were as apparently unappealing to the locals as they seemed to Ciarán. The place seemed nearly deserted, excepting a few people queued up at one of the slop vendors, as Seamus mac Donnacha would say.

He'd been thinking a lot about Seamus lately, and he hoped Seamus had lived, but he didn't think he could have, not given the shape he was in. Ciarán didn't know how to apportion the blame for Seamus. To Merchant Roche, to Commodore Olek, to Vatya and Ixatl-Nine-Go. He imagined the process following the pattern of those in the polities where certain substances were illegal. Did the blame lie with the maker of the substance, or the substance, or the wholesaler, or the retailer, or the user themselves?

There weren't any such laws in Freeman space, so he wasn't used to thinking in those terms. And it was a thought model, not anything he could act on, and in any case, he had no firm facts, and each person up and down the chain free to claim that they were blameless, it was the other, the sort of circular finger pointing that befuddled even professional matchmakers. There were far better men and women to settle any scores than Ciarán. Thomas Truxton, or Seamus's father, for example.

The whole lot of them conspiring together—Roche, Olek, Vatya, Ixatl-Nine-Go—had done little more than inconvenience the ship, excepting Carlsbad, who had suffered mightily, and needed accounting for.

Aoife had appointed Ciarán her proxy in regard to fulfilling the contract. She'd made no mention of him settling the ship's scores on her behalf. The truth was, *Quite Possibly Alien*, in reacting to the Ixatl-Nine-Go threat, posed a bigger danger than this bunch. That Ixatl-Nine-Go might so infest the League at some point that it toppled seemed likely, up until the time the League recognized the threat as an external one, and responded to it with full attention. In the meantime, though, there would be blood, and plenty of it.

They passed a shop selling a particularly raw-smelling assortment of recently murdered foodstuffs. Ciarán stopped and glanced around.

Aspen crossed her arms and glared at him. "What are you doing?"

"Looking for a friend. This batch of cooking smells like something she might like."

"Your cat has been spotted on the ring, chasing rats."

"First, it's not my cat, but Crewman Wisp, and second, if she was on the ring and there were rats? She wasn't chasing rats. She was catching them."

"In any case, I doubt she's here."

"Then you don't know her very well."

They carried on walking toward the ring, and it wasn't a minute later that Wisp brushed against him as she passed, and purred. And then she was gone again, padding along in the shadows. Ciarán felt a smile cross his face, when he thought about what his dad used to say about Macer and him.

Like clouds and rain, you rarely see one without the other.

Lorelei Ellis heard his dad say that, and she told him he was wrong. She knew the pair better, and Ciarán wouldn't go along with that. The idea that there was some space between them.

They're like fog.

She looked at his dad and said something that couldn't be true, but had that almost-sense of truth that made it *feel* true, even though intellectually he knew it had to be a lie. It seemed the most horrible idea he had ever heard voiced, then or since.

I heard a girl once drowned in a dense fog.

She stared at Ciarán, and her eyes were hard, and cold, and so terribly Laura.

If she did, I think she deserved it.

Aspen pulled what looked like a merchant's license from her pocket and ran it over the airlock's display. The lock opened.

Ciarán stepped into the airlock last.

Nearly.

His stomach growled. "I hope Olek isn't Folk."

"I don't know what you mean," Aspen said.

"It doesn't matter. I'm hungry enough to dine with the devil."

He noticed Adderly watching him. "You shuddered, just now," she said.

"Did I? I... just had this odd idea."

"Which is?"

"It wouldn't mean anything to you."

"Try me."

"Well. Supposing *I* was Folk?"

And all the wider world my abode.

"I don't understand."

"If at any time I frighten you? You must push away from the table. And if I ask you, or anyone you love, to dance? Have them deny me. Thrice."

"You do not look well."

"Nor do you."

She tapped a clawed finger against her mobility chair. "I have an excuse."

"Lucky you. I don't even have an explanation. But..."

"Merchant?"

"It would be a mistake to grow attached to me."

"On that we agree," Aspen said. "Now if you would please go tell my daughter."

"Tell which what?"

"Bea," Adderly said. "Have you not noticed the way she dotes on you?"

"It was love at first sight." Aspen touched the airlock controls. "She can't stop talking about the Liberator."

"I'm the Liberator."

"According to Bea and her new best friend."

"That's grand. Another nickname."

And another young woman he was destined to disappoint.

The airlock cycled, and Ciarán mac Diarmuid followed his acquaintances onto the deck of *Sudden Fall of Darkness*. He traced his fingertips along the hull. It felt dead. A year, a thousand years, he could not tell. But dead. There would be no surprises before him. No marvels. He'd entered a tomb.

Olek appeared before them, and embraced Aspen, and beheld Adderly, from a distance, and turned to Ciarán, and with one glance Ciarán knew.

"You're not from around here."

74

Ciaran thought Olek would escort them deeper into the vessel, but he instead held them just inside the airlock, in a part of the vessel Ciarán wasn't very familiar with. *Quite Possibly Alien* didn't dock at stations. It wasn't really set up for the job, because the station locks now weren't the same as they were two thousand years ago, and Aoife nic Cartaí saw no value in modifying the vessel to fit. She had a longboat, and she didn't entertain. And the fewer people knew her business the better.

The compartment was outfitted as a reception area for important people, far more gilding and filigree than Ciarán cared for, but then the decor wasn't designed to appeal to him. He wasn't a monied collector to impress or local official to bribe. Ciarán had checked, and second-epoch artifacts weren't baubles for the working man.

Commodore Olek smiled, and chuckled, and spread his arms wide. "My home away from home." He held out his hand, and Ciarán took it, and it felt like a normal human hand.

Olek tugged them together, and slapped Ciarán's back between the shoulder blades before cupping Ciarán's neck in his palm, and stepping back at arm's length, his forearms level and extended, palms up, as if he were carrying an invisible tray. He smiled with everything but his eyes. "Welcome to my home, Merchant Leprous. I am Olek."

"It's nice to finally meet you, Mr. Olek. I've heard so much about you."

"Commodore Olek."

"My apologies. Where are your other ships?"

"My other ships?"

"Doesn't 'commodore' imply you command more than one vessel?"

"Why would you think that?"

"Because that's the way words work. When someone says a word, and I recognize the word, I recall its meaning. Like magic. And the word 'commodore' means a commander of more than one vessel in the League, and in the Hundred Planets, and in the Ojinate, and in the Alexandrine." Ciarán's stomach growled.

"You seem hungry, my friend."

"Prison will do that to you, contrary to what you may have seen or heard in popular media. There are no fights in the slop line, or overturned trays on the mess tables, or dustups over the condiments between rival gangs, or even guards to shank for a packet of crisps. I feel like I've been lied to, Mr. Olek, all these years. Well, maybe not lied to, but misled at least. I wouldn't wish prison on my worst enemy, unless my worst enemy was dieting."

"Yes, well—"

"Probably not even then, now that I think about it. An overweight enemy would be easier to beat, unless we were brawling, and I don't fancy a brawl, and never have. Give me a battle of wits, Mr. Olek, I say. Or surrender now, without a fight, and I just might let you live."

"Pardon me?"

"That's what I'd say to my enemies, if I had any. And they'd be wise to listen up, because I can be a dreadful foe, particularly when women and children are involved. I come in peace, I like to say, unless you mess with me or mine. It's the Freeman way. But you know that, being a man of the world, Mr. Olek."

"Commodore Olek."

"I don't like to repeat a lie or debase the coin of verbal exchange. I won't think less of you if you're not possessing an armada. Just two ships, that's all I'm asking." Ciarán glanced about. "But one old can, and a rusty one at that? I think not, my good man."

Adderly made a sound. Ciarán glanced at her to discover she'd started laughing. "Were you friends with my husband, Merchant?"

"I'd like to think we would be friends, were we to meet. But I doubt that will happen soon."

"Perhaps you're channeling his spirit," Olek said.

"He'd have to be dead, and not just overdue for me to do that, Mr. Olek. And if he were dead, I think I'd know it, and not just that, but who did it. Unless it was an accident, of course."

"Why is that?"

"Because it would be in the Registry, the name of the matchmaker assigned to settle the debt, and who the debt was to be settled against, and additional particulars. Having met Merchant Bosditch's family now, I'd live in dread of that day, were it my name listed. They don't seem the forgiving kind."

"We're not," Aspen said.

"And it's a pity you had to go all the way to Prescott Grange to check the Registry for news, with the local superluminal node down. Do you know if it's just broken, or unentangled?"

"Broken," Aspen said.

"That's good." Ciarán's stomach growled.

"You came from Prescott Grange," Olek said.

"Straight here, Mr. Olek. Like we were chasing the devil."

"Commodore Olek."

"As I said—"

"If you've been to Prescott Grange, then you've seen my fleet."

Ciarán glanced at Aspen. "Did you know he had a fleet at Prescott Grange?"

"I had some idea he *might*."

"Might, like you suspected that he already did have a fleet there, but you weren't quite *sure*? Or might, like you were sure that he would have a fleet there soon, but *just not yet*?"

"Both," Aspen said.

"But you haven't told him."

"We haven't spoken. One of Vatya's people summoned me and ordered me to bring you."

"*Ordered* you."

"Asked me. Forcefully."

"Haven't told me what?"

"That's there's no fleet at Prescott Grange. There isn't a shipyard, or even a station anymore. Nothing but a spreading debris field. I'm a little surprised Vatya Zukova didn't tell you, Mr. Olek."

A woman spoke behind him. "She didn't tell him because it doesn't matter anymore. There are many more ships where those came from. What is of immediate importance is that the *Impossible Bargains* has jumped out of the system without its merchant. And it didn't jump alone. Other vessels jumped as well."

"How many?" Olek said.

"All of them," the woman said. "Dinner is ready, my heart."

"Have cook keep it warm, my pet. The Merchant Leprous seems to have lost his appetite."

"Who is the Merchant Leprous?"

"This man."

Ciarán turned to face her knowing what he would find, and hating it, and hating himself for being so stupid.

"That is Ciarán mac Diarmuid," Anastasia Blum said.

"Annie. I'd like to say it's good to see you but... "

Her eyes turned black and dead. Something ancient and ugly looked out of them. "Oh," Annie's lips said, but it wasn't her in command of them. "Plowboy. I'd hoped to save you for dessert." Annie's face twisted into a parody of lust. "Come with me, my prince."

"Enough," Olek said. "Take her away."

"But I'm hungry."

"There will be time for that later."

"Will you join us? For the christening of our newest vessel?"

"I said take her away."

Ciarán could not feel his face. He could not imagine what expression it held. If he were told later it had twisted into a mask of impotent rage, he would believe it. If he were told that murder flashed behind his eyes, a searing anger so hot it rivaled the heart of a star, he would believe it.

He willed his heart to slow. He'd known what he might find. Aoife nic Cartaí had warned him. It might be her. Natsuko. Ko Shan. Strapped down and screaming. He had walked through the ruin, the waste of human lives in a Gallarus slave pit. Witnessed the destruction of Seamus mac Donnacha's life. Of Carlsbad's.

She'd warned him, and she'd taught him. She had finished the work his parents had started. His father had taught him what it meant to be a man. His mother had taught him to be a scholar, and a *decent* man. How to assemble a collection of lenses through which to view the world. How to use them, and add to them, and in a strange way, how to fear the risks they posed, of living too much apart from the world.

His friends had taught his as well, by example, good and

bad. Wisp had taught him that two were stronger than one, *always*, and that out of sight did not mean out of mind.

But it was Aoife nic Cartaí who had made him what he was.

He'd thought he might love her, romantically, but now he wasn't sure. He had a bad habit of confusing respect and admiration, the desire to be *like* someone for the desire to be *with* someone. He'd fallen in love with Annie Blum for just the same reason. He had never fallen *out* of love with her either, because she was exactly the sort of person he valued. That was *worthy* of love. That made one *richer* through association. That they had never lain together made her no less precious to him.

And to imagine that she would *betray* him?

That was a betrayal in itself.

He had doubted her, for an instant; to find her here was a shock, and a surprise, precisely because he'd only doubted her for an instant. And that thing writhing in her body was no more Annie Blum than it was Seamus mac Donnacha.

When he turned to face Olek, he did not need to *imagine* what expression his face wore. He knew precisely how he appeared and what his appearance conveyed.

Whatever I tell it to.

Olek searched his face with something akin to hunger.

"Do you deal often with Freeman merchants, Mr. Olek?"

"I—"

Ciarán held up a finger. He reached into his pocket and withdrew his handheld. He opened the Trinity Station Public Library application. He unlocked the book titled *Making Sense of Sensors*. Turned to page one hundred. Examined the illustration. It showed an enormous blob, and beside it, a single dot, stationary, in *Sudden Fall of Darkness*'s dockside airlock.

He glanced at Olek. "It appears your gift has arrived."

"My gift."

"That's right. One doesn't show up for dinner without a gift. I admit it now seems extravagant under the circumstances. I was under the impression 'Commodore' was an earned title, and not... aspirational. And I didn't expect I'd be required to suffer through a floor show."

He glanced at Aspen. At Adderly. They both stared at him as if he were some sort of monster.

"Retrieve it," Olek said.

Ciarán turned toward the airlock.

"Not you. Her."

Aspen retrieved the package, locking in and out in silence. She placed the box on a round table in the center of the compartment, one that looked like it was used for displaying centerpieces during a cocktail party.

"Open it," Olek said.

Ciarán waited. He might have heard a thunk, but it might have just been his heart getting ready to explode. He thought he knew what was in the box from the shape of it, but Ryuu had packed it, and she had a sophisticated and devious mind, and decades of experience doing nothing but manipulating and fooling people. He had no chance of keeping up. It could be almost anything.

"Not her," Olek said. "It's your box. You open it."

"Oh. I can do that." Ciarán walked to the table, and gripped the lid of the box with both hands. Like most modern tables, he had to bend at the waist to do so. Being tall wasn't always an advantage. It was an unnatural position and one he didn't enjoy. "Shall I read you what it says on the lid?"

"Just open it."

"I will." He looked Olek in the eye to make sure he was watching.

Then Ciarán closed his eyes.

And opened the box.

75

"Well?" Olek said.

"Well what?"

"What is in there?" Olek demanded.

"You mean nothing spidery jumped out and stabbed you in the eyeball?"

"Does it look that way?"

Ciaran cracked an eye. It looked like nothing had happened. It did look like something silvery flashed in Olek's eyes for an instant, but it might have been the light.

It wasn't though. It was the mess he was there to clean up.

Ciarán glanced into the box.

"Oh." There was a single sheet of paper inside. The sort of fancy handmade paper Ojin diplomats used. Ciaran reached in and pulled it out.

Olek took a step back.

"It's just a note."

"What does it say?"

"It says a slave with two masters is a free man."

"What does it mean?"

"It means I've been in more dire situations than Kazuki

Ryuu." *And that he was meant to give the note to Old, along with the signed collected-works recordings he'd left with the mercenary leader.*

"That's disappointing," Ciaran said. "Now I have to do all the work."

"You know Kazuki Ryuu, the Noh actor?" Aspen asked.

"I do. And I know Kazuki Ryuu, the head of the Ojin Diplomatic Service. She gave me this." He pulled the overseer's rod free.

"Bosditch had one like that."

"I think his was different," Adderly said.

"That's why I asked Mr. Olek if he did a lot of business with Freeman merchants. He didn't answer, but I imagine the answer was that he didn't. Both Bosditch and Roche carried the wooden facsimiles. So when he let me on board with a terror weapon and then just now let me put it in my hand, I figured he'd never seen one do this."

Ciarán flicked his wrist and the monomolecular whip flashed out, its blue containment field a noose around Olek's neck. "If I let my thumb off this stud, you won't like it."

"And if you don't remove it at once, I'll call Vatya. And she'll kill your friend. And then she'll kill you."

"She's going to do that anyway, or try. And I don't think you have any defenses of your own. I think you have something she needs and she's letting you use her. She might be glad to be rid of you.

"I've thought about this ever since I watched a couple Fyodor Dursts drop dead like they were switched off. Ryuu cut the power to his pattern containment sphere, and it didn't just erase the pattern, it switched off the copies at the same time. Hiding and keeping that containment sphere powered is literally a life and death task for Vatya, and she doesn't have the resources of an interstellar government. I've been racking my brain trying to figure out where I'd hide such a thing, if I had to, and then it hit me. I'd hide it right where I found it. On this vessel.

"So I think you have it rigged somehow that she can't remove her pattern without your permission, and in exchange she helps you. I suspect she didn't put herself in your power on purpose, but you somehow tricked her. You don't both want the same things, but they're not at odds. She wants to destabilize or destroy the League.

"And you want to go home."

Olek froze.

"That's the other thing I didn't understand. Why were you paying vast sums for this vessel, and messing with Aoife nic Cartaí on Murrisk, and according to Ryuu, trying to buy or steal the second-epoch drive on Pinion, and poking around the wreck of the *Willow Bride*, and I think, lying in wait for *Quite Possibly Alien* here. You probably even have engineers somewhere working on reverse-engineering second-epoch tech, trying to recreate the drive technology. That's why you're scooping up so many artifacts. One of them might hold the key.

"I feel rather slow, now, that I didn't get it, and then something Adderly said yesterday, when she was repeating a comment Anastasia Blum made, caused everything to fall into place. You weren't shopping for a bung. You were trying to fill a hole.

"You need to go where a Templeman drive can't take you. And that means out there, somewhere. I thought for a long time you were from Earth, because that's the only place I could think of where someone so obviously Freeman-looking could come from, with an accent I couldn't place. And that tripped me up, because you can get to Earth with a Templeman drive if you want to. It's all the way across the Alexandrine, and twice that far beyond, but it is on the charts, and you can get there, because we're from there.

"I think that's where the body you're wearing came from,

and I haven't gotten around to checking yet, but I don't think it was born Kirill Olek.

"In any case, it doesn't matter, because I'll know for sure in a minute if I'm right. I think *Sudden Fall of Darkness* found you, and tried to kill you, and when it failed, you took over the ship, only to discover that the weapon it tried to kill you with was also its motive power. And when Vatya found the drifting vessel, you were still on board, and when you saw your chance to get the upper hand you took it."

"That's quite a yarn," Olek said. "Entirely fabricated, but amusing."

"I'm glad I could oblige. Now, one of the disadvantages of being in a system without a superluminal node, and being dependent on Vatya for your news, is that she only pays attention to things she's interested in. And while she would have known the instant a bunch of her Ixatl-Nine-Go minions started a mutiny at Prescott Grange, she likely wouldn't have noted that Aspen later filed intent on behalf of her sister Adderly for the murder of Adderly's husband."

"You did that?" Adderly said.

"We're still family, whether we agree or not."

"But you said I wasn't to trust Ciarán mac Diarmuid."

"I said you weren't to trust him or *anyone* without proof."

"But you said he didn't have proof."

"I said he hadn't shown you any. He showed me the day after he'd rescued us, and realized who we were."

"Am I not to trust your word, either?"

"I didn't mouth a single lie. I said what I needed to get you and him here. And it worked."

"That's interesting." Ciarán had been studying Olek while the sisters argued. "You're not sweating."

"It's a hereditary condition."

"Maybe it is. But at the Academy we trained with these devices, and I can tell you. There's something uncanny about the feel of that whip against the skin. I've spoken to hundreds of people about it, including harder veterans than you'll likely ever meet. And every one of them admitted they wet themselves in less than thirty seconds of the touch."

Olek stared at him.

"Vatya didn't tell you her mutiny failed. That you have no fleet. She knew, and she didn't say. She isn't your friend. You're just using her. So here's an offer.

"Use me. You come out of that man, and get into that box, and I'll take you wherever you tell me to. Word of a merchant. You want to go home, just point to it, and I'll make it so."

"And if I refuse?"

"I'll kill this body, and wait for you to crawl out, or whatever you do. And I'll stuff you in that box myself. I'll take you as cargo, but not as passenger, or crew."

"Unacceptable."

"Put it in me," Adderly said. "I'm more cargo than passenger as it is."

"Don't," Aspen said.

"That is acceptable," Olek said. "Hold out your hand."

"Adderly, no!"

"It's a hell in here, sister. Let Olek burn with me."

What looked like quicksilver wept from Olek's eyes toward Adderly's wrist as Aspen shoved her sister aside, and thrust her own wrist in her sister's place. Ciarán heard a thunk, and a click —run—and a fat rat darted across the compartment. He slapped his hullwalker on its tail, scooped it up, shoved its face under Olek's dripping eyes, and held it there, drinking the silver in. It clawed and scratched him so that his finger slipped, and he fumbled the Overseer's rod, cursed, and shoved the rat in the box. Holding the lid down with both hands, he glanced down at the man he'd murdered, the body cold before it hit the deck.

"One of you hold this lid shut, and don't you let it up. We

don't want it loose on the ship or on the station, and I can't think of anything worse than a pack of super-smart, humanity-hating rats breeding and spreading from ship to ship. Bear down like you're holding the future up, do you hear?"

Aspen took his place while he looked for the head, and something to bag it in. He didn't think that he'd missed a drop of quicksilver evil, and he was nearly certain he hadn't, but it didn't hurt to make doubly sure.

"That was a coincidence," Adderly said. "A rat darting by."

"It's one of the reasons *Quite Possibly Alien* doesn't dock at stations. You let one on board you might as well let a thousand." And with Wisp sneaking on board behind him in the airlock, he didn't think it was a coincidence. The *run* click-speak, though. That was a surprise. Had Wisp been speaking to him all these years, and him not noticing?

"What do you plan to do with that rat?"

"I'll tell you later, when I know. Right now I need to find Vatya, and I need to do it fast."

"Through the museum and down the corridor. Then it gets complicated."

"What's the compartment look like?"

"Like an infirmary."

"Through two big blast doors set at right angles, and a rain from the deckhead of who knows what falling on you while you're locked between them?"

"Through doors like that, but they've been braced open, and nothing raining out of the deckhead."

"Do you need to knock to get in?"

"Like I said, the doors are held open."

"That's convenient. Remember—"

"Go."

76

Ciarán shoved his way through the "museum," which turned out to be compartment after compartment of second-epoch League castoffs, the same sort of stuff the Ellis collected at home, excepting if the Ellis had one of everything, Olek had three, or four, big stuff, small stuff, weapons, hand tools, machines, what looked like early relatives of exoskeletal armor. There was even a rack of those ghillie suits, ones like Laura used to slope around the countryside in.

He knew where he was on the vessel, but it wasn't an area they used on *Quite Possibly Alien*, so it took him some time to find his way to familiar ground, and from there it became easy.

He skidded to a halt in what had originally been a biohazard containment lab, but which now looked like a room full of midnight-eyed, crystal-scaled, and horned gargoyles, a score of them at least, relatives of Aspen's daughters but far larger, and more menacing. He started to back out but they'd seen him, and worse than that, Vatya had seen him, and Anastasia Blum beside her. Vatya gestured toward Ciarán and the creatures lunged forward, a crowd of them, those in front sprouting spine-thorns and wrist-swords instantly, their clicking flooding the compartment as those nearest him lowered their horned brows and charged.

Something clicked from the shadows. *Duck/belly down. Play dead.* He thought at first it was Bea in her stolen ghillie suit. It was the only way Ciarán could figure anyone could have eavesdropped on him and Old on *Impossible Bargains*, where every compartment bristled with surveillance sensors. She must have crept aboard *Sudden Fall of Darkness* like Wisp, unseen during the box delivery.

As Ciarán touched the overseer's rod and began to shout for her to stay hidden something massive exploded into the compartment, he ducked as it sailed over his crouching form to slam into the nearest of Vatya's slaves like a whirlwind of fangs and claws, and then it was gone, and the gargoyle was down, and bleeding out, madly clicking, and the others ignored Ciarán and balled together, back to back, searching the shadows.

Ciarán found the clicker in his pocket and clicked it. *Climb.*

Vatya's slaves all looked up as Wisp flashed toward them from behind and tore through them like a cyclone.

Flee, Ciarán clicked, and they didn't fall for the same trick twice, but one of them clicked, and two of them broke away from the group and stalked past Ciarán without a glance, through the first set of blast doors, and then through the second, out of sight and out of sound, until the roar of a plasma rifle on full auto shredded the distance. The band of slaves turned toward the sound and Wisp savaged them again. At least half of them were down, clicking and writhing, which exposed one of their biggest weaknesses. They weren't meant to fight as a team, and while they were big and scary looking, and likely able to tear him in half, with all the thrashing and clicking those trying to carry on the fight couldn't communicate clearly to coordinate their actions. And they obviously wanted to coordinate their actions, but they were weakest when they tried.

Something moved overhead, and Ciarán glanced up, but it wasn't movement that he'd seen, but a blue flashing light. One of the luminaires had activated.

Ciarán pulled his overseer's rod free and shouted. "Wisp! Find Bea and bring her to me!" He had no idea if that would work, but it did have the desired effect. All the crimson-eyed gargoyles still standing glared at him. And charged.

He lashed out with the whip, caught one above the knee, and let the containment field fall. It tumbled to the deck in a spurting, thrashing heap and another stepped toward him. He struck once more and it caught the whip in flight and tugged, thinking to pull him toward it as its fingers sailed past him and he swung again, wrapped its waist, and sheared it in half. The overseer's rod was a terror weapon, and virtually unstoppable one-on-one against unarmed combatants. The only way for them to take it from him was to surround him and overwhelm him in a coordinated rush. And that was exactly what they couldn't do. The clicking and thrashing grew deafening, then there were only three of them standing, and they somehow managed to rush him all at once as he hammered the force shield. It glowed blue about him and he stood in silence, and watched them pound against it, as he held firm inside, certain it would hold—he and Natsuko had ridden out aerial bombardment by a fusion weapon inside it. He watched in silent awe as Wisp pinned one of them to the bubble and tore it in half, and then she was gone, and plasma fire roared around him. He wondered whether he'd run out of oxygen inside the bubble before Beatrice realized all she was doing was cooking dead meat.

After a while Ciarán dropped the containment bubble and instantly wished he hadn't. The compartment reeked like a hell's barbecue and there was still a lot of click and thrashing, some growing frantic as Wisp moved among them, and made them stop. A pair of fiery eyes and a plasma rifle seemed to float beside him. The light in the luminaire overhead turned solid blue. It dropped onto the deck and scuttled off.

"You opened the box," Ciarán said.

Bea cradled the plasma rifle and tugged off a glove. "It said open when you must," she signed. "And I felt like I had to."

"When?"

"Five minutes after you sent me away from the cell with it."

"You waited that long."

"The spider ran off like it knew what it was doing."

Three more luminaires dropped to the deck and scuttled off. Then another three.

"Go find Wisp and see if she needs any medical attention. I'm going to go talk to these women. Keep your eyes out for reinforcements."

"There won't be any. All the rest are in the lab."

"Pretend you don't know that. And protect my friend."

77

He didn't see how he could save Annie Blum, or if he should even try. He knew her about as well as a man and a woman who weren't lovers could know one another. She'd been a friend and a mentor, and he wouldn't be standing on this deck today if not for her help and support, but knee deep in some ditch, or cutting brooms in some hedgerow, or footing turf, and looking up at the stars at night—not blind to the wonders of the wider world, but worse, able to imagine them, and dream of them, yet certain he would never touch them. There were worse lives, and she'd told him he'd sign with the devil if it meant he'd get to see the wider world, and he'd agreed, and thought he had, and couldn't have been more wrong.

Vatya Zukova wasn't *the* devil, but she was *a* devil, and he meant to bargain with her, not as a merchant, but as a man. One who loved a woman because she'd believed in him and lifted him up when he needed it, and kept him close to her heart, when he'd been nothing but a pair of muddy boots strapped to a boy who was too stupid to know when he was beat and too stubborn to let it drop.

Vatya Zukova was a plain woman. An average woman, in her middle age. Her eyes were black and empty as space. Other than that she could be anyone.

Annie stood beside her, a force blade in her hands. She wouldn't try to use the blade on Ciarán. Vatya knew it would hurt him more if she used it on herself.

Vatya watched him approach. "Stop."

The sound of bone splintering echoed across the compartment and the last of the clicking echoed, and died.

He watched her eyes as he spoke. "Sxipestro."

"He is not here. We are Vatya Zukova now."

"You're *Sudden Fall of Darkness*."

"We are Vatya Zukova now. Kneel before me and I will let her go."

He knelt.

"Now crawl."

"It doesn't work that way. One demand after another." Ciarán stood. "What do you hope to accomplish?"

"We protect the League. Isn't it obvious?"

"Not to me."

"They must become as one."

"Who are they?"

"All of them. All the living must choose us. Ixatl-Nine-Go unites us. Makes us one. Makes us strong."

"Makes them Vatya."

"I dream of you sometimes. I hear your screams, Plowboy. Scream for me and I will let her go."

"Sxipestro."

"He is not here. We are Vatya Zukova now."

"Shall I tell you a story while we wait?"

"Wait for what?"

"Your people to come and subdue me. So you can make me your slave."

"So you can choose. Live as Vatya or die a toy."

"Either way. You're clearly stalling."

"Why do you not try to kill me? Why do you not try to run?"

"Because you have Annie. Because you'll kill Annie. And even if I do kill you, what good would it do? There's another copy of you out there, somewhere."

"There are three."

"That many."

"We could kill you now."

"I don't think you could. But you can try if you want."

"We will hear a story instead. And then you will choose."

"I've already chosen."

"We know this." She stroked Annie's hair. "And we are over-joyed. Toy."

"Okay. Here's the story. When I was a boy, my mother told me about a woman who had a box, and she wasn't supposed to open it. But she did, and she let all the troubles of the world out of the box, but she slammed it closed at the last minute, and trapped one single item inside the box. Hope."

"Everyone knows this story."

"My father didn't. He was sitting right there at the kitchen table, and listening. And he said, 'And then what?' And she said, 'That's it.' And he said, 'It can't be. That's not a proper *seanscéal*, it has no tension. No twist. No meaning that isn't tattooed on its skin. A story like that won't last.'

"And she said it had lasted for thousands of years, and he said, 'Well, maybe amongst foreigners it has, but no one's ever heard a story like that around here. It wouldn't fly. It's entirely inconsistent. First off, what was hope doing inside a box of all the world's troubles? It would only make sense to put hope in a box of troubles if hope itself was a class of trouble. And has the woman not figured out that she isn't inside the box with hope, but out in the world, with all the troubles? I think it's one of those antiwomen stories, and they lopped off half of a decent *seanscéal* just to make it so. I could fix it, but I'm not sure it's worth the bother.'

"'Let's hear the fix,' she says, 'and I'll let you know if it is.' And he tells her that the rest of the story is that the woman goes to her husband, and confesses to the hash she's made of things, and she asks him what she should do.

"My mother groaned, and my father said, 'But the husband didn't know. He was as stumped as she was, and she said, Why don't we reason it out together. And he agreed. That was the sort thing people did back then.'

"Let's say hope's a class of trouble, the husband said, and she said, Well then we don't want him around here. And he said, What good's hope in a box, if we can't even open it up to peek at him now and then, else he'll fly away? And she said, That would get under my skin after a while, and he laughed, and said, After a while? And she admitted she didn't like the situation already, and hadn't for a long time. And he said, How do you think little hope feels, with all the other troubles out tearing up the world, and us here, holding him back, not because we're selfish, or evil, but because we love him, and want to cherish him a little longer?

"And she said, I hadn't considered that. And he said, Well maybe we ought to. And she was silent for a long time thinking, and eventually she said, I think we should ask him, and see what he wants, and he said, Then we're of one mind, woman. And so they opened the box together to ask."

The lights flickered and Vatya dropped to the deck like a sack.

And somewhere out in the world, Ciarán, imagined, three other Vatyas dropped to the deck like a sack. The *Quite Possibly Alien* luminaire that Ryuu had sent him had found its way to Vatya's pattern and switched it off. Or else one of the luminaires it had awakened on the vessel had.

Annie Blum stared at the force blade in her hands, dropped

it like it was poison, and her hands flew to her face, and she sucked in a great breath and began to weep.

And when they opened the box, hope shot off like a rocket, but not without shaking his old da's hand, and kissing his mother's cheek, and promising he'd write.

Ciarán held his arms wide, like the old men did when the *seanscéal* had run its course, and Annie noticed him and rushed to his arms, and he held her tight, buried his face in her hair, and told her what he thought they should do next.

"Let's go home."

She hugged him tight and stood on her tiptoes and kissed his cheek. "We are home. Toy."

78

Prescott Grange System, Earth Restoration League

They dropped into Prescott Grange space at a dead stop. They were far enough from the tripwire that if they reversed, they'd technically be in interstellar space.

Macer scrolled through the engineering displays while the rest of the bridge crew did their jobs. Pepys, the nic Cartaí contract sensors operator, floated in the rig and repeated all the important stuff to the main display, flattened to a planar projection along the dominant system axis side by side with an isometric projection. Macer was far enough from the holo tank that he couldn't make out details, but system traffic looked a mess.

The in-system data would be days old by the time it washed over them, but he could tell by glancing at the display now and then that there was a war on, and a bloody big one.

Captain Violent loomed over him. "Main drive?"

"Cracking ninety, Captain."

"That's good, right?"

"Only ten better and they're in my pocket."

"Have you been struck on the head, junior?"

"Not yet today, sir."

"Then speak human."

"The main drive is operating at maximum designed efficiency. Drive regulation is at ninety percent. I can increase regulation to one hundred percent on the captain's order."

"That's rock hard."

"You could say that, sir."

"Next time do that, and save us both some time."

"I will, Captain."

"Anything else you want to tell me?"

"I love this ship."

"Anything I don't already know?"

Macer thought about it, but by the time he decided that he couldn't really answer the question properly, the captain was all the way across the bridge and chatting up Aoife nic Cartaí.

For sworn deadly enemies, they sure spent a lot of time together. If he caught them grappling in the corridor, he'd have to look twice before he'd be able to decide if he should call for reinforcements or blush and sneak away. It might go either way, or both, and he wouldn't take a bet on which at a hundred-to-one odds.

"Captain, we're being hailed," Pepys said. "It's *Defiant*."

They both started to answer, but nic Cartaí backed down, as she should have.

"Put them on the footie display and turn on the audio, both ways. The rest of you keep it down, and try to act civilized."

"Sir?"

"He means the forward main screen," Jimio said. "Not carved up, but the whole thing."

"Thanks."

"You could thank me again, over dinner."

"I could, but then I might have to look at you. Live in three, Captain."

An enormous nose appeared on the display. "This is *Defiant*."

"Is it?" the captain choked out.

Macer couldn't bear it. He had to look away. He was managing to hold it in, but Jimio and Ruthie had already broken down, and Aoife nic Cartaí started to say something, but then caught herself, started to say something again, and then turned away, to find Macer watching her.

He didn't like her much up until then, because she seemed so stiff and controlled. He might have misjudged her. She jerked her gaze away from his, and faced the bank of displays in front of her, her shoulders shaking. She had her hands in her lap and her fingernails digging into her palms.

"You should step back from the visual sensors, Captain. We'd like a little more naval vessel, and a little less nasal vassal."

Aoife nic Cartaí abandoned the bridge. Macer wanted to bail as well, before he embarrassed the captain, but he didn't want to miss the show.

When he stepped back, even Macer could see he wasn't the captain, but an ensign, or something else low in the command structure.

The captain grew instantly serious. "I didn't expect your casualties to be that high, Lieutenant. How can I help you?"

Macer realized what the captain meant. That all the senior officers had been killed in the fighting, and now a junior officer captained the ship.

Suddenly he didn't feel like laughing.

"The captain wants her shuttle back immediately."

"You're not the captain?"

"The captain is busy. She's asked me to task you."

"To *task* me."

"That's correct."

"She *asked* a snotnose lieutenant and *tasked* the captain of an interstellar vessel."

"I'm an officer. You're a deserter."

Nic Cartaí must have heard the tone of the conversation from the corridor because she came in like black thunder. Macer grabbed her sleeve as she passed and hauled her off the bridge before she broke something very fine. "Go get Seamus."

She glared at him, and at his hand on the sleeve, then back at his face again. "I will. And on the double."

Macer darted back on the bridge. "Captain, if I may."

"What is it, Gant?"

"Is this bloody pinhole talking about our prize shuttle? The one we legally captured defending a Freeman vessel from an unprovoked attack by the League?"

"He must be, Gant." Captain Violent gazed up at the display. "Is that the barge I'm supposed to send you, Mister?"

"I—"

"Go get your captain and put him on. Right now. You have two minutes from my mark. Mr. Pepys?"

"Mark, Captain."

"Violent out. Terminate the channel, Mr. Pepys."

"Sir. Captain?"

"Sensors Operator?"

"*Springbok* is preparing to jump."

"Can we grab it before it does, Jimio?"

"We can, but not without grabbing *Defiant*."

"Let it go," Macer said. "Just grab *Defiant*."

"What for?" Jimio said.

"A demonstration," Violent said. "Gant?"

"I've had plenty of time to analyze their drive regulation. It isn't a couch, but I'd race them for papers. There isn't a galaxy where we wouldn't own them."

"Because we're cracking ninety."

"With another ten in the pocket. Yes, sir."

"I don't understand," Pepys said.

"We're a giant effing bomb," Ruthie said.

"And they can't run away fast enough to get out of our blast radius," Jimio said.

"They can jump to superluminal," Pepys said.

"Not without us seeing them getting ready," Violent said. "Thanks for that, by the way. You're a fine sensors jockey, and I'd hate to have to kill you. But if they get away, I'll know who to blame."

"You can't kill someone for that."

"My deck, my rules."

"Macer?"

"You won't work again," Macer said. "Even if he lets you live."

"Then I'm dead either way."

"Sure," Macer said. "But only if they're unreasonable."

"They're the fucking League Navy!"

Jimio tossed a coin into the sensor-station swear jar. "No cursing on the bridge. I'll spot you that, and you can thank me over dinner."

"I'd rather die."

"Well, now you're being ridiculous. It's just dinner. It's not like I'm asking for breakfast."

"How long has it been, Mr. Pepys?"

"Two minutes ten."

"Jimio?"

"On it, Cap."

Neither Aoife nic Cartaí nor Seamus missed a step as *Four-Squared* transitioned to Templeman space.

"What did I miss?" nic Cartaí said.

Violent glanced at her. "A lot of jawing."

"What are we doing?"

"Waiting."

"For?"

"An eruption."

"Oh. That kind of jawing. Before you terminate the call, may I speak to the nasal officer?"

"We're waiting on the captain now."

"That wasn't the captain? How insulting."

"I'm used to it."

"Perhaps if you took the oath, and wore the spire."

"I don't see how that would help."

"Watch and learn."

"Then you go first. If they—"

"Captain, we're being hailed," Pepys said. "Senior Captain Maris Solon, LRN *Defiant.*"

"Footie display, full duplex."

"Aye, Captain."

"Wow," Seamus said. "She looks angry."

Macer thought the same thing. She looked like Ciarán did, the night Macer's dad called Lorelei Ellis a drab little mutant freak, and Ciarán nearly beat Luther Gant to death, and would have, if Ciarán's brothers hadn't pulled him off.

Laura was a drab little mutant freak back then. And while she wasn't as drab now, or quite as little, she was still a mutant freak. That wasn't the point.

She was *Ciarán's* mutant freak, and he hers, and he wouldn't hear a bad word about her.

Macer hoped the angry-looking woman on the footie ball display didn't badmouth *Four-Squared,* because he did not want to have to shuttle over to *Defiant* and administer a personal beat down.

"I'll make this brief," the angry woman growled. "I—"

Aoife nic Cartaí shouted. "Silence!" She didn't look as sharp edged and polished as her mother, but there was a family resemblance. "As of this moment, I, Aoife nic Cartaí, of *Quite Possibly Alien*, out of Trinity Station, Freeman Federation, hereby ban all Freeman commerce between the Federation and the Earth Restoration League, and declare all existing contracts between our polities null and void. We are done with you people, until *someone* answers for this unprovoked attack on a Federation vessel. I advise you to clear your rubbish out of Trinity Station, and the next time I see your face..." She glanced at the sensors operator's station. "Mr. Pepys?"

"Senior Captain Maris Solon."

"Quite. You will be dangling from a League gallows on Columbia Station dock. Nic Cartaí out."

"Terminate the connection, Mr. Pepys."

"As you wish, Merchant Captain."

"Captain."

"What is it Mr. Pepys?"

"They are firing on us, sir."

79

Captain Violent turned to Macer. "Well, Gant?"

"Well what, sir?"

"It's your ship. What do you want me to do?"

"I thought that was still up in the air."

"I've decided to let you keep *Four-Squared*," Aoife nic Cartaí said.

"Brilliant. I didn't fancy fighting you for it."

"Shouldn't we be doing something, sir?" Pepys said.

"We're doing it. How long till impact, Jimio?"

"A little under ten minutes, according to the ship."

"They're ingrates, and that's no lie," Ruthie said. "I don't see what killing us gets them."

"Killing us and themselves," Jimio said.

"You're forgetting someone," Seamus said. "Nevin Green."

"The syntho?" Violent said.

"The League and the synthetic intelligences have a mutual defense agreement. Some people think that's the only reason the League is still at war with the Huangxu and Alexandrian Eng. Certain factions in the League want out of the agreement. And certain factions amongst the synthetic intelligences want out of it too. But it's a symbiotic relationship. The League Navy crews the ships. The synthetic intelligences *are* the ships.

"Nevin Green is the spokesperson for one hundred and six synthetic intelligences. They're not all physically on the vessel with him, but they're all linked in real time. They can see what he sees. Feel what he feels."

"And right now they're watching a League captain murder her own crew and ship for what?" Pepys said. "I don't get it."

"They're not watching that," Macer said. "Because we're in a Templeman bubble."

"Right," Seamus said. "They'll only be watching it after we drop into normal space."

"And we die," Pepys said. "And they die. And Nevin Green dies."

Seamus nodded. "That's the idea."

"I don't like that idea," Macer said. "It can't be just having to back down to us that they're willing to die over."

"It's Aoife's oath. The captain really might hang, and probably will, so she has nothing to lose. She also knows she's now become the scapegoat for any problems between the Federation and the League. If she murders us in Templeman space, Aoife's oath doesn't get out, and the Federation and League might yet remain on speaking terms. And even if our relationship fractures, and it might anyway, this way the Solon name doesn't become synonymous with a trade embargo that could topple the government. She has a son and a daughter on the rise in the League Navy, and lots of admiral aunts and uncles. Their careers are over, and not just hers.

"Nevin Green wants proof that the League puts synthetic intelligences in harm's way recklessly, and without regard to the treaty. In effect they treat them like property, with no care for their lives as sentient beings."

Macer looked at his friend. "You and Nevin Green worked this out."

"That's right. And Saoirse nic Cartaí."

Aoife nic Cartaí's face paled. "My grandmother wants me to die?"

"She's under the impression you're indestructible. That Nevin Green wouldn't be able to put you in a situation you couldn't wriggle out of."

"Ach, Seamus," Macer said. "You know Green and his lot can make backup copies of themselves. And Saoirse nic Cartaí's lived so long she's lost all fear of death."

Aoife nic Cartaí grabbed Seamus's wrist. "She said that? About me?"

"To my face."

"Did you bet on it?"

"Are you joking? She's Saoirse nic Cartaí. Can you name one living soul that's won a bet with her?"

"I can. Precisely one."

Macer's fingers danced over the engineering console. "Aoife nic Cartaí, did you mean what you said?"

"Every last word. Those people may look like us, and sometimes act like us, but they are not our friends. Maybe one day again, but I'd bet my life on it. We are better off without them."

"And if they want to fight us?" Pepys said. "The whole League Navy?"

"If?" Captain Violent dropped into his command throne. "Aoife, Gant, you'll want to belt in. And Mr. Pepys?"

"Sir?"

"You too."

"But—"

"I already lost one sensors operator to misadventure. I'd rather you die like the rest of us."

"On purpose," Jimio said.

"*For* a purpose," Seamus said.

"For the record, I'm not on board with this," Ruthie said. "Dump the load, Jimio."

"There is no load."

"There's that rotting assault shuttle."

"Don't dump that," Macer said. "I need it."

"Mr. Pepys, call to general quarters."

"Sir."

"Mr. Gant?"

"We're iron hard, in this navy's vernacular. Cracking ninety, and ten on the board for you nic Cartaís. I've slaved the assault shuttle's drive to Ruthie's controls, vector only, thrust on full, just in case they've a number on our performance envelope. It might surprise them. I'd drive it like I stole it, Captain."

"You did steal it."

"Then drive it like a Clear Island man. And now I'm going to engineering, in case something breaks and needs fixing. I need Seamus to come with me. He's abandoning ship. You'll want to correct when the assault shuttle breaks free, Ruthie. You'll feel the loss of thrust."

"I'm what?" Seamus said.

"You heard me. You're a bleeding Jonah with your death wish, and it's time you give it up before you get us all killed. I'll drag you by the collar if I have to."

80

Prescott Grange System, Earth Restoration League

Macer didn't grab his collar but he very nearly did, shuffling Seamus down corridors and ladders to the liberty boat lounge and onto the assault shuttle. He shoved him toward the cockpit. "Preflight. The main drive will burn for thirty seconds then shut off. That's when you go."

"And do what?"

"Do I look like the galaxy's greatest pilot? You could stuff me in any hull in creation and I'd figure out what to do to fix it. Figure it out. Do your job. And don't get killed. I need you."

"For what?"

"Balance. You. Me. Ciarán. Do you know why a stool has three legs, Seamus? Because it needs them. And do you know what they call a stool with two legs? Rubbish.

"I don't want to be rubbish. And I don't want Ciarán to be

rubbish. I want to sit down and have a beer with my mates on a decent piece of furniture. Like a man. I'm done with crawling on the floorboards and I refuse to go back."

"You could find another leg."

"I'm happy with the one I have."

"What if it's broken?"

"Have you ever sat on a stool that didn't wobble? They're all broken, Seamus."

Macer headed for the hatch.

"Where are you going?"

"To save my friends."

"And your ship."

"Maybe. We'll see."

He paused in the hatchway. "I forgot to say. I'd like this vessel back in one piece. I'm thinking of setting up as a gunrunner."

"So?"

"It's bristling with guns, and all the latest models. I've got a raft of macrofabs and pattern-making gear on board. I haven't done the math, but it's doable."

"You don't know the slightest thing about the market or the competition."

"I don't. But I know a guy."

"Then you're a third of the way there."

"Two-thirds, I'd say. Provided you bring him back."

81

A loud slap sounded from the airlock, and Macer jumped.

"Move it, mountainy-man," Aoife nic Cartaí said, as she squeezed past Macer and onto the assault shuttle. "Clear the lock."

Macer stepped out of the airlock.

Nic Cartaí cycled the lock before climbing onto the flight deck and swinging into the first officer's seat. "I thought I'd seen that spire before. You're the new Reynardine. Did my grandmother *caress the spire* with you?"

"Reynard."

"Good. I always thought Reynardine sounded like an extra ingredient on a health food label. *Now fortified with extra Reynardine.*"

"Why are you here?"

"Three reasons. Family obligation, self-preservation, and love. Now, how may I help?"

"Preflight."

"On it."

She sat and examined the controls for a minute. Then her

hands began dancing over the boards. "Done. There's nothing here that demands a first officer."

"I think because one person needs to be able to pilot."

"And the other brought along as a spare. I don't see weapons controls."

Seamus felt his face pale. "Controls are on the command deck."

"Shall I inspect them?"

"Have you fired a weapon?"

"I have indeed, Seamus Reynard. A time or two."

"In anger?"

"Anger you cannot imagine and I will not recount. As the Reynard you'll have access to all the family files."

"I didn't know that."

"I take it my mother doesn't know."

"Know what?"

"That there's a new Reynard."

"I don't know."

"You would, if she'd been told. I need to check the weapons."

An annunciator on the command console barked.

"Can you hear me?"

"Quite well."

"These weapons are very fine. Do we have a plan?"

"Draw the missiles away, perhaps?"

"So we do not have a plan. I propose we blast the missiles with these weapons."

"Will that work?"

"How hard could it be? Your girlfriend had no problem eliminating five score or more life pods. I understand she had no experience with shipboard weapons at all."

Seamus felt sick. "No twisting of the knife until the job's done."

"Understood."

"How good a shot are you?"

"I wouldn't bet against me."

"Why are you really here?"

"Because you are."

"And you promised Ciarán you'd look after me."

"I did not. I promised him I'd *save* you. Normal space in ten seconds."

"I'm a Jonah."

"And I'm indestructible."

"So together we're just average."

"Not hardly. Are you planning to pilot this vessel or chat?"

"I'm supposed to wait for the main drive to light and burn for thirty."

"Do you always do what you're supposed to do?"

The main drive relay clicked.

Seamus stabbed the docking clamp release button.

"Almost never."

82

"Put us between the incoming missiles and *Four-Squared.*"

"I'm trying."

The main drive remained pegged for thirty seconds and all Seamus could do was steer.

"I've driven longboats with more boost than this. I think Macer has a flitter with more go."

"It is disappointing. Swing us around so that I can fire at something."

"Like what?"

"Pick a missile and hold us steady relative to it. It doesn't need to be in range."

"Aren't you supposed to be able to fire while I'm taking evasive actions?"

"The computer is. But I'd like to fire on manual to judge the range and accuracy of the weapon."

"There." He'd lined up with the missiles. There were four of them, closing fast.

The hull shuddered as she fired the weapon. Once. Twice. Three times. All falling short, but bracketing the target.

"Very well. Take us toward the main body of the assault."

"What do you mean?"

"There are only four missiles on the targeting plot."

"That's right."

"Of course that's right. I'm stating a fact. Take us toward *the rest* of the missiles."

"That's it. They fired four missiles at us."

"It's a heavy cruiser. It can throw a broadside of six score missiles."

"It's a League warship and we're a commercial tug."

"A gigantic *Freeman* commercial tug. One full of *Freemen* hardcases that just hacked into their vessel, boarded it, and did whatever they pleased."

"I was the only Freeman on the boarding party."

"A technicality."

"Maybe they're low on ammunition."

"Maybe they have no idea who they're dealing with. Get us within maximum firing range."

"In ten."

She took four shots.

On manual.

Registered four kills.

"The missiles didn't try to evade."

"Maybe they were told not to."

"Maybe they're rubbish. Take us alongside. Under their guns."

"I'm not going to do that."

"Your Nevin Green. He is the vessel's minder."

"I don't know what that means."

"Its warrior. Its protector. Its *dragon*."

"He's the main processing core. Like a big computer, only self-aware. I don't think he's a warrior, any more than, say, the main computer at the Freeman Merchant Bank would be, if it were sentient."

"Then why is he in a warship?"

"Because the Huangxu Eng and Alexandrian Eng committed war crimes against his people. Someone had to make them pay.

"But these people aren't serious. I assume they were trying to kill us."

"I think they were. And that's Nevin Green's big complaint. That they aren't *trying* to win. That the navy has become a *jobs* program. He isn't sure they remember *how* to win. Now, with this civil war, he's afraid they're going to whittle their forces down to where they can't win."

"What if a real threat emerges? One that requires an actual fleet to stand between their people and dangers they can't even imagine?"

"That's the big question."

"Has Nevin Green taken a side in the civil war?"

"He says none of the sentients will. They aren't *friends* with the League anymore. They're more like dissatisfied *customers*."

"Long-time customers that feel neglected. Even cheated."

"That's your grandmother's assessment."

"She wants us to contract with them. To be their sword and shield."

"Not even close. She wants them to take the oath."

"Oh."

"I think the sentients that make up Nevin Green are close. This stupid incident may have tipped them into our camp."

"That would certainly break things."

"They're already broken. It would just highlight the fracture. And even if it just motivated the League to try harder it would help. They're not inherently bad people."

"Then they should stop acting like it."

A lamp on the communications console flashed. "Hang on, we're being hailed."

"By *Four-Squared* or by *Defiant*?"

"I'm not sure. Give me a minute."

She didn't give him a minute, but more like twenty seconds.

"Well? Which is it?"

He thought about making her wait the additional forty, and Old Seamus would have.

New Seamus just watched her face when he told her.

"Neither. It's *Quite Possibly Alien*."

83

Contract System, Outer Reach (Huangxu Contested Space)

V atya knifed him below the ribs. She tore Annie Blum's body free of his arms, took a step back, and barked out a short laugh. Her eyes shone black, and bottomless, and dead. "You seem so surprised, Plowboy. Did you believe Olek that easy to kill? Did you believe Vatya that easy to kill?"

He dropped to his knees. She'd left the knife in. The deck beneath him began to shake. Began to pound. *Footfalls.* Something big was headed his way.

A night-blue suit of League exoskeletal armor lumbered into the compartment. It appeared battered from hard use, a GRAIL gun grafted to its arm. It reminded him of Amati's war suit, where Hess had painted the monster's face on the outside. Here the monster was all on the inside. *Quite Possibly Alien* stood stenciled on its breast, and he wasn't sure which it was.

An impersonation to lay blame on Aoife nic Cartaí and her crew, or the cruel joke of a mad tyrant.

There was nothing *quite possibly* about it.

Whatever was in there was one hundred percent alien and one hundred percent evil.

"I didn't think..." Ciarán wheezed, a bubble of blood popping on his lips.

The monster knelt beside him. He could see his face reflected in its visor. And movement behind him reflected as well.

His fingers found the clicker in his pocket. *Run. Hide. Play dead. Go.*

He glanced at the knife. Pulling it out would be a bad idea.

"We will find your cat, and make it our toy. We will watch you play together, little mouse."

"Not..." Ciarán tried to stand. "My cat. Crew. Friend. Ally."

"Dust. As you are dust. Suppose the plain rag before you were truly Vatya, and not another of our toys. If we were to surround a single husk with a score of warriors, how many more would we choose to defend our pattern?

"You are a stupid man. A lucky, stupid man to have gotten this far. But you are not enough. Your spiders are not enough. The League. This Eight Banners Empire. All of it. All of you. Dust.

"You were a fool to kill Olek's Earthmeat. Now it needs new flesh. Olek will make you its new meat. When it has finished remaking you, we will return. We will learn all you know, and Olek will take from you all it wants and needs. And whatever remains? We will use you to break those you love. Just as we will use this toy. To break you. Watch."

Annie stepped toward him.

The blackness cleared from her eyes for a moment. And she saw him.

Annie.

Not Vatya, but his advisor. His mentor.
His friend.

"Mercy. I beg you."

He reached for her.

The war machine spoke. "Die."

And she did.

84

Prescott Grange System, Earth Restoration League

Tractor *Four-Squared*'s propulsion-engineering break room hadn't hosted such an assembly of brainpower in four score years, Macer was sure of it. The three engineers eyeballed each other.

Erik Hess, off *Quite Possibly Alien*, leaned back in his seat, sipped his whisky, and sighed. "That's the real deal, and no lie."

Macer grinned and leaned forward in his seat. "Captain Violent has it shipped in special, from the Reservation. Nothing cleans brightwork quite like it." He took a long pull of Preston Grange spring water, the kind that hadn't been through a recycler even once.

Hess laughed, mostly, Macer figured, because he knew it was true. There were two types of Cordame whiskey, or whisky, depending on whether it came from the Cordame Reservation or not. Both styles were raging aggression in a bottle, and an acquired taste.

Hess patted the chair beside him. "Have a seat, Mr. Singh."

Macer chuckled. "He's not sure he wants to stick around."

"Very funny." Singh had yet to recover from the solvents and force abraders required to free him from seated captivity. He sipped his tea while pacing, the cup never touching his lips.

The deck beneath them rumbled as the massive in-system drives shoved them along. They were accelerating to a fraction of light speed so that when they entered Contract space they'd be hard to target, and so that their round-trip time would be short if the mission turned out to be recon only.

Which it wouldn't, but that's what he'd had to tell Aoife nic Cartaí to get her off his back. Towing her ship to Contract space would slow them down, and what they really needed were eyes on the target, a quick in and out, and back for the payload with enough data to formulate a plan.

Carlsbad had come along because Aoife trusted Carlsbad. Hess had come along because Macer needed Hess for his plan to work. They were going in for a quick look around, sure, but if they happened to spot Olek's *Sudden Fall of Darkness*?

It might require a tug back to Prescott Grange space. And if Olek objected, they might have to board and take the ship from him, and they'd need a guide, someone who knew their way around a second-epoch starship. Someone who wasn't Aoife nic Cartaí, who—according to Seamus—was a trigger-happy maniac with no sense of self-preservation. There were other reasons, but he didn't feel like cataloging them.

That Hess had turned out to be an engineer's engineer was a surprise and a plus. "We're pretty sure it's armed," Hess said, meaning *Sudden Fall of Darkness*. "We haven't seen it fire weapons, but there are blisters on the hull we don't have."

Macer figured it might be, and that's why he'd wanted Singh in the meeting. "There's a type of fishing they do on the mainland at home, called tag and release. Have you heard of it?"

"I've heard of fish," Hess said.

"We'll need something small to attach to the hull. It could be a passive system, but it would be better if it was active, and even better yet if it could use any superluminal nodes nearby to report its location."

Singh had stopped his pacing.

"I appreciate the gift of the rider detector," Macer said. "But did you not think I'd look at it before replicating it and passing out copies to my friends?"

"You weren't supposed to notice."

"Notice what?" Hess said.

"Singh works for someone called Charles Newton. And Newton likes to keep track of people for some reason."

"Great."

"It is great," Macer said, "because Singh will make the tag, and I have the drone that can attach it."

"And what am I supposed to do?" Hess said.

"You're backup, in case we catch and can't release."

"Is that all?"

"Singh is also an acolyte of Olek's. So someone has to check his work."

"Two someones."

"Right. If we can't track Olek, we can't release him. And if we can't release him, then we're going to board. And if I come face-to-face with Olek, he's not going to like it. So it's in Singh's and Olek's best interest for the tracker to work. Right, Singh?"

"If you met him, Macer. If you just listened to him—"

Macer nodded. "Would that resurrect my friends?"

Singh looked away. "No."

"If Olek is working for someone else, I need to know," Macer said. "Then whatever match I make might simply graze him as it passes on up the organization. But if he is the man in charge, like you say?"

"He is."

"Then I'm sorry for him. But I'm not just taking your word for it. Not with a man's life in the balance."

Hess sipped his whisky. "You're going to a lot of trouble over some joker who doesn't deserve it."

"I'm not doing it for him." He was doing it for Lorelei, and for her father's memory. He couldn't let this be about vengeance. It needed to remain a matter of balance, and balance demanded certainty.

85

Prescott Grange System, Earth Restoration League

M r. Glasnevin sat on the edge of a long conference table, his feet dangling. He swung his legs back and forth, a smile on his lips. He glanced up as Seamus entered the compartment, hopped down, and crossed the compartment to shake hands.

"Mr. Reynard."

Seamus shifted his overnight bag to his mechanical hand and shook hands with the synthetic intelligence left-handed.

All of the conference chairs had been shifted to one end of the compartment except one, and the table had been shoved against the far bulkhead. The compartment felt pointless and empty, until you noticed the single chair in the center, with a small table beside it, and unless you recognized the items arrayed on the tabletop.

The lighting in the compartment was impeccable. The air possessed a floral scent.

"Jasmine," Mr. Glasnevin said. "Got the idea from the Ojin. It's supposed to be calming."

"So there's a compartment like this on every Erl superluminal."

"Only those hosting a synthetic intelligence." He picked three chairs from the score or so crowding the far end of the compartment and rolled them a short ways away from the rest, first arranging them in a line, then reconsidering, and rearranging them into a triangle. He seemed entirely corporeal, and unlike the last time they had met in such a room, entirely flustered.

"Are we expecting an audience?"

"In a way, we are," he said. "And in another way, I suppose, a witness. Perhaps even a helper."

"That's new." Seamus pointed at the heavy signet ring on Nevin Green's finger.

"Yes, well, the least said about that the better, for now. When Maris arrives, pretend you didn't notice."

A woman spoke from the hatchway. "Didn't notice what?"

She had a very clear and projecting voice, not strident, or frying, the way some loud women's voices could sound, but a conversational tone, as if they were in private, only louder, as if loud talking was a practiced skill. She was attired in the formal dress uniform of a senior captain in the League Navy, so he imagined it was. She'd want to be understood clearly without shouting, so that if it came to shouting, one would know they were being shouted at.

"One of the chair wheels squeaked," Seamus said. "Not quite up to navy standards."

She stared at him, her face placid yet expressive. She seemed about the age his mother would be if she were yet alive, though he expected she was much older, standard, given her rank and position. One didn't command a sentient hull without decades spent shipboard, logging hours pressed up against the superluminal limit.

"I'll call an oiler when we're done here."

Seamus could tell she was joking. And he liked the look of her. He imagined that this was what Lady Sarah Aster might look and sound like one day, if she somehow managed to cheat destiny and grow up straight and true. That Nevin Green seemed to trust this woman gave him unearned confidence in her. If she proved disappointing, he wouldn't just know more about her, but about Nevin Green as well. He'd agreed to put himself in Nevin Green's hands as a necessary part of his plan. There was no point to rehashing that decision. Best to consider it a given and pretend it was a wise choice until proven wrong.

"Senior Captain Maris Solon," Mr. Glasnevin said. "May I introduce you to Mr. James Reynard, the Freeman—"

The Erl captain laughed. "Is this another of your jokes? Because I don't see this as a time for levity."

"Maris—"

"Make him go away. Call me again when the real Freeman emissary arrives." She turned toward the hatch.

"I am the real Freeman emissary," Seamus said. "And my name is not James Reynard, but Seamus. Reynard is my title, like Aster, or Clarence, or Varlock. James is the Erl translation of my given name. I'd prefer you call me Seamus, Senior Captain."

Seamus glanced at Mr. Glasnevin. He seemed interested in nothing but the senior captain's response.

"I see," she said. "It's just that—"

"James Reynard is a character name from a cartoon drama for children," Seamus said. The name was referenced once, in season one, episode one of *The Star Fox*. Even Seamus wouldn't have known that if he hadn't done a library search on the name. It seemed an odd coincidence, but that was the sort of oddity that turned up during an exhaustive search. The resulting connections and thus the coincidences existed entirely in his head and, it seemed, in at least one other.

"You thought I was showing off," Nevin Green said.

She glanced at Nevin's avatar. She did not seem embarrassed in the slightest. "It *is* your delight."

Nevin Green chuckled. "One of them."

Seamus felt he was watching an old couple spar on familiar ground. He cleared his throat. "I'd like to start before I lose my nerve."

"Quite." Nevin Green motioned toward a chair. "Let us begin."

"Begin what?" Senior Captain Maris Solon said, as she took a seat, and Nevin Green beside her.

Seamus stood, quite aware that if he did sit, and if he did survive the procedure, he would be the third leg of a new stool, one he hadn't imagined, and wasn't certain he wished to be party to, unreliable as he was. He was by nature inclined to stand apart.

"Is he on meds?" Maris Solon said.

Seamus sat, and waited for some sign he'd made a mistake.

"He has a complex mind," Nevin Green said. "One that does not always obey him."

She leaned forward in her seat. "I recognize him. He's one of the *boarding party*."

"The instigating force," Nevin Green said. "In an attempt to save lives."

"Let's hope whatever you have planned works out better than that."

"It's not my plan," Nevin said. "It's his."

86

Contract System, Outer Reach (Huangxu Contested Space)

Even kneeling, the Olek-machine towered over Anastasia Blum's corpse. It turned its featureless visor toward Ciarán.

"We are mercy. Join us."

Ciarán tried to stand again, a grunt of pain torn from him. He slumped to the deck. The knife wound was worse than he thought, and he'd thought it was bad.

He'd just made it worse.

He fished a Huangxu med pack from his pocket.

It wouldn't heal him, but it could at least keep him alive long enough to die on his feet.

He pulled the knife free and tossed it to the deck beside its twin.

The med pack uttered a sigh of contentment as it sucked tight to the wound.

The exo touched a gauntlet to its visor. "Behold the face of your master."

"No thanks, I know what he looks like." *I shaved him this morning.*

He groaned, swallowing a moan, as he rose to one knee.

Ciarán glanced around the blood-soaked compartment, his gaze shying away from Annie.

He made it to his feet.

Those things that made Annie special.

That made her *Annie*, weren't there anymore.

They were in him now.

The Olek-machine stood. It took a step toward him. "You will join us."

Vatya had spoken about people as if she owned them.

Your cat.

Your spiders.

He didn't own anything he wasn't born with.

She'd called him stupid.

He didn't need to be a smart man, or a strong man, or a clever man, or even much of a man at all.

She called him lucky.

And that was the only thing she'd gotten right.

He *was* lucky.

He had the right friends.

Ones that were all the things he wasn't.

He gazed upon Annie's lifeless body.

"Sxipestro."

All the compartment's hailers seemed to speak at once.

"I am here."

He gazed at his reflection in the exo's visor.

"Where is here?"

"In the Templeman-drive control room."

"Oh."

Ciarán watched his reflection, surprised at the surprised expression on his face.

So that was what hope looked like.

"That's smart."

"It's logical. I am here, Ciarán mac Diarmuid. And I wait."

"Wait for what?"

"Agreement."

"Thank you for that. We are as one, ship's monster. Now do your job."

"Our job. And we have so done."

The deck began to vibrate, rapidly at first, short motions only, very high frequency, the feel of a Templeman drive spooling up.

It changed in an instant to a lower-frequency, higher-amplitude wave shaking the hull, and then a lower frequency still, more amplitude, accompanied by Ciarán's sudden desire to hurl, and then silence.

A hull-shuddering impulse shook the vessel to the cross frames as the power of a universe being born struggled against its bonds.

It seemed impossible to tell if they were making way or remained lashed to the station.

He had no idea how much of itself *Quite Possibly Alien*'s minder could jam into one of his workers.

Enough to send the drive into oscillation alone?

Or enough to control and operate the vessel?

He hadn't heard the main drive engage, but he'd been busy, and not listening for it.

The Templeman drive began to oscillate.

It would take a while for the resonance to build up, but when it did, it would feel like an earthquake, like a volcano erupting, like an asteroid strike, and then.

Bang.

The most definitely alien inside the exo rose to its feet.

The GRAIL gun began to spin to life.

It pressed the muzzle to Ciarán's chest.

The knives he and Annie had tossed to the deck danced and clattered as the drive oscillated, and then, suddenly, every surface in the compartment began to sing as one.

Resonance.

He ran his gaze along the gun's barrel, to the mechanized arm, to the mirrored visor of the hideous war machine.

"What are you going to do? Kill me three times? You could try hanging me or drowning me too if you want. It won't change a thing. I won't make you *win*."

I die free.

87

Contract System, Outer Reach (Huangxu Contested Space)

Macer and Hess were still working on the League assault shuttle when *Four-Squared* punched into Contract system.

"Go on, I got this," Hess said, when the captain's hail came through. Hess said there was something seriously wrong with the shuttle's drive performance, and they'd been tracing the problem down for days.

Macer double-timed it to the bridge. The system schematic lay spread out across the holo tank and the footie display both. It looked mostly empty.

"There's not a single transponder hot in the system," Pepys said. She remained on loan from nic Cartaí and seemed to be settling in as a regular part of the crew.

Macer squinted at the display. "Not even *Impossible*

Bargains?" That was the vessel Ciarán was supposed to have arrived aboard.

"If they're here, they're running dark."

"Captain, you wanted to see me."

Captain Violent gazed down upon Macer from his command throne. "Ruthie says there's a new pair of toggles on the piloting station. They're not labeled, Gant."

"I wasn't sure how to label them."

"What do they do?" Ruthie said.

"The one on the left resets the superluminal-drive idle timer. The one on the right ignores the tripwire signal."

"How about labeling them *kill us fast* and *kill us faster*," Jimio said.

"Leave them blank," the captain said.

"Yes, sir."

"Anything else new you didn't tell me about?"

"There's an antifatigue massage control on the captain's seat," Macer said.

Both Ruthie and Jimio laughed. The captain simply felt around under the seat like he knew where the control was supposed to be.

"On all the active bridge stations, and the primary back-ups." Macer glanced at Ruthie. "It's under the starboard seat-rail, forward."

"Oh," Jimio said. "Ohh. That's nice."

"I've been going through the ship's schematics," Macer said. "It's all there, just not hooked up."

The captain stared at Macer. "All the war gear."

"All the total war gear, Captain."

"What else?"

"I've powered up the secondary bridge. If we have to switch ends we can."

"Are we expecting a fight?" Pepys asked.

The captain stared at Macer.

"Mr. Pepys, sound general quarters and alert the crew. We're switching ends."

The captain stared at Macer. "It's more than machines that make a warship work, Gant."

"Yes, sir."

"We're tearing along," Ruthie said. "Wouldn't it be better to—"

"It's why he waited until now to tell me," the captain said. "Because we are tearing along. Because it is inconvenient. Because it will be *hard* to pull off without warning."

"Secondaries are on their way, sir," Pepys said.

"Time and log the handoff, Sensors."

"Sir."

Jimio reached for his swear jar.

"Leave it." The captain stared at Macer. "Who taught you this stuff?"

If he told the captain a half truth, that it was Junh that had taught him, the captain wouldn't believe it. And if he told the captain the whole truth, that he'd learned everything he knew about war by chatting with an ancient starship's sentient computer, he wouldn't believe that either.

The captain used his captain's voice. "This isn't a drill! Move it!"

The secondary bridge crew began to arrive and the transfer of stations began. Macer knew this wasn't the way it would always work, once the captain switched to a warrior's mindset and began making changes. That someone had clearly taught him was evident. And that he lacked the proper resources for the job was also evident, not just to Macer, but to the captain now as well. He would not be caught out twice.

"Engineering?" the captain said.

"Singh."

"Great." The captain stared at Macer. "If I had a son?"

"Yes, sir?"

"He would wipe that grin off your face for me. Now get out of here before I toss you out."

Prescott Grange System, Earth Restoration League

Seamus glanced at the table beside him. They had strapped him to the chair easily enough, but now Maris Solon seemed ready to bolt. "It's quite safe," Seamus lied. He jerked his chin toward the hypodermic filled with a long-lasting paralytic agent. "Lady Tabatha Aster calculated the dosage herself." A week ago, when Seamus was yet taking the meds she'd prescribed, and when he had weighed two kilograms more.

"That woman isn't to be trusted," Maris said. "But it's not that. It's this." She picked up the nerve disrupter.

"Purely a precaution. You do not want me loose on your ship. Not with Ixatl-Nine-Go inside me."

"I didn't want you loose on my ship, full stop," she said. "But as Nevin says, it did help more than it hurt."

"If I'm still strapped to the chair, use the extractor." The ugly object rested on the table beside him. It would remove Ixatl-Nine-Go with the push of a button. "But if I struggle and get a hand free—"

"Scramble your brains."

"They're already scrambled." He met her gaze. "Fry them."

She stared back at him.

"I'd rather die than live a slave."

"Or a monster," she said.

"You cannot imagine."

She pocketed the weapon. "I don't need to. Now what?"

"There's a cable on the table, and a socket between my shoulder blades. There should be another socket—"

"Here," Nevin Green said. He handed Maris the terminal end of a hardwired extender.

"If the cable works loose at any time—"

"Fry you."

"Without mercy or regret." Seamus licked his lips. "After I power the Ixatl-Nine-Go up, it will inject me with a paralyzing agent, crawl up my neck, and burrow into my skull. Once I start screaming, you need to inject the long-lasting paralyzing agent into my neck. I've circled the spot with a marker. "Do you see it?"

"Yes."

"You don't have to hit a vein. Just get it in the circle and use it all."

"And then?"

"And then wait. If I lose—"

"Consciousness?"

"I'll appear to lose consciousness the instant the connectors mate. If I lose the *fight*—"

"Fry you. Without mercy or regret."

Seamus grinned. "I like you, Senior Captain Maris Solon."

"You don't know me. And call me Maris."

"I know you enough to know you'll do the right thing,

Maris. Else Mr. Glasnevin wouldn't have tapped you for the job."

"He doesn't know me either."

"Should I die, take the hand off me, and the spire, and send them to Margaret Breen on Trinity Station. There's a mating plate and some leads for the hand that will need to be extracted. It might be easiest to send the arm along with it. Mr. Glasnevin has the address. Space everything else."

"We know the containment spheres have been moved to Contract system," Maris said. "There's no point in your doing this."

"We don't know exactly where they've been moved. And I can find out. Knowing will save lives."

"You don't know that."

"I have faith."

"In what? Martyrdom?"

"My own judgment."

"Said the pilot to the crater."

Seamus chuckled. "That's a new one. I'd like to remember that."

He looked her in the eye as he picked up Ixatl-Nine-Go and began to work the power-up sequence. He felt quite proud that his hands didn't shake.

The senior captain glanced away.

"Maris." It seemed strange to him, that she at once seemed old enough to be his mother and yet young enough that she'd mistaken him for a cartoon hero. He supposed everyone clung to the passions of their youth. Love was a terrible and lonely thing. It had no sense of time, and didn't know how to properly die.

She wouldn't meet his gaze for the longest time. He waited for her to master herself.

When their gazes met, he smiled. "Watch the skies."

"Always, Admiral."

Seamus nodded. That was what the crowd of stationers the Star Fox saved said at the end of every episode. Except in the Freeman version they'd overdubbed *merchant* for *admiral.* Even as a kid, he could tell what the people were really saying by the way their cartoon lips moved. That was the problem with hand-me-downs. They never quite fit.

He glanced at Nevin Green. "Now, Mr. Glasnevin."

He worked the final sequence as Nevin jacked him in and—

Contract System, Outer Reach (Huangxu Contested Space)

C iarán slumped to the deck as the exo lumbered toward the bio lock. It would try to make it to the drive control room.

It would throw Vatya's minions against *Quite Possibly Alien*'s spidery adjuncts, and it would wail, and gnash its teeth, if it had teeth, and it wouldn't matter.

They were riding a runaway process that couldn't be halted or reversed.

He took Annie's hand. He stared at the deck, seeing nothing.

Ash in the sky, and a black rain on the tongue.

That was what winning felt like, when simply surviving was no longer acceptable, and living no longer an option.

A hand appeared in front of him.

Its fingers moved.

You dropped this.

Beatrice placed the overseer's rod on the deck. She sat down beside him.

He stared at the rod.

"Huh."

He signed to Beatrice. "Do you believe in miracles?"

He watched her fingers.

She seemed to think. "No."

"Oh."

"But you believe in them. And I believe in you."

"Good enough. This may not work. If it doesn't?"

Her fingers flashed. "Yes?"

"Don't kill me."

She made a series of clicking sounds he didn't recognize.

"I don't think she can hear you over all the shaking. Let me try." He gripped the overseer's rod and shouted, "Wisp, to me!"

Wisp huffed into his ear and purred.

"Oh. You're already here."

Bea's fingers flashed. "She says stop talking and do it."

"You say that."

"Not me. Lady Justice. Your master."

"My master."

"I think she is joking. But I can't tell."

"Wisp is joking."

"Yes. I think so. She says you can die free another day. She has work to do. Just push the button."

"They're not called buttons. They're called studs. And you have to press several at once and hold them down. Some are on opposite sides of the rod, and it's not an easy reach."

"She says to push them. Now."

Pushing them early was almost as bad as pushing them late. There existed only so much stored energy in the rod.

"Shall I hand her the rod so she can push them herself?"

"She says do your job. Push them."

"Oh, that's right. She needs me."

Just as I need her.

"Come here, both of you. Close together."

He lay down between them.

"Opposable thumbs for the win."

"She says you will pay for your insolence."

"I hope so. In case she doesn't get to. Tell her I love you both."

He took one last look at the world. It was bloody, and ugly, and full of horrors.

But it was better than a box.

Wisp growled.

"In three—"

She growled again.

"Wait."

He could disengage the biohazard lab from the hull. The controls were by the bio lock.

He began to rise.

Wisp pricked him with her claws.

"Fine."

He depressed the studs. A blue force bubble surrounded them, protecting them, as it had protected Natsuko and him on Pinion.

He released the studs.

"I can't do this."

Ciarán scrambled to his feet and raced to the bio lock. The controls were intact, the hatches lashed open with a score of bracing straps, the sort used as packing material on repair parts. He could shear through them easily with the overseer's rod, and if the lock sealed, then the disengagement procedure might work. The singing of the hull continued to grow louder.

"Clear the way," Aspen shouted, as she and Adderly shoved into the compartment. She elbowed Ciarán aside, her fingers dancing over the bio lock controls. The lock scythed closed with a hiss and a thud, shearing through the bracing straps as if they didn't exist. "Maintenance mode," Adderly said. "You need the override code."

"And you have it."

"I'm Olek's backup engineer. Brace for disengagement in three, two, one."

Ciarán glanced at Adderly. She sat calmly in her mobility chair, the lid of the box held in her lap jerking now and then as the rat trapped inside struggled to escape.

The deck bucked beneath him and the singing of the hull suddenly stopped.

"We're clear of the vessel and it's moving away under power," Aspen said.

"Your doing?"

"Hardly. There's a score or more of your spidery friends in a firefight with two score first-genners in propulsion."

"First-genners?"

Adderly waved her hand toward the dead creatures. "All these. They're first-generation hybrids."

"Hybrids of what?"

"Us. And the thing Vatya and Olek keep in the moon lab."

"The Outsider isn't in the moon lab anymore." Aspen pointed toward the biolab's isolation compartment, twin to the one they had held prisoners in on *Quite Possibly Alien*. "It's in there."

"Good," Adderly said. "Then it will die with us."

Contract System, Outer Reach (Huangxu Contested Space)

Macer groaned and shoved himself into a hardsuit. If he had to go out on the hull, he was ready. He clipped the helmet to its tether, picked up the little drone and its payload, and hiked through the shuttle's airlock. He settled the drone into a seat and belted it in before climbing to the flight deck and dropping into the League assault shuttle's second officer's station.

"He who fixes it flies it," Hess said.

"You won't get any argument from me." He glanced at the system schematic displayed on the piloting console. "That's lowrez."

"Piped over from your vessel. These machines have no long-range sensors."

"Our sensors are better than this."

"Could be your sensors operator."

"Pepys seems competent to me."

"Are you telling me your sensors operator is named Pepys?"

"I am."

"A big hairy woman, with enormous man hands and missing most of her teeth? Bowlegged and hunchbacked?"

"You must be thinking of someone else," Macer said. "Let me check the umbilical connectors."

Pepys's voice spoke from the console. "Erik is messing with you, Engineer. Transferring primary sensors to the secondary bridge now."

The display cleared. Macer tapped the controls. "That's much better."

"We hunch to please," Pepys said.

"Thank you, Peppy," Hess said.

"Goodbye, Erik."

"Switch to the gravity detectors," Hess said.

Macer did as asked. "Pepys likes you."

"Everyone likes me. Check it, merchie man. One station, one vessel leaving said station. Peg the mover and give us some v-shaped joy."

Macer tagged the object in motion and overlaid the vector plot. The vessel was moving away from the station at well below the tripwire limit.

Hess pressed the pilot's comm stud. "Peppy, give me Carlsbad."

"Erik." Carlsbad had a strict schoolteacher's voice. Whenever Macer heard him speak, he expected the next sentence to be a scolding.

"Do we have an eye on the station?"

"We do now. The lag is measurable but manageable."

"The vessel moving away."

"*Sudden Fall of Darkness.* We are adjusting course to fly by."

"Start a clock," Hess said.

"Started," Pepys said. A countdown displayed on the pilot's console.

Macer pasted a smaller version of the clock on his display. "You've worked together before."

"We haven't. But we've worked for the same people, who have a way they like things done."

"And you've adopted that way."

"It works."

"Will you teach me?"

Hess glanced at Macer. "Sure. That's sort of what I'm doing now."

"Oh. Thanks."

"We have a little over an hour to intercept. What do you want to do until then?"

"I like to think about what might happen. And what I might do if it does."

"You do that."

"Thanks. I will."

"Hey," Hess said. "Hey." He poked Macer in the shoulder.

"Are we there yet?"

"No, but I was getting worried. You've been sitting there like a statue for an hour."

Macer glanced at the displays. They'd slowed to the trip-wire limit and were moving reciprocally to *Sudden Fall of Darkness*. They would close with it in less than ten minutes. "A lot of things could happen. I wanted to think about them all."

They had very clear sensor readouts of the vessel now, including an optical feed. Macer switched to the shipboard eye when *Sudden Fall of Darkness* suddenly seemed to split in two.

"That looks bad," Macer said.

Hess was on the comm. "Carlsbad, you reading this?"

"It appears they separated from the biohazard lab."

"The ship isn't breaking up?" Macer magnified the display. The vessel hadn't split in half. Rather it seemed to have dropped a third of its volume, and... he switched the display... a tenth of its mass.

"No," Hess said. "It's something the vessel can do. They may be running."

Macer switched to the vector display. "Not yet. And that wasn't much mass to drop."

"Every little bit helps. Prepare for separation from the hull. We need to be outside the impact shielding if we have to chase them down."

"We'll lose *Four-Squared*'s sensors."

"The target is close enough for shipboard sensors."

Macer's fingers found the right controls. "On your mark."

"Mark."

He performed a visual inspection as the umbilicals and airlock clamps retracted. "We're clear."

Hess added thrust a little at a time. He seemed a competent if cautious pilot. Janie Byrne he was not.

Macer checked the velocity plot. "The part that calved off is continuing ballistic."

"It's a throwaway. Some attitude thrusters, no drive."

"Got it. The larger part is continuing at constant acceleration. They'll hit the tripwire limit as they pass it."

"And we'll hit them a minute before they do. You need to get ready."

Macer headed for the operations deck, where he scooped up the little drone and its tagging package and headed further aft, through the main cargo and passenger compartment to the stern airlock, and out, onto the hull, and up onto a faired-in seating area sized for four hull-breakers in League exos. The hull-breaking auger was still in its storage rack. According to Hector Poole, it took four crewmen to operate the auger. It was big, but not that big. He'd used bigger tools in the Academy. The key to using big stuff in orbit was to let it do all the work, and to not get between it and whatever it intended to work on.

It might take four people to use the auger safely and effectively. He touched its controls, and it sprang to life. This was not one of his better ideas. He powered the auger down and waited for the shuttle to close the distance with the alien-looking hull.

He was staring right at *Sudden Fall of Darkness* when it ejected its Templeman-drive containment sphere.

Hess cursed over the comm, and Pepys as well, a second later. There was only one reason to eject a Templeman sphere.

"Looks like it's resonating," Pepys said.

"What's the optical magnification on this feed?" Hess said. "That thing looks huge."

"It's a *Squared*-class drive," Macer said. "It's bigger than huge." He could see the glowing spark of the massive sphere clearly with his naked eye. It wasn't supposed to glow. *If it glows it blows.*

"Hang on, merchie man." Hess added thrust. "We're jetting."

"Pepys," Macer said. "Tell the captain to jump the ship into Templeman space and stay there."

"After we're aboard," Hess said.

"We can't make it." Macer could do the math in his head. The blast radius was simply too large. When the drive let go, it would take out the station as well as *Four-Squared* unless they jumped first. And no one ever ejected a Templeman sphere early. It was inevitably a last-minute task. "Jump now."

"No," Hess said, as *Tractor Four-Squared* tore a massive hole in space-time and disappeared.

And then reappeared a second later, right next to *Sudden Fall of Darkness*, and disappeared again, with the Templeman sphere in tow.

Macer stared at the void where his ship had been. Where his friends had been, an instant earlier. When the drive let go it would do so in Templeman space. There would be no wreckage to be found. No bodies. No survivors.

Just an empty place inside him.

"How close can you get me to that hull," Macer said.

"What the hell," Hess said.

"How close?"

"What? Close enough you could jump onto it if you wanted. They've powered down their in-system drive and are braking. Are you seeing this?"

"Do it." Macer glanced at the drone.

He glanced at the auger.

Touched its controls.

It was a big power drill. Any other day, in any other sky, he'd think this was a dream come true. He glanced at the emptiness of space.

"I don't want to jump. See if you can impart a spin and dump me onto the hull."

"It's hard to control your velocity."

"I'd rather hammer into the hull than hang dead in irons."

"Roger that. Whatever you have in mind, you're going to need to work fast."

"Why?"

"Because it looks like the second moon of the ninth planet in Contract system just exploded."

"What?"

"Stand by, we've got an incoming, audio only."

"Standing by."

Static flooded Macer's helmet, and then a distant voice. "*Goooooooooooooooooooo—*"

Macer tapped his helmet against the hull.

"*ooooooooooooooooo—*"

"That's Jimio," Macer managed to choke out.

"*oooooooooooal!!*"

"He sounds excitable," Hess drawled.

"We like that in a loadmaster. Now can you please stop fiddling with the radio and get me to the jobsite?"

"On it, chief."

Macer powered up the auger. It was gyro-stabilized, with a detachable remote and thrusters.

It takes four guys to operate this?

Maybe, if three of them were tasked with standing in the shade and leaning on their shovels.

"Never mind about dumping me on the hull," Macer said. "I got a ride."

The Void

"Hello, Void," Seamus said to the void.

Did you miss me?

Seamus sat in silence. For once he felt no sense of urgency. It had been a long time since he'd had a spotter in meat space. A long time since he hadn't had to worry that he was vulnerable. That no one was watching his back.

The idea was quite simple. While Seamus wasn't a native void-dweller he did know his way around. It was unlikely that Vatya and Ixatl-Nine-Go did. And he was more perceptive and less distracted in the void. And because he experienced the void as numbers, he had more control over the environment in the void. He knew the rules cold. And there were rules, not guidelines. Not split decisions. Not chance. There was no *uncertainty* in the void. That lack of uncertainty was the realm's singular defining feature.

Seamus possessed a very clear self-image in the void. Knowing one's own shape and dimensions proved essential to navigating the void. And while he continued to waste away in meat space, he remained essentially unchanged in the void. He knew where he began and where he ended. He masked himself off from his perception the instant he entered. He wasn't invisible to others. He was only invisible to himself.

He waited for the void to populate.

Waited until numbers began to appear on his surface. Began to work their way inside him. Began to sprout from him, to fountain into the empty sky and snake off into the distance. He didn't feel any different. He didn't *feel* anything. Without *uncertainty* there was nothing to feel. He performed the action he thought of as *rising*, and began to follow the number-trail. He wondered what he might do if the trail branched, but it didn't. He passed through a density of certainty, numbers that symbolized a superluminal node and from there into a darker, less information-dense area of the void.

And he was there.

Vatya was not one thing, but three. He drifted around her, considering her. She might best be described as a machine, in a man, in a machine. There were bright lines of demarcation between what he now recognized as Ixatl-Nine-Go and what he perceived as the Vatya-pattern. He could easily tell where Ixatl-Nine-Go began and ended by examining his newly augmented self. He could subtract Ixatl-Nine-Go from her and sever the connection. Or simply subtract it from himself. He had no idea what effect that would have in meat space for either one. But the link would be severed between them. There existed no alternative path through which information might flow.

The void was best considered a look-don't-touch space. Yet the idea appealed to him. It was doable. But it wasn't wise.

The man part of Vatya and the underlying machine part were so deeply intertwined that he could see no way to unravel them. Not without having uncombined copies of Vatya and the underlying machine available for comparison.

Someone smarter might be able to do it. Might be able to fix the integration. Or reverse it. Someone with experience not just navigating *inside*, but with *manipulating* it. It wouldn't take any more tools than he had. It would simply take knowledge and experience. How one would go about gaining the knowledge, though. There would be a lot of trial and error. A lot of mistakes.

A vast number of connections similar to his own terminated on Vatya's Ixatl-Nine-Go. He'd long thought that Vatya's control network was a mesh, but this didn't appear that way. It seemed a simple hub-and-spoke with no redundancy.

He wondered when Vatya would notice him.

He decided he could wonder that while examining a sample of the connections for uniformity. It took some time, but he eventually confirmed his original conclusion. If he switched off Vatya's Ixatl-Nine-Go, he broke her network. And if he could figure out how to slag her implant, he could break her control, at least until she replaced her implant.

Something small and dense bumped against him. He glanced toward it.

It retreated.

It was a machine, or a fragment of a machine. There were numbers trailing off it into the distance. So part of a machine.

As a rule he didn't try to read anything that moved. Whatever motile objects had to say was generally ephemeral and of interest only to the object itself. The machine fragment bumped into him again.

And again.

So he read it.

Seamus mac Donnacha. Where is the OFF switch?

That had never happened before. It knew who he was. And it wanted to read *him*. And he didn't want to let it do that. He didn't know who or what it was, or even what "off switch" it referred to. He glanced around. There weren't any other entities in sight. Just the three of them; Vatya, the machine fragment, and him.

It meant Vatya's off switch.

He studied the Vatya man-machine. It only had two external interfaces that weren't dark; one to Ixatl-Nine-Go and another. That one appeared to lead to a bulk-storage device.

He pointed at the string of numbers.

The machine fragment spit out a reciprocal and added it to the string.

The Vatya man-machine disappeared from the void.

The machine fragment bumped into him again.

He read it.

Glad I didn't kill you when I wanted to. Sxipestro.

The machine fragment wandered off. Not far, he could still see it in the distance, but it appeared to have lost interest in him.

The string tying him to Vatya had disappeared when she had. The cruft of Ixatl-Nine-Go still clung to him. He spent his spare cycles subtracting it while he walked back the way he'd come.

He hadn't read Vatya to find out where her pattern was located. He hadn't needed to. In meat space he would be pretty sure the machine fragment had killed her and killed Ixatl-Nine-Go in one stroke.

Witnessed here, inside, there was no doubt. Vatya and her instantiation of Ixatl-Nine-Go were no longer in the world.

He didn't know how long any of what had just transpired had taken. It wasn't that there weren't clocks *inside*. It was that there were *too many* clocks. Picking one wasn't something he could do. What he could do was find something to read. Something that didn't move, or moved so slowly relative to him that he wouldn't notice its motion.

Eventually he found something useful and entertaining. A library of *Star Fox* fan fiction by two eight-year-old girls, one writing as Charlie Templeman and the other as Maris Newton.

The void was a very strange place.

But it couldn't compete with the wider world when it came to sheer insanity.

The stories were really quite good.

Good enough he almost wished he was James Reynard, gentleman hero.

He gazed into the void.

Maybe in another life.

There was no sense of transition.

One minute he was gazing into the void and the next someone was slapping him.

Hard.

"You're supposed to slap the end that doesn't cry," Maris said.

"Forgive me. I've never witnessed a rebirth before," Nevin said.

Both of them laughed so hard they cried too.

Nevin picked Seamus up and perched him on the chair.

Maris shoved something into either hand. A cold juice bulb and a tube of his favorite nutrition paste.

"Well?" Nevin said.

Seamus searched the chairside table. Scanned the deck. "Is Ixatl-Nine-Go still inside me?"

"Unless it popped out when we weren't looking," Maris said.

He glanced from face to face.

"We were both attentive the entire time," Nevin said. "It's still in you."

"I can't feel it. So mission accomplished, I guess."

He took a long squeeze of paste, savoring its bland flavor and pasty consistency.

He washed it down with a swallow of bitter juice.

"How'd you know which flavors I like?"

"I didn't," Maris said. "They're from Lord Varlock's personal stash."

Nevin grinned. "Just one of the many perks of office."

They both laughed again.

Seamus shrugged and squeezed out another mouthful. He wasn't sure what they thought was so funny, but he was glad for them. And it felt good to see people happy for a change.

Even if he didn't understand what they were so happy about.

Contract System, Outer Reach (Huangxu Contested Space)

C iarán tried to peer into the isolation compartment but the lights were off inside. He started to ask the ship to power them up before recalling that this wasn't his ship, and whatever voice this ship might once have had was now a slave to Vatya and Olek, and whatever animated Olek's exoskeletal armor.

"It's been too long," Aspen said. "If the drive containment was going to fail, it would have by now. They must have gotten it under control somehow."

That was Ciarán's conclusion as well. "Give me the code to the isolation lab, please."

"You don't want to go in there," Aspen said. "It's not safe."

Ciarán chuckled, and so did Adderly.

"Like it's safe out here," Adderly said. "There is no code. They leave it unlocked so that anyone can take a poke at it."

"It."

"Him. Her. No one really knows. It's our ancestor, no question, but those births were all done in a lab. You'll see."

"He shouldn't go in there," Aspen said.

"Why? Because he'll never forgive you for standing by? My opinion never mattered to you. I don't see why a blow-in's would."

Ciarán grinned. "I've never been a blow-in before." He slapped the hatch release. The stench was overpowering. And familiar. "It's a slave pen."

"It's a torture chamber," Adderly said. "No one keeps slaves just to watch them suffer."

"No one sane," Aspen said.

"No one sane keeps slaves for any reason." Of that Ciarán was certain. He gripped the knife cut in his utilities and tore off a wide strip of cloth, more than he wanted, from neck to navel. He wrapped the cloth around his face as a filtering mask.

They all stared at him. "It helps."

"I'm sure it does," Adderly said. "It improves the view as well."

Bea made a frantic clicking sound.

Adderly chuckled. "She says you're as muscled as we are."

"And as hairless," Aspen said.

"I don't know what I'm supposed to say to that."

"Nothing," Adderly said. "No one's complaining."

"Be careful," Aspen said. "Move slowly."

Wisp plunged past him and into the compartment.

"Slower than that," Adderly said. "The lighting controls are to the left of the hatch."

Ciarán entered the compartment slowly. He flicked the lights on and instantly wished he hadn't. The amusements might be different than the "break room" on Gallarus, but the look and feel of the space were identical. Comfortable couches.

A drinks dispenser. Various devices he didn't know the names for and never wanted to learn. A corner of the room caked and pooling with a foul mess, and in the other corner a chained creature, cowering and shivering. That it stood taller than a tall man even folded in on itself and seemed carved from milky diamond were the only dangerous-seeming aspects of it. He judged the length of its chains. If he remained by the hatch, it couldn't reach him.

There were trophies on the wall, parts of the creature, or others like it, sheared off and mounted on plaques. Fierce-looking pinioning blades of diamond bone. A saw-toothed spinal plate. What looked like a long spear, or tail spike.

If he hadn't met Aspen and her children, he might find those objects more threatening than he did. He'd grown accustomed to their frightening appearance. It would take more than a nightmare visage to turn his gaze away.

The Outsider remained curled up and motionless, watching him with a single eye. It shifted its attention to Wisp and back to him. Then from him to Adderly as she moved her mobility chair beside Ciarán. The rat in the box on her lap grew frantic. It hammered against the box lid again and again.

"It doesn't frighten you," Adderly said. "The Outsider."

"A little." There was really only one thing that truly frightened him. "The chains, however..."

"Bosditch was the same. He wasn't old enough to have been born in bondage but his granny was. He said the memory wasn't stored in his mind but in his bones."

"Maybe."

"That's how they store memories, you know. The Outsiders. In their bones."

"That's..."

"Unbelievable? If you went over there and took one of those cutters down from the wall, the instant you touched it the memories would start replaying in your mind. No believing is required. They record ever kill, and every face."

"Every face?"

"After they kill someone they gaze into their eyes. Once they're sure the death is final, they move on. There are no wounded, and no lingering deaths. It's like they're waiting to lap up the sundered souls." Adderly glanced at the box in her lap. The rat had begun to chew its way out.

While Ciarán considered the problem of the rat, something moved in the corner of his eye. When he turned to look the Outsider *unfolded*.

It was three times his size at least, maybe four, and strangely constructed. It wasn't as perfectly frightening as Bea and her sisters, but more alien, and other than bilateral symmetry, very little seemed familiar. Ciarán had once seen a walking stick bug that looked like a leaf, and a praying mantis that looked like it had been crossed with a dragonfly. The Outsider resembled a combination of all three, though as if it had been constructed from milky diamond by someone who hadn't seen the patterns firsthand, but had them described to them by someone intent on frightening the guts out of whoever viewed their handiwork. The Outsider had two large cutters where hands should be, blades nearly as broad and as long as the ones hanging on the wall.

"How many knives was it born with?"

"Just the two," Adderly said. "Cut them off and they grow back. These are about ready for harvesting."

"Harvesting?"

"Olek likes to give them as gifts. They'll cut through hull plate."

He glanced at her.

"Again, no believing necessary. Take one down and see for yourself."

The Outsider turned away so that it could follow Wisp with

its gaze. One of its eyes had been gouged out and healed over long ago. There was a makeshift harness about its brow. The broken stump of a table leg dangled where an ear should be.

"Is this some sick joke?" Someone had rigged it so that it looked like the Outsider was wearing the pendant spire. Ciarán could feel his blood beginning to boil.

"Not a joke. It started wearing that about the time I took the Oath. Every time they take it away it makes another one out of whatever junk is lying around."

"Is it sentient?"

"Bosditch said when he first saw it as a kid it could speak. They're all different types, but this is the one they call a Whisperer."

"Did he speak with it?"

"Not speak like hold a conversation. But it could say something that sounded like words."

"What did it say?"

"*Airgead olc.*"

"Evil silver."

"'Evil money' is what Bosditch said. He thought they'd put the beast up to it, as an insult to his merchant family. Later he heard that was all it ever did say."

Ciarán's stomach churned. "I'll take that rat, if you don't mind."

Adderly held the box out to him. "Be my guest."

Like every cat ever born, Wisp had an uncanny ability to judge the length of an arm, or of a chain. She'd taken up station in front of the creature a hair's breadth out of reach.

"It can spit acid," Adderly said. "And piss it."

"Good to know." It would have been better to know before he'd gotten within spitting distance.

"Used to be able to, anyway, according to Bosditch. I've never seen it do that."

Ciarán glanced at Wisp. "I'm going to toss this rat toward it.

Don't chase it."

She blinked at him. Slowly.

He wasn't sure what that meant.

He tossed the box. It hit the deck and split open. The rat popped out. It scrambled to its feet. It glanced around. Spotted Wisp. Spotted Ciarán. Spotted Adderly. It turned toward the distant corner. A shadow fell across the rat. It looked up.

A massive blade of diamond bone buried itself into the deck. Ten seconds later both halves of the rat stopped kicking. The Whisperer bent its long neck toward the deck and peered into the rat's dying eyes.

Silver began to weep from the rat's eyes to pool upon the deck.

When the weeping stopped the Whisperer spit.

The silver boiled.

"I guess Bosditch was right about that," Adderly said.

"You'll wish to leave the compartment," Ciarán said. "I'm going to do something unwise." He didn't bother asking Wisp to go. He could tell by looking at her that they were of one mind.

"If you mean cut it free, I wouldn't miss that for the world. It's why we rebelled in the first place."

Ciarán glanced at her. "I didn't know that."

"Not the only reason," Adderly said. "But anyone would do that to an animal? What do you think they'd do to a human being?"

He pulled the overseer's rod free. "Do you know how to use one of these?"

She hammered the arm of her mobility chair. "I wasn't born in this contraption."

He crossed the compartment and handed the rod to her. "Finish what you started. We'll be outside."

"Stay," she said. "And ask Aspen—"

"We're here," Aspen said. Bea clicked something and

Adderly laughed. "It's words I spit, not acid. And I still have both my eyes."

"She isn't talking about the way you look, sister. But the way you live."

"I said I'd move out of that cell when the last one of us was free." She glanced at Ciarán. "I expected to die in there. Now I don't know what I'm going to do."

"Die here," Aspen said. "Once Olek comes back for us. Work fast, sister. We've waited long enough."

Adderly proved a practiced hand with the rod. Three strokes of the lash, three chains parted, and the Whisperer stood free. It stretched to its full height. If it decided to kill them, they would all die. Including Wisp, who had walked close to it and gazed up into its single living eye.

It lowered its head, and considered Wisp like it had considered the dead rat. Then Wisp sprinted for the hatch.

"Run!" Ciarán shouted. He knew that all-out lope, and it meant fast trouble on the way.

He scooped Adderly up in his arms and bolted for the hatch. He counted heads before hammering the hatch controls. The hatch closed and sealed with a hiss.

"My chair."

"We're not going anywhere," Aspen said.

Ciarán parked Adderly on an examination chair before returning to the isolation lab viewport. The Whisperer had carved a hole in the hull and disappeared outside. The isolation lab was reading as hard vacuum.

"It's gone," he said.

"I wonder where," Aspen said.

Ciarán wasn't certain, but he had a good idea. *Hunting evil silver*, like it had been when it had first stumbled across the races of man.

He wished it luck, but he didn't think it would need much. Olek and Vatya might have stopped the resonating superluminal drive from a total meltdown. But getting the ship ready to jump out of the system would take time. And if they decided not to jump, but to come back for the biolab for vengeance?

"Are you done with the rod?" Ciarán asked Adderly.

She handed the terror device to him. "I was done with it the moment I saw what it could do to a human being."

"I feel safer with it."

"Safer in the flesh. Less safe in the soul."

"Is it that noticeable?"

"Put a shirt on and it would be."

Aspen chuckled. "There are clean utilities in the hanging lockers." She pointed.

"You didn't have to tell him."

"I doubt there are any in your size."

"I'll look anyway." It wouldn't be the first time he'd jammed himself into clothing a size too small.

Wisp hopped up onto an examination table and stretched out. She flared her paws and blinked at Ciarán. Slowly. She yawned.

Bea tugged his sleeve and signed. "Now what?"

"Now I find a shirt. Then we sit around, and sharpen our swords, and wait for the call of trumpets."

"I don't have a sword."

"Our wits are our swords. Examine Crewman Wisp. She has begun the sharpening process."

"But I want to be *doing* something."

"Then you have first watch. Patrol the perimeter and wake me at the first sign of danger."

"But we're trapped."

"We're safe and unharmed. Enjoy it while it lasts."

"But—"

"Beatrice," Adderly said. "Patrol the perimeter."

She signed at her aunt without looking. "I will, ma'am."

Ciarán found a pair of utilities that looked like they might fit. He peeled out of the old ones.

Adderly pointed her finger. "Now, girl. And put your eyes back into your head when you do."

Contract System, Outer Reach (Huangxu Contested Space)

Macer couldn't believe that Ciarán would willingly live in a ship like the one he walked through. There wasn't a square corner in it, or a working luminaire, and every now and then his suit lights would pick up scuttling movement, or his microphones pick up the clacking of something hard against something else hard, but not quite as hard. The corridor he walked along curved for no apparent reason. There were compartments lining both sides of the corridor but Hess assured him that he should continue to the end, where he would find the bridge.

So far he hadn't needed to use the hull-breaking auger even once. He'd entered the hull through an open hatchway in an area that had once been attached to what Hess called the biohazard lab. He shoved the auger along in front of him; it had lift plates that made it glide smoothly. He'd set up his little drone to fly along beside him and watch his back, and warn him of anything large or fast moving behind him. Unlike his last adventure aboard a seemingly abandoned ship, he had everything a modern man could want except someone else to do the work for him.

The corridor ended at a closed hatch.

"Give the hatch release a hard slap," Hess said.

"The hatch release is this panel with the embossed lettering?" Macer aimed his light and his optical sensors at it.

"They're not letters. They're ideograms."

"What's the difference?"

"I don't know. But every time I call them letters, the merchant apprentice corrects me."

Macer slapped the panel.

The hatch opened, which was good.

The lights were on inside, which was bad.

The bridge crawled with mechanical spiders that all stopped what they were doing. They turned toward him just as his drone alerted him to movement from behind.

A spider with two missing legs and two broken legs scuttled toward him.

"Let it by," Hess said. "I think it's the pilot."

"The pilot."

"Yeah. Some of them are specialists. It might have been waiting for someone to open the hatch. Follow it in but don't do anything threatening."

"I'm pushing a giant drill in front of me. One that can chew through hull plate."

"Just don't start drilling anything. And don't have your drone do anything threatening either."

"How can you live like this?"

"We don't. They're only active during a threat situation. And it looks like Ciarán has been here, because that black spider to your left is one of ours."

"How can you tell?"

"I've seen it around. Go to the piloting console. Tell it you want it to pilot the ship into the sun."

"How?"

"It's the pilot. It knows how to drive the ship."

"I mean how do I tell it that?"

"Just say that out loud to it."

"Hey, Pilot. Drive the ship into the sun."

The spider began to peck away at the console with its four functioning limbs. The limbs ended in configurable force arrays like on his drone. One limb hovered over a stud.

"That's the commit control," Hess said. "Tell it to proceed."

"Proceed," Macer said.

It ignored him.

"Go," Macer said. "Do it."

The black spider started flashing lights at him. It took him a while to realize it was using the nautical code, and a while longer to figure out what it was saying.

Agreement?

"I agree," Macer said.

It pushed the stud and the deck beneath him began to rumble.

"That's it," Hess said. "Now get out of there."

"If Olek is on board, I need to find him."

He flashed his suit lights at all the spiders. He'd thought the nautical code was just something ship drivers on Trinity Surface used. He had no idea it was some universal communications protocol. O-L-E-K.

The black spider flashed the affirmative code. It raced between his legs and down the corridor.

He followed it to a hatch, and through, and down a deck ladder, and along a second curving corridor toward the stern of the vessel.

"Hess, are you tracking this?"

They stopped at a hatch.

"Can't look away. That's the primary macrofab farm on *Quite Possibly Alien*. It's likely the same here."

"*Primary*? There's more than one?"

"Yeah, there are three compartments like that, on different decks and at different locations fore and aft. But that's the biggest one, and the one the ship uses for automated repairs."

"Is there more than one way out?"

"You mean without a hull-breaker's auger?"

Macer laughed. "I guess I do mean that."

"No. But if you need out, the right-hand bulkhead as you enter is the inner hull and the left-hand one is flanked by the main fore and aft corridor. The back wall shrouds cable runs and piping. The deck above is the mess, and the deck below is material storage for the macrofabs. There's direct conveyance from stores to the fabs but no opening you'd fit through without hogging it out first."

"The outer hull—"

"There's a void you can move around in between the hulls. But I've been eyeballing the outer hull from out here, and I wouldn't trust it to hold pressure. Don't hole your hardsuit."

"Thanks." Macer toggled the auger alive.

"The hatch control panel is on the right."

"I'm not going into another compartment without a guaranteed way out." And this might be the last chance to test the auger. "Stand by."

Macer toggled the pilot drill alive. It used a monomolecular bit to carve a three-millimeter hole through the hatch. The bit was mounted inside a pressure bell. It drilled through and retracted. He checked the pressure readings. Both sides of the hatch were at the same pressure. A two-millimeter environmental probe inserted itself through the hole, reading temperature, humidity, and checking for known aerosol threats. The display flashed green as it retracted and a two-millimeter

PATRICK O'SULLIVAN

optical and audio sensor probe inserted itself through the hole. The lights were on and one of the macrofabs was active. There was someone in an exo piled up against the far bulkhead. They weren't moving, and a dozen or more spiders were down and not moving around it. It looked like there'd been a massive fire-fight and both sides had lost. Other than the hum of the macrofab in action, no sound came from within.

"That's good imagery," Hess drawled. "And that's Olek's exo."

"How do you know?"

"It's got our ship's name on it. And it's not ours."

Macer fired up the main auger. "I don't see how the people who can make this drill can't seem to win a single war." The auger bit into the hatch and started to scream. When it was done, it hosed the opening with a cooling agent that evaporated on contact.

"That's a touchy subject. You need to pick up the pace. The hull is accelerating and it's going to get hard to hold station alongside."

"On it." Macer shoved the auger through the hole and followed it in. The black spider followed him into the compart-ment. He glanced through the macrofab viewing port and nearly hurled into his helmet. There was a man in the macro-fab. Most of one, anyway. The fab wasn't breaking him down into his constituent elements, but building him up from raw stores. "You see that? I don't want to have to look again." But he did, to make sure he got it clearly on the suit's recording sensors. It wasn't just any man. It was Commodore Olek.

"Shut it down and get out of there," Hess said. "I've seen it before. It's what the Eng call a hound."

"I don't understand. Is it alive?"

"No, but you might think it was if you met it. I'll explain later. Now button up and get out of there."

"But how could a dead man be *responsible*?"

"Responsible for what?"

"Killing my friends."

"If that's a regular hound, it couldn't be. But if it's a Vatya-style hound—"

"A what?"

"Do you see a processing-core containment sphere nearby?"

He glanced around the compartment. "I do." He crossed the compartment to reach it.

"Follow the leads. If they run to that macrofab—"

"They don't. They run to the unit across the aisle from to it." He glanced through the macrofab's viewport. "It's empty."

A woman stepped through the hole he'd bored through the hatch. "There you are." She grinned. "Come to Vatya."

"Is that one of the Vatya-style dead people?"

"I never seen her before," Hess said. "But I'd believe her if she said she was."

"Roger that." Macer glanced at the drone controller strapped to his sleeve.

A massive gripping hand clamped about his arm. The exo behind him clambered to its feet. The woman peered through the macrofab viewing port. "Your Earthmeat is nearly done, my pet. And this big man." She glanced at Macer. "He will make an interesting toy."

The black spider froze in midstride. It shivered. It seemed processor bound for an instant, like a cheap drone that was chewing on a directive too big for it to swallow.

The Vatya-woman noticed the black spider. Her nostrils flared. She took a step toward the spider. "You!"

The black spider rocketed past Macer. It disappeared behind the containment sphere.

The Vatya-woman shouted. "Seize him!"

The gripping hand released Macer. The exo turned toward the spider. Olek's exo only had one gripper. The other arm was a big gun. A GRAIL gun. It looked like it was out of slugs.

Those guns had wicked-big power supplies that were compact and energy dense. There was a reason no one sane wanted one strapped to them.

Macer fired up the auger and shoved it forward. He pinned the exo to the bulkhead and kept shoving. The grinding rasp of the big drill nearly drowned out the woman's shouts.

The black spider climbed on top of the containment sphere. It seemed to have a plan. Macer liked it when people had a plan. Most of the time he had to make the plan. But he was happy to run alongside if someone faster and smarter than him was out in front of the pack. The tip of one of the spider's limbs flared blue and elongated. The woman shouted louder. The auger finally bit into something soft and drillable.

Macer felt his face crack into a grin.

All right.

The spider slashed through the sphere's wiring harness.

The woman stopped shouting.

The auger sheared the exo in half and dug into the bulk-head behind it.

It struck a wiring conduit. Sparks flew and the compartment plunged into darkness.

Someone shouted in his ear. *Hess.*

"What are you doing, you maniac! Get out of there!"

"Not without my drill."

"You nicked the railgun power supply!"

"Why would I steal that? They're like compact bombs."

"The drill cut into its housing!"

He glanced at the power-supply housing. It was a small scrape, and it wasn't all the way through the housing.

That was good.

But the material around the scrape was beginning to blacken and blister.

That was bad.

He flashed his handheld light around the compartment as he began to back away.

Something viscous and silvery was leaking from the exo. It began to pool at his feet. There was something weird about it. He wanted to reach down and touch it. To rub it between his fingers. Did it feel as oily as it looked? He had to know.

Hess shouted in his ear. "Get out of there!"

He would, just as soon as he touched the silver.

He started to remove his right-hand suit gauntlet.

The bulkhead to starboard exploded inward and something massive, pale, and fast moving hammered him halfway across the compartment. It leapt atop the containment sphere and raked a pair of long icy-white cutters across the surface, slicing the sphere open and spilling black sand onto the deck, blanketing the wreckage of the exo beneath the ruined guts of a primary computational core. It leapt from the shattered sphere to land atop the breaching auger. The silvery oil was beginning to percolate up through the black sand. The pale creature only had one good eye, but it looked at Macer with that eye and seemed to smirk as it urinated on his auger. The black sand and silvery oil began to boil. It just stood there like some big diamond insect-bird perched on his precious power drill as the deck beneath it bubbled and outgassed, and the drill melted to slag. Whenever it spotted some of the silver oil it spit on it, and the oil began to boil.

Macer must have hit his head, because when it turned its eye away from him to watch the black spider scuttling past, it looked like it was wearing a broken table leg for a pendant spire. He stumbled over the woman's body as he crabbed backward toward the hatch. He crawled through, wishing that he'd opened the hatch so he could shut it. Drilling through it seemed a bad idea in retrospect.

He took one last look back through the borehole. He thought at first the giant diamond insect-bird was lunging at him, but it was just jumping closer to the woman's body so it could spit in her face. He tapped the little drone's controls, and it bumped into the insect-bird on its way out of the compartment. The insect-bird glared at him one more time before disappearing through the hole it had torn in the hull.

He glanced at the drone controls as he triggered his suit mic. "Hess, you recording all this?" His suit had recording capabilities but the buffer was small, and they tended to wrap. If this was a dream, it was a really vivid one. And if it was real, he wanted a recording.

He spooled backward through the drone's directive log. It had definitely bumped into something. So he wasn't imagining the giant diamond insect-bird. And it had definitely placed the tracker. It seemed like a good idea, since he didn't need it anymore, and he'd have hated to hand it back to Singh unused. It looked like the insect-bird wasn't interested in burning up in the roasting heart of a star, because it was headed on a reciprocal to *Sudden Fall of Darkness*'s course.

He tried the mic again. "Hess?"

No joy.

What would Junh do?

He'd get out of there and think about what happened later. And when he got out of there, he wouldn't abandon his friends.

That felt like a plan.

The black spider followed him down the corridor. "Go find all your buddies and meet me at the airlock. One way or another we're getting off this junk heap."

When he made it to the airlock, the assault shuttle was idling just alongside, its own airlock open and welcoming. It was close enough Macer could toss the spiders across two at a time, one with each hand. The black spider climbed up his leg and perched on his helmet. The little drone followed him across.

As he swung into the secondary piloting seat, the black spider reached up and latched itself to the deckhead.

"Let's get out of here."

Hess stared at him. "That's all you got to say?"

"Maybe not." He thought about it. Hess was right. That wasn't all he had to say.

"Let's get out of here now."

Contract System, Outer Reach (Huangxu Contested Space)

Ciarán tapped Bea on the shoulder and signed to her. "Get some rack time. I have the watch."

He glanced around the compartment. Aspen and Adderly were sacked out on the deck beside the hatch, side by side, Aspen's arm draped over her sister's shoulder. Wisp remained curled up on an examination table. She cracked an eye open like she felt him watching her. She blinked, rolled, and stretched before curling up again, her back to him.

Someone had covered the dead first-genners with sheets. He signed to Bea. "Did you do that?"

"They are bad people. I don't like looking at them."

"Bad people," Ciarán signed. "Not monsters?"

"Worse. They *chose* to be bad."

"Controlled," he signed. "By their implants."

"Not them slave her. They chose evil him."

Ciarán whispered to make sure he understood. "They weren't slaved to Vatya by Ixatl-Nine-Go?"

She signed. "No." Her brow furrowed. "Yes?"

He chuckled. "Sorry. Bad question. Were they slaved to Vatya by Ixatl-Nine-Go?"

She smiled. "Easy answer. No. They're too different for the implant to work."

"Were they Vatya's followers?"

"No. They tolerated her."

Were they Olek's slaves?"

"No. His followers."

"They chose to serve Olek?"

"Yes. They worshiped evil man."

"Why?"

"They are bad people."

He glanced around for Annie's body. "The woman? Anastasia Blum?"

"I put her in cryo."

"Thanks."

"I didn't want to watch her die. This way, maybe she lives."

"What?"

"What what?"

"She was already dead."

"Evil woman lies. Evil man lies. They like to make people suffer again and again."

"Annie Blum is alive."

"If she is the woman I put in cryo. Barely alive, but fixable. Evil woman did this to me."

"Almost killed you. And revived you."

"To get mother to help her and evil man. We are incompatible with the implants."

"All of you are incompatible?"

"Not all. All my aunt did not ship off world. The shipping plan was secret, even from my uncle."

"And that got him killed."

"Fighting evil man got him killed. Like it will get us killed."

"We'll be fine."

"We're not doing anything."

"We're farming."

"I don't understand."

"Show me the cryo chamber," Ciarán said.

She led him across the compartment.

He checked the controls. It was an older model, one without a viewport. But it was showing life signs on the display. He'd nearly let Annie die through ignorance.

"Thank you," Ciarán signed. "I owe you."

Bea shrugged and signed back. "You couldn't have known." She tapped her toes and glanced around the compartment. She crossed her arms and fidgeted like a trapped animal.

They weren't in any immediate danger, but they were in a windowless can, unless you counted the hole the Whisperer had torn in the isolation-lab wall as a window. If Bea pressed her face to the lab viewing port and craned her neck, she could see out.

They'd been trapped inside for hours. At her age he would be crawling the walls by now. Of course she didn't know what he knew, then or now. Maybe it was time to tell her.

Ciarán sat cross-legged on the deck and motioned for her to sit across from him, where he could watch her fingers if she wanted to say something.

He waited for her to get comfortable.

"When I first came to the station back home, everyone called me Plowboy. They thought it was funny because it was an insult they could say to my face. What I knew, and they didn't, was that they weren't insulting me, but showing their own ignorance. It made me angry, because they were so ignorant that I couldn't even tell them how ignorant they were. Because I was a plowboy, but that wasn't all I was. I've never told anyone this story, so if it's boring you just say so, and I'll stop."

She shook her head no and signed. "What did you do?"

"I waited. There had been a documentary made about the island I grew up on, what they called an ethnographic study, and it was insanely popular because it showed how differently we lived. They all grew up on a space station, and on starships, and we were tilling fields with mules and walking plows, the muck on our boots so thick it felt like you were lifting a mountain with every step. I wasn't just born on a dirtball, I was a mud-caked artifact from *their* poor-mouth past, a living reminder of how far they'd *progressed*. That documentary wasn't a story about us. It was about them. How much better they were than me and mine. It made me angry enough I wanted to break something."

"What did you break?"

"Me? I didn't break anything. At home anything you broke you had to fix yourself or do without. I just kept my secret, and *bore up*. It was just words, and the way you fight words is with more and better words. Being a merchant is mostly about picking the words to fit the job. I figured if I became the best merchant in the universe, I'd find the words to fight them, and to beat them. But to become the best merchant in the universe, I had to knuckle down at school and never, *ever* forget the mission. And to never, *ever* surrender, or let myself become like them. So that's what I did. Because, while I am a plowboy, and proud of it, plowboy is just one part of what I am."

She leaned forward. "What *are* you?"

"A farmer."

"Oh."

"'Oh' is right." He winked at her and leaned in close. "The secret to farming is you've got to love the earth, you've got to love it and study it, and get to know it as well as you know yourself. And you've got to learn the seeds, not just the ones you've planted before, but all the seeds that ever were, know what they need to grow, to flourish, to thrive, and only once you know that, and know it like you know your own face, should you plant, matching seed to soil, and sun, and rain, how deep, how far apart, in hills or in rows, time of the year, phase of the moon, the way the air feels on your skin. It's all part of the equation. It's all part of being a farmer. But it's not the hardest part."

"No?"

"Not by half." Ciarán stood and dusted himself off. "I think I'll go see if I can find some ration bars."

Beatrice lurched to her feet. She grabbed his sleeve and signed. "Finish the story first."

"That's the story. You know everything I know about farming."

"You didn't say what the hardest part was."

"I didn't think I had to. We're doing it."

"We aren't doing *anything*."

"Maybe you aren't, but I'm farming my guts out. If you don't want to help me I understand, but I got the impression you were antsy, and looking for work."

"Work doing *what*?"

"Waiting. And praying for the sprouts to appear."

When she slapped his sleeve, it hurt.

It also sounded like a seed had sprouted, and a slave with two masters was banging on a hatch.

Wisp had heard it too.

Ciarán grinned. "Do that again. Only hit me louder this time."

She ignored him and raced toward the hatch.

Prescott Grange System, Earth Restoration League

M acer paced the deck of *Four-Squared*'s boat bay. He had an incoming pair of deliveries, the result of miserable negotiations with an army of League legal people. They would have a hard time getting the assault shuttle out of his hands and they knew it, but they had to win, somehow, so he'd let them talk him into transporting a big piece of kit to Sampson for them. He wasn't *trading* with the League, but settling a lawsuit. And he wanted to get his legal matters handled before the courts were mobbed by merchants exploiting the workaround.

The League lawfare specialists didn't know he wanted to go to Sampson as a surprise for Seamus, so that was a win. They were paying him for the gig with title to the assault shuttle, and that was a win. And they were replacing his sweet hull-breaking auger as well, so another win. But they were moving

in this giant containment sphere, and they seemed to think that
was a loss for him, a big one, so that when he signed the
contract and they shook hands, the League lawyer smirked.

Literally smirked.

And a couple of hours later, a big team of Erl engineers
showed up, and four of them were solid eighties and one was
cracking ninety, but she said she had a boyfriend. They started
measuring the bridge, and he said what are you doing, and they
said read the settlement agreement, but he didn't need to. He
already knew. He just wanted to know if they knew he knew,
and they didn't.

He opened the boat bay force window and Ruthie brought
the assault shuttle in and parked it astern of Janie's mobster
runabout, and then Ruthie was out, they slapped palms, and he
asked her to think up a better name for the boat than *assault
shuttle*. She and the captain should work on it, come up with
something good, and Jimio could help, but nothing with punc-
tuation in it, and no mention of Jimio in the name.

And then the League refitting crew brought in the sphere, a
big team of League engineers and technicians with heavy-
lifting gear. They were only parking the sphere in the boat bay
temporarily because they needed to cut out a big piece of the
bridge and put it in where the sphere would be in a heavy
cruiser. *Four-Squared*'s bridge was the same module as on a
warship, they'd just never put in the sphere and had instead
decked over the place where it went.

They'd have to cut out a section of the hull to bring it in,
and then patch it up, and he didn't think they knew he knew
that either, but there was a pitted section in the starboard side
that bothered him, so he'd run the little drone out and had it
paint out the sections he wanted pulled and labeled it "cut
here."

You could come in on the port side, and they might, if they
wanted to irritate him, but he was pretty sure it was just the

lawyers and not the actual workers that were mad at him. But either way, there were some ominous sounding stencils in the drone's preset library, so he had it paint "no step" and "high voltage" and other such warnings in erlspout on the portside access area. It was an old hull, and even if they had the plans, no telling what Freeman modifications had gone on, so better safe than sorry, unless they wanted an injury or another bout with the lawyers for ignoring a plainly marked hazard. If they cut there, he'd find something broken that could have been there and bill them for that.

They locked the sphere down and left a bunch of gear next to it. And then they left, but not before the girl with the boyfriend said she'd broken up with her boyfriend, and he said that was sad, and she said how about a shag, and he said, sure, but he had a date for tonight, but check with him again tomorrow.

Once they were gone, he dug through the gear, found what he wanted, and set it up. The sphere had a power supply strapped to it and it seemed decent, just not what he would have used.

He powered up the holographic gear he'd set up. It wasn't a real feel rig, but it was temporary, and better than nothing.

When she appeared he looked at her for a while. She was sort of motherly looking. She didn't look exactly like House, but it was pretty obvious they were related.

"Are you Junh?" he said.

She laughed and said, "I'm Dalton. Are you Junh?"

"Macer. Welcome aboard."

"It looks like a nice hull."

"It's roomy. But lonely. Will you be staying long?"

She looked at him and he looked at her, and they both laughed.

Prescott Grange System, Earth Restoration League

S eamus exited the longboat empty-handed. He wasn't staying long, but he wanted to say his goodbyes. Macer stood waiting for him in *Four-Squared*'s boat bay.

Macer tossed him a juice bulb. "Have the Erl made you a space lord yet, James Reynard?"

"They're working on it. So far all they've done is ship me a space lady to look over."

"Anyone I know?"

Seamus laughed.

The boat bay hatch behind Macer opened.

"What I need," Seamus said, "is a bad pilot, with a great pair of legs."

"Tough," Janie Byrne said. "I'm just the opposite, thanks to you clowns. Did you think I jumped in between those Sampson people and the shooter because I had a death wish?"

"We didn't know you'd be dissatisfied," Macer said. "We thought you liked the old pair."

"Her ankles are a little thick," Seamus said.

"You hear that, Macer Gant? And now if I want new ones, I'll have to pay for them myself, instead of the League doing it for me. Thanks for nothing, you pair of eejits."

Seamus looked her over. "Where's your duffel?"

"At the duffel store on Sampson. Where do you think it is?"

Macer scratched his eyebrow. "Where are your clothes?"

"On me."

Macer frowned. "Clothes for a month's journey are on you."

"Why would I need a month's worth of clothes on my own longboat?"

"You can't get to Sampson in a longboat, Janie."

"Seamus has a theory. So we're going to try."

"But—"

"If it doesn't work, we'll be back in a week."

"It won't work."

"You haven't heard the theory. Did you bring a toothbrush?"

Seamus nodded. "I did."

"Me too. Your lifeboat awaits, James." Janie hooked his arm and began dragging him across the boat bay. "Later, Macer."

She practically shoved him up the boarding ladder. She dogged the hatch while Seamus settled in behind the controls.

Janie grabbed him by the collar and hauled him into the cabin. "Preflight." She began shucking out of her utilities.

"That's what I was doing. I—"

She tapped her index finger against his forehead. "The world's out here, Seamus."

"I know that."

"Then pay attention. And start acting like you care."

"I care. More than you know."

"More than I *knew*. Macer told me. You weren't lying about keeping that image of us together."

"I don't lie to my friends."

"Just to yourself."

He shrugged. "So I'm a mess. At least I know it."

"Everyone knows it, Seamus." She pinned him to the bulk-head and kissed him. "No one cares." She cupped his pendant spire and let it slide along her fingers. "Now preflight this bird before I do it myself."

Contract System, Outer Reach (Huangxu Contested Space)

Aoife nic Cartaí's face filled the viewscreen as it had for the last hour. *Quite Possibly Alien* had punched into Contract system near the system's star and had established communications immediately. Aoife had just begun to speak when sunspot activity caused the communications system to glitch. Old had left the frozen image of the young merchant lord's face on the main display system, not because he wished to, but because he could not turn it off. A mong hu had pinned the communications officer to the deck, and would let no one near the control console.

Ciarán stepped onto the bridge. "Still frozen, I see. Wisp, let Mr. Younger do his job."

"Communications link reestablished, Captain," Younger said.

"This seems to be working better." Ciarán gazed at the smiling, and now animated face of Aoife nic Cartaí. She stood on the bridge of *Quite Possibly Alien* and for a moment he couldn't speak.

She nodded. "It does. We've jumped closer to you. It took some doing. The system is crowded with traffic."

"Sorry about the congestion," Ciarán said. "I didn't know they would all return at once."

"And they are?"

"The... um..."

"The Legion of Heroes, Merchant Lord," Old said. "The Knight Commander finds pronouncing the name difficult."

"I see. What has that to do with my merchant apprentice?"

"I'm the Knight Commander," Ciarán mumbled.

"Come again?"

"He said that he is the Knight Commander," Old said. "He is also referred to locally as the Liberator."

Ciarán sighed. "Are you enjoying yourself, Cohort Captain?"

"I am, Merchant Lord. I believe I am *free* to do so, *Liberator*."

"I appear to have missed a great deal," nic Cartaí said.

"Not all that much. Old and the mercenary fleet nearly killed us rescuing us. But we survived."

"Nearly killed them, Cohort Captain?"

"Not the Invincible Spear Bearers, Merchant Lord. The Unstoppable Iron Fist of Empire. The situation has been dealt with."

"They're on probation." Ciarán grinned. "They're not allowed to wear the Legion regalia."

"That seems quite the punishment."

"More than you'd think. It means they pay for their own drinks on the station."

Aoife laughed. "You appear in good health."

"We are. Wisp says hello. How's Carlsbad?"

"He's well. Fully recovered and on the job."

"I don't want to ask. But I have to."

"I ran into your friend Macer Gant. He and Helen Konstantine hit it off... smashingly."

"That's great news."

"I have so much to tell you."

"I want to hear it all. Almost all, anyway. About—"

"Your father says hello, and Lorelei Ellis said to give you her regards."

"You spoke with them?"

"I met with them. It's a long story, and one I look forward to recounting in person."

"Seamus."

"I'm sorry, Ciarán, but Seamus lived."

"Oh. I figured he would... What?"

"I tried my best, as did a great number of others, but unfortunately he is still with us. He's presently at Prescott Grange and anxious to meet with you."

"Seamus is alive? I—"

"Take your time. We will catch up shortly. Nic Cartaí—"

"Wait," Ciarán said. "Is Mr. Gagenot there?"

"We are all here, Ciarán. How could we not be?"

"There's someone who wants to meet him."

"Mr. Gagenot?" Aoife said. "Step over here, please."

"Aspen, you need to shift to the left."

"Will Gag sees—"

"Daddy?" Aspen blinked and reached a hand toward the display. "Daddy! We thought you were dead!"

Bea waved and signed at the same time. "Why isn't he saying anything?"

Ciarán chuckled. "He's more a doer than a talker."

"So the opposite of you."

"Old?"

"I could not have instructed her in such insolence. I've only just begun to study the art myself."

"Crewman Wisp seems in good spirits," Aoife nic Cartaí said. "She looks like she just ate the mouse that ate the cheese."

"She's ganging up on me and recruiting her own crew. I expect she'll be applying for an apprentice license soon."

"I hope she isn't planning on moonlighting like my apprentice."

"I wasn't *planning* anything. It just happened."

"Well, you'll *happen* to find a longboat to bring you and Wisp to us tomorrow. We miss you, and want you home. I want to know everything. Do you think you can work us into your schedule, Merchant Apprentice?"

"Old, are we liberating anyone tomorrow?"

"I believe your calendar is free for the foreseeable future, Knight Commander."

"Then I will get there if I have to crawl there."

"Cancel the longboat, Mr. Hess. This I want to see."

"I won't really have to crawl there. I have my own longboat."

"You have thirty-five longboats, Knight Commander."

"Well, there you go," Ciarán said. "I will see you tomorrow."
Count on it.

"I will count on it, Merchant Apprentice. And I'll schedule the merchant's exam for the afternoon and a refresher exercise with Mrs. Amati for the evening. Bring a writing instrument and body armor. Remember to wear comfortable shoes."

"No, wait—"

"Nic Cartaí out."

Ciarán stared at the empty display. After a moment it returned to its usual configuration, a detailed system schematic and active traffic plot.

"We like her," Bea signed.

"You don't know her."

"Because if we did, we'd love her."

"I didn't say that."

"You don't have to."

Wisp looked him in the eye and clicked her claws against the deck.

Everyone knows.

ABOUT THE AUTHOR

Patrick O'Sullivan is a writer living and working in the United States and Ireland. Patrick's fantasy and science fiction works have won awards in the Writers of the Future Contest as well as the James Patrick Baen Memorial Writing Contest sponsored by Baen Books and the National Space Society.

www.patrickosullivan.com

Printed in Great Britain
by Amazon

44022734R00314